P9-DWH-402

the
invisible
circus

Nan A. Talese
doubleday   new york   london   toronto   sydney   auckland

the
invisible
circus

jennifer egan

PUBLISHED BY NAN A. TALESE
an imprint of Doubleday
a division of Bantam Doubleday Dell Publishing Group, Inc.
1540 Broadway, New York, New York 10036

DOUBLEDAY is a trademark of Doubleday, a division of
Bantam Doubleday Dell Publishing Group, Inc.

This novel is a work of fiction. Names, characters, places and incidents
are either the product of the author's imagination or are used
fictitiously. Any resemblance to actual persons, living or dead,
events or locales is entirely coincidental.

Book Design by Gretchen Achilles

Library of Congress Cataloging-in-Publication Data
Egan, Jennifer.
  The invisible circus / Jennifer Egan.—1st ed.
    p. cm.
  1. Teenage girls—United States—Fiction. 2. Hippies—United
States—Fiction. 3. Sisters—United States—Fiction. 4. Death—
Fiction. I. Title.
PS3555.G292I55   1995
813'.54—dc20   94-6205
                                                        CIP

ISBN 0-385-47379-6

Copyright © 1995 by Jennifer Egan

All Rights Reserved
Printed in the United States of America
January 1995

10 9 8 7 6 5 4 3

For my mother, Kay Kimpton
and my brother, Graham Kimpton

Acknowledgments

I would like to thank the following individuals for their advice, encouragement, and efforts on my behalf: David Herskovits, Monica Adler, Bill Kimpton, Nan Talese, Jesse Cohen, Diane Marcus, Tom Jenks, Carol Edgarian, Webster Stone, Virginia Barber, Jennifer Rudolph Walsh, Ruth Danon, David Rosenstock, Kim Snyder, Don Lee, Julie Mars, Ken Goldberg, and David Lansing.

I am grateful as well to the National Endowment for the Arts, the New York Foundation for the Arts, and the Corporation of Yaddo for their support.

Above all, I owe thanks to Mary Beth Hughes, whose faith, wisdom, and insight are essential to this book.

"... for the present age, which prefers the picture to the thing pictured, the copy to the original, imagination to reality, or the appearance to the essence ... *illusion* alone is sacred to this age, but *truth profane* ... so that the *highest degree of illusion* is to it the highest degree of sacredness."

—Ludwig Feuerbach

"Exultation is the going
Of an inland soul to sea,
Past the houses—past the headlands—
Into deep Eternity— ...

—Emily Dickinson

part one

one

She'd missed it, Phoebe knew by the silence. Crossing the lush, foggy park, she heard nothing but the drip of condensation running from ferns and palm leaves. By the time she reached the field, its vast emptiness came as no surprise.

The grass was a brilliant, jarring green. Debris covered it, straws, crushed cigarettes, a few sodden blankets abandoned to the mud.

Phoebe shoved her hands in her pockets and crossed the grass, stepping over patches of bare mud. A ring of trees encircled the field, coastal trees, wind-bent and gnarled yet still symmetrical, like figures straining to balance heavy trays.

At the far end of the field several people in army jackets were dismantling a bandstand. They carried its parts through the trees to a road, where Phoebe saw the dark shape of a truck.

She approached a man and woman with long coils of orange electrical cord dangling from their arms. Phoebe waited politely for the two to finish talking, but they seemed not to notice her.

Timidly she turned to another man, who carried a plank across his arms. "Excuse me," she said. "Did I miss it?"

"You did," he said. "It was yesterday. Noon to midnight." He squinted at her as if the sun were out. He looked vaguely familiar, and Phoebe wondered if he might have known her sister. She was always wondering that.

"I thought it was today," she said uselessly.

"Yeah, about half the posters were printed wrong." He grinned, his eyes a bright, chemical blue, like sno-cones.

It was June 18, a Saturday. Ten years before, in 1968, a "Festival of Moons" had allegedly happened on this same field. "Revival of Moons," the posters promised, and Phoebe had juggled her shifts at work and come eagerly, anxious to relive what she'd failed to live even once.

"So, how was it?" she asked.

"Underattended." He laughed sardonically.

"I'm glad it wasn't just me," she said.

The guy set down his plank and ran a hand across his eyes. Blunt, straight blond hair fell to his shoulders. "Man," he said, "you look a lot like this girl I used to know."

Startled, Phoebe glanced at him. He was squinting again. "Like, exactly like her."

She stared at his face. "Catnip," she said, surprising herself.

He took a small step away.

"You were friends with Faith O'Connor, right?" Phoebe said, excited now. "Well, I'm her sister."

Catnip looked away, then back at Phoebe. He shook his head. She remembered him now, though he'd seemed much bigger before. And beautiful—that intense, fragile beauty you saw sometimes in high school guys, but never in men. Girls couldn't resist him, hence his name.

He was staring at Phoebe. "I can't believe this," he said.

While Catnip went to extricate himself from the work crew, Phoebe struggled to catch her breath. For years she'd imagined this, a friend of Faith's recognizing her now, grown up—how much like her sister she looked.

Together she and Catnip crossed the field. Phoebe felt nervous. There were blond glints of beard on his face.

"So you're what, in high school now?" he asked.

"I graduated," Phoebe said. "Last week, actually." She hadn't attended the ceremony.

"Well, I'm Kyle. No one's called me Catnip in years," he said wistfully.

"How old are you?"

"Twenty-six. Yourself?"

"Eighteen."

"Eighteen," he said, and laughed. "Shit, when I was eighteen, twenty-six sounded geriatric."

Kyle had just finished his second year of law school. "Monday I start my summer job," he said, and with two fingers mimed a pair of scissors snipping off his hair.

"Really? They make you cut it?" It sounded like the Army.

"They don't have to," he said. "You've already done it."

Traffic sounds grew louder as they neared the edge of Golden Gate Park. Phoebe felt like a child left alone with one of Faith's friends, the uneasy job of holding their interest. "Do you ever think about those times?" she asked. "You know, with my sister?"

There was a pause. "Sure," Kyle said. "Sure I do."

"Me too."

"She's incredibly real to me. Faith," he said.

"I think about her constantly," said Phoebe.

Kyle nodded. "She was your sister."

By the time they reached Haight Street, the fog was beginning to shred, exposing blue wisps of sky. Phoebe thought of mentioning that she worked only two blocks away—would be there right now if not for the Revival of Moons—but this seemed of no consequence.

"I live around here," Kyle said. "How about some coffee?"

His apartment, on Cole Street, was a disappointment. Phoebe had hoped to enter a time warp, but a sleek charcoal couch and long glass coffee table dominated the living room. On the walls, abstract lithographs appeared to levitate inside Plexiglas frames. Still, a prism dangled from one window, and tie-dyed cushions scattered the floor. Phoebe noticed a smell of cloves or pepper, some odor familiar from years before.

She sat on the floor, away from the charcoal couch. When Kyle shed his army jacket, Phoebe noticed through his T-shirt how muscular he was. He took a joint from a Lucite cigarette holder on the coffee table and fired it up, then lowered himself to the floor.

"You know," he croaked, holding in smoke as he passed the joint to Phoebe, "a bunch of times I thought about dropping by you and your mom's. Just see how you were doing."

"You should've done it," Phoebe said. She was eyeing the joint, worrying whether or not to smoke. Getting high made her deeply anxious, had paralyzed her more than once in a viselike fear that she was about to drop dead. But she thought of her sister, how eagerly Faith had reached for everything—how Kyle would expect this of Phoebe. She took a modest hit. Kyle was bent at his stereo, stacking records on a turntable. *Surrealistic Pillow* came on, the rich, eerie voice of Grace Slick.

"She remarried or anything, your mom?" he asked, resuming his seat.

"Oh no," Phoebe said, half laughing. "No."

As Kyle watched her through the smoke, she grew self-conscious. "I guess that phase in her life is kind of over," she explained.

He shook his head. "Too bad."

"No, she doesn't mind," Phoebe said, wondering as she spoke if she knew this for sure. "She's sort of past the age of romance."

Kyle frowned, toking on the joint. "How old could she be?"

"Her birthday's next weekend, actually. Forty-seven."

He burst out laughing, spewing smoke and then coughing

with abandon. "Forty-seven," he said, recovering himself. "That's not old, Phoebe."

She stared at him, stunned by his laughter. "I didn't say she was old," she said. The pot was confusing her.

Kyle's eyes lingered on Phoebe. Smoke hung on the air in folds, dissolving slowly like cream into coffee. "What about you?" he said. "How've you been?"

"Fine, thanks," she said guardedly.

By the time they finished the joint, the room seemed to pulsate directly against Phoebe's eyeballs. Her heartbeat echoed. The pillows exhaled a cinnamon smell when she leaned back.

Kyle stretched out flat, hands cradling his head, legs crossed at the ankles. "I want to talk about it," he said, his eyes closed, "but I don't know how to."

"Me too," Phoebe said. "I never do."

Kyle opened one eye. "Not even with your mom? Your brother?"

"I don't know why," Phoebe said. "We used to."

"Plastic Fantastic Lover" came on, meandering and druggy, invading Phoebe's mind with fluorescent splashes of color. They listened in silence.

"So . . . did you ever find out what happened?" Kyle said at last.

"You mean, how she died?"

"Yeah. How it happened exactly."

As always when the subject turned to Faith, some pressure inside Phoebe relaxed. She took long, peaceful breaths. "Well, everyone says she jumped."

Kyle sighed. "In Italy, right?"

Phoebe nodded. After a pause she asked, "Do you believe it?"

"I don't know," Kyle said. "I mean, the way I heard it—you'd know better than me—it would've been pretty hard to fall there by accident."

"Except no one saw."

Kyle raised himself on his elbows and looked at Phoebe. She

gazed back at him, very stoned, trying to pinpoint what exactly had changed about Kyle since the old days.

"But I mean, why?" he said. "You know—why?"

He looked so earnest, as if he were the first person ever to pose the question in quite this way. It made Phoebe laugh, softly at first, then convulsively, tears running from her eyes. "I'm sorry," she said, wiping them on her sleeve. Her nose was running. "Sorry."

Kyle touched her arm. "I just wondered what the story was," he said.

"Yeah," Phoebe said, sniffling. "Me too." Laughing had relieved her, the way crying did.

"You think it was an accident," Kyle said.

"I'm not sure."

He nodded. The subject was closed, somehow. Phoebe felt as if she'd lost a chance. It was her own fault, she thought, for laughing.

They drifted into silence. Phoebe's thumb and middle finger were sticky with resin. Kyle relit the roach, and when he handed it over, she smoked without hesitation. Finally Kyle let the nub of roach drop to the floor and sat cross-legged, the fingers of one hand pressed to the other. "You look like her," he said. "I guess you hear that a lot."

"I don't hear it," Phoebe said, confused as to why. "Because" —she laughed, realizing—"well, I mean, no one sees us together."

Kyle smacked his forehead, clearly mortified.

"But I wish they did," Phoebe said. "Say that."

He left her, crossing the room to the window. Phoebe stretched, reaching toward the ceiling in her painter's pants and desert boots so the muscles pulled at her ribs. She was very stoned, but today it seemed all right. She even felt a loopy sort of confidence as she lay on her side, watching Kyle squint through his prism. A nylon thread attached it to the window. He twisted it, scattering smudges of rainbow light. King Crimson's song "Moonchild" came on.

"I just had a weird feeling," Kyle said.

"What?"

"I thought, if you told me right now you were Faith, I bet I'd believe you."

Phoebe turned her face away to hide her pleasure. She still wore Faith's clothing sometimes, frayed jeans and lacy flea-market blouses, a crushed velvet jacket with star-shaped buttons. Nothing quite fit. Her sister had been thinner, or taller, her black hair longer—something. Try as Phoebe might to bridge the gap between herself and Faith, some difference always remained. But one day that difference would vanish, she believed, part of a larger transformation Phoebe was constantly awaiting. She had thought it would come by graduation.

"I'm leaving for Europe pretty soon," she lied, seized by a desire to impress and dazzle Kyle. "A long trip."

"Oh yeah?" he said from the window. "Where to?"

"I'm not sure. I thought I'd just go, you know? Kind of be spontaneous." There was some truth in this; Phoebe did intend to go one day to Europe, retrace her sister's steps. She had always known it. But she'd enrolled at Berkeley for the fall semester, chosen five courses and even dorm space.

"I'm all for spontaneity," Kyle said, sounding envious.

So had their father been. In his will he'd tried to ensure it, providing Faith and Phoebe and Barry five thousand dollars each after high school, to explore the world. "Do it first," he'd said, "before you get tied down. Do things you'll tell stories about the rest of your lives."

"Just go, you know?" Phoebe said, losing herself in the lie. "Just take off."

Kyle moved to where she lay, his bare feet sticking on the polished floor. A knee cracked as he eased himself on the cushions beside her. Phoebe shut her eyes.

"You're beautiful," he said, touching her face. Phoebe opened her eyes and quickly shut them. She felt giddy, as if the room, like Kyle's prism, were twisting on a nylon string. He leaned down,

kissing her mouth. Phoebe kissed him back, some blind part of
herself rushing forward. She was still a virgin. Kyle's mouth had a
sweet, applesauce taste.

He adjusted the cushions and stretched out beside her. As he
touched Phoebe's breasts through her T-shirt, she sensed his confidence, and it helped her relax. Kyle took her head in his hands,
his palms cool at her temples, and Phoebe heard behind her covered ears a rushing, seashell noise. Kyle eased himself on top of
her. She clung to the muscles along his spine, the heat from his
body seeping through Phoebe's clothes to her skin. The coiled
strength of his stomach moved gently as he breathed; his erection
pressed her thigh. She opened her eyes to look at him. But Kyle's
own eyes were clenched shut, as if he were making a wish.

"Wait—wait," Phoebe said, squirming out from beneath him.

Kyle resisted her at first, then sprang to his feet as if a stranger
had entered the room. Phoebe heard his shallow breathing. She
sat curled like an egg, chin on her knees. Kyle moved to the couch
and hunched at one end. "Shit," he said.

But Phoebe had lost track of him. There was something she
needed to remember. She shut her eyes, forehead pressed to her
knees, and saw Faith and her friends swallow tiny squares of paper and sometime later start laughing, crazy weeping laughter that
in Faith soon turned to helpless sobbing in her boyfriend's arms—
"Wolf" he was called for his brown skin and white teeth, brown
hands on her sister's head, "Shhh," stroking her hair as if Faith
were a cat, "Shhh." Shirtless under a soft leather vest, his brown
stomach muscles reminding Phoebe of the shapes on a turtle's
shell. And then Faith was kissing him, Phoebe watching, uneasy.
"Come on," Faith said, and tried to stand, but she couldn't; she
was sick, her eyes feverish. "Come on." Kissing, kissing, but Wolf
saw Phoebe crouched beside him, and their eyes locked.

"Faith, wait," he said. "Babe, hold on."

But finally he helped her up, Phoebe creeping behind them
into the hall, where they tottered to the far end, her mother's

white bedroom door swinging shut behind them. Then silence. Phoebe waited in the hall for the door to open up again, growing frightened as the minutes passed—her sister was sick, could hardly walk! After their father got sick that door was always shut, sweet medicine smells in the hallway. Phoebe threw herself down on the rug and lay there in a kind of trance, the white door burning a hole through her head until finally after what seemed like hours she ran at the door sobbing, cool smooth paint against her cheek, but still she didn't turn the knob. She was too afraid.

Then footsteps. Phoebe jumped back as Faith opened the door, her sister's eyes wide and black, drops of water sticking to her lashes. Hugging Phoebe close, "Baby," rocking her gently, "Baby, baby, what's happened to you?" Smelling of soap—had she only been taking a shower? And Wolf, the hero, watching Phoebe with such pain in his face, as if he'd hurt her. No, Phoebe wanted to say, no, no, but how could she speak when she understood nothing, when everyone was mysterious?

Now Phoebe looked at Kyle, miles away on the couch. It was always this way—something she needed to remember pulling her back, like an undertow. A white door sealing her off, reminding Phoebe that her present life was unreal and without significance. What mattered was hidden from sight. At times she hated remembering, wanted nothing in the world but to rush forward into something of her own, lose herself in it. But this wasn't possible. The only way forward was through that door.

"Do you miss her?" Phoebe said into the silence.

Kyle groaned up from the couch and sprayed water on the leaves of several spindly marijuana plants leaning toward an ultraviolet bulb. Delicate threads tied them to stakes. "Sometimes I feel like she's still back there," he said. "In that time. I miss it like hell."

"Me too," Phoebe said, an ache in her chest. "Even if I wasn't really there."

"Sure you were there."

"No. I was a kid."

There was a long pause. "I wasn't there, either," Kyle said. "Not totally."

"What do you mean?"

"I kept circling, circling, but I never quite hit it."

This admission made Phoebe uneasy. "You were there, Kyle," she assured him. "You were definitely there."

He grinned, seeming heartened. He sprayed his mister into the air, granules of vapor catching the light as they fell. Phoebe heard the cannon, fired each day at five o'clock from the Presidio military base. "I better go," she said, wobbling to her feet. One of her legs was asleep. It was 1978. Faith's boyfriend Wolf lived in Europe now. Phoebe's mother hadn't heard from him in years.

Kyle waited, hands in his pockets. "I'll give you a call."

"Okay," Phoebe said, knowing he wouldn't.

She walked carefully down the macadam steps to the street, gripping the rail. Sunlight glittered in the trees. There was a distant cable car prattle, silence around it.

"Hey," she heard overhead. Kyle was leaning out his window. "I forgot, I wanted to give you something in case you get to Munich. I've got a cousin over there."

Phoebe shielded her eyes. She'd forgotten her Europe story, and was startled now to hear it repeated as fact.

"C'mon back," Kyle said.

Phoebe retraced her steps. Kyle handed her a joint wrapped in fluorescent pink rolling paper. It felt dry and light in her hand.

"Tell him it's the same stuff we smoked at Christmas," he said, copying from an address book onto the back of a receipt. "Steven + Ingrid Lake," Phoebe read, with an address. The telephone number seemed short on digits. She rolled the joint carefully inside the address and slipped it in her wallet.

"Tell Steve to stay clear of the anthills," Kyle said, laughing in the doorway. "He'll understand."

Descending the stairs a second time, Phoebe felt a curious

excitement. As far as Kyle knew, she was going to Europe—next week, tomorrow—and this thought amazed Phoebe, thrilled her with a sense that anything might happen.

On the street she looked up. Kyle was watching her from his window again, absently touching the prism. "When are you leaving?" he said.

"Soon," she said, almost laughing. "Next week, maybe." She turned to go.

"Send me a postcard," he called.

Phoebe found herself smiling at the bony Victorian houses. Europe, she thought. Birds, white stone, long dark bridges. Going all the places Faith had gone—exactly, one by one. Her sister's postcards still lay stacked in a shoebox underneath the bed. Phoebe recalled awaiting them feverishly, right from the day her sister and Wolf had first left, a summer day not unlike this one. They'd driven to the airport in Wolf's truck, with a girl who'd already paid him for it. Phoebe had stood on the sidewalk a long time after they'd gone, wondering what would happen to them. She'd been wondering ever since.

Her sister died on November 21, 1970, on the rocks below Corniglia, a tiny village on the west coast of northern Italy. She was seventeen; Phoebe was ten. Traces of drugs were found in Faith's body, speed, LSD, but not enough that she would have been high at the time. If her neck hadn't broken, they said, she might have lived.

If Phoebe could string together the hours she'd spent circling this event, they would surely total years. She lost herself in these contemplations, her own life falling away like a husk as she sank into the rich, bottomless well of her sister's absence. And the longer Phoebe circled, the more certain she became that a great misunderstanding was at work; that if Faith had taken her life, she'd done it without a hint of the failure or hopelessness the word "suicide" implied. When Phoebe thought of her sister's death, it was always with a curious lilt to the heart, as if Faith had been lifted into some more spectacular realm, a place so remote she could reach it only by forfeiting her life. Like kicking away a ladder. Where was the failure in that?

Phoebe's mother, Gail, had flown to Italy and returned with Faith's ashes in a box. She and Phoebe and Barry scattered them from the clifftops near the Golden Gate Bridge, a place where their family used to picnic. Phoebe remembered staring in disbelief at the silty, uneven chunks, like debris left in a fireplace. Her hands had been sweating, and as she tossed fistfuls into the wind, the finest powder stuck in the creases of her palms. No matter how hard Phoebe shook, the powder remained. Afterward she'd locked the door to her room and gazed for a long time at her open hands. The house was quiet. Phoebe stuck out her tongue and lightly ran its tip along her palm. The taste was sour, salty. Horrified, Phoebe fled to the bathroom and scoured her hands and mouth in the sink, staring into the toilet and willing herself to be sick. Lately she'd wondered if what she tasted that day was her own sweat.

A white door at the end of a hallway. "Come on," Faith had said, reaching for Wolf. They closed it behind them.

Phoebe pacing outside, driving her toes deep into the soft rug. Terrified—of what? That her sister was gone. That the door would never open. That when finally it did, she would find herself alone in a bright, empty room.

two

When Phoebe rode with her brother in his Porsche, they played a tacit game of chicken: Barry accelerated steadily, knowing it scared Phoebe, wanting her to ask him to slow down. Phoebe would plunge straight into the jaws of death before she gave him that satisfaction. When they rode alone together, grim silence would overwhelm them as the needle edged across the speedometer, Phoebe begging God please for one red light. How long can this go on, she would think, before something happens to us? But she wasn't giving in.

"Honey, calm yourself," their mother said when Barry began gunning the engine three blocks out of the driveway. "I'd like a few more birthdays after this one."

The day was warm and clear, rare for a San Francisco June. Barry was duly elated. He'd been planning their mother's birthday for weeks, proposing first a long weekend in Hawaii, then a hot-air balloon ride, finally an all-day sail on a chartered yacht. "I'm your mother, not the CEO of Sony," she'd chided him, laughing gently so Barry wouldn't take it wrong. "Why not a picnic?"

At twenty-three, Phoebe's brother was a millionaire. The seed of his wealth had been their father's five thousand dollars, engorged by careful investments while Barry was at Berkeley. After graduation he'd used the money to start a software company, and when Phoebe last asked, his employees had numbered fifty-seven. He owned a four-bedroom house in the hills outside Los Gatos, and showered Phoebe each holiday with gifts that left her weak with gratitude, a Prince tennis racket, a digital watch, a string of real pearls that radiated a faint pink glow in certain lights. Barry often dropped the names of important people he'd met at parties, always stressing how they'd sought him out, how some moment of unique communication had transpired. According to Barry, his employees were off the genius charts, his products so phenomenally great that customers were nearly fainting away at their computer terminals. Against her better judgment, Phoebe found herself believing him sometimes, adopting Barry's view that the center of the world was not New York or Paris or Washington, D.C., but a software company near Palo Alto.

"Where are we going?" Phoebe called from the backseat as the Porsche entered Golden Gate Park.

"You'll see," Barry said. He was talking to their mother. Chips, Phoebe heard, bytes (of what? she idly wondered). She opened her window and breathed the wet, eucalyptus smell of Golden Gate Park. It had been exactly a week since she'd met Kyle here, and like most stoned memories, the encounter had a sketchy, dreamlike quality. But the feeling of telling Kyle she would go to Europe, having him believe her—that Phoebe couldn't forget.

She reached over the back of her mother's seat and touched her frosted hair. Exquisite though her mother looked to Phoebe, an outdatedness made her beauty seem muted in the outside world, inactive. Phoebe loved this. It unnerved her to look at old snapshots of her young, glamorous mother smiling coyly up from under hat brims. She remembered her parents together, how her father would lie with his head in her mother's lap or playfully slap her behind. She remembered Claude, too, her mother's single lover in a widowhood filled with meaningless dates—the dazed openness that had fallen on her mother in Claude's presence, a tension between them filling the room like a charge. But Phoebe loved her mother best as she was now, wistful, out-of-step, her laugh tinged always with sadness, as if things were only funny in spite of themselves. Phoebe saw her mother as still in mourning and treasured the safety this made her feel, like falling asleep knowing someone else will always be awake, keeping watch.

Barry parked beside a clearing full of fruit trees whose leaves were so new they looked wet. He unloaded the car, waving away their offers of help. Barry was dark-haired and tall, his eyes pure black, as if the pupils had sprung wide in some moment of panic and never snapped back. The trait was arresting in photographs— "That's your brother? God, what a fox," Phoebe's friends had been saying for years when they saw his picture—but in life something cut the effect. He moved childishly, neck outthrust, arms loose at his sides, looking always ready to duck.

Barry assembled their picnic, a lavish, daunting array of Brie and red pears, roast beef and bagels and stuffed grape leaves. There was Dom Pérignon in an ice chest, a tiny pot of beluga caviar. Their mother kicked away her espadrilles and sipped her champagne, flexing her white toes. The skin of her calves was so dry it shone like a glaze. "I could do with a few more days of this," she said.

When they'd all eaten slices of Phoebe's carrot cake, Barry returned from the car with arms full of gifts. He piled them before their mother, a heap of gold foil and green ribbons. "Goodness," she said.

Phoebe's own gift was hidden in the pocket of her corduroys, a silver necklace from Tiffany for her parents' twenty-fifth anniversary. It would have been Tuesday. "You go first, Bear," she said, knowing he would like that.

Barry selected a box. Their mother opened it slowly, at pains not to tear the wrapping. She always opened gifts in this same careful way, yet afterward would crunch up the untorn wrappers and toss them away without a thought. "Makeup," she said, peeling the gold aside.

"They're the latest colors," Barry said. "It's a whole set."

Rows of tinted ovals sparkled like the watercolor sets Phoebe had used as a child. "I haven't worn much makeup in years," their mother said.

"Not to worry," Barry assured her, proffering a second gift. It was long and flat. Inside lay a card.

" 'A gift certificate,' " she read. "For a complete makeover?"

"What it is, is," Barry leapt in, "they figure out what goes best on your face, then they teach you how to do it."

"A paper bag would suffice in my case," their mother said, putting an arm around Barry. "Honestly, honey, you really spent time on this."

The next box revealed another gift certificate, this time for a hair salon. Their mother rumpled Barry's hair. "Excuse me," she said. "I'll have you know this style was the rage in '65."

But Barry seemed not to hear. He loomed over their mother, handing her presents as fast as she could open them. Phoebe gazed overhead at the fresh new leaves, furious. How rude, she thought, how totally insulting. Had Barry lost his mind?

Another gift certificate, this time for the Centurion, a clothing shop on Union Street. "This is too much," their mother said. "You've gone completely overboard here!"

"And now," Barry said, foisting upon her a final box, "to bring it all home, present number five."

Their mother opened it and frowned. "Fashion coordinator," she said. "It sounds like a machine."

"No, no, it's a guy," Barry explained. "You bring him with you to the store and he helps you choose what to buy. He knows what styles are 'in.' "

There was a beat of silence. Their mother looked up from the flurry of gold wrapping, and Phoebe glimpsed in Barry's face a flash of distress, as if the weight of so many gifts had suddenly borne down upon him. "I don't mean it badly . . ." he said.

"Of course not," their mother said, turning to Phoebe. "He's right, isn't he? I have become sort of a frump."

"You're not a frump," Phoebe said.

"I hope you'll really use this stuff," Barry said. "I mean, not just throw it in a closet or something." His eyes lingered on Phoebe, as though divining her urge to sabotage him.

"It's funny, actually," their mother said. "I've been thinking for months about trying to . . . revitalize my appearance."

"Really?" Phoebe said, taken aback.

"Honestly. But I had no idea where to start. Your timing is sort of uncanny, Barry."

Phoebe mulled this over uneasily. It was several moments before she remembered her own gift and pried it from her pocket.

"More presents," her mother said. "Such extravagant children."

Barry looked on in silence. Already Phoebe sensed his resentment, his fear of being upstaged. Their mother unwrapped the tissue slowly, opening the box to find the small blue Tiffany bag. "What a beautiful little bag," she said. "I'm sure I can use this for something." She was going slowly, balancing Phoebe's one gift against all of Barry's, making it last more than an instant.

Her mother loosened the bag's drawstring throat and found the necklace: a solid drop of silver on a slender chain. "Oh," she said. "Oh Phoebe, this is beautiful. Help me put it on." She lifted her hair and Phoebe fastened the clasp around her mother's neck, so the drop of silver rested in the shallow cup between her collarbones.

"Nice," Barry said, shifting on the grass. "That's pretty, Pheeb."

"It's spectacular," their mother said, kissing Phoebe's cheek. Phoebe caught the smell from inside her blouse, tart from her lemony perfume. Their mother always smelled the same.

Phoebe kept her eyes on her mother, waiting for her to acknowledge the true meaning of the necklace. Probably she would manage this without Barry's ever knowing—just a glance to remind each other of the vanished years stretched taut beneath them.

Their mother shut her eyes and tilted her face to the sun. Phoebe peered at her until she opened them. "What is it?" her mother said, straightening.

Phoebe just stared. She heard a distant pulse of bongo drums.

"Sweetheart, is something wrong?" Phoebe kept her eyes wide open. "Phoebe?"

"Don't you get it?" Phoebe cried, exasperated.

"Get . . ."

"Silver." It astounded her, having to say it.

Her mother touched the necklace. "Yes, I—I love silver."

"Think. Sil-ver," Phoebe said, drawing out the word. "I can't believe you don't understand!"

"What's to understand?" Barry cried. "Jesus, Phoebe, she said she liked it."

Her mother's hands fluttered at her neck.

"Silver! For your twenty-fifth."

But even now, her mother's face remained empty. Phoebe felt a pulse of fear deep in her stomach.

"Oh, I see," her mother finally cried, with relief. "Our twenty-fifth, of course. But that was last year."

Phoebe sat upright. "Last year? How?"

"What was last year?" Barry said.

"We were married in '52."

" 'Fifty-two! I thought it was '53."

"It doesn't matter, honey. Really, it makes absolutely no difference." Her mother still seemed off-balance. "Goodness," she said, "you frightened me."

"Cut. Cut!" Barry said. "Will someone please explain what this necklace has to do with you and Dad getting married?"

"Silver," their mother said. "That's what you give on someone's twenty-fifth wedding anniversary."

Barry leaned back, staring fiercely at the trees. "Got it," he said.

"It was a sweet thing to do," their mother said, but without the conviction Phoebe longed for.

Barry did not reply. Phoebe followed his gaze to a long, rainbow-striped kite twisting just above the trees. A muscle jumped near his jaw. "Don't be mad, Bear," she said.

"Oh, I see. Now it's my fault."

Their mother's shoulders fell. Phoebe sensed her defeat and blamed herself, getting the year wrong. She looked at the trees, an old man tanning his face and chest with a blinding foil bib. Beneath all this lay a frame of past events, a structure upon which the present was stretched like a skin. A mistake in that frame made the world appear senseless—clouds, dogs, kids with fluorescent yo-yos—how did they fit? What did they mean? " 'Fifty-two," Phoebe said, trying to calm herself. "I can't believe it was '52."

Barry opened his mouth to reply, then exhaled. Their mother took Phoebe's hand in her own, slim and warm, full of strong veins. Phoebe relaxed. Her mother saw the frame; she saw everything.

It was time for their mother to go to her office. She worked often on weekends, a fact that drove Barry to paroxysms of rage at her boss, Jack Lamont. They rode in silence to her building, on Post Street. "I have the most wonderful children in the world," their mother said, kissing them both as she left the car. Phoebe remained slumped in the backseat, leaving Barry alone in front. As he roared down Pine Street, running lights the instant before they turned green, she shut her eyes, trying to pinpoint when exactly it was that she and her brother had first turned against each other. But no matter how far back she went, it seemed already to have happened.

In the driveway Barry killed the engine. "I want to talk to you," he said, leading the way to the house. All Phoebe's life they had lived in this same sprawling Victorian on Clay Street. In recent years it had gone a bit to seed, the paint dull and chipped, overgrown trees leaning drunkenly at the windows. The third floor had been sealed off years ago, rented out as a separate apartment.

Barry followed Phoebe into the kitchen. "Sit," he said, pointing at a chair. She obeyed, heart racing. "This has to end, Phoebe. You know it."

"What?" Phoebe said. But he was right. She did know.

"You and Mom," he said. "How you've been living."

"But you're hardly ever around."

"That's right," Barry rejoined with energy. "It's physically painful for me to come inside this house! I mean, Jesus, Phoebe, it's been years and nothing's changed; it's like *Great Expectations.*"

Phoebe listened in dread. He was right, she thought, he must be right. She'd read *Great Expectations,* but couldn't think which part he meant.

"You, I'm not worried about," Barry went on. "You're about to start college. But Mom, Jesus. Alone in this house, that asshole boss eating up all her time and she's forty-seven years old, Phoebe. Think about it. Forty-seven."

"But I'm not going to leave her," Phoebe cried. "She won't be alone ever."

It was the wrong answer. Barry veered toward her, nearly wild-eyed. "Phoebe, don't you get it?" he shouted. "You have to leave, that's my whole goddamn point! You're not what she needs anymore."

"So that's why you gave her that stuff," Phoebe said, angry now. "So she can catch a new husband before it's too late."

"To put it crassly." There was a pause, then Barry went on in a quieter voice. "After Faith, I don't know, Mom just froze. It's tragic."

"You mean because of that one guy?"

"The only guy since Dad! And Mom was in love with Claude—"

"I don't want to talk about this."

"But after Faith died she just—"

"Stop it, Bear." Phoebe covered her ears. But she could still hear him.

"—cut him off. Like she thought she couldn't have that anymore. Like some kind of punishment."

He had never said anything like this before. Phoebe was amazed. "She dates," she finally said, addressing a straw placemat. "Mom goes out."

"Yeah, she goes," Barry said with scorn. "Then she comes back to you, this house—"

"We live here! What else can she do?"

"Let go," Barry said, his voice hushed. "Just, let go."

"Of what?" Phoebe asked fearfully. "Each other?"

"All of it. Dad, Faith, the whole number. Just"—he flicked open his hands, a flash of white skin—"let it go."

Phoebe rested her head on the table. Barry moved close and touched her hair, and something in Phoebe relaxed, trusting him. "You'll be amazed how easy it is," he said.

"What if we don't want to?"

The question seemed to stall him. Phoebe raised her head, then sat up. "I mean why?" she said, confused. "For you? Because you say?"

"Of course not for me—for you," Barry said, moving away from her, "you and Mom."

"But we're perfectly happy. You're the one who's upset with things, Bear. I mean, wait a second," Phoebe said, pushing away from the table to stand as the realization broke across her. "I know why you're saying this stuff, it's because of Faith."

"Bullshit," Barry said, uneasy.

"You want her gone," Phoebe said, the very words inducing a reeling sensation. "You want to stamp her out!"

Barry opened his mouth, speechless, and Phoebe knew she'd touched something. "You want her gone so you can be everyone's favorite."

The shadow of her brother's beard was blue against his skin. "You don't know what you're talking about," he said.

"You're scared," Phoebe said. "I see it."

They watched each other across the kitchen. Phoebe felt a surge of power over Barry that spent itself abruptly. "Forget it, Bear," she said, moving near him. They relaxed against each other, a rare moment. Even their hugs were normally tense.

Then Barry moved her away. "Fuck it, Phoebe. You didn't hear one thing I said."

"I did," she said. "I tried."

He laughed at her. "You refuse to try," he said, "which mystifies me, because what've you got to lose?" He waited. "Nothing! Don't you get it? This is nothing. You're sitting on nothing here." He left the room.

"It is not nothing!" Phoebe yelled after him, but Barry was out the front door, slamming it behind him so the floor shook. Phoebe heard the lash of his engine for several blocks. She imagined the freedom Barry must feel, ripping along the freeway toward Los Gatos, blasting his tape deck. She wished she knew how to drive.

Two or three months after their father died, Barry had decided one Saturday to clear out a basement storeroom for an inventing workshop. Their father's paintings crowded the little room: hundreds of canvases, many painted in the last months before he died. Nearly all the paintings were of Faith. Barry decided to throw them away.

He stacked a first load into an enormous cardboard box and dragged it out to the street. Faith was outside, trimming beds of ivy with a large pair of clipping shears. Phoebe slumped beside her on the warm brick path, twirling ivy stems like propellers and letting go, watching them fly for a second.

"What's in the box?" Faith asked when Barry came toiling along the driveway.

"Some old stuff of Dad's."

Faith went to the box, still holding her shears, and looked inside. She pulled out one of the paintings, a portrait of herself in the backyard. In the picture she was smiling. "Bear, what are you doing with these?"

"Throwing them out."

Faith seemed confused. She'd hardly been able to eat, and the shears looked heavy and dark in her hand. "Put them back," she told him.

"There isn't room."

"Put them where they were, Bear. Back in the basement."

"I'm throwing them out!"

"They were Dad's!" Faith cried.

Barry pushed past her, dragging the box behind him over the pavement. It made a loud scraping sound.

"Stop it," Faith cried. "Just—give them to me."

But something had happened to Barry. "I want them out," he hollered. "I'm sick of these things!" There were tears on his face. He seized a painting from the box and threw it into the street. There was Faith, face-up on the concrete. She shrieked as if she'd felt the impact. Barry took a second painting and tried to break it with his hands. Phoebe ran at her brother and held his arms, but he shook her off easily, pulled three paintings from the box and hurled them as far as he could. Two rolled in cheerful somersaults before toppling over. Barry was a fierce, wiry boy, and he moved quickly. Portraits of Faith soon littered the street: pastels, water-colors, wet-looking oils.

Faith was sobbing. She waved the shears in Barry's face. "Stop it," she screamed, "or I'll kill you!"

Barry paused. He looked at the shears, then smiled. He broke the painting over his knee. Faith plunged the shears into her own thigh.

Then everything stopped. Barry's face went so white Phoebe thought at first that her sister had killed them both. There was a long, almost leisurely pause when none of them moved, when the day tingled around them.

Then everything happened at once: Faith sank to the ground. Barry tore off his T-shirt and tied her leg in a tourniquet. Phoebe pounded wildly on the door of their neighbor, Mrs. Rose, who ferried them to Children's Hospital in her clattering station wagon. There were shots, stitches and lots of questions. It was a game, they'd all insisted—instinctively, without plan or discussion among them—a game that had gone too far.

It had always seemed to Phoebe, looking back, that on that day something shifted irreversibly among the three of them. As Faith lay in the emergency room, bleached from loss of blood, Phoebe saw in her sister's face a kind of wonderment at the power of what she had done. It was spring 1966. That fall Faith would start high school, and within a year would be immersed in what had become, in retrospect, the sixties. But when Faith and Barry fought, none of this had happened yet. Faith was thirteen, wearing green cotton pants. She knew nothing of drugs. Even the first of so many boyfriends had not yet crossed their threshold.

After the fight Barry kept out of Faith's way. He would watch her from a distance, following her movements with his dark eyes. He was afraid of her. And Faith, after that day, no longer seemed frightened of anything.

Phoebe went upstairs to her sister's old room and shut the door. After Faith died, their mother had tried to clear this room out, but Phoebe raised such a clamor she agreed to wait, and a few months became a year, then two; it was somehow too late.

For the past three years Phoebe had slept here. Just slept. Her clothes and possessions she kept in her old room, down the hall.

Phoebe knew her mother disapproved of this arrangement, for she never came in Faith's room to perch on the bed and talk, as she had before.

Faith had draped her ceiling in reams of blue batik. Glass pyramids lined her shelves, scarabs and rare beads and miniature gold incense burners. Outside the window hung a cheap set of wind chimes, cloudy, peach-colored discs reminiscent of Communion wafers. They'd come from the sea, Phoebe thought. Their sound had the giddy unevenness of children's laughter, or some fine thing splintering into pieces.

Phoebe flopped on the bed, still in her Wallabees, listening to Faith's chimes and feeling the house pull in around her as it always did when strangers left it. Faith's room was full of pictures, snapshots of toothless grins and Christmas trees, birthday cakes suspended above the upturned faces of children in party hats. Faith had loved pictures—photographs, their father's drawings, it made no difference—she'd craved any glimpse she could catch of her own life reflected back at her.

Objects crowded the shelves of her sister's closet, a Mexican straw hat embroidered with flowers, a cowhide wallet, flesh-colored arrowheads from the rain-soaked fields around St. Louis, on and on it went, down, down, until at the very bottom lay— what? Phoebe didn't know. But something. The key to a mystery was buried among the forgotten moments of her sister's life, times when Faith had leaned in a doorway or slumped on her bed fiddling with an alarm clock. Alone in this house Phoebe often heard a faint humming noise, some presence beneath her, around her. Faith's room was the entrance to it.

Maintaining the room was not easy. Pictures dropped from the walls, dust gathered in the batik. Phoebe knocked it into clouds with a broom, then vacuumed it up from the rug. Twice she'd taken down the batik and washed it by hand, hung it in the yard to dry, then reattached it exactly as it had been, or close. But despite her best efforts, there was a kind of erosion in the room, a sagging and curling and fading she was powerless to halt.

Phoebe rarely had friends to the house, aware that in most people's eyes she would look like a nut. Yet this mystified her—for how was living in your sister's room any crazier than surrounding yourself with life-sized posters of Roger Daltrey hollering into a microphone, as her friend Celeste did, or following the personal lives of Starsky and Hutch, or sleeping on a street curb overnight to get decent seats to a Paul McCartney concert? Being obsessed with total strangers was considered perfectly normal, yet on the few occasions when outsiders came into Faith's room, Phoebe glimpsed herself through their eyes and was terrified. So she kept them out.

Barry had this same effect. Much of what he'd said was true—detritus from their mother's brief courtships filled their house, weird breakfast cereals from a man in market research, record albums by someone's punk rocker son, their grim mechanical sound suggestive of auto assembly lines. But these dates were little more than anecdotes for Phoebe and her mother to laugh about, how one man had confessed to a previous life as the lapdog of the British Queen Mother—"Can you imagine?" Phoebe's mother cried, flinging off her pumps as Phoebe writhed on the bed, shrieking in horrified delight. "A dog? And he tells me this?" By ten-thirty she was usually back at home listening to Phoebe talk about the quaaludes and LSD she'd seen people take, how her friends had raced cars on the Great Highway and had sex among the cattails beside the school playing fields. For with each revelation Phoebe also was saying, I didn't do this—they did, but not me—assuring her mother that she was careful, separate, likely to live forever. Phoebe often sensed that she and her mother had struck a kind of bargain, each gaining something crucial from the other by keeping her outside life at bay. They often spent Saturday mornings together at her mother's office, Phoebe doing homework at the boss's big desk. Afterward they would eat a late lunch somewhere fancy, each drink a glass of Chardonnay, and as they walked to the parking garage through the oceany wind, Phoebe would feel the magic of their lives—what spectacular things awaited them.

It was a mystery: what throbbed up from the basement, what rang in Phoebe's ears, alone in this room. Something had happened to Faith.

The sixties had been named and written about. In the public library Phoebe had spent hours poring over old *Oracle*s, leafing through scholarly and journalistic accounts of the "Love Generation." But she read with a restless, uneasy suspicion that these analyses were leading her further from the mystery's core, not toward it. Often she found herself drifting instead to the fashion magazines, leafing through *Vogue* and *Harper's Bazaar* where models lazed in their inadvertent beauty, Lisa Taylor and Patti Hansen, Janice Dickinson glancing furtively over one shoulder while being yanked down a narrow street by a small black schnauzer on a leash. Where was she going? Where were all of them going, so gorgeous and distracted, the trees grainy— Yes! Phoebe would think, her breath quickening as she flipped the pages. Yes. Another world gleamed through these images. Phoebe searched the pages half expecting to find a picture of Faith.

She curled on the bed and closed her eyes, longing for sleep, but the chimes distracted her. Barry was wrong, she thought, he was wrong and she was right, she and her mother were right. It all made sense. Phoebe thrashed on the bed, searching her mind for the righteous indignation she'd felt in the kitchen with Barry. But it was gone. And instead she felt the other thing, a queasy vertigo, as when her mother had failed to comprehend the silver necklace. Phoebe opened her eyes and looked at Faith's room, the pictures and trinkets she'd struggled for so many years to keep intact. I'm right, she thought, it all makes sense. And then: How long can I go on like this?

Her mother's boss dropped her off at seven o'clock. She was cheerful, sunburned. "God, I've been freezing to death in just that

damn sweater," she said, tossing her clothes on the bed and heading for the bathroom.

Phoebe perched on the toilet seat, yelling back and forth to
her mother while she showered. The delicate scent of her soap
rose with the steam, and Phoebe was so relieved she was back.
Fog had surrounded their house, browsing coldly at the windows.
She lowered the shades.

Her mother pulled on a sweatsuit and they went downstairs to
make a cheese soufflé. Phoebe tore the lettuce leaves. She'd never
really learned to cook, but was a good assistant.

Taking turns, they beat the egg whites in a hammered copper
bowl while a Brahms piano concerto roiled through the house.
Phoebe noticed a gold serpentine chain on her mother's wrist.
"Were you wearing that before?" she asked.

Her mother paused, holding the whisk. "Isn't this something?" she said. "It was sitting on my desk, all wrapped."

"Jack?" Phoebe said, incredulous. The only birthdays her
mother's boss remembered were the ones she reminded him of.

"I know. I almost fell over."

"Did he—I mean, did he watch you open it?"

"No, he disappeared. I think he was embarrassed."

"Maybe it wasn't from him."

"No, it was. I mean, I thanked him. It's nice, don't you
think?"

After dinner they carried bowls of Häagen-Dazs upstairs to
her mother's giant bed. A rerun of *The Rockford Files* was on.
True to form, Jim Rockford fell in love with the woman he was
trying to protect and his old dad was threatened by thugs outside
the silver trailer. Phoebe fought sleep but finally gave in.

Her mother woke her. "You're pooped," she said. "Go to
bed."

"Wait, I want to see the end," Phoebe muttered, sitting up
and rubbing her eyes. She searched the screen for Rockford.

"The show's all over, sweetheart," her mother said. "This is
just news. It ended while you were sleeping."

three

While Phoebe's father was painting her sister, Faith, Phoebe would bang objects sometimes to try to catch his attention, or rustle leaves if they were outside. Her father looked, but only for a second.

She tried disappearing, wobbling into the bushes in her bare feet or hiding up in her room, waiting for someone to call, but no one did.

Finally, in frustration, she went back to them. Faith reached for Phoebe without even moving her head—she was good at sitting for paintings. Phoebe slumped against her sister and, out of nowhere, she was happy. Their father grinned. "You've been ignoring us, squirrel," he said.

Afterward Phoebe would run to look at the canvas, thinking she might be in the picture, too, but there was only Faith. And sometimes not even Faith was fully visible, just a hint of her face, a shadow or else nothing at all. But even then Phoebe saw her sister hidden among the trees or windows or abstract designs, like a secret. She was always there.

"It's a gesture," their father said, "an expression you make with your body."

Diving lessons. A gigantic turquoise swimming pool, water syrupy-looking in the thick summer light. Three boards, the highest a virtual skyscraper attempted only by the seasoned teenaged divers, doglike boys with short legs and long tapered torsos, girls whose slender bodies curved toward the water like birds diving for fish, entering it with so tiny a splash that they left an impression not so much of having dived as of having ascended.

"Sure you're scared," their father said. "Don't fight it, that's the trick. Walk into your fear. Let everything go and you'll get it all back, I promise."

Phoebe listened, mystified. She was too young to dive except from the pool's edge, but her father's face she understood. He climbed on the lowest board and bounced, handsome in his faded trunks, his muscular body more like the boys' than the half-melted physiques of the other fathers. He could still do a one-and-a-quarter, though he'd been much better back in the seminary. "Don't fight the fear—let it swallow you," he called, still bouncing. Their heads bobbed as they listened.

Abruptly he stopped and climbed off the board. "You poor kids," he said. "You just want to get wet."

From a reclining chair he watched them practice, gathering Phoebe absently into his lap, calling over her head to Faith and Barry. "You're not ready for that," he said when Faith headed for the middle board. She tried anyway, hitting the water sloppily, legs flapping back over her head. "She's a show-off. That's not enough," he remarked to Phoebe, adding with a laugh, "Too bad."

For ten days each July, they came to St. Louis to visit Grandma and Grandpa in the mansion where their mother grew up, and while their mother played bridge with old friends or golfed with Grandpa, their father drove them to the country club. Thick grass surrounded the pool. You could have your lunch brought there: cottage cheese, salade niçoise. No money ever changed hands; you just signed "3342" with a tiny yellow pencil and the bill went to Grandma and Grandpa. Early evenings, tanned and showered, martini in hand, Phoebe's father would lift her into his arms to wait for her mother on the club's flagstone terrace. As he gazed down at the sloping green lawns and egg-shaped flowerbeds, Phoebe felt his happiness. Behind the chugging locusts she heard the faint thump of tennis balls, like a heartbeat. There was a warm sweet smell of cut grass. He was happy. Phoebe drank her Shirley Temple, saving the cherry for last. Summer heat on her bare arms, filling the sky with strange, imaginary colors. It looked like heaven.

But he never painted enough. Driving the stakes of his easel deep into the lawn, their father would gaze up at the towering elm and walnut trees outside their grandparents' house, everyone hanging back, letting him alone. "I can't believe this is all I've done," he'd say, panic in his voice at the discovery that he'd spent his vacation drinking cocktails, charming the club wives with his lean handsomeness, his roguish air of having come from somewhere else, someplace less fastidious. Now the vacation was over. Tomorrow they would fly home.

"I'll bring them to the club today," their mother said. "You stay and paint." But no, no, he would take them. He was dying to escape.

Beside the pool their father lay back in a chair and closed his eyes. Phoebe and Barry and Faith clustered helplessly around him, frightened of a world that could reduce their father to such despair. Phoebe stared at his tense, unhappy face and wanted to help, but she felt so small. He couldn't see her.

Faith kept glancing at their father, fidgeting with the straps of her bathing suit. Finally she rose to her feet. With dread in her face she walked slowly to the highest diving board and climbed its steps. She looked tiny up there, eleven years old, slim and deeply tanned, slightly knock-kneed. "Dad," Barry said. Their father opened his eyes and rubbed them, followed Phoebe's and Barry's stares and sat upright, muscles tense in his neck. Faith stood a long time at the end of the diving board. A few teenagers waited impatiently below, craning their necks to see what was taking so long. Please do it, Phoebe thought. Please, please do it. Faith gave a tentative bounce. Then a clarity came to her movements, a stillness; she leapt high in the air, spread wide her arms and arced into a swan dive, head straight down like an arrow's head, pulling the wand of her body toward the turquoise water. Her splash was minute—in years to come Faith would never again match that first, perfect dive, a fact that galled her—and their father leapt to his feet. "That's it!" he cried. "Jesus, you see what she did?" He was grinning, his despair gone, and Phoebe knew the day was saved.

Faith must have known, too. She rose from the water, steamy chlorine footprints on the pool's concrete lip, grinning from ear to ear as they all waited, and suddenly Phoebe was angry—why her? Why always her? Then, without warning, blood poured from her sister's nose over her mouth and chin and neck, spattering the wet concrete, as if by accident she'd breathed out blood instead of air. Faith frowned, raising a hand to her face. "Oh," she said, and there was a beat of confusion before their father bolted to her side, laid Faith gently on the grass and sent Barry running for ice, a wet towel.

When the nosebleed finally ended, Faith slept for a solid three hours. Their father moved her tenderly into the shade of a tree, but she didn't wake; she was exhausted.

Phoebe and Barry went swimming, then ordered grilled cheese sandwiches for lunch. At the sight of Faith's thin, sleeping shape, Phoebe felt something move in her stomach and was ashamed of herself for having wanted her sister to jump.

Phoebe's ragged memories of her father made her angry at herself; she should have watched more closely, should have memorized whole days from his life. She remembered the strength of his arms, the rough, easy way he would lift her to his chest—absently, as if she were a cat he wanted to put outside—would toss her into the air or spank her without warning, so startling Phoebe that her crying came as an afterthought.

His dark mustache was unexpectedly soft. Mornings when her father and mother were still in bed, Phoebe would burrow between them, inhaling the milky warmth of their flesh, softer after hours of sleep.

Grandma and Grandpa O'Connor still lived in the Southern California town where Phoebe's father grew up. Mirasol was mostly Navy—Grandpa had been a military policeman—and the small olive-colored house where these grandparents lived could not have contrasted more starkly with the others' St. Louis mansion. But Mirasol had the ocean. Sea wind rattled the doors of the neighborhood church, grains of sand fell from prayer books. As Phoebe watched the priest break the Host, she would think, That could have been my father. He'd almost become a priest. Phoebe imagined his strong arms lifting the golden chalice to drink the blood of Christ, placing a pale Host on the tongue of each parishioner, murmuring "Amen" to their "Body of Christ." But to Grandma and Grandpa O'Connor's lasting sorrow, her father had refused a place at Holy Cross Fathers at Notre Dame and gone instead to Berkeley, where by his own account he endured his electrical engineering courses so at night he could play the bohemian, sketching nude models in paint-spattered art studios.

Afterward he'd moved to San Francisco, lived in North Beach and worked the construction jobs that had cost him some hearing on the left side. On weekends he would set up his easel behind the Maritime Museum and paint the old blue-eyed Italian men who played bocci. Phoebe's mother had met him there, on a trip to San Francisco with friends from Bryn Mawr, a graduation present from her parents. After their wedding Phoebe's father took an engineering job at IBM, the job Phoebe came to believe had cost him his life.

Phoebe grew up surrounded by sketches of Faith: in their mother's arms at the hospital, at home in her crib, on a rabbit skin, splashing in her bath, in a high chair, car seat, playpen. Beside the vivid record of her sister's childhood, Phoebe's own existence felt shadowy, and this confused and enraged her. Seven years younger, she grudgingly endured stories of how Faith had lunged for everything in sight with her small, star-shaped hands: bees, hornets, broken glass, diamond earrings. Everyone spoke of her daring, how when her father pushed her on the swings Faith would egg him on, yelling "Higher! Higher!" until at four years old her swing overshot the bar it was attached to, wavered in midair and dumped Faith onto the sand.

Their mother screamed, bolted from the bench where she'd been rocking Barry's stroller and ran to Faith, who lay crumpled in a heap. "Gene, how could you push her so high?" she cried.

"She told me to," he said, shaken, abashed. "She kept saying 'Higher.' "

Faith was white-faced, her lips dry. Grains of sand fell from her hair. "Look at her," their mother chided, lifting Faith up. "Honestly, Gene, she's four."

"Not hurt," Faith whispered. When her parents eyed her skeptically, she insisted, "Not hurt."

Years later the grandparents still would tease her, asking, Does it hurt? Does it hurt? No way, Faith always said, laughing. She was famous for that.

Phoebe tried in small ways to match her sister's daring, taking little chances on her trike or with the neighbor's dog, but Faith was always older, always doing more. When her sister's exploits led her into trouble, Phoebe felt a surge of guilty satisfaction. Once Faith came home crying after a hunting trip in Sonoma with their father, a dead rabbit clutched to her chest. "Well of course it's dead. You shot it, for Christ's sake," their father said, exasperated, but Faith hadn't meant to: she loved to shoot clay pigeons but had never hunted, and failed somehow to realize that firing at a flash of brown fur would lead to something dying. She buried the rabbit in the backyard among the other beloved family pets ("Killed by me," read its epitaph, inked on kindling wood with Magic Marker, and underneath that, "i am sorry, Bunny"). Years later Faith still mentioned the incident, that poor rabbit she'd murdered, by accident.

On the Osage River one Sunday: someone's pier, slippery wooden slats, Faith pushing with the other kids until a boy sent her flying into the river with her sun hat on, in front of all the parents. Faith emerged dripping river water, laughing crazily under the sopping hat, waited until her assailant wasn't looking and then threw her weight against him so the boy slipped, fell unevenly into the water, smacking his head on the pier as he went down, a big gash just above the left eye. Faith's horror at the sight of his face running with blood, all the parents leaping from white grille chairs in a single motion. They rushed to the boy, whose eye was saved by half an inch—less—and while they rallied to get him to a hospital, Phoebe followed her sister to a hidden corner of lawn, powerless to stop her sobbing. Phoebe felt afraid then, touched by the bad thing Faith had done. Her sister disappeared for the rest of that day. They found her at nightfall, coiled tightly in a spare bedroom, fast asleep. Their father carried her to the car. Back at Grandma and Grandpa's, Phoebe stood outside her parents' door and overheard them arguing. "I'm saying stop encouraging her," her mother said. "You see what happens."

"How do you mean? Encourage her how?"

"I mean she does it for you. That wildness? Come on, Gene. You know perfectly well that's for you."

Her father's voice was hushed, furious. "You think I told her to knock that kid in the river?" he said. "I don't tell her to be wild, Christ Almighty. She just does it."

"You don't have to tell her," her mother said. "Any fool can see it makes you happy."

Remembering her father, Phoebe pictured a man always struggling to carry too many things at once, children, briefcases, rolls of un-stretched canvas. She saw him leaping up the garage stairs late for dinner after a poetry reading by one of the Beats he so admired, Lawrence Ferlinghetti, Gregory Corso, Michael McClure—all were his acquaintances. He'd even been present on the legendary night when Allen Ginsberg challenged a heckler to take off his clothes, then flung off his own before a stunned audience. Often their father painted late at night, stealing an hour or two when they'd all gone to sleep. He'd be up the next day before anyone, clean-shaven, smelling of limes. With dark circles under his eyes he kissed them all good-bye and drove downtown to his other life, the one he despised.

Weekends, he would haul his easel and canvas and paintbox to the cliffs near the Golden Gate Bridge. If Phoebe walked slowly enough, her father would sling her into his arms and carry her, too. Their mother followed with the blanket and camera and picnic basket, herding Faith and Barry. Only when they'd all fin-ished eating would their father set his canvas on the easel and stand before it anxiously. Often he couldn't paint, couldn't make himself even begin and finally gave up, resting his head in their mother's lap. But occasionally Faith would wander over and hand him a glittering purple flower she'd picked from the ice plant and something would hit him just right. "Baby, can you stay there a minute?" he'd ask, and always Faith would; Phoebe couldn't re-member her sister ever refusing in favor of some game or a fort she and Barry were building, though there must have been times when she'd wanted to. Or maybe not. Maybe nothing of her own could compete with their father's need of her, her unique and seemingly bottomless power to save him.

Now and then Barry would emerge after hours alone in his room holding a machine, which he would show their father. Phoebe always dreaded these occasions, for try as their father might to look alert, machines were his work, and he loathed them. "You made this stuff in school, right, Dad?" Barry would say, always hopeful at first. "You got any ideas of how I can make this go backwards?" When he realized their father was only half listening, Barry would fall silent. "Forget it," he'd say, and storm off, leaving their father startled, with no idea what he'd done wrong. No! Phoebe wanted to holler outside her brother's door. No, no, no! He made everything worse. She felt such a terrible pain, knowing what would happen, unable to stop it. It left her sick. She pitied her brother and wanted no part of his weakness.

Their father was always struggling, always tired, but there came a time when he struggled harder to do what he'd always done, when suddenly he was exhausted. The circles under his eyes turned dark and moist as clay. Even his skin seemed weaker, bruising at the smallest impact. Phoebe and Barry and Faith no longer wumphed against him when he tottered home from work; now they seized his legs and held them tightly, filling him up with their strength, replenishing what IBM had drained away.

When Phoebe was five, she looked across the dinner table one night and saw her father sleeping. Her mother crouched at the oven with Faith, easing a toothpick into a chocolate cake. The kitchen was warm, an arc of steam on each windowpane.

"Daddy," Phoebe said softly. He didn't move. His lips were white. "Daddy?"

Barry sat beside their father, pouring salt on the tablecloth and arranging it in piles with his fork. Normally their father would have stopped him—the salt mounds were a regular battle between them—and Barry wore a smirk of incredulous triumph at what he was getting away with. He looked up at their father, whose head hung to one side. They heard his labored breathing. Barry grinned at Phoebe and pulled a few hairs on their father's arm.

Faith galloped back to the table holding her cake between two red potholders. At the sight of their father she stopped. "Mom," she said.

"Good Lord," their mother said, dropping into a chair and

gathering their father to her, so his head lolled against her shoulder. "Let's get you to bed." He nodded, rising slowly from his chair.

When their parents had left the room, the three of them stared at one another, unsure how to react. Barry's grin still hung tentatively on his face. But Faith looked afraid and Phoebe felt it, too, like ice water down her spine. The cake plate still hung in Faith's hands, forgotten.

The next day was Sunday. Monday their father would go to the doctor. There was a false heartiness in the air, too much loud, bright laughter.

After church they went to Baker Beach. Normally the waves were bloated and sodden, pulling away from the gritty sand with a sound like deep-frying. But today the sea was flat, silvery as a lake.

Their mother leaned against a log, one arm around their father. Faith and Barry rolled up their pants to wade and Phoebe ran behind them, shrieking when the icy water touched her feet. Barry wanted their father to walk with him to the far end of the beach, where giant mussels and purple starfish clung to the rocks.

"Don't think so, Bear," their father said. "Not today." Barry looked crestfallen, and their mother offered to go. They set off, padding over the thick sand.

"Want me to sit for you?" Faith asked.

"I'm beat," their father said. "You draw me for a change."

"Okay," Faith said with energy. She sat, the big pad covering her legs. She held the stick of charcoal between two fingers and looked at their father. They both laughed shyly. "It's hard," Faith said.

"Damn right it's hard," he said, closing his eyes and resting his head against the log. "Just draw what you see."

Phoebe leaned against her sister. Together they took in their father's pale, spent face. Faith made a few lines, charcoal trembling in her fingers. The longer their father's eyes stayed shut, the more nervous they became. They had to keep him awake.

Faith stood up. The pad dropped to the sand, and their father's eyes snapped open. "I'm going swimming," she said, slightly breathless.

Phoebe looked up, surprised. This was not a swimming beach.

"In your clothes?" their father said.

"I wore a swimsuit." She pulled off her sweater, hurrying, whipping off her stretchy pants to reveal a blue one-piece with a white ruffle along the bottom. The wind made her shiver.

Their father sat up. "I'll be damned," he said. "If you'd told me, I would've worn mine."

"But you're tired," Faith said.

"Not that tired."

Phoebe felt relief. Faith moved nervously on the sand. "Will you watch me?" she asked.

"Sure I'll watch. Just don't go too far out."

"But watch." Faith was always asking to be watched, having reached that age when nothing seems quite real without an audience.

Faith walked toward the sea. "She's nuts," their father said, and laughed. "Your sister is one hundred percent crazy."

They watched Faith slowly enter the water. She was twelve, fragile in her adolescence: small breasts that astonished Phoebe whenever she caught sight of them, the slightest indentation at her waist. Phoebe saw from how slowly her sister walked that the water frightened her. So what, she thought anxiously. Get in.

Her father leaned against the log and gathered Phoebe into his lap. The top of her skull fit perfectly under his jaw. Together they watched Faith wade deeper into the water. "It must be cold as hell," he remarked.

Faith turned to look back at them. "Are you watching?"

"We're watching," he yelled. "We're wondering when you're going to dunk your head."

The instant he said it, Faith dove underwater and began to swim. With careful strokes she moved parallel to shore, first the crawl, then the breaststroke. She turned around and came back the other way, doing the backstroke and sidestroke. Now and then she paused, calling out to make sure they were watching. Phoebe fattened their father's yell with her own—she was happy, Faith was keeping him awake.

"You must be freezing to death," he shouted.

"I'm not," Faith cried through chattering teeth. "I'm warm as a desert."

But gradually Phoebe felt her father's head grow heavy above her own. Faith did the butterfly. "You see that?" she called. But the wind had risen, her voice was faint. Their father's eyes must have fallen shut.

"Daddy?"

Phoebe raised her arm, but apparently her sister couldn't see it. "Dad?" Faith called again. When there was no reply, she resumed swimming, faster now and away from shore. Go on, Phoebe thought, Faster! She felt unable to move, as if she could act only through Faith, as if her sister's movements included her. Go, go, she thought, watching Faith's shape grow smaller. Good! He would have to wake up now.

The next time Faith stopped, she looked tiny. If she called out, Phoebe couldn't hear. Faith lingered there, looking back toward shore as if waiting. Phoebe felt ready to explode with the urge to run to the water, shout that their father was sleeping again and Faith had to do something. But he rested so solidly against her, pulling long, deep breaths, and Phoebe felt paralyzed—not frozen so much as absent, without a body of her own. Go, she thought, Keep going. And as if hearing her, Faith began swimming again. It became hard to see her sister through the cold glitter of sunlight on the ocean. Phoebe thought she stopped once more, but couldn't be sure.

It worked. To Phoebe's vast relief, their father stirred behind her. He rubbed his eyes, shook his head and looked out to sea. He looked up and down the beach. "Where's Faith?" he said.

"Swimming."

He leapt to his feet, holding Phoebe under her arms. He set her down on the sand.

"Jesus Christ," he said. "Where is she?"

It hadn't occurred to Phoebe that Faith herself might be in danger. Now a sick, guilty feeling swelled in her stomach as her father bolted to the water's edge. She followed slowly.

"Faith!" he bellowed at the top of his lungs. "Faith!" His voice cut the wind, and the force of yelling so loudly made him start to cough. "Faith," he cried over and over again. Then he stood, one hand shielding his eyes, and stared at the water. "I think I see her," he said. "I think she's out there."

He turned to Phoebe, who waited timidly at his side. Her father's pants were soaked to the thighs. He took Phoebe's arm and walloped her behind so quickly and efficiently that she hardly knew what was happening until it was over. "How could you let her get so far out?" he shouted helplessly. "Why didn't you wake me up?"

Phoebe began to sob. She had no idea why.

Their father resumed calling out to Faith. He hollered until he had almost no voice left, then he coughed and coughed, unable to stop, until, to Phoebe's horror, he doubled over and vomited into the water. Afterward he wiped his mouth and began shouting to Faith again.

She was swimming back. Phoebe saw her sister's tiny arms plowing the sea. Their father's face was gray; he looked on the verge of collapse. He stood back from the water, breathing hard. Phoebe clung to his leg, and absently he cupped a palm over her head. "She's coming back," he said. "You see her?"

Finally her sister emerged from the water, frail and exhausted, nearly gasping for breath. From the look on their father's face, Faith must have known she was in trouble. "You said you'd watch," she said, without confidence.

Their father slapped her across the face, his palm making a loud, wet noise against her cheek. Faith looked stunned, then tears filled her eyes. "That didn't hurt," she said.

He hit her again, harder this time. Phoebe, standing to one side, began to whimper.

Faith was shaking, her thin limbs covered with gooseflesh. With each breath her ribs stood out like a pair of hands holding her at the waist. "Didn't hurt," she whispered.

He hit her again, so hard this time that Faith bent over. For a moment she didn't move. Phoebe began to howl.

Then he lifted Faith into his arms. She clung to him, sobbing. Their father was crying, too, which frightened Phoebe—she'd never seen him cry before. "How could you scare me like that?" he sobbed. "You know you've got my heart—you know it." He sounded as if he wanted it back.

Phoebe put her arms around whatever parts of them she could reach, her father's wet pants, Faith's slippery calves. A long time seemed to pass while they stood like that.

Finally their father lowered Faith onto the sand. She looked up at him, her teeth chattering violently. "Daddy, are you going to die?" she said.

There was a pause. "Of course not," he said. "There's nothing wrong with me."

"You're not scared?"

"No, I'm not scared. Why, are you scared?"

Faith took a moment to answer. Phoebe thought of her father coughing, vomiting into the waves. She wished she hadn't seen it.

"No," Faith said slowly, "I'm not scared."

He was dead within the year.

four

After her father died, Phoebe sleepwalked among the other second-graders, cut off from the high spirits that buoyed them through games of jump rope and tetherball and two-square. Her own legs felt so heavy. Even her head felt heavy. She wanted to take it off and leave it somewhere.

She had never believed their father would die. After he became sick, she went to church with Faith every day, lounging beside her sister on the pew, content to swing her feet and gaze at the dangling Savior and pretty candles while Faith took care of the praying. Phoebe hardly bothered to pray, and when she did, it was often for some greedy purpose; much on her mind were those Kiddles that came inside plastic perfume bottles, each with its own scent. She had Lilac and Lavender, but was desperate for Rose. She didn't worry much about their father. She was powerless to help him and therefore not responsible; Faith was acting for both of them. Phoebe left the church feeling cleansed by her sister's feverish prayers, satisfied, as Faith seemed to be, that whatever cure she was working could only result in their father's recovery.

After he died, Faith stopped brushing her hair and a giant rat's nest formed in back. She didn't care. Loose, soundless tears slipped from her eyes when their mother tried to comb it. She was racked by stomach pains, prompting Dr. Andrews to limit her diet to boiled rice and saltine crackers. Weight fell from her like layers of clothing. She disappeared. And only then did Phoebe realize what a brilliant, magical world the old Faith had granted access to. Neighborhood games had formed around her spontaneously—statuemaker, spud, capture the flag—lasting over days in the rapturous hours between school and dinnertime. Their house had been a labyrinth of secret passageways Faith never tired of searching for, tapping floorboards, prying at moldings in the zealous belief that any moment a wall would slide away to reveal underground cities, treasure chests gorged with pearls and silver. Barry tried to fill the gap of their sister's absence, tried rallying the neighborhood for a treasure hunt one Saturday, but the effort fell flat. He wasn't enough. Gradually the neighborhood gang began to disperse, and Barry retreated to his room, stung by his failure.

A deadening sameness bore down on them. The floorboards and walls of their house no longer trembled with hidden passages —it was just a house. Their street was a street, Phoebe's room a room, not a honeycomb of hiding places. Their mother was constantly hugging them, smoothing their hair, but she moved like someone underwater, so pale that Phoebe saw blue veins on her temples. In losing their father they had somehow lost one another —Barry's door always shut, Faith drooped alone before the TV set. Try as they might to be cheerful at dinner, eventually the silence always won, snuffing out conversation like the fog that overwhelmed their house each night, obscuring every other house from view. Phoebe wanted to scream, kill that silence for good, but she felt buried under the ordinariness of everything in her life —a carton of milk, a stick of butter—they were bricks being laid on top of her one by one. She began closing the door to her own room, losing herself among *The Chronicles of Narnia, Alice in Wonderland, Peter Pan,* magic worlds that seemed to Phoebe far less magical than Faith's had been until their father died.

Retracing the steps of their father's life was one of the few activities Faith still found worthwhile. Phoebe liked going with her to prowl his North Beach bachelor haunts. "Dad sat on this same bench," Faith said in Washington Square, across from the Church of Sts. Peter and Paul, whose white façade he'd loved to paint. "He lay on this grass." And Phoebe shared her sister's awe at touching the very things their father had touched. He was gone forever, but he was everywhere. It felt miraculous.

Nowadays young people lounged in Washington Square wearing colorful outfits, smoking, playing guitars. Faith was too shy to approach them, but they fascinated her. She speculated that they must be painters, or the Beat poets their father had so admired. She used Phoebe as a prop, piggybacking her around Washington Square for a better look at its bohemian occupants. After their father died, these were Phoebe's happiest times.

The following March, 1967, their mother went on her first business trip to a film festival in Tucson. She departed with great misgivings, leaving Phoebe and Barry and Faith in the care of an old friend of Grandma O'Connor's named Mrs. McCauley, sweet but hard of hearing, who insisted they eat everything on their plates. With a knowing flap of her plump hand, Mrs. M. (as they called her) dismissed Faith's lingering stomach ailments and ladled extra corned beef hash on her plate. Faith was slowly getting better; though still frail and rather quiet, she'd started high school and even had a boyfriend, Wolf, at whose house she ate dinner the remaining nights until their mother came back.

After dinner Phoebe would pace nervously up and down the silent hallway past her brother's door, which was always shut. One night, in desperation, she knocked. Barry opened the door an inch or two and peeped out. "Heya, Pheeb," he said through the crack.

He turned and went back in his room, leaving the door ajar.

Phoebe hesitated, then decided this must be an invitation to enter. Barry's room looked unfamiliar, its red rug and bubbling fishtank. She couldn't remember the last time she'd seen it.

Barry sat at his desk. "What's up?"

"Nothing."

Though she and Barry were only seven and twelve, there was a wariness between them that seemed always to have been there. "What're you doing?" Phoebe said. "Homework?"

"Nah, I finished." He was scrutinizing something on his desk. When Phoebe approached, Barry hunched protectively over whatever it was, so she went instead to the fishtank. There were eight or nine fish, two frilly black with ugly bulbous eyes, her favorite. "Can I feed them?" Phoebe asked.

"I already did."

"Okay." Phoebe watched the fish in silence, overcome with despair. Plants fluttered in one corner of the tank, jostled by silvery bubbles that rose to the water's surface and vanished.

"Actually, Pheeb?" Barry said. "You can if you want. Feed those guys."

With a tiny key he unlocked a drawer beneath the tank, where, to Phoebe's surprise, his fish food was kept. She sprinkled a few flakes on the clean water, anxious not to abuse her privilege. Only when the fish had gulped these down did she dare add more. "See, Bear?" she said. "They're hungry."

Mysteriously, the tension between them eased. Phoebe began exploring her brother's room, which, despite Barry's savagely guarded privacy, was arranged as if for an audience. An ant farm, a Southern plantation house with a field of miniature corn, some creature's brain inside a jar, plastic dinosaurs romping among miniature trees and cottonball clouds—shelf after shelf of displays.

Phoebe sensed her brother's dark eyes following her, his pleasure at having captured her attention. She grew bolder, moving close to the shelves, even touching things, filled with a desperate wish to please him. She inquired about the cargo planes and battleships he'd built, animating her voice as she remembered their mother doing when Barry was younger and would still show his projects to the family.

"I've got something that's better than everything else put together," Barry said, moving back toward his desk. "But it's a secret. You've got to swear not to tell."

"Swear on the Bible," Phoebe declared. She followed her brother to the desk. Spread across it were thin sheets of creased, rather ancient-looking paper covered with cryptic blue sketches. Phoebe heard her brother breathing behind her.

"They're Dad's," he said in a hushed voice. "From engineering school."

Phoebe stared at the sketches. She felt Barry poised to spring at her reaction, and it made her nervous. "Are you going to try and make one?" she asked.

His whole face lifted in a grin. He unlocked a desk drawer and, with a flourish, removed a wallet-sized board with a frazzle of knobs and wires erupting from it. A black electrical cord emerged from one end like the tail of a rat, and Barry plugged this into a fixture above his desk. He turned a switch and a small blue light winked on, accompanied by a shrill siren-like noise. Grinning feverishly, Barry raised the volume. He made the siren a buzzing noise, then turned to Phoebe in triumph.

She looked at him questioningly. "What is it?"

"A sound generator," Barry said. "Back when Dad was in school, you needed vacuum tubes to make these things. Now you can use transistors, so they're a lot smaller and they don't break so easily."

"How did you make it?" she said over the buzzing.

"It was hard," Barry told her with relish. "I had to order the parts from this store in New Jersey, Edmund Scientific. Then I just figured it out, you know? Studied Dad's sketches."

He was flushed, dark eyes fastened to the small machine. He turned a knob and the buzzing sound became a loud ringing. "Think about it," Barry hollered over the racket. "You know? I mean, think about it, Pheeb."

Phoebe was overwhelmed—by the whispery trace of their father, which seemed caught against its will in this shrill contraption; by her own fragile closeness to Barry, which seemed in constant jeopardy.

"I'm going to make them all," he said rather grimly. "Every single one."

Phoebe nodded, smiling at her brother. Her head ached. Much as she longed to share in Barry's awe, she wished he would turn the thing off. She tried to imagine their father here—his reaction to the leftover drawings, even Barry's machine. And she knew that he wouldn't give a damn.

"So, what do you think?" Barry said, leaning close.

"It's great," Phoebe said. She felt a panicky urge to get away from him.

"Really?" With his neck thrust forward and thin, smudged hands, Barry looked so meager, so peeled away. Phoebe felt an ache of pity, for herself and Barry both. "Really, Pheeb?" he said. "You're not just saying that?"

"It's the best," Phoebe lied. She felt ready to cry. "Daddy would be so happy, I know he'd be so happy."

"You think?" He was grinning now.

Phoebe nodded miserably. The tortured machine whined on. A faint smell of melted plastic tinged the air. When Mrs. McCauley tapped on the door to announce Phoebe's bedtime, Barry unplugged his treasure and spirited it away.

The dullness of Phoebe's bedroom met her like a blow: polar bear wallpaper, rows of faded stuffed animals, a wicker chair that crackled when you sat in it. Mrs. McCauley tucked the sheets tightly around her, as if fastening Phoebe in for a violent ride. "It's nice, you and your brother keeping company," she said. "He needs it." Phoebe turned on her side, eager for sleep. Mrs. McCauley lingered a few moments in the wicker chair, humming faintly, then departed in her slow, stiff gait.

———

Phoebe woke in darkness to noises downstairs. Her bedroom was over the kitchen, and for some minutes she lay still, fearful that thieves had broken in through the back door and were heading upstairs to murder her. Then she heard music. Curious, Phoebe rose from bed and crept barefoot down the back stairs in her nightgown, hugging the banister. She heard unfamiliar voices; then, to her astonishment, she heard her sister's laughter.

Phoebe stopped in the kitchen doorway, amazed. The room looked like a church, pitch dark except for dozens of white Christmas candles spilling their syrupy light across its walls. Organ-like music snaked from the radio. Faith and Wolf leaned at the stove, their backs to the door, surrounded by unfamiliar people who appeared to be in costume: a slim, dark-haired girl like the Queen of Spades in her floor-length purple dress of crushed velvet; another girl with ropes of white-gold hair and a sparkling white pants suit. The man nearest the door wore a top hat, his cut-off jeans exposing an abundance of deeply sunburned flesh. It was he who first noticed Phoebe.

"Greetings," he said, tipping his hat. "Your hair wants cutting."

Phoebe stared at him, jarred by the familiar phrase. Then she remembered: the Mad Hatter's first words to Alice in Wonderland, a scene she'd read only that morning.

"It's rude to make personal remarks," Phoebe said, reaching for Alice's response. "Don't you know that?"

The man's face went still with surprise. Then he threw back his head and laughed, mouth open, his round tongue the same pink as his sunburned legs. Everyone turned. "Who is this groovy kid?" said the sunburned Hatter.

Faith went to Phoebe and knelt beside her. As Phoebe clung to her sister, she felt the rapid pulse of her heart. "Is it morning?" she asked.

"Almost," Faith said, breathless. Her cheeks were flushed. A tiny painted rainbow began above her left eye and curved around her cheekbone. "We're making breakfast to eat on the roof and watch the sunrise."

"What about Mrs. M.?" Phoebe said.

"She's sleeping," Faith whispered, crossing her fingers. "I told her I was staying overnight at Abby's house."

The strangers watched Phoebe very kindly, as if the mere sight of her standing there in her nightgown were somehow pleasing. Finding herself at the center of attention gave Phoebe a jittery pleasure. One man wore a magician's crimson velvet cape and held in his palm two silver balls, which made dense clicking noises as he rolled them together. Another man looked like Jesus, in his thick beard and sandals. He'd been rolling skinny yellow cigarettes; now he lit one so the tobacco sputtered and crackled, took a puff, then offered it to his neighbor. "What a beautiful kid," said Jesus, breathing odd, sweet-smelling smoke. Phoebe blushed to the neck.

"C'mere, beautiful," Wolf said, pulling a chair to the stove. "Come help the chef."

Shyly Phoebe approached him. In the candlelight Wolf looked like a warrior chief, deeply tanned even to his hands. His skin had a wonderful smell, like her father's leather boots when he'd left them out in the sun. Wolf lifted Phoebe onto the chair, his warm hands on her ribs. Phoebe noticed a tiny gold hoop in his earlobe.

The eggs were warm, as if they'd just been laid. Phoebe cracked a luminous shell, letting the yolk and white slide into a glass bowl. Wolf added vegetables to the buttered pan, and the blend of smells became intoxicating: sweet cigarette smoke, buttery vegetables, a rich, oily scent of the candles. The White Witch rose from her chair and began to dance, floating in the music as if it were liquid. The sunburned Hatter snored gently, his top hat upright beside his head on the kitchen table. The Queen of Spades perched on the lap of a man in a harlequin shirt, a Joker from the same pack of cards she was queen of.

"Who are they?" Phoebe whispered to Faith.

Faith shook her head, gazing into the room. "I don't know," she said.

"But where did they come from? How did you find them?"

"They found us," Faith said. "Or we found each other, I guess. At the Invisible Circus. We were all at the Invisible Circus."

It made perfect sense—these costumes, the crazy good humor of everyone. Phoebe loved the circus, and was crestfallen that her sister would go to one and not bring her. "A three-ring circus?" she asked.

Faith smiled, turning to Wolf. "Was it?"

"Bigger," Wolf said. "Four-ring, I'd say. Maybe five."

"Five rings!" Phoebe turned away in fury.

"Oh no," Faith said. "She thinks—no, Phoebe, it wasn't— they called it a circus, but it was just a party, a big party in a church. Then it got closed down."

"No animals?" Phoebe said warily.

"No, nothing like that at all," Faith said. "More like a grown-ups' funhouse."

Phoebe thought of Playland, an old funhouse out by the ruined Sutro Baths where their father used to take them: a revolving tunnel you couldn't walk through without falling and bruising your knees, the blasts of air that shot up through tiny holes in the floor. There were long, perilous slides of polished wood that you descended on potato sacks, getting raw white welts where your skin touched the wood. Faith and their father had loved going to Playland, but beneath its smiling good cheer Phoebe sensed a grimacing, sinister core.

Faith took Phoebe's hands in her own. "Something is happening," she said softly. "Can you feel it?"

"What?"

"I don't know, but I feel it. Like this vibration underground." Her voice trembled, as if the vibration were running through her body.

"What are you talking about?" Phoebe said.

"Everything's changing," Faith said. "Everything's going to be different."

Things had already changed—too much. "I like how it is," Phoebe said.

"No, this is better," Faith said. "This is history. You can't stop it."

"What? What is it?" Phoebe asked, frightened now.

Faith ran shaking fingers through her hair. "I don't know," she said. "But it's going to be huge."

"Don't try and tell it," Wolf said gently, stirring the vegetables. "She'll know when she knows."

"It's here," Faith said, shutting her eyes and holding both hands suspended near her breasts. "Phoebe. Can you feel it?"

Phoebe turned to look at the room. The White Witch, the Queen of Spades and the Joker were all dancing now, moving their arms like swimmers. Phoebe tried to imagine what they felt, suspended in the warm, silky music—it seemed a pleasure she'd known herself, once, a long time ago. The music came faster, cymbals, voices, laughter. Candles dashed their light against the walls.

"Something happened," Faith said. "I don't know what it was."

Phoebe found herself smiling. She was happy, a delicious warmth beginning in her stomach and seeping out through her limbs like the taste of a candy. "In the court of the Crimson King . . ." chanted the radio singers, the scene like something from an old book, Sir Lancelot and Queen Guinevere, Aladdin. The dancers' bodies rippled like flames. Where am I? Phoebe thought, remembering nights at the amusement park in Mirasol, bathed in colored light, riding her father's shoulders so high she could touch the paper Chinese lanterns with her fingers. Where am I? Wondering felt so much better than knowing the answer.

"I can," Phoebe said, extending her arms as if to cross a tightrope. She was Alice, downing the potion, waiting to see what would happen. "I feel it."

"Daddy would love this, wouldn't he, Pheeb? He'd love it,"

Faith said, and Phoebe knew instantly that Faith was right; whatever this was, their father would approve wholeheartedly. She pictured him leaning back against a counter, arms crossed, a look of hungry pleasure on his face. Phoebe stood on her toes, lifted from her chair by a swell of joy and comprehension: her sister knew the way, she always had.

There were footsteps on the back stairs. Barry appeared in the doorway, fully dressed. He stood a moment, taking in the candles, the strangers, the unrecognizable kitchen. Phoebe glimpsed the scene through her brother's eyes and saw how strange and fragile it was, how it might whirl away as suddenly as those children stepping back through the wardrobe out of Narnia, into their real lives.

"Bear," Faith said. "We're making breakfast."

Barry glanced at his watch. "Six-thirty A.M.," he said, flicking on the overhead light. The bright, empty glare startled them, making everyone blink. Someone lowered the music, and the dancers fell still.

"All Mom's Christmas candles," Barry said. "All used up."

"But we can buy more," Faith said. "Christmas isn't for almost a year."

Barry eyed her grimly. "I think these people should leave."

Wolf turned off the stove and went to him, slinging an arm around Barry's slight shoulders. "Come on, man," he said, "this is once in a blue moon."

Phoebe watched the struggle in her brother's face. Barry admired Wolf, wanted badly to be liked by him. But he hated giving in to Faith. "It's not my blue moon," he said, pulling away from Wolf. "Or Phoebe's. We were just sleeping."

"But you can be part of it, Bear," Faith said. "Look, Phoebe's helping us cook—you can join in, too, why not?" It seemed less an invitation than a plea.

Wolf tried to touch him again, but Barry withdrew, glancing fearfully at the strangers. "What's going on, Faith?" he said. "Did you take drugs?"

"Aw Christ," said the Queen of Spades, hoisting herself on a counter and crossing her legs in disgust.

Barry flinched. Then he stuffed his hands in his pockets and looked at the floor. "I want everyone to leave," he said. "Now. Or I'm calling the police."

Wolf shook his head. "That's not the way."

"Barry, please," Faith implored.

But at the mention of police the group roused itself, the White Witch pulling a macramé bag from under the table, the sunburned Hatter smoothing his hair and restoring his top hat. Faith smiled beseechingly at everyone. She looked frantic. Phoebe felt her sister's desperation, her fear that the one good thing she'd found was about to be taken away. The Invisible Circus, Phoebe thought, the Invisible Circus, chanting the words to herself like a spell. But the group was standing now, ready to go.

"Phoebe," Barry said from the doorway.

Her own name startled her; she'd forgotten that she herself was a presence in the room. She was standing barefoot on a kitchen chair. From the doorway Barry held out his hand. "Come on, Pheeb," he said. "Let's wait upstairs."

Phoebe turned helplessly to Faith, but all expression had dropped from her sister's face like a pillowcase sliding to the floor. She looked as she had for months, indifferent.

"Come on, Pheeb," Barry said. "It's okay now."

He spoke as if they were alone, but Phoebe felt the eyes of everyone but Faith upon her and stood paralyzed, anxious to please all of them, to rid herself of this unfamiliar power. She pictured herself imprisoned among Barry's locks and drawers and keys—that wretched sound machine, their father's forgotten sketches—while the Invisible Circus sailed away without her.

Barry dropped his hand, uneasy. "Phoebe?"

"I'll come up later, Bear."

Something sagged in Barry's face. He stepped backward through the doorway and hovered outside it. Phoebe stared at her bare feet, aware of having made an irreparable move. When Barry turned and bolted upstairs, she felt relief.

Now the group went hysterical, giddy. The light flashed off, someone turned up the music, and a frenzy of dancing overcame them. The candles had never gone out; now they flung their honey light with rebellious zeal. Clutching the Mad Hatter's hot, sunburned fingers, Phoebe danced without shame, music rocking her limbs like the bubbles moving the plants in Barry's fishtank. She felt a breathless, manic joy. "Hurry," Faith cried as light streaked the sky. "Hurry, let's get outside."

They blew out the candles and scrambled upstairs with their plates of eggs, three flights, then a last narrow flight to the roof. Bursting into the open air, they threw themselves down on the pebbled tar and ate ravenously, tearing bread from two enormous loaves that Wolf had bought off a bakery truck. The roof was flat, and from its height a spectacular view arrayed itself, the scalloped shores of Sausalito and Tiburon, glassed-in houses flashing like ore. The Golden Gate Bridge was a slender red skeleton. The magician walked on his hands, cape dragging behind him. The sky seemed nearer than usual. Phoebe felt as if she could catch the gassy pink clouds with her hands.

The wind blew up through her nightgown, chilling her bare skin. Wolf set down his plate and lifted Phoebe into his lap, rubbing her arms to warm her. She felt very small, as if Wolf's body were a hand, she a leaf or an acorn clutched within it. "Poor Phoebe," Wolf said, holding her tightly. Phoebe didn't know why he'd said that, but did not contradict him. If Wolf knew how happy she was, he might let go.

Faith darted around the roof, arranging piles of torn bread for the seagulls. Wind shook the jeans on her skinny legs, lifting her dark, tangled hair above her head. When the loaves were gone, she stood apart from the group and began jumping in place, facing the bay and just leaping, arms stretched to the sky, feet pounding the gravel. Everyone watched her at first, nodding, smiling at this overflow of spirits. Phoebe's gaze remained on her sister long after the others' had wandered. She couldn't look away.

Eventually Faith stopped jumping. Flushed, she lowered herself to the roof beside Phoebe and Wolf, a calm over her like a veil. The others were drifting to sleep, tangled together like cats. The Queen of Spades sang "Now I Lay Me Down to Sleep."

"Maybe Dad can see us," Faith said softly, looking at the sky. "Maybe he's watching."

Phoebe looked up. And yes, the sky and sunlight seemed fuller than on the other days, alive with their father's watchful, humorous gaze. Phoebe stared into the fresh white sun and offered herself. Not alone—alone she was nothing—but as part of Faith, a small shape included within her sister's outline. It hurt. Her whole body ached as if it were dissolving. Phoebe kept her eyes open as long as she could, then shut them. The darkness relieved her. "Poor thing," Wolf said, rocking her to sleep.

five

Phoebe's mother had worked for Jack Lamont since 1965. He was a film producer, best known for *White Angel,* which won Best Picture in 1960. Phoebe had never seen the movie.

She found Jack impossible to like, handsome though he was with his deep tan and pale blue eyes. A terrible chill seeped from beneath his warm-looking skin. "Hiya, Pheebs," he'd say when she came in the office, then the pale eyes flicked away and that was it, her moment had passed. She would always be his secretary's daughter. "He's shy, that's all it is," her mother said, but that wasn't all. Jack was a man in complete control of his life.

Her mother had started as a part-time typist for Jack when their father was first diagnosed. Later she became his full-time assistant and now, thirteen years later, effectively ran his life. No decision he made was too sublime or mundane not to warrant her involvement: cutting partners from a deal, choosing restaurants on the Riviera (where she'd never been), Mexican golf resorts, birthday and Christmas gifts for his far-flung children. It filled Phoebe with pride that a man as cool and self-possessed as Jack could depend on her mother so heedlessly, as if her very touch ensured good fortune. Yet she resented the way his life loomed over theirs, his emergencies wiping out long-held plans in an instant. Barry claimed their mother had all the disadvantages of being Jack's wife, without the benefits. "Benefits!" their mother snorted when he aired this theory. "There are no benefits to marrying Jack." He was thrice-divorced, still engaged in legal skirmishes with his last ex-wife. "On the payroll" was his term for the fractured array of steps and exes and halves whom he still supported; if nothing else, their mother said, you had to admit the man was generous. ("Guilt" was Barry's dour construction.) As for the wives, Phoebe's mother still lunched with all but the third, who was keeping her distance until the legal matters were settled. Jack married interesting women, her mother said, although the throes of divorce sent him reeling into the soothing embraces of sweet, empty-headed starlets.

Phoebe's mother complained about her boss, but Phoebe knew she loved the job. She was co-producing a film with Jack— her first—a documentary on the life of one of Faith's heroes, Che Guevara.

Monday morning was drenched in fog, as if the city itself were still dreaming. Her mother drove, Phoebe sitting uselessly beside her, as always. She still hadn't learned to drive. Her mother discouraged it, citing their solitary car, but Phoebe knew the true reason was fear for her safety. Not driving embarrassed her. Like all her mother's restrictions it divided Phoebe from her peers, but she accepted it as she did not smoking, watching enviously as friends mouthed perfect silky rings, gulping down luscious French inhales like whipped cream.

"I've been thinking," Phoebe said, "about maybe going somewhere."

Her mother glanced at her. "Like where?"

"Europe."

"What for?"

"Just, I don't know. Just travel. Maybe start college a year late."

There was a long pause. "This seems a little out of left field," her mother said.

"I know it," Phoebe said bitterly. "Because I never do anything."

"Sweetheart, you're about to start college," her mother said, brushing Phoebe's hair from her eyes. "That's something."

"Everyone does it."

"So?"

"So I don't want it," Phoebe said, startled by her own vehemence. "I want something real to happen to me. I feel like a zombie, I swear to God. Like I can't wake up."

There was a long silence. "I'm relieved you're saying this, Phoebe," her mother finally said. "Frankly, I've been worried about you."

Phoebe was caught off-guard. "Why?"

"Just, lately you seem so cut off," her mother said, almost timidly. "Since school ended, you hardly seem to call anyone, even when they call you."

"But I saw people last week—"

"What about Celeste? You used to see so much of her. Then not going to graduation—"

"You said you understood!"

"I know it," her mother said, thoughtful. "I've been a big part of the problem, looking back."

"What problem?" Phoebe cried.

"I was always afraid you'd run wild and something would happen . . ." her mother said in a thin, quiet voice. "I've held you back."

Phoebe had lost her bearings. She sat in silence.

"You know, I hadn't planned on telling you this quite yet," her mother said, "but lately I've been giving some serious thought to selling the house."

"Really?" Phoebe said, uncomprehending.

"Just, it's so big, and soon I'll be the only one living there. I've been dreading telling you, frankly," she said with an odd laugh.

Phoebe jerked upright in her seat. "What do you mean?" she said. "You mean sell our house?"

Her mother turned to her in alarm. "It's just a thought."

"How could you even think that? Sell the house?" Phoebe's voice filled the car.

"I haven't sold it. Honestly," her mother said, flustered. "I was thinking aloud."

They'd been idling at a curb, but now her mother reentered traffic as if to flee the subject. Phoebe felt wild. Selling the house was the wrong thing, the worst possible thing. "So I guess I can go," she said, incredulous.

Her mother looked blank.

"To Europe."

"No, sweetheart. No. I meant that I understood the impulse."

"You can sell the house but I can't go to Europe?"

Her mother shook her head, clearly puzzled. "It's a bad idea, Phoebe, isn't that obvious? Of all things—that?"

It was like yesterday, with the silver necklace. The hidden world was there, but suddenly her mother couldn't see it.

"You let Faith," Phoebe said.

Her mother glanced at her. It was a bad thing to say. A long silence fell while they pulled over at Oak and Masonic, where Phoebe got out each morning for work. Her mother wore a silk blouse with a bow at the neck, her Diane Feinstein blouse, she called it. In the Panhandle, purple-clad figures performed Tai Chi on the wet grass.

Her mother rested her elbows on the steering wheel. "Just getting her out of this city seemed like a godsend."

Phoebe nodded, anxious to agree.

"I thought Wolf could take care of her," her mother went on. "But that was too much to ask, even of him."

Phoebe kept nodding, a jack-in-the-box. "That makes sense."

"Does it?"

Her mother turned to her. In the bare morning light her face looked slightly swollen, large-pored, as if it had been bruised at one time and never quite healed. Phoebe felt the weight of her response.

"It does," she said, shaken. "Mom, it totally does."

The fog was beginning to thin. Houses emerged with colors replenished. Phoebe left the car, waving as her mother pulled into traffic. She watched the back of her pale head until the Fiat disappeared, then walked to work full of vague foreboding.

The Haight-Ashbury intersection had vanished.

Nostalgics were to blame, their zealous removal of the street signs having finally persuaded the city to stop installing new ones. From inside the café where she worked Phoebe often saw tourists traversing Haight Street with maps aloft, aware that they were close, so close, but unable to find the dead center they sought.

Much remained of the sixties: whole-food stores with their bins of knobby fruit, head shops, an occult store full of shrunken heads and tinted crystal balls. But Milk and Honey, where Phoebe worked, had nothing in common with these places. It was a new café full of red neon hearts and white tile, owned and run by gay men. Being neither gay nor male, Phoebe of course was on the outside, but the feeling of this was easier, somehow, than being on the outside where she should have belonged. She listened with passionate interest to her colleagues' tales of growing up in strait-laced American towns where they'd dated cheerleaders and made faggot jokes, bluffing their way through one life while they dreamed of another. And here it was. They'd found that promised life and nothing could take it away from them now, or so it seemed.

A new guy was starting today, and Phoebe would be training him. She'd worked at Milk and Honey for over a year, finishing high school at noon, then riding the bus to the Haight. Except for the manager, Art, she'd been here longer than anyone.

The new guy was good-looking, which explained Art's more

than usually high spirits. "This is Phoebe O'Connor," he said, introducing them. "Phoebe, Patrick Finley. I suggest you talk about your Irish roots."

Phoebe and Patrick exchanged forced smiles. Patrick was tall, dressed in jeans and a white T-shirt. Phoebe wouldn't have guessed he was gay, but he must be—she'd never known a straight guy to work here.

"Phoebe is training you," Art explained to Patrick. "She's our paragon of virtue, aren't you, dear?"

Phoebe blushed. "Not exactly."

"Well, no, not if you count all the bodies buried under your house," Art said merrily.

"They're deep," Phoebe said, trying to get into the spirit of it.

But Art's attention was entirely on Patrick. "She's never smoked a cigarette," he said. "Can you imagine?"

"Not once?" the stranger said softly, meeting Phoebe's gaze. She shook her head, feeling more than usually shy. His eyes were a bright, hungry green.

"She's training to be a nun," Art went on. "Although I will say I've seen her drunk."

Phoebe looked at him in alarm. At the Haight Street Fair a few weeks before, she'd gulped down several glasses of sangria in the bright sun and started to cry while watching the motley parade of hippies—their worn-out faces and eyes that seemed bleached from one too many blinding sunrises. Art had put his arms around Phoebe and hugged her. "It's a long life, kiddo," she remembered him saying.

"But why am I surprised? All Catholics are drunks," Art went on, winking at her. "Even the priests."

"Especially the priests," Patrick murmured.

"What makes you think I'm a Catholic?" Phoebe said, relieved that her drunken tears had been kept a secret.

"It's written all over you, dear," Art said, kissing her cheek.

The morning rush began. Phoebe felt sorry for new employees, that bumbling, incompetent phase, but Patrick seemed used to it. She guessed he was in his mid-twenties. Phoebe taught him her forte, caffè latte, which she made with such consummate skill that the coffee and milk formed separate shifting layers inside the glass mug. Often these efforts went unnoticed by customers, who stirred her masterpieces without so much as pausing to admire their perfect layers.

When the crowd ebbed, Patrick retreated to a nook outside the view of customers. He took a Camel from his pack and tapped one end against the counter. "Can I?" he asked.

"Sure. Everyone does."

He lit up, eyes falling shut an instant as the smoke met his lungs. "You're smart not to," he said, exhaling. "It's ugly."

"Oh, I don't think so," Phoebe said with feeling. "I love to watch people smoke."

Patrick burst out laughing. "Are you serious?"

Phoebe nodded uncertainly. She hadn't meant to be funny.

Patrick took a deep pull on his cigarette, rolling the smoke from his mouth back into his nostrils. "I'm surprised you don't just do it, then," he said. "It's not like there's a waiting list."

"I promised someone I wouldn't." This was her usual line.

Patrick stubbed out his cigarette, running both hands through his dark hair. "Well, they did you a favor," he said.

At two o'clock Phoebe hung up her apron, brushed her hair and left the café for her lunch break. On the corner a guitarist was strumming "Gimme Shelter" on a threadbare electric, an amplifier sputtering beside him. He wore a black leather coat tied at the waist, yellow bell-bottoms and grubby platforms. The clothing looked older than he did.

Clustered at his feet were the vagabond kids who populated Haight Street. Now and then one of them would appear inside Milk and Honey asking for a lemon slice, which Phoebe had learned only recently they used to dilute heroin before shooting it into their veins. These kids were younger than she, far too young to have witnessed the sixties, yet Phoebe felt they were linked with that time in a way she was not, and envied them for it. She still gave them lemons whenever they asked, though Art had forbidden it.

Phoebe continued walking to Hippie Hill, a hump of coarse grass just inside Golden Gate Park. She climbed to the top and sat cross-legged, unwrapping her bran muffin and coffee. Normally she read during lunch—she loved to read and did so quite uncritically, taking each book as a prescription of sorts, an argument for a certain kind of life. But today she ate mechanically, staring down at the trees. Sell the house? Now, after so many years? It was crazy.

And she wasn't "cut off." She'd gone with a group of people last week to *The Rocky Horror Picture Show,* where a piece of bread landed in her hair, then on to a Broadway disco where an eel-like man plied her with watery cocktails in exchange for the dubious privilege of wriggling opposite her on the seething dance floor. She wasn't "cut off." But try as Phoebe might to blend with her peers, it felt like bluffing, mouthing the words to a song she'd never been taught, always a beat late. At best, she fooled them. But the chance to distinguish herself, impress them in the smallest way, was lost. At her vast public high school Phoebe had felt reduced to a pidgin version of herself, as during "conversations" in French class—Where is the cat? Have you seen the cat? Look! Pierre gives the cat a bath—such was her level of fluency while discussing bongs or bands or how fucked-up someone was at a party.

She was not a presence at high school. If someone thought to include her, Phoebe was included, but if she stood up and left mid-party, as often she had, phoning a taxi home among the bright potholders and fruit-shaped magnets of someone's kitchen, few people noticed. Handed a hit of acid once, she'd slipped it into her pocket (kept it to this day), but nobody caught the move. "Hey, were you okay with that?" they'd asked days later, for apparently it was powerful, someone had flipped out. Phoebe pictured herself in the eyes of her peers as half ghostly, a transparent outline whose precise movements were impossible to follow. During free periods she had no place to go. Often she simply wandered the halls, feigning distraction and hurry, afraid even to pause for fear that her essential solitude would be exposed. A glass case full of old trophies stood near the school's front doors, shallow silver dishes from state swim meets, faded ribbons; they were dusty, inconsequential, no one looked at them. As an excuse to stop walking, Phoebe sometimes would pause before that case, pretending a trophy had caught her attention—I'm nothing, she would think, I could disappear and no one would notice—her face reddening in shame as she stared at the meaningless trophies and waited for the bell to class.

But tortured as Phoebe was by her own irrelevance, deep within herself she saw its necessity. For all that surrounded her now was barely real. What about Faith? she would remind herself, walking the smudged halls or eating her lunch alone in the hospital-smelling cafeteria; what about the student strike of 1968? All that was forgotten. Even the teachers who had been there seemed barely to remember. What a nightmare, they would say, rolling their eyes; you kids are much better. But what about Faith O'Connor, who organized the strike and gave a speech in the courtyard? Well, maybe, they'd say. Let's see . . . squinting at the window as they reached for some blurred memory to match Phoebe's encyclopedic descriptions of her sister; but no, incredibly enough, no one remembered Faith, either. They saw nothing but the present. And sometimes even Phoebe would forget, dancing to the Tasmanian Devils or Pearl Harbor and the Explosions; for a moment everything but her immediate surroundings would slip from her mind. But something always brought her back—jerked her, like discovering she'd overslept—and Phoebe would remember that her present life was nothing but the aftermath of something vanished, at which point its details would simply shrink. Her life shrank even when she fought to hold it still—clinging to a boy named Daniel in his car during a school dance, watery music faintly audible from the gym as they lay across his front seat, fog crystallized like sugar on the windshield. She'd liked him all year. Daniel's breath on her neck, ribs splayed beneath her like a fan, and suddenly a different world seemed to offer itself to Phoebe, bones and flesh, all she wanted was this— Yes, she thought, this was enough—but already it was starting to slip, she was slipping from Daniel even as she clung to him, something she needed to remember like distant footsteps in the corners of her mind. "Hey, you still there?" he asked, but Phoebe wasn't, could barely make out Daniel's startled face as she drew away, full of anger, feeling as if someone had robbed her.

Afterward, as always, Phoebe was relieved she had escaped— even when Daniel avoided her eyes in the halls, for he was nothing, all of this was nothing. She had to resist. If Phoebe lost herself in her own small life, it would be like dying.

At six-thirty Phoebe and Patrick hung up their aprons and left Milk and Honey together. The sun was low. Outside the door they paused. The street was empty, caught in the pause between day and night.

"Thanks for the help," he said.

"You did great."

"I don't know. The first day's always a bitch."

"No, you did."

They stood in silence. Phoebe felt depressed, anticipating the empty night ahead. Her mother was busy.

"I've got a car," Patrick said. "You need a ride someplace?"

"No, thanks," she said, then wondered why she had. It would be better than taking the bus. But Patrick had already turned.

"Okay. See you."

Phoebe was going the same direction, but felt stupid following Patrick when they'd just said good-bye. She lingered outside Milk and Honey, watching the night staff set up. When Patrick was out of sight, she headed for the bus stop at Haight and Masonic. There was a party on Ocean Beach that night, but those parties were always the same, surf toppling in, a wavering line of bonfires strung across miles of cold sand. Phoebe stopped at a pay phone and fished through her tip money for a dime. She dialed her mother's office.

"Sweetheart," her mother said, "how was work?"

"It went fast. Mom, I can't remember," Phoebe lied. "Are you busy tonight?"

"I am, unfortunately," her mother said, lowering her voice. "We've got a director in from Germany."

"Does it go late?"

"No, just cocktails, although I don't know, we may go on to dinner. Why, are you at loose ends?"

"Not really. There's a party."

"Well, that might be fun. Why not go?"

Phoebe said nothing, remembering her mother's worries about her.

"Well, you're welcome to join us," her mother said. "Would you like to?"

Phoebe declined. An evening with Jack Lamont she could do without. Besides, it was probably dressy.

"All right then, I'll see you later on. If I'm back early, we can watch some TV. Oh, but you're busy."

"But I might be home though. *Kojak*'s on."

Her mother paused. "Sweetheart, is something wrong? Your voice sounds funny."

"I'm outside."

"Okay. Well, have fun at your party. And please be careful— promise you'll call a taxi home. I'll reimburse you."

"But Mom?"

"Yes?"

"How late will you be back? Maybe I won't go."

"I'm not sure, honey. I wish I could tell you, but I just don't know."

Phoebe could think of nothing else to say. "Okay," she said.

"Bye-bye. I'll see you tonight."

"Bye."

Phoebe continued slowly toward Masonic. Abruptly she stopped, turned back around and headed for the bus downtown, to her mother's office. She wanted to see her. Just see her, just for a minute, then she would go home.

The bus came quickly, floating on its electrical wires. From the crest of each hill Phoebe glimpsed the East Bay blinking across the water. Torpid planes floated overhead.

She got off downtown. The air was linty, opaque. Her mother had warned her repeatedly that cars crashed more often at dusk than at any other time, and Phoebe crossed the streets with care. Nearly a block from the office she was startled to see her mother standing outside the building. Just waiting there, in her white suit. Phoebe stopped. The sight of her mother alone on the street, unaware of her own presence, was strangely compelling. She felt a childish urge to hide—it had been a favorite game of Faith's, positioning herself and Barry and Phoebe in different parts of a room to eavesdrop on their parents; the wild hope of hearing things they weren't supposed to know. Of course, their mother and father heard their sniggering, the rasp of Barry's asthma. "Where are those kids?" their father would growl, causing a leap of delicious fear in Phoebe's stomach. "Where are those kids, so I can hang them out the window by their toes?"

Phoebe flattened herself against a wall. Her mother's back was turned. She faced downtown, where a soap-bubble moon had risen between two buildings. Her mother tipped back her head to look at it. This was strange, watching her watch the moon. Phoebe felt a little guilty.

Someone else came outside—Jack, Phoebe thought at first, then recognized the bouncing, tentative stance of Marty, her mother's new intern. Phoebe had met him twice—very eager, determined to make his own films. His ears stuck out.

Typical Jack, Phoebe thought, making everyone wait. She could see him now, telephone wedged between shoulder and jaw, flapping them out the door as he lit a cigarette. She heard her mother's and Marty's voices, but not their words. It began to seem absurd, skulking here while her mother made conversation with a boy hardly older than Phoebe. She longed to leave her hiding place and join them, but how to explain her arrival? Say she'd changed her mind and wanted to come with them, in her torn jeans and berry-spattered T-shirt? She could imagine Jack's reaction.

A car pulled up alongside her mother—their own boxy Fiat. To Phoebe's surprise, Jack climbed out. He wore a dark blazer, shiny buttons catching the glare from the streetlight.

The three stood talking for several minutes. Phoebe's mother's voice was high, silvery. Jack kept laughing, which seemed unlike him. Phoebe began to feel desolate, stowed away in her corner, furious with all three of them for leaving her out. She wished she'd just gone home.

Finally Marty handed Jack a folder and went back inside the building. Jack and her mother waved. Then her mother turned and looked right in Phoebe's direction—Phoebe's heart contracted like a fist. But her mother hadn't seen. She turned to Jack, who caught her hands in his own and swung them. Then Jack took Phoebe's mother in his arms and kissed her mouth.

Phoebe was so stunned that she simply stared. It seemed possible this was not her mother after all; as a child she'd made that mistake in department stores, clutching the legs of strange women whose skirts resembled her mother's. A man and woman were kissing—they could be anyone, Phoebe thought, filled with brief chaotic hope. But there was the Fiat, lights still on, the left one slightly dimmer, their own without a doubt. It all felt irreconcilable, dreamlike. The kiss seemed to last so long. Afterward Jack and her mother hugged, folded together like a single body under the streetlight. Phoebe shut her eyes.

When she looked again, they were getting into the car. Jack took the driver's seat. The windshield clouded their faces. The car drifted away from the curb behind a bus, heading in Phoebe's direction. She flipped to face the wall, shoving her cheek to the plaster and holding very still, not turning around until the traffic had gone and the street was silent.

Phoebe stayed where she was for some time. Her mind felt curiously empty. She began walking aimlessly, toward Polk Street, feeling only a numb, dizzy sensation, as if she'd been hit on the head.

Phoebe reached a block lined with male prostitutes her own age or younger, crotches bulging, faces riddled with acne. One boy leaned against a parking meter, smoking. Phoebe approached him. "Can I bum a cigarette?" she asked.

At close range the boy's face looked uneven, as though poorly assembled under hasty conditions. "I've only got this one," he said, pulling it from behind his ear. "You want it?"

Phoebe took the cigarette. The boy's hands were thin, freckled. They trembled a little. "Light?" he said.

She nodded, placing the cigarette between her lips. It was filterless, and mixed with the tobacco was an oily taste from the boy's hair. He struck a match and held it for her. Phoebe let the smoke wander from her mouth. "Thanks," she said.

"Sure."

Phoebe puffed, gently inhaling. A swell of dizziness stunned her. She smiled at the boy and he smiled back, his teeth gray, the bottom ones missing in front. "So long," Phoebe said.

He nodded. As Phoebe wandered down the block, she thought she felt the boy's eyes on her. At the end of the block she swung back around, expecting to intercept his gaze. But the boy was facing the street, eyeing the slow parade of traffic.

six

Phoebe walked quickly, trying to hold the fragile emptiness in her mind. Down Polk Street to O'Farrell, then into the Tenderloin, where prostitutes in hot pants and feather boas sauntered up to cars with the wary swagger of lion tamers. The air smelled of sweet, ripe things gone bad. Phoebe's hands shook from the cigarette, and she threw the butt in the gutter.

But she kept thinking about her mother.

Again and again the scene played through Phoebe's mind: her mother and Jack holding each other in the half-dark; herself, invisible, watching them. It had the terrible, fated power of a dream.

For years when she felt ignored at school, Phoebe would tell herself, I always have my mother, and imagine herself back at home, how funny she was, talkative, how lost her mother would be without her.

Phoebe walked up lower Powell toward Union Square. The air was heavy with fog, cold points of moisture on her face. The ocean felt so near, black and deep, ships' foghorns crowding the night with their plaintive, guttural cries. Phoebe gazed at the palm trees flapping above Union Square and felt a tightening around her heart. This would never have happened to Faith.

And Phoebe saw, with a dreadful clarity, that in the end she'd failed to interest her mother enough, failed to hold her attention. Some flaw within herself made her extraneous to everyone. She stopped on a corner overwhelmed by a terrible pain. It was her fault, her own fault. She'd done everything wrong.

Wait, she thought, but wait—walking again, faster now— maybe she'd misunderstood, maybe the deal with her mother had been that they each would live a secret life and not tell the other, but Phoebe hadn't realized—she'd failed to live the secret life and now her life was only this, a hundred empty years stretched uselessly behind her.

She entered Union Square. This was not a place you went at night. Phoebe sat on a bench and looked at the empty square. Overhead, white fog swept past. How could she make up the time?

A young black woman ambled through the square in thigh-high magenta boots, a silvery wig on her head. When the woman was some distance away, Phoebe left her bench and followed her from the square, up Stockton Street. She'd done this many times before, followed people who she sensed could lead her to shadowy, interesting places. Always at a distance. The woman turned inside a hotel lobby near the entrance to the Stockton Tunnel, and Phoebe continued on through the white, echoey tunnel, ignoring the elongated whoops of boys in passing cars. She emerged in Chinatown and turned down Broadway, heading into the thicket of strip joints and X-rated bookstores she was always straining to see through her mother's car window. The night world glimmered around her, its colored light garish, too bright for ordinary life, like stained-glass windows. Phoebe passed the Condor, where the famous Carol Doda danced; Big Al's, where tired-looking girls in spike heels and bathing suits were poised at the entrance before red velvet curtains, music pulsing out from behind them. Phoebe allowed herself only a glance, not wanting to draw attention, but she longed to stare at the women, to part the curtains and peer inside. Between this world and her own cautious life lay a barrier, transparent, impermeable. One day Phoebe would cross it. At the Casbah a whispering man in a fez muttered indecipherable promises about the belly dancers within; wasted punk rockers lounged outside the Mabuhay Gardens, chains of safety pins running from their noses to their earlobes. What a relief it would be finally to cross, like walking into a wall of oncoming headlights rather than leaping aside, releasing yourself to the luminous swirl of water under the Golden Gate Bridge. Pure surrender. And afterward, catharsis. She would be on the opposite side of her life.

Phoebe turned off Broadway and went inside a bar. It had a close, velvety feel, like a jewelry box where the ballerina twirls. Small round tables crowded the shadows. Phoebe sat on a stool and ordered a martini. She'd never had one before, only the residue left on olives her father used to feed her at the country club, a vile, medicinal shock she'd endured as the price of the olive's deliciousness. "On the rocks or straight up?" the bartender asked.

"On the rocks." She liked saying it. The time had come for a hard, different life. Spotting a cup of pickled onions on the bar, Phoebe added, "With onions, too."

"You want a Gibson," the bartender said.

"A martini."

"With onions it's a Gibson."

"Oh. Then no onions."

"I mean," he laughed, "I can make you a Gibson. I'm just saying."

Phoebe's face filled with heat. "Okay."

"Okay what? A Gibson?"

She nodded. A certain weight of attention seemed to be gathering upon her, but she didn't look around. The bartender set an empty triangular glass on the bar, then paused at the approach of another man, quite short, neatly dressed in a brown pin-striped suit. His companion, a woman whose hair was arranged in a pale, translucent ball, sat at one of the small tables. Her face resembled a tabby cat's.

The man in brown flicked his eyes at Phoebe. "You got some ID, miss?"

Phoebe looked at the bartender. The brown-suited man did the same. "You gotta card 'em, Eddie, I keep saying," he said. "You're my eyes and ears."

Phoebe wormed through her bag for her wallet. It was hard to feel much confidence producing her fake ID, a wrinkled card with a blurry photo, making the unlikely claim that she was a twenty-three-year-old Las Vegan. The brown-suited man took it, studying the card in the light from the bar. His hands were beautifully manicured. "No can do," he said, handing it back.

"Aw, give her the drink for chrissakes," said the tabby-faced woman. "Drive yourself crazy, Manny, what for?"

He turned on her fiercely. "I got cops up my ass," he said. "June's the worst month, you got all these goddamn proms over at the Hyatt."

The woman breathed smoke like a retort. "She look to you like she's going to a prom, Manny?"

Phoebe slid off her stool and made for the door, ears ringing. A disaster, a complete disaster.

"Go to Paddy O'Shaughnessy's, sweetheart," the woman called after her. "Sansome and Jackson. They got happy hour till eleven."

Phoebe did not go to Paddy O'Shaughnessy's, she went home and started to pack. A determination had seized her: to flee the city, the country, her life. From the closet of her old room she yanked the backpack her mother had bought her for an eighth-grade trip to Yosemite, a hail of dust and pine needles raining down from its waterproof canvas. Phoebe opened a window and shook out the pack over the backyard, turning her face to the wet air and closing her eyes.

What could she do? She could vanish.

They would hardly notice.

She began rounding up things she remotely imagined needing across the world: the passport she'd gotten for a trip to Mexico with her mother, calamine lotion, the hit of acid she'd been handed at a party and kept for months in its white envelope. Birth control pills some doctor had given her, cough medicine, a snakebite kit, a book of Charles Dickens stories. She lay on the floor and groped under the bed for the box of postcards Faith had sent from Europe. At one time Phoebe could recite these by heart, but memorization had dulled their effect. Two years ago she'd put the cards away, determined not to read them again until she had reached the places they were written from. She fished out the box and slipped the cards in a manila envelope, which she packed.

Phoebe turned now to Faith's bulletin board, a frenzy of newspaper clippings curled and brown with age. Though she'd dusted them frequently over the years, she rarely looked at their contents: stories on the Tet Offensive, the March on the Pentagon, the assassinations. Now she had an urge to take the clippings down, protect them from whoever might come in this room when she'd gone. She began unpinning articles. Some crumbled like ash in her hands. The magazine pages were heartier, John F. Kennedy's shooting in a series of freeze-frames—Jackie holding the President's head, then crawling in her short skirt over the back of the moving car—each moment so still, so deeply familiar, like images from Phoebe's own dreams.

She removed a newspaper clipping and held it in her hands. OAKLAND DRAFT PROTEST. A BLOODY ATTACK BY POLICE— CLUBS, TEAR GAS, BOOTS. MANY ARE INJURED. 20 ARRESTED.

The headline was dated Wednesday, October 18, 1967, a picture below it of three cops in riot gear beating two protesters with clubs. One of the victims, a boy, had just been hit and was falling, knees giving way, head bent—he looked as if he were kneeling to pray. Beside him, Faith was lunging—toward the cops (as she claimed)? Away from them? It was hard to say. A billy club was inches away from hitting her head. The picture had darkened with

time, so that even the white hexagonal patch on the thigh of
Faith's jeans (her irrefutable proof) had melted into the basic fact
of violence, five people jammed together in what had proved to be
a historical conflict.

Phoebe remembered the envy she'd felt, gathering her lunch
bag and books for third grade while her sister sat at the kitchen
table, a washcloth full of ice on her head.

Barry hunched over the newspaper, cupping one hand around
the picture as though it were homework he feared they might try
to copy. "That's you?" he kept asking, skeptically.

"Look at the jeans," Faith said.

She had gotten in the newspaper. Now she wasn't going to
school, she was going to the doctor.

"Can I see it?" Barry asked.

Faith lifted the washcloth from her skull and leaned forward
shyly, offering them her head. Barry set down his books and
moved near her, Phoebe following right behind, standing on tip-
toe to peer at the wound.

"Wow," Barry said with relish, parting Faith's hair for a better
view. "Sick."

Phoebe touched the lump on her sister's head. It was hot,
moist. Beneath the bruised skin, she felt a pulse.

"That's got to be a concussion," Barry said.

"I hardly felt a thing," Faith said from under her hair, and
Phoebe heard the excitement in her voice. "My teeth knocked
together."

Barry held Faith's head in his hands. As Phoebe pressed her
palm to the wound, she found her eyes wandering again and again
to the newspaper picture. Faith was here in this kitchen but she
was there, too, in the news. Phoebe stared at the image: protesters
and police, the billy club descending toward her sister's head like
a magic wand.

Months later, Faith read aloud to Phoebe about the general strike
in Paris—students wandering the streets pulling the hands off

public clocks, stopping time, Faith explained, because time literally *had* stopped, a new phase of history was beginning. "Think
about it, Pheeb!" her sister cried, leaping from her chair and dragging it to the kitchen clock, where she snapped off both its hands.
Afterward she seemed unsure what to do with them. She put them
in her pocket.

That evening, their mother slid a casserole dish in the oven
and glanced at the time. "My God," she said, "what's happened
to our clock?"

It stared from the wall as if stunned. "I was stopping time,"
Faith said.

A bubble of laughter broke from Phoebe's chest. Then they all
were laughing, Faith the most.

"If breaking a clock could stop time," their mother said,
"there wouldn't be a single one left."

Faith took the clock's hands from her pocket and set them on
the counter, useless things, like insect legs. "I love you, Mom," she
said.

Jealous as Phoebe felt, she was transfixed by everything her sister
did, dating the Hell's Angel while she and Wolf were apart, Zane,
he was called—everyone appalled because of rumors Faith had
repeated about the Angels' initiation rites, which included killing a
man and drinking a woman's menstrual blood. Then Zane appeared at their house in a leather jacket that groaned and
squeaked each time he moved, as if it were alive. He seized a quart
of milk from the refrigerator and drank it straight from the carton,
gulping in a kind of trance until the carton was empty (which was
better, Phoebe argued later, than putting it back in the fridge after
he'd already drunk from it). Then he crumpled the carton in his
fist and placed it in the garbage pail with surprising gentleness.
Their mother forbade Faith ever to see him again, but Faith
vowed with a passion quickened by adversity that she would move
to Alameda, where Zane lived with five other Hell's Angels. She
was sixteen and a half. Their mother gave in.

Zane's motorcycle had seemed to Phoebe the pure embodi-
ment of evil, a black-silver machine the Devil himself might ride,
snorting, throbbing, belching sour-smelling fumes that wafted in
through the windows of the house. In envy and revulsion she
watched her sister straddle the seat and peel away, her hands buried in the thick leather of Zane's jacket. One Saturday, when their
mother was at work, Phoebe followed Faith down to the street
and begged to be taken along. "Baby, no, Mom'll murder me
alive," Faith said, but Phoebe persisted, finally aiming her whining
appeals at Zane himself, until he ordered them both to shut up
and lifted her onto the seat.

By the time they hit the highway, Phoebe was paralyzed with
terror—not of crashing so much as the speed itself, which seemed
likely to pulverize her. Wind pounded her head, yanking her hair
—which she pictured leaving her scalp in tufts—and forcing itself
inside her mouth so her cheeks flapped against her teeth. She tried
to scream, but the wind shoved her voice back down, gagging her
on it. In agony Phoebe clung to Zane's leather jacket, and even the
man inside it, while Faith sheltered her from behind.

On a cliff they finally stopped. Phoebe's knees had locked,
and Faith had to pry her loose from the bike. The world felt still
enough to break. Phoebe gaped at her sister, awaiting some acknowledgment of the horror they'd just suffered, but Faith's
cheeks were flushed, her eyes bright. On shaking legs Phoebe followed her sister and Zane to the cliff's edge, stared down at the
glittering sea and promised God she would never, never again ride
on a motorcycle. Yet strangely, as the peaceful minutes passed,
Phoebe found herself recalling that terrible speed and beginning
perversely to long for it, not so much with her brain as with her
lungs and stomach and legs—unthinking parts of herself that had
adjusted to the machine's gnashing rhythms and now craved them.
Gradually her hunger sharpened, a deep, inexplicable urge for the
very thing she dreaded—for the dread itself. "Come on," she finally cried. "Let's go more."

At these words Zane's face parted in the first and only real smile Phoebe ever saw upon it. He squatted beside her, handsome, scary, his eyes oddly spent, like burned-out flashcubes. His breath on her face was boozy, medicinal. Rather shyly Zane asked Phoebe her age. Nine, she told him. He started to laugh, a rusty untried sound like an old car door swinging open and shut. "Nine years old, shit," he said to Faith. "She's gonna end up crazier than you."

Riding back, he really let fly, showing off for his crazy girl-friend's crazy little sister, leaning into such drastic turns that Phoebe's ear seemed nearly to graze the pavement.

For weeks after, Phoebe would lie in bed thinking jealously, achingly, of Faith and Zane sawing the world in two on that bike, the violence of its speed, the unwilling pleasure that had risen from her legs through her stomach and finally to her throat, pushing up from behind her tongue like fear or nausea, but it wasn't all bad. It was good, too. It was all mixed up.

Remembering her times with Faith, it seemed to Phoebe that over and over again they had approached a border that, since her sister's death, had moved out of range. Occasionally, by accident or sheer force of will, something propelled them across it. Yet much as Phoebe longed for the intensity of those times, her own life remained stubbornly apart from the world of events. Governments, armies, networks of underground crooks—their very existence struck her as impossible, dizzying. How had it all been organized? Who was in charge? She was left feeling that the news took place in another world, far from the quiet, incremental one where she led her life.

With one exception: the kidnapping of Patty Hearst had riveted Phoebe like no other news event in her lifetime. She'd been fourteen when it happened, had neither heard of William Randolph Hearst nor read much further in his newspaper than "Question Man." But that winter she'd scoured the *Chronicle* and *Examiner* each day for news of the heiress, discussing minute developments with her friends on the telephone, even dreaming of her. During the year when Patty was in hiding with the SLA, Phoebe and two other girls had spent several Saturdays in search of her, combing the Sunset and Richmond districts, giggling crazily as they peered through strangers' curtains for a whisper of Patty's black beret, the long shadow of her rifle. Patty's later account of rape and torture and brainwashing had done little to alter Phoebe's vision of her: a dull, privileged girl drawn irresistibly toward an invisible border, then crossing it into a dark, transcendent world.

Phoebe stacked the bulletin board's contents in the box where Faith's postcards had been and slid it back under the bed. Then she stood in the midst of Faith's room and listened to her sister's chimes. She heard the front door open—was it? Yes! Phoebe ran into the hallway, leaning over the banister to listen for her mother's steps . . . yes? But no, it was just the overgrown tree knocking against the roof. But wait, wasn't that her mother's car? Phoebe listened, every nerve trained on the street awaiting the sound of tires, the jolt of the garage door starting to open. Her false relief left a terrible emptiness behind it. Phoebe went back to Faith's room, realizing, as she surveyed the half-filled backpack and piles of clothing, that she had no desire to go anywhere. She was bluffing, arming herself in the hope of calling her mother's bluff, forcing her to give up Jack and come back to Phoebe.

Disgusted, Phoebe resumed her packing. She packed the white sundress it was always too cold to wear in San Francisco, a bottle of Chanel No. 5, extra shoelaces. Shorts—did people wear shorts in Europe? Mascara, though she didn't need it, her mother said, her eyelashes were so dark. She sat at her desk and penned a letter to Berkeley announcing her decision to defer her admission until next year. She sealed the letter and stamped it. But all this felt preventative, like her father keeping a bag packed for the hospital after he got sick—"How often does it rain if you carry your umbrella?" he'd say, trying to sound jovial—in hopes that preparing himself would protect him from having to go.

Phoebe left her backpack in Faith's room and went downstairs to the living room. Their father had been an avid collector: etchings of Connecticut River yachts, ivory backgammon sets, relics of a patrician America to which neither he nor anyone else Phoebe knew had the slightest connection. She paced the room. Her mother was out with Jack. Phoebe touched a gold clock under a dome of glass, a carving set encased in a pair of mock dueling pistols. She opened the cupboard where her parents' wedding china was kept and took out a dish of Florentine marble eggs. She held the eggs in their alabaster dish, awaiting the hum, the swell of promise to rise from beneath the house and lift her up. But the house felt cold.

Phoebe brought the marble eggs to her father's love seat and lay down. An exhaustion overcame her. I'll sleep here, she thought, lulled by the foghorns, and felt a sudden hush. She placed one egg in each eye socket, the sensation of cold marble dense, final somehow, like coins on the eyes of the dead.

seven

It shocked Phoebe to find her mother in the kitchen as always the next morning, reading the *Chronicle* in her white terrycloth robe. "That was so odd," she said, looking up when Phoebe appeared in the doorway.

"What?" Phoebe was alert.

"Last night. Finding you asleep on the love seat."

"God, I forgot."

"I could tell you were in the house because your purse was by the door, but I couldn't find you," her mother said. "I got absolutely terrified."

"What time was this?"

"I'm not sure. Pretty late."

Something should certainly be different, but everything seemed as usual: the smell of coffee, Bach melodies filing neatly from the radio. KDFC San Francisco, KIBE Palo Alto, *Your Radio Concert Hall.*

"What were you doing down there?" her mother said.

"Thinking," Phoebe said. She sat down. Oatmeal bubbled on the stove.

"Did you go to your party?"

Phoebe shook her head. She glanced at the headlines: OPEC promising not to raise prices in '78, NATO planning billions more for defense. A grainy photograph of Aldo Moro, the ex–Prime Minister of Italy who'd been murdered by Red Brigade terrorists the previous month. Phoebe remembered the story only dimly, but the blurred, grainy face of the dead man struck her as poignant. "Look at him," she said. "That poor guy."

Her mother was stirring the oatmeal. "Who?"

"Mr. Aldo Moro. They kidnapped him, and when the prisoners weren't set free, they shot him and left him in the street."

Her mother shook her head, dropping bread in the toaster. She went to the window and stretched, her spine cracking gently. The sound made Phoebe look up. She noticed the gold serpentine bracelet sliding down her mother's wrist as she reached her arms overhead. She must have worn it to bed.

"Look. The sun," her mother said, yawning.

"I guess you don't really care."

"About what?"

"Aldo Moro."

Her mother turned to her. "What kind of a question is that?" she said. "It's terrible, yes, but I don't feel personally about it. Why, do you?" She looked incredulous.

Phoebe said nothing. Heart pounding, she carried breakfast to the table, hot cereal and toast, a creamer of milk, brown sugar in a blue ceramic dish. In her mother's every gesture she sensed a turning away, the loss of some hold Phoebe had had on her before. She felt powerless to stop it.

Her mother returned to the paper. While she read Herb Caen, Phoebe glanced at the soft collar of her robe, the shadowy tops of her breasts. In the attic, she'd come across some old nudes her father had painted of her mother in the fifties, and been startled by her mother's alien, painted flesh, the bright nipples, stomach and hips that seemed to flow, as if the skin were actually moving. It was not the same body she'd seen dripping after the shower or sucking in its breath to zip up a skirt.

"Have some toast," her mother said, nudging the plate. She'd moved on to Art Hoppe.

Phoebe lifted a piece to her mouth, wishing her mother would look up. "Did anything funny happen last night?" she asked.

Her mother glanced at her. Phoebe saw the tiredness in her eyes. "Funny how?"

"You know, just sometimes Jack is funny. Like he does funny stuff."

Her mother's expression went flat. "No. Nothing funny happened."

Phoebe saw this was the wrong tack but couldn't seem to stop. "You know, like that time when he put out his cigarette in the middle of that guy's steak, or—"

"Jack is not a clown, Phoebe, all right?"

The toast turned to sand in Phoebe's mouth. She stood up. Dishes rattled in her arms as she brought them to the sink.

"I'm sorry," her mother said. "I'm just bored with the jokes about Jack, aren't you? After all this time?"

Phoebe began to cry.

"Sweetheart," her mother said.

Phoebe stood in the kitchen and wept. Her mother left her chair and enfolded her in a familiar, soothing embrace. "Hey, I wasn't so bad," she said. "I'm tired and I barked, that's all."

"I'm tired, too," Phoebe sobbed.

Her mother held her another moment, then let go. "You seem awfully tense," she said. "Is something wrong?"

Phoebe shook her head, ashamed of having cried. "I have to go," she said. "I told them I'd come in early today."

"Let's have supper tonight," her mother said. "Get dressed up and go someplace nice, drink some good wine. We haven't done that enough lately." Phoebe sensed her mother's gaze playing over her anxiously.

"Okay," she said, pulling on her down vest, which she wore even in summertime.

"If you want to," her mother said. "But if you have other plans, we can wait . . ." She was searching Phoebe's eyes.

"I don't have any," Phoebe said.

She was working with Patrick again. Phoebe nodded hello and donned her apron without a word. He took the hint. They worked the morning rush in silence.

During a lull Patrick shared a cigarette with Art. "Can I have one?" Phoebe asked them.

"Of course, dear," Art said.

"No, I mean it."

Patrick cocked his head, took a filtered Camel from his pack and gave it to Phoebe. She felt both men's eyes on her as he lit it. She inhaled deeply, feeling a blow of white dizziness. When she looked up, the men were still watching her. Art looked worried.

"So I'm smoking," Phoebe said. "So what?"

"What about your promise?" Patrick asked.

Phoebe leaned weakly against the counter. "Promise?"

"Not to smoke."

The information seemed to take a moment to reach her. "Oh," she said. "It broke."

Phoebe spent her lunch break on the phone in Art's office. She called her father's lawyer, Henry McBride, whom she dimly remembered having known as a child. Come down to the office, he told her, sign the papers anytime. Her check for five thousand dollars would arrive about two weeks later.

"There's no way I could get it today?" Phoebe said. "Or tomorrow?"

Henry McBride laughed. Phoebe imagined him, white hair, boozy red nose. "Sorry, my love," he said.

Phoebe called Laker Airways, whose flights to London proved to be booked solid through the rest of summer. Alone, she might

get on standby, the man said, but he couldn't guarantee it. Phoebe
returned to work feeling oddly relieved; for the moment, at least,
there seemed no way she could leave the city.

She shared another Camel with Patrick when their shift
ended.

Phoebe had long viewed herself as the sole audience for her
mother's unfashionable beauty, a subtlety lost on the fools she
dated and Don Juans for whom she was nobody, a middle-aged
woman in eyeliner. But tonight she sensed a keen awareness of her
mother in every man they encountered, from the young valet who
parked their car to their waiter, whose gaze never strayed from her
mother's face while he recited the specials. Pair after pair of moist
eyes, and Phoebe saw what drew them: a new liveliness sharpened
her mother's features, dissolving her usual wistfulness like a mist
burning off around her. Her long bare neck and delicate wrists
seemed too exposed. Phoebe wanted to hide them.

"A Sancerre? Does that sound good?" her mother asked.

Phoebe nodded. The restaurant was new to her, a bustling,
elegant place on Union Street, French waiters, specials scribbled
carelessly on small chalkboards and propped at each table. No
doubt her mother had been here with Jack, Phoebe thought, and
felt a sudden, uneasy need to entertain her.

"How's work?" she asked, buttering her bread with care.

"Well, it's been great . . ."

"Are you—"

"We're—"

"Go on . . ."

They shared an edgy laugh, both gulping their wine.

"I was going to say, we're having our first rough-cut screening
of the Che Guevara project next week. So that's exciting."

"Wow," Phoebe said, oppressed by her mother's frequent use
of the word "we."

They studied their menus and ordered, then her mother
straightened the heavy silverware beside her plate. "I have some

other news," she said, obviously nervous. "Surprising news, I think."

Phoebe's heartbeats scattered. She was going to be told. A terrible dread overwhelmed her. She didn't want to hear it, now or ever.

The waiter arrived to replenish the wine, and Phoebe left for the bathroom. She stared in the mirror at her white face and gray, nervous eyes and wondered what she was so afraid of. Finally she returned to the table, threading her way among couples toward the solitary figure of her mother. Jazz played, the sound like insects diving against a lightbulb.

The appetizers had arrived. Phoebe attacked her foie gras, barely looking up. She speared a bite for her mother, who swallowed it distractedly. Her own dish lay untouched.

"Mom, why don't you eat?"

Her mother gave a tense laugh. "I'm afraid," she said. "Isn't that funny?"

"Of what?"

"Telling you. My news."

Phoebe was flushed from eating so fast. Sweat trickled from her underarms, seeping into her silk dress. "Then maybe you should wait."

Her mother studied her. "That's an odd suggestion."

It was hopeless. Phoebe let the last bite of foie gras slide down her throat and slowly wiped her mouth. "Never mind," she said. "I know what it is."

"I'm not sure you do, Phoebe."

"Jack?" Her throat was dry. "You and Jack?"

Her mother inclined her head as if Phoebe had spoken too loudly. "I'll be damned," she murmured, lifting a fork to poke at her crab salad. Phoebe waited uneasily to be asked how she knew, but apparently her mother was too rattled to wonder. "Well," she said with an empty laugh, "so much for my big announcement."

Phoebe wished she'd simply feigned surprise. Several moments passed in silence. "For how long?" she finally asked.

"A month or so. A little less. At first I couldn't believe it myself. I wanted to make sure it was something real before I told you, so I wouldn't shock you over nothing."

"Wow," Phoebe said. "You and Jack."

"I can imagine how bizarre this must seem," her mother went on, with more confidence. "After so many years, all my joking and complaining about him. But I think when you see us together—he's a wonderful man, I can't tell you how happy he makes me."

There was no need. Before Phoebe's eyes a metamorphosis was in progress, her own mother merging seamlessly with a glamorous stranger from old photographs. Apparently that other woman had lain in wait all these years, beneath her mother's wistfulness. She'd been biding her time.

"What I thought," her mother said, finally beginning to eat, "was that maybe we could all do something together this weekend, go somewhere nice, Mount Tamalpais or Stinson, have Barry drive up—"

"Barry knows, too?"

"I told him today. We had lunch together."

"I'll bet he was thrilled," Phoebe said, surprised by her own bitter tone.

Her mother looked startled. "He was pleased for me," she said, then fell silent. "Anyway, how does that sound?" she asked, tentative now. "A drive somewhere, the four of us?"

"It sounds fine," Phoebe said. "Just, it seems so . . . weird. You and Jack."

Her mother took Phoebe's sweating hand in her own long fingers, smooth and cool as bandages. "I know it, sweetheart," she said. "Believe me, if someone had told me a year ago this would happen, I'd have said they were out of their mind. But I think if you saw us together . . ." Phoebe's look must have discouraged her, for her mother withdrew her hand. "Please keep an open mind," she said. "That's all I ask."

"I'll try."

"Sweetheart, you make it sound as if I were asking your permission," her mother said gently. "You realize that's not the case."

"Of course," Phoebe said miserably. "Who cares what I think?"

Her mother watched her in silence. Phoebe glimpsed herself through her mother's eyes—a problem, a wrinkle to be dealt with. She was filled with sudden, angry frustration. "So what about Dad?" she said. "Does he just fall by the wayside?"

"Phoebe, your father died thirteen years ago! I think by any standard this would be considered a respectable mourning period."

In spite of herself Phoebe smiled. Her mother smiled, too. It's already over, Phoebe thought, none of this makes any difference. She felt a wave of panic. "But how can you even look at someone like Jack, after Dad?" she cried.

There was a rare, unmistakable jerk of anger in her mother's face. "That shows how little you knew your father," she said.

"I didn't know my own father?"

"Not if you think he was perfect."

"I don't think that. But Jack—"

She was silenced by the arrival of their dinners. Phoebe glanced at the soft-shell crabs without recognition.

"Look," her mother said in a hushed voice. "You adored your father, you were a little girl when he died, fine. I've never questioned that. But you haven't the slightest idea what sort of husband he was, so please"—she shut her eyes—"please don't presume to tell me."

"You and Dad weren't happy?"

"I'm not saying that! We were in love, we had wonderful times, but he was a difficult man and we had problems like every couple. You have no right to compare him to Jack, whom you hardly know, as if your father were some perfect ideal. I promise you, he was not."

Phoebe looked at her hands, remembering her parents' warm

bed with its milky smell of sleep, what a comfort it had been to lie there. "You feel guilty," she said. "That's why you're saying that."

"Guilty? For dating another man after thirteen years?"

Her father bursting through the kitchen door breathless, the rattle of new paint tubes in his briefcase, dinner cooling on the kitchen table. The hope and strain in his face. "Because he never got to paint," Phoebe said, and experienced in that moment a thrill of relief. All her life she had known this, they all had. But no one had said it.

Her mother's face tightened. She stabbed at her fish, then set down the fork. Phoebe felt the weightless exhilaration of having gone too far. A fight would be unavoidable now, and she wanted it. She wanted to fight with her mother.

"I think we'd better change the subject," her mother said. "Because in about one minute I'm going to say something I'll regret."

They eyed each other across the table. Their anger bent the air.

"Go on," Phoebe said. "Say it."

Her mother narrowed her eyes and sipped her wine. "How closely have you looked at your father's paintings?" she asked.

"What do you mean?"

"Phoebe, they're bad. He was a terrible painter. There was passion galore, it was sweet to watch, but he had zero talent. Why else do you think he never had a single gallery show or even sold any paintings, for God's sake, except to my parents? You think he was the first painter in the world who had to work for a living?" She paused, breathing shakily. Phoebe listened in speechless amazement. "I would never have said this to you, Phoebe—haven't, in all this time. But for you to blame me, blame our family for your father not succeeding as an artist, well, that's just wrong. I can't let you think it. He invented that myth to comfort himself."

"I don't believe you," Phoebe said softly. "I don't believe he couldn't paint."

"The proof is hanging on every wall of our house."

Phoebe felt a sudden, drenching wooziness. Something had begun that she felt powerless to stop. Her exhilaration leaked away, leaving her frightened—of her mother's anger, of her own grinding urge to push things further, punish her. "Let's go home," she said.

"Fine."

They sat in silence while her mother paid the check. The untouched meals were lifted away. Back in the car her mother fixed her gaze on the road, blue drop earrings leaping at each turn. Phoebe saw the pearlized gleam of her makeup—not for Jack, not for anyone but Phoebe—and was sick with regret at having wasted this night, tossed it away. What hope was there now of winning her back? Phoebe studied her mother's sad face in the street light and felt only pity. Seizing this chance with Jack—why not? Taking Phoebe out to dinner to give her the big news, to celebrate. Now there was just the ashy disappointment of a ruined night.

Phoebe longed to apologize. She opened her mouth more than once, willing the words to come, but a weight seemed to push them back inside her. Too much had happened; to apologize now would mean accepting the terrible thing her mother had said about her father. Impossible! If her father couldn't paint, then where was the sense of his life? Even trying to imagine him in this new, shameful light left Phoebe dizzy. It couldn't be. It simply could not be.

Her mother led the way up the narrow steps from the garage, high heels jabbing the bare planks, the hem of her coat jerking with each step. Inside the house she turned to Phoebe. "Sweetheart . . ." she said.

Phoebe moved toward her. They stood for some time on the dark landing, hugging in silence. Phoebe breathed her mother's lemony perfume, her powder, the warmth of her skin.

"What I said about your father," her mother said, still holding Phoebe, "I'm sorry I said that."

"You mean it's not true?"

Her mother hesitated, and Phoebe's arms loosened around her. "You're not sorry," she said.

They withdrew from each other, but slowly. In the darkness Phoebe saw only the whispery outline of her mother's face.

"The apology is for telling you something you didn't need to hear, because I was angry," her mother said, hanging her coat over the banister. "But I'm not going to stand here and lie to you, Phoebe. Frankly, at eighteen years old I think you're better off knowing your father was not a talented painter than believing he was some kind of martyr. I promise you, if the man had stayed a bachelor to his dying day, he'd have ended up an engineer. Because that—that!—was what he really did well."

She climbed the stairs to the second floor, Phoebe clambering behind her. "You don't know that for sure," she cried. "For all you know, if he'd stayed a bachelor, he might still be alive!"

"Now what in God's name is that supposed to mean?"

"You know what it means!"

They faced each other in the upstairs hall. Light fell at one end from her mother's bedroom where Phoebe had left it on after borrowing stockings. "I haven't the faintest idea," her mother said. "Tell me."

"Because IBM made him sick," Phoebe said, angry at the quaver in her voice.

Her mother snorted, turning on her heel. "That's ludicrous," she said, heading for her bedroom.

Phoebe charged after her. She felt crazed. How could it be ludicrous? That was the story of her father. With every move, every gesture—for years—her mother had confirmed it. "Mom," she pleaded, "I can't believe what you're saying."

"I can't believe what *you're* saying," her mother replied. "You're telling me your father got leukemia, a blood disease, from working as a manager at IBM? What, from chemicals or something? What are you saying?"

"No! You know!" Phoebe was shouting. "Everyone knew, because he—" Explaining felt useless. "Not chemicals, but—"

"What? Radiation?"

"No, no! Because he hated working there."

"Oh please," her mother said. "Spare me."

Phoebe felt as if she'd been struck. Her mother sat on the bed and pulled off her pumps. She set them side by side on the polished floor.

"This is crazy," Phoebe said. "Everyone knew. Dad knew it, Faith totally knew . . ."

"What Faith knew is meaningless," her mother said with a sad, bitter laugh. "She believed whatever he wanted her to, poor thing."

She rose from the bed and hung her shoes on a rack inside the closet door.

"Faith did not," Phoebe said, "believe everything."

"Oh, I'm not blaming her," her mother said, unzipping the side of her dress, "not for a second. Children always think their parents are gods— what else do they know? It's our job to keep the truth in perspective, otherwise you end up loving your kids because of how they make you feel about yourself. And that's not love, that's egotism, pure and simple."

"What are you talking about?"

"I'm saying your father used Faith to bolster all kinds of myths about himself—it was her main function in his life."

Phoebe stared at her mother. She was aware of the two of them sliding, drifting somewhere dangerous. She was lost, yet each unfamiliar step had its own eerie logic, and against it Phoebe felt powerless. "Dad loved her more than anything," she said, shaking her head.

"No question. But if he'd loved her less, he'd have been a better parent."

"Why?"

"He made her responsible for his happiness. It was too big a burden—for anyone, much less a child. Not that Faith didn't try, God knows, sitting for him hours on end . . . Sometimes I'd think, He's not painting Faith at all, he's painting himself—Gene O'Connor, the great unrecognized artist—directly onto her brain. And that he did very well, I must say. When all was said and done, she was his masterpiece."

Phoebe felt panic closing in. She looked around the room, but the familiar objects of their lives appeared tainted now, unrecognizable. Even her mother seemed altered, a stranger, like the naked woman in her father's paintings.

"If he'd lived, I'm sure everything would have been fine," her mother was saying. "Faith would have rebelled eventually, and she and your father would've found each other again on different terms. But Faith never had that chance—she was completely dependent on him when he died, completely, utterly unable to cope without him."

Phoebe's head throbbed. A wild, animal urge to defend herself rose in her. "It made you jealous," she said instinctively, "how much he loved Faith."

There was a pause. "That's true," her mother said, in a different voice. "It did." And this seemed to sadden her, tire her somehow.

"You were jealous."

"Of course I was. Neurotic love is so powerful, at times it eclipses everything else. Yes, I was jealous, Barry certainly was. You were, too, I think, although you don't seem to remember it."

"Not me," Phoebe said.

"Fine," her mother said. Clearly she was sick of talking. She sat heavily on the bed in her terrycloth robe, as if waiting for Phoebe to go. But Phoebe wasn't leaving, not until she'd found a way of fighting back. There was something she needed to remember, some moment of weakness in her mother, recently—then it came to her: yesterday in the car when they'd talked about Faith's going to Europe. Her mother explaining herself to Phoebe, then asking if she understood. The unnatural weight of her answer.

"You let her go," Phoebe said.

Her mother looked up, startled.

Goosebumps rose on Phoebe's scalp and traveled down her spine. "You let her go."

Her mother lifted her hands to her face. And Phoebe knew she'd found it, her worst fear. Found it and said it aloud.

"You did," she said, amazed. "You let her."

Her mother opened her mouth to speak. Then something broke in her face and she began to cry, leaning into her hands. Phoebe watched her coldly at first. Fine, she thought, let her cry, but her mother's despair soon awoke in her a queasy guilt. "Mom," she said, hovering uselessly a few paces away, afraid to go near. Her mother wept and wept. Phoebe remembered how she'd looked at the beginning of the evening, that overflow of high spirits—gone, forever, it seemed—Phoebe had stamped them out. She thought of Claude, years ago, big, laughing Claude, how her mother had laughed when he was there, laughed and laughed, and then Faith had died and the laughter, too, had died. When she thought of Claude, Phoebe had to remind herself that he was still alive somewhere.

"Mom," she said again, and moved closer. She felt a terrible pressure in her chest. Everything was broken. And now the person who had broken it was broken, too.

Her mother raised her head, tears and makeup staining her face. "Go away, Phoebe."

Phoebe didn't move. There had to be a way of undoing this, of going back.

"Please go," her mother sobbed, waving Phoebe away with her face half hidden, as if she were ashamed to be seen. When Phoebe didn't move, her mother rose suddenly from the bed and pushed her, trembling hands on Phoebe's shoulders. "Please go," she said. "Leave me alone, please."

"Wait," Phoebe said. "Mom wait—"

She held up her hands, but her mother kept pushing, a confusion of shaking arms. "Why won't you leave?" she sobbed. "Is there more you want to say? Did I do something else? Please, just say it and go." Talking made her choke. She began to cough, covering her mouth with one hand, finally turning her back to Phoebe out of some automatic politeness. A wave of nausea rolled through Phoebe at the sound of her mother's helpless coughing.

When finally her mother rose straight again, she seemed to have coughed away fear and hysteria both. She faced Phoebe calmly. "You're right," she said. "You're right, I let her go. But it wasn't then."

Phoebe listened in dread.

"I let her go when I let him crush her. Because that's what he did."

She looked at Phoebe evenly, a kind of strength in her face.

"I watched it happen," she said. "It started as soon as she was born. He loaded her down. I knew it was wrong, all that time. But she seemed to thrive. Still, I should have stopped him."

She paused, gazing at Phoebe, full of calm. "Do you hear this?" she said. "Are you listening?"

Phoebe just stared.

"Well, there it is," her mother said, breathing deeply. "There it is."

But Phoebe felt nothing. Only when she found herself outside in the hallway, her mother's white door shut behind her, was she conscious of having left the room.

eight

All morning Phoebe debated whether to leave a note. She debated while mailing her letter to Berkeley, then waiting in a pink-and-orange booth at Zim's in Laurel Village for Gibraltar Savings to open; she debated while walking home in the soft gray fog with the entire contents of her bank account—$1,538, saved from a year of work at Milk and Honey—in traveler's checks. The round-trip Laker Airways standby ticket would cost almost $500. How long could you manage on a thousand dollars? Phoebe wondered. Well, as long as possible, and after that maybe she would find a way to get her $5,000.

Phoebe had lain awake for much of the night. At times she'd considered calling someone, asking to borrow money. Barry had plenty, of course, or her friend Celeste, who worked at a travel agency. But everyone seemed at such a distance, as if Phoebe had known them years ago and had no claim on them now. As if she'd already left.

Her mother slipped from the house well before seven. From her bed Phoebe listened to her faint steps, the front door swinging

softly shut. Her mother wanted only to escape her. She would get
her wish.

Finally Phoebe did write a note, on a sheet of her mother's
thick, creamy stationery. *Dear Mom,* she wrote:

1. *I'm sorry.*
2. *I love you.*
3. *I'm going away now which is the best thing.*
4. *I will be careful.*

Love,
Phoebe.

It was done. Everything was done. She had only to get to the
airport.

The shuttle bus left from O'Farrell Street, in the Tenderloin.
Phoebe called De Soto Cab, which lately had edged aside Vet-
eran's in the hierarchy of her affections. She'd been calling cabs
for years from parties she wanted to escape, foggy phone booths
above Ocean Beach. But she was always headed home. It felt
strange, giving the address as her departure point.

Phoebe set her backpack inside the front door and sat on the
love seat to wait. From the kitchen she heard the ringing phone:
Art, no doubt, calling to find out why she hadn't shown up for
work. All morning it had rung. But finally it stopped, and as Phoebe
waited for the taxi she began, for the first time since seeing her
mother with Jack, to feel a sense of hope. Finally she was going,
heading into the world. Phoebe stood, anxious to take a last look
around the house, fix it in her mind. She circled the living room,
gazing at an ostrich egg on its onyx stand, a hand-blown glass horse,
the marble eggs from Florence—and all at once she felt a faint pulse
from deep within the house, beneath the floorboards, beneath the
earth below, and it came to Phoebe that she wasn't leaving after all,
she was merely sinking deeper within this house, entering its hidden
world. As if, after years of nudging and prying and tapping, a wall
had at last swung wide and she were stepping through.

part two

nine

London felt tropical. Dense, steamy air filtered the sunlight to watery yellow. The sound of church bells was everywhere.

With a map she'd bought at the airport, Phoebe guided herself through the tangle of streets. She was exhausted. She'd arrived this morning on the overnight Laker flight, after her second night in a row without sleep.

She'd had trouble finding the youth hostel, in part because it was tall and white like every house in Kensington, gleaming with wet-looking paint. When she finally discovered it, at 11 A.M., the hostel had closed for the day. But a man let her come inside to leave her backpack and use the bathroom, where she'd splashed water under her arms and brushed her teeth.

Phoebe's exhaustion made things blur and run. She liked it. There was a clovery scent to the air, an intoxicating smell of flowering trees. It made her feel drunk.

The streets of Kensington curved; she had to keep checking her map. Phoebe did this furtively, not wanting to look like a tourist. In her dark sunglasses she felt incognito. She carried Faith's postcards in her purse, along with her sister's photograph, a small notebook in which to document her progress, her passport, more than twenty English pounds, a thousand dollars in traveler's checks and the hit of LSD in its small white envelope. Tired though Phoebe was, a manic energy coursed through her as she walked. The taxicabs looked like limousines. Tiny oval-shaped parks were tucked in the middle of city blocks, encircled by locked gates. Peering through the brambles, she caught the glint of wet grass and long crimson branches. Once she heard the gentle *thock* of tennis balls and glimpsed someone's white leg.

In Knightsbridge Phoebe stared through sparkling windowpanes at silk handkerchiefs arranged into fans, neckties and smoked fish, old ladies still in their overcoats drinking tea, their hair faintly blue, like skim milk. It was all England. Everywhere she looked—England. Tabloid salesmen bellowed headlines around wet stubs of cigars, red double-decker buses sailed past. You could get on a plane and get off in England. It was miraculous.

What amazed Phoebe most, though, was the light. It seemed to pour from all directions at once, forming gleaming points on every window and leaf, heightening colors to surreal intensity. She felt she could *see* for the first time in months, as if the fog that engulfed San Francisco each night had enshrouded her mind, too, obscuring her thoughts, and now had burned off. What remained was this light, a mesmerizing clarity that made Phoebe feel she had arrived in a different land. It was just as she'd hoped.

Dear Mom, Phoebe and Barry, The first thing we did was we went to Harrod's like you said Mom what a trippy place!! You're right those Food Halls are so intense. I bet they haven't changed from the 50's when you and Dad came. Wolf and I got some funny looks I can tell you that. People in London are pretty uptight they don't like jeans with patches but when I took off my poka dot jacket they

were nicer. We ordered you a cake maybe you already got it.
I hope it's not stale they promised it would stay fresh. It has
raisins. Love, Faith

Inside Harrods Phoebe found herself searching the crowds for a familiar face. She felt welcomed, expected, if not by a person, then by the city itself. Her own presence so rarely seemed momentous to Phoebe that the sensation electrified her. She felt almost high entering the Food Halls, lush columned rooms that gave the impression of being glass-rooved and flooded with sunlight. The walls were of glazed tile, orange, green, turquoise. Meats were displayed on marble slabs, stuffed with herbs, tied in string like precious bundles, huge gleaming livers and pale veals, lamb shanks, lamb legs, venison, crimson steaks, guinea fowl with loose velvety skins folded sumptuously around each breast and wing. The very food seemed to give off light. Men in straw hats stood behind each counter, holding long knives.

Phoebe wended her way to the bakery. Cakes big as hats, glazed, draped in shredded coconut or curls of chocolate, studded with fat raisins, cakes whose frostings gleamed like the shining white houses in Kensington. *We ordered you a cake maybe you already got it. I hope it's not stale they promised it would stay fresh* . . . Here it was. Faith and Wolf had been in this very store eight years before, this very room, their sandaled feet had walked upon this same gray marble floor, perhaps touching the spot where Phoebe stood now. She felt a kind of wonderment. At that moment a loudspeaker suddenly crackled to life. "Attention all customers," said a woman's English accent. "The store must be evacuated. Kindly move toward the nearest exit doors as quickly as possible."

A stillness fell. "All customers are asked to leave the premises at once. The store must be evacuated. Kindly proceed . . ." People began gathering their parcels and moving briskly from the room. Phoebe looked around in confusion. "Attention all customers . . ." Was the store closing for the day? But obviously not.

Baffled, she followed the crowd into a central area filled with mirrored cosmetics counters, where hundreds of shoppers were already gathered. She heard the terse, complicit whispers of people in danger and experienced a thrill of fear. Something was the matter. Light poured in from the street, but the bottleneck of departing customers forced her to a standstill some distance from the doors. She began to grow nervous. Yet at the same time, she felt strangely exempt from any real danger. "All customers are advised to move toward the nearest exit doors. The building . . ."

"What's going on?" Phoebe asked a man beside her, who carried a round loaf of bread under his arm.

"Bomb threat, I'd imagine," he said. "Happens fairly often."

"Wow, a bomb?" Phoebe said. Everyone seemed so docile. "I guess 'threat' doesn't mean there's really a bomb, though."

"Rarely," the man said. "Mind you, they do go off now and then." From his half-smile Phoebe sensed he was baiting her, and tried to assume an air of indifference. The doors looked very far away.

"You're American," the man observed. He pronounced it "Amer-ee-can."

"Yes," Phoebe said. "I got here this morning."

"You haven't got many terrorists in America, then."

"Terrorists?" Phoebe said, startled. "No. Well, I mean, Patty Hearst was a terrorist . . ."

He frowned. "Who's that?"

"She was this rich heiress, but then she was kidnapped by terrorists and she became a terrorist, too. It was incredible," Phoebe said, aware as she spoke that it didn't sound particularly incredible. The man said nothing. "Are there a lot of terrorists in London?" she asked.

"We've got our share. Mind you, the French have it worse; they've got bombs exploding every time you turn round over there."

A smell of anxiety and humanity filled the vast room. Phoebe wanted to escape. The man had a kindly, defeated air. She pictured his children leaping on him like monkeys before he'd had a chance to put down his loaf of bread.

"So . . . what're they trying to do? The terrorists in London," she asked.

"Depends which ones," said the man. "The IRA hate the Brits, full stop. The Pal-ee-stinians want hostages freed, or they're taking revenge over some bloody thing. Then you've got kids all over Europe that haven't got a clue, just sod capitalism and that. Cooking up bombs and carrying guns around—that's the bit they really enjoy."

"I'm sure they have better reasons than that," Phoebe said, feeling oddly defensive on the terrorists' behalf.

"Avoid boredom?" he said with a short laugh. "Best reason in the world."

Finally they neared the doors. Phoebe felt a sudden, odd reluctance to leave the danger behind. She pictured the terrorists observing this commotion from some hidden place, and longed to slow down for them, flaunt her fearlessness.

At last they pushed through a door to the street. Phoebe looked around for the man she'd been speaking with, thinking he might have paused to share with her the triumph of escape. But he'd disappeared. The crowd, still flooding from the doors behind her, forced Phoebe to move on. Policemen crowded the sidewalk, black helmets strapped beneath their chins like bonnets. Phoebe slowed, resisting the crowd's momentum. Customers still leaving Harrods were caught in the press of bystanders pushing toward it. The policemen's short-tempered warnings did little to quell the crowd's desire to move nearer the trouble. And Phoebe felt it, too —here was the world of events, a place she knew only from pictures, from newspaper stories. Overnight she had reached it.

You see this lagoon well believe it or not we went swimming in it the water was totally clean just a little green from

algae. The ducks weren't scared they came quacking right up
to us. But the English cops totally freaked and about eight of
them stood in a row hollering for us to get out with their
oval hats down over their eyes and we said No No you
should come in the water's so nice it would do you good but
they blew their whistles and kept yelling so finally we came
out with the ducks paddling after us. What a crazy day I was
so happy!! Love, Faith

The trees of St. James's Park hung like velvet drapes, heavy,
dense, sunlight spilling between their leaves and soaking the
bright grass. Phoebe walked to the water's edge and looked at the
ducks, their crisp, bright markings like costumes.

She circled the lagoon. It was large and sprawling, curved
bridges spanning its narrowest parts. In the middle a spray of
water shot straight into the air. A nervous excitement coursed
through Phoebe. Following Faith's directions filled her with a
keen anticipation, though for what she had no idea. Objects
seemed to leap at her, charged with significance.

Phoebe bought a ham sandwich, chocolate cake and a green
apple. She carried her tray to a small stone table outdoors and
devoured the food, ravenous. After finishing her meal, she opened
her notebook and wrote: "July 2, 1978. In England everything is
more real. The money is colorful, the coins are heavy like real
gold, the parks are greener, the people have beautiful accents.
There are terrorists all over, and bomb threats. Nothing is the way
I'm used to. This is the real world and I'm totally alive, for the
first time ever."

Eating left Phoebe exhausted. She found an empty cloth chair
on the grass and sat down, taking Faith's postcards from her purse
and fanning them in her hands like a deck of cards. There were
eighteen in all. Phoebe looked at the postcard of St. James's Park,
then at the park itself. A part of her had not believed she would
ever actually sit here, as if the real places would vanish, like mi-

rages, just as she reached them. Now, for the first time in years, the ground felt so solid under Phoebe. She let her eyes fall shut, sunlight warm against her lids, sounds of birds and children and distant traffic lulling her to sleep.

Phoebe woke at six-thirty with a parched throat. Earlier, a boy had shaken her awake to collect money for the chair, but his accent had been hard to comprehend and there were moments of confusion before she'd managed to produce the desired coin. Now Faith's postcards littered the grass. Phoebe scrambled to gather them up, afraid one might have blown away—but no, all eighteen were there. She tucked them back in their envelope. A ghostly population of empty cloth chairs scattered the grass. The sky had clouded over. Shivering, Phoebe stood.

Quickly she left the park, dogged by a sense of having lapsed, missed something important. She soon found herself under the overhead tracks at Charing Cross station, murky air illuminated by the greenish light from tiny fish-and-chips shops. Railway workers in blue uniforms and boots tossed half-smoked cigarettes into the gutters. Their speech, like that of the boy who had wakened her, was impossible to decipher. From the station doors came a dank, breathlike smell and a gush of human traffic. Phoebe stood in the shadows and watched. No one looked at her. She stared into the flood of oncoming faces and waited for one to sharpen into focus, to be singled out as in a movie crowd scene. People poured through the doors, hurrying to get home. Finally she turned away.

The youth hostel would be open now. Phoebe took the tube to the Gloucester Road station, where an Indian man at a fruit stand displayed a pyramid of figs dusted white with powdered sugar. There were rows of red apples, each wrapped in a tissue.

Trees tossed and bent in the wind. It felt like rain. Phoebe looked at the swollen sky and thought of her grandparents' house in St. Louis, that promise of a violent storm, sticks and leaves dashing across the grass as if for cover. "It's going to be a bad

one," people would say, but always with a certain excitement at
the thought of watching the storm lash itself against their windows.

Phoebe walked in the direction of the youth hostel. She
passed a small stone church, dandelions tossing in its graveyard.
The long, crooked street blurred. She stopped to rub her eyes and
suddenly felt that her sister was very near, not a memory or an
echo but Faith herself—laughing, reaching—what else but her sister's presence could explain the excitement Phoebe had felt since
arriving in London, the swell of promise? It was Faith who
brought these feelings, who always had. And Phoebe knew, then,
that her journey would only be complete when her sister had finally revealed herself. Faith would simply appear, burst from nowhere as when she lost patience during games of hide-and-seek,
exploding the stillness by leaping from behind a curtain or beneath a couch, announcing, "Time's up, you couldn't find me."

A coldness broke in Phoebe's lungs, like inhaling helium from
a balloon. She froze mid-step. From across the street a tall, eccen-
tric house leapt at her in flashes of orange brick. She searched the
grainy air, half expecting to see the familiar form of a skinny leaping girl with dark hair. An old woman hobbled by, clutching a
frilly black umbrella, and as the woman passed, so did the feeling,
unmistakably as a wind shifting course. Phoebe resumed walking,
a weakness in her legs, an odd, buttery flavor at the back of her
throat. It was raining. Yellow squares of light had appeared inside
houses. From a high window came the sound of a piano, notes
floating down solid as leaves, then vanishing. The rain felt so
good, the wet dress clinging to Phoebe's legs. Her old life was
gone. Gone forever, the years alone in San Francisco, years of
waiting, looking for a sign, they had floated away like the thinnest
dry husk, leaving Phoebe newly born in a strange land.

ten

Dear Mom and Phoebe and Barry, Amsterdam is the be all end all. London was nothing compared to this. Wolf and I are crashing in an empty building where all these squatters have been living for months. The cops don't do one thing it's the opposite, they're our guardian angels. We're like a family, everything is spiritual and when someone leaves maybe you won't ever see them again but so what, even in that little time you can still love them. At night the stars are so pretty. Love, Faith

Phoebe stayed in London a week. But the longer she remained, the more the thrill of her surroundings seemed to fade. She began to fear that her own presence was erasing her sister's, blurring it to vagueness. Simply to go where Faith had been was not enough, to stand there, flanked by other tourists, groups of singing children—not enough. Phoebe worried that her own hesitating nature had kept her from making some crucial leap, entering fully the danger and intensity of that first day, with the bomb threat. She left London determined to push herself harder.

She arrived in Amsterdam in the morning with two Australian sisters, Diana and Helen, whom she'd met on the overnight boat. They left their bags in the train station lockers—check-in time at the youth hostel was not until afternoon—and walked to the Dam, Amsterdam's central square. Phoebe noticed a number of young people asleep on the shallow concentric steps surrounding the War Monument, a giant white cone that brought to mind a pillar of salt. She watched with interest as they shook themselves awake, coughing, rolling cigarettes, finally tottering to their feet and stretching skinny arms toward the sky so their tie-dyed shirts lifted up and their shrunken bellies met the sun. She felt a burst of excitement. These were hippies.

All morning Phoebe thought of the sleeping hippies while she trekked with Diana and Helen through the Rijksmuseum, looking at paintings of moist-eyed burghers in stiff lace collars. At two-thirty, when the sisters returned to the station for their backpacks, Phoebe seized her chance to escape them. The official youth hostel was rumored to fill up fast, and they wanted to be there when it opened.

"We'll save you a place if we can," said Helen, the younger sister, who was always offering kindness. "We'll leave your name at the desk."

"Great," Phoebe said, nodding and smiling and wishing they would go.

> *Dear Mom and Phoebe and Barry, Wolf is gone but I don't miss him. I was made to live in Amsterdam. The craziness here is beyond anything. Maybe I'll become a Dutch citizen. Just kidding Hee Hee. Love, Faith*

The number of hippies in the Dam had grown since the morning. Phoebe paused at a florist's stall, watching as they lounged against the War Monument and milled in groups, some entering and leaving the Dam in the brisk manner of drug dealers. One man with dreadlocks thick as wrists played a hoarse-sounding guitar; a blond girl leaned against him, her tangled hair glittering like cut wheat. Phoebe felt the same jealous awe she'd felt for the Haight Street kids who asked her for lemons. She wanted to be on their side.

Phoebe reached in her purse for Faith's picture. It did not seem impossible that one of these people would remember her sister. But her own appearance felt too neat. The peasant skirt and huaraches were ludicrous, insufficient, and shyness tightened like a hand at Phoebe's throat. The space between herself and these gypsies loomed, unnavigable.

The flower vendor eyed Phoebe inquiringly over his buckets of red tulips. She left the stall and crossed the Dam toward the group, Faith's picture in hand. But at the last moment she lost heart, swerving away from the gypsies and out of the Dam altogether, down a narrow street leading toward the canal. Her heart was pounding; there seemed no room for air in her chest. She went to the canal and stopped on a bridge to regroup. Okay, she thought. Okay. In a minute I'll go back.

A few feet away stood a guy Phoebe recognized as one of the sleeping bodies she'd watched come to life that morning in the Dam. She eyed him furtively. His profile was mostly obscured by hair, a wavy pale blond that might have been angelic but for its thinness. Two dirty strings were tied at his wrist. He was leaning over the bridge, staring at the water.

"Excuse me," Phoebe said.

The man started so violently that Phoebe jumped, too. He began to laugh, a harsh, croupy laughter that sounded like coughing. His face seemed unnaturally small, shrunken almost, a child's face on a man's body. Yet he didn't look young.

"Goh, wat hib ga me bang gemaakt!" he said.

Phoebe was taken aback. She hadn't fully registered the fact that these people might speak another language. "I'm sorry, I don't understand," she said.

"American?" He regarded her with interest. When Phoebe nodded, he said warmly, "American is best."

"Thanks," Phoebe said, quizzical.

"Then comes Australia, New Zealanders, then South African. Oh, and Israeli also is great."

"You know them all?"

"Sure," he said. "Everyone comes to Amsterdam."

He turned back to the water, gazing at the canal as if some worry lay hidden there. "So . . . you live here?" Phoebe asked.

"Yes. I am living here."

A pause fell. The man looked up and down the canal. Phoebe thrust Faith's picture before him. In it, her sister was laughing, her mouth open, a string of white shells hanging crookedly around her neck. The shells were from Fiji; their grandparents had sent them each a set.

"Did you ever know this girl?" Phoebe asked.

The fellow took the picture and studied it. His fingernails seemed unusually long for a man. He looked at Faith, then at Phoebe. "Is you?"

"No, my sister. She came to Amsterdam eight years ago."

"Eight years," he said, laughing his gritty wet laugh. "Come on, eight years ago I am this." He flattened a hand at his thigh, indicating the height of a child.

"Oh," Phoebe said. "I thought you were older."

"Everybody thinks," he said rather proudly. "Actually, I am eighteen."

"Me too," said Phoebe.

There was an awkward pause. The guy turned back to the water. Phoebe restored the picture carefully to her purse.

Suddenly he turned to her. "You have some minutes?" he asked, twisting his forearm as if to consult a watch. But there were only the two dirty strings.

Phoebe hesitated. "What for?"

"We can make a visit to Karl. He is staying in Amsterdam more than ten years. He knows everybody coming here."

"Sure," Phoebe said. "Yes, I'd like to meet him."

"Some little walk," he said. "Is okay?"

She felt a shadow of anxiety. "All right."

"So. Please come." He flicked his gaze along the canal a last time, then began walking swiftly away from the center of town. Fighting her reluctance, Phoebe fell into step.

"Nico," he said when she asked his name.

Phoebe's anxiety eased as they walked. Along glistening greenish canals the narrow houses sat unevenly, as if floating. Boxes of bright flowers hung in their windows. The day was warm, bits of white fluff poised delicately on the water.

Nico walked in silence. Twice he and Phoebe passed groups of other young people clearly from his world, and both times the strangers behaved identically: they muttered something to Nico, eyes brushing Phoebe as they passed. She had an uneasy sense that her situation was recognizable to them in some way. "Who were they?" she asked after the second encounter.

Nico just shrugged. "You know. People," he said.

After a baffling series of turns, they reached what appeared to be a student neighborhood. Layers of torn posters were pasted across buildings, and outside corner bars young people sat cross-legged on the pavement, drinking beer from dark bottles.

"Not so much more," Nico assured her.

They turned onto a quieter street. Garbage floated on the canal, plastic bottles, soaked sheets of newspaper. An upside-down doll, pink legs groping up from the murky green. The houses here seemed more drastically uneven than those nearer the Dam, as if they were bobbing directly on the water. Phoebe had to trot every few paces to keep up with Nico. Again the anxiety seized her; how would she find her way back?

They turned again and the canal disappeared. The street narrowed. Abruptly Nico stopped. "Okay," he said.

"I hope he's home," Phoebe said.

"Yes, I am hoping also."

They walked up a few steps to a red wood door with a pane of glass at its center. Nico rang the bell. He rang it in a particular way: two short rings, one long, then another short. Each ring followed a pause, like something landing a long way down.

Phoebe heard a sound overhead and glanced up, catching a flash of dark hair from a high window. A moment later the front door jerked open as if released by a hook. Nico pushed it wide into a cool, dusty foyer. The floor was a coarse-looking marble covered with dry leaves.

"So," Nico said, leading the way up a cramped staircase. Phoebe followed, nervous yet determined. There was no stopping now; if she lost this opportunity, she would despise herself. At the second landing Nico stopped, breathing hard. "Please," he said, motioning Phoebe ahead.

Landings came and went. Finally, on what seemed a sixth or seventh floor, the staircase ended. Nico seemed virtually undone by the climb. Drops of sweat glistened through the hairs of his eyebrows, and he breathed in quick, shallow gasps. Phoebe decided he must be unwell in some way.

"Okay," he breathed. "So we meet Karl."

"Fine." Phoebe was looking forward to different company.

Nico pounded on the door, calling out something in Dutch. It opened quickly, and Phoebe glimpsed a set of striking, almost womanly features before their host about-faced without a word, leading the way down a narrow hall. Nico and Phoebe followed him into a room that struck her immediately as a place where one person had lived for many, many years. At the focal point of the room stood a large black sewing machine on a table, surrounded by bright, jumbled fabrics piled so high that they seemed on the verge of overwhelming the machine itself. The remainder of the room was overgrown with plants, ivy around the windows, lily pads floating in a shallow tub, long vines dangling from hanging pots. A breeze pulled the algae smell of the canal inside and made the leaves and stems shiver gently.

"Welcome welcome," said their host, smiling broadly. He was beautiful, olive-skinned with an Asian lilt to his eyes. He wore a pair of loose Turkish pants belted with a cord of brightly colored yarn and a short-sleeved black T-shirt. "Please," he urged Phoebe, "take a seat."

Oriental carpets covered the floor, a kaleidoscope of golds and crimsons and blues overlapping crazily, disappearing near the windows beneath a heap of pillows piled like a kind of bed. Phoebe chose a cushion at the edge of this mass and folded her legs underneath her.

Karl spoke to Nico curtly in Dutch. With military swiftness the boy turned on his heel and disappeared through a curtain of beads into another room, where Phoebe heard cupboards being opened, a running tap.

Karl seated himself at the sewing machine. "You are visiting Amsterdam the first time?" he inquired politely.

Phoebe told him yes. Slivers of muscle flicked in Karl's arms as he poked through his mountain of fabrics. His hair fell to his chest, heavy and dark as an Asian's hair, but wavy. Phoebe guessed he must be forty.

"What are you sewing?" she asked.

"Everything," he said. "I am a tailor."

His accent was strange to Phoebe, clearly not Dutch, for it was nothing like Nico's. His English sounded British, in fact, but underneath that a deeper accent leaned at the words.

Karl pried a green velvet vest from the heap, threaded a needle and began sewing a square yellow button on it. Nico returned to the room holding three beers, wisps of steam rising from their throats. Karl addressed him sharply in Dutch and the boy answered meekly, then seemed on the verge of returning the third bottle to wherever it had come from. But Karl waved a hand and grinned, suddenly easy. Nico sank onto the cushions near Phoebe, cupping both palms protectively around his bottle.

"You are traveling alone?" Karl asked, finishing with the yellow button and snapping the thread with his teeth.

"No," Phoebe said instinctively. "My friends are at the museum."

Nico began prattling in Dutch. Karl listened with more patience than he'd shown his friend thus far, nodding over his sewing, asking occasional questions. Phoebe listened, too, hoping for some familiar word, some clue to what they were saying.

Finally Nico pushed at her arm. "Show him," he said. Phoebe looked at him. "The photo."

She'd forgotten it. Hastily Phoebe produced the picture of Faith and brought it to Karl at his sewing machine. He glanced at it briefly and nodded. "Sure," he said. "I remember."

"You do?" Phoebe cried.

"She was here some years ago, yes?"

Her heart flinched. "Eight years."

Karl pressed the pedal that operated the sewing machine and began coaxing a piece of blue fabric under the needle. The machine was an old black Singer, curved like a woman's waist, the name in gold lettering.

"So . . . you knew her," Phoebe prompted him.

"Knew her, no, I did not. I remember her," Karl said. "There were people coming, people going all the time, but that one I do remember." After a moment he added, "Dead?"

Phoebe stared at him. "How did you know?"

"If she is alive, then why you are coming to me with a picture in your hand?" He flashed a white grin, his needle greedily gobbling the fabric. "OD?"

"Oh no," Phoebe said, but stopped short of divulging the truth. "So," she said, at a loss, "I mean, what did you think of her?"

Karl turned the fabric under the needle to pull it through in another direction. "You know, there were so many people," he said. "She was a nice girl. Fun, a little crazy? Beautiful," he said. "Lots of boyfriends."

"Did she ever come here?"

Karl worked the pedal, prompting the machine's rhythmic mutterings to increase in speed and pitch until they seemed to verge upon speech. When he lifted his foot from the pedal, a hush fell over the room. Karl shut his eyes. "Yes. I think yes," he said, opening his eyes again. "I can remember her there." He pointed to the cushions beneath the windows. Turning, Phoebe was surprised to see Nico, whose presence in the room she'd entirely forgotten. He sat erect and pale. Karl laughed at him, muttering something in Dutch.

"She was actually here, in this room?" Phoebe said, overjoyed. "I can't believe it."

"I'm not saying for sure, you understand me," Karl said, resuming his sewing. "She was here maybe one minute."

But a minute was enough, a minute was everything. Spellbound, Phoebe watched Karl's hands sift among his silks and linens. "She was here," she said.

Though the sun was still high, it had a worn-out feeling about it. Karl pried open a nugget of tinfoil, breaking off a piece of something brown and damp-looking inside. He placed it in the tiny copper bowl of a long Chinese pipe, lit, puffed, and passed the pipe to Phoebe. The smell was strange. She took the pipe and deeply inhaled the soft smoke, sweet inside her throat. God knew what it was. She returned to her spot on the cushions and passed the pipe to Nico, who accepted it halfheartedly. Karl did not resume his sewing. He leaned over the pile of fabrics and looked straight at Phoebe for what seemed the first time. Yet even now his gaze was absent, as if her face were merely a resting place for his eyes.

"Do you ever miss those times?" Phoebe asked.

"What times?"

"You know. The sixties." The term sounded foolish.

Karl sucked at the pipe, eyes narrowed. "It was good," he said, breathing smoke. "Like falling in love. Sure, you want the beginning. But you know already the end."

Phoebe took the pipe. The smoke was soft as felt in her lungs. "What's the end?" she asked.

Karl shrugged. "Same like everything," he said. "Goes too far, becomes the opposite."

Phoebe puzzled over this. She tried passing the pipe to Nico, but the boy waved it away impatiently. He looked dreadful. Phoebe was suddenly very high, and not a high she recognized. The room appeared smeared. She blinked to straighten out her vision. "Opposite of what?" she said, her voice seeming to waft in from a distance.

Karl lifted a pile of fabric scraps from his lap and set it on the floor. Then he spoke with sudden intensity. "You want peace, finally you take guns to find it. Use drugs for opening your mind so everything will come inside—now you think only where to get more smack. You love to live, but you die and die and die—so many dead, from that time," he said. "Like your sister." And as he looked at Phoebe, something opened in Karl's eyes like a camera shutter, as if, for a moment, he actually saw her.

Then he looked away. Phoebe took a long hit of satiny smoke from the pipe. The fishy canal breeze filled the room. Things becoming their opposites, yes, she thought, it made sense. Karl's voice sounded oracular, the single and absolute voice of truth. Opposites, she thought, yes . . .

Nico broke the thread of her meanderings. He lurched from his seat and crawled toward Phoebe across the cushions, his face gray, moist with sweat. Revolted, Phoebe tried to draw away but achieved this only by faint degrees, her motion stalled by the drug.

"Look," Nico said, smiling uneasily. He was still on all fours, his face thrust toward Phoebe's. She smelled a terrible sweetness on his breath and thought of hospitals, the sweet smell that covers death. "So look, okay?" he said. "I am brought you here."

Phoebe turned to Karl, expecting him to heap scorn upon Nico for this grotesque performance, but Karl was sorting with renewed absorption through his heap of fabrics. "Yeah," she finally conceded to Nico. "You brought me . . ."

"So now, if you have some money, I have none."

"Money!" Phoebe said. She turned again to Karl, but clearly he'd removed himself from this discussion. "Why should I give you money?" she asked, more querulously than she would have liked.

"Because how you would come here without me, yes?" Nico said in a high, trembling voice. He looked ready to explode.

Karl was sewing again, cocooned in the whir of machinery. Clearly he'd seen this moment coming, agreed to it beforehand. Some larger plan was revealing itself. Phoebe felt a shudder of awful comprehension, as if a part of her had known all along, and been silenced. Alone in an apartment with two strange men, in a foreign country. Her heart clambered against her ribs, but her stymied brain lagged behind it, thickened by the drug. "Well— how much?" she asked Nico.

"Maybe, let's say fifty guilders?"

Phoebe was too stoned for arithmetic. It seemed like a lot. She opened her purse and took out her wallet. Only seventy guilders remained of the money she'd changed at the station that morning. "Here," she said, handing Nico two twenty-five-guilder notes. Through the sleepy flow of her thoughts certain piercing worries were beginning to penetrate—time, banks, paying for the hostel— like the prickling of a numbed limb regaining sensation. But more painful still was her injury over Karl's betrayal, his willingness to abandon her to this parasite.

Money in hand, the whimpering Nico became a man of action. He sprang to a shelf obscured by wandering Jew and opened the lid of a black lacquered box. There was a sudden pressure in the room. Phoebe felt it bodily, a ripple of sickness, a faulty quiver in her heartbeat. But she was afraid to move, to call attention to herself in the smallest way, for fear of causing an explosion.

Nico returned to the cushions holding a syringe. Of course, Phoebe thought. Of course. She stared at the rug, hearing the babble of Karl's sewing machine. Here was the underground world, here it was; after a lifetime of stolen glimpses, she was right in its midst. A sense of deep inevitability bore down on her. Nico sat on the cushions near her, holding a teaspoon to which he added liquid from an eyedropper. He flicked a plastic cigarette lighter and held its flame beneath the spoon. A faint, sweet burning filled the air.

Karl left his sewing machine and knelt beside Nico. He filled the syringe with the liquid from the spoon, then yanked the yarn belt from his Turkish pants and knotted it tightly around the boy's arm, just above the elbow. He took Nico's forearm in his hands and held it, touching the tiny eruptions of scabs with the gentleness of a doctor. Phoebe turned away, her amazement eclipsed by horror, but as the seconds passed, she felt compelled to look again. She whirled back around. Gently, almost lovingly, Karl pushed the needle into Nico's flesh.

Karl eased the plunger down. Nico's eyes fluttered shut and he sighed. When Karl withdrew the syringe, there was blood at the bottom. He set it on a windowsill. Nico gazed at Phoebe, his face so peacefully settled that for the first time all day he looked his real age. "Cheers, okay?" he said softly. His eyes kept falling shut, despite his valiant efforts to keep them open. Again and again they closed, Nico rocking slowly forward, then catching himself, jerking back, drooping to one side and jerking straight again. He looked like a jack-in-the-box.

Karl moved close to Phoebe. She noticed his forearms were scarless, full of long rivery veins. He touched Phoebe's shoulder in the same gentle way he'd touched Nico's arm. No, Phoebe thought, no, but she was so tired, the drug had sapped all the energy from her body, and now a part of her longed, like Nico, to shut her eyes and hand herself over. Karl pushed her backward onto the cushions, stroking her hair, glancing toward the open window, where a church bell rang faintly. Then, in a swift, effortless motion he flattened himself on top of her. Phoebe lay still, not paralyzed so much as dulled. Someone was calling out instructions; she strained to catch them. Nico continued bobbing from side to side, teetering between sleep and wakefulness. Phoebe

wished she could lay him down flat. Karl began to kiss her, pushing his tongue deep inside Phoebe's mouth, pressing himself to
her leg. From below the windows she heard children. She wanted
Karl to stop, but the fierce efficiency of his desires seemed to
muffle her own. In a single, fluid gesture, he lifted her skirt and
eased aside her underpants. She felt his bare hand.

Phoebe shrieked, and the hand withdrew. Nico's eyes blinked
open. He stared at Phoebe, seeming about to speak, then was
folded helplessly back into sleep.

"Hey," Karl said, moving his long body to one side of Phoebe.
"Hey, so relax." He touched her bare thigh. She saw the shape of
his penis through the Turkish pants and began groping for support, wanting to stand now, certain even in her murky state that
no redemption awaited her. But she couldn't stand, Karl was making it hard to balance. "Hey," he said, as if Phoebe were a cat lost
among the cushions, and even now she felt a longing to believe he
was somehow good, if she could just . . . find her balance . . .
Karl's breath at her ear— No. She clawed the cushions, the struggle giving her focus; for an instant the murkiness cleared and she
felt a charge of bright terror— No! She had to stand up, a sound
was moving through her, up toward her throat. It emerged painfully, like a bubble breaking. "Stop," she cried, a strangled sound,
then louder, "Stop!" fighting him now, fumbling to her feet, but
Karl just laughed and leaned back looking up at her, not even
trying anymore, his laugh not cruel so much as surprised that a
stupid, meaningless thing was costing him this much trouble.

"Get out of here," he said.

Clutching her purse, Phoebe tottered down the narrow hall,
past photographs, drawings under dusty glass, the shadowy kaleidoscope of Karl's life. She opened the door and careened down
the curving staircase to the lobby, half expecting him to pursue
her, but no, he wouldn't. Outside, the light broke painfully against
her eyes and she reeled, thinking she might be sick. There was a
pain between her legs, a burning, as though he'd chafed her.

Phoebe rounded a corner, half ran, half fumbled alongside the canal until she was gasping for air. When she noticed people watching her, she slowed to a walk. She felt a horror of being discovered, as if fleeing the scene of her own crime. For some time she wandered without direction, trying to still her panicked breathing. She thought of going to the police, but she'd forgotten where Karl even lived, had never known in the first place—doubtless the reason for all the twists and turns she and Nico had taken on their way. And anyhow, what did she have to report? Drugs were legal in Amsterdam as far as she knew, and Nico hadn't robbed her—she'd given the money freely. But why? Why not leave the apartment right then, when things started to turn? Why go there at all? It was her own behavior, more than theirs, that Phoebe couldn't bear to recall—so vulnerable, so easy. She saw this now with a painful clarity. And of course they'd seen, too. To people like them, a weakness like hers must be obvious, must cling to her like a smell.

Beneath everything else lay a single, terrible fear, worse than the needle or what Karl had done to her: the possibility that he'd lied about Faith, had not really known her at all. Phoebe's mind touched this thought and instantly veered away. It wasn't possible. She'd seen in his eyes that he was serious.

Still, the adventure had been a failure. An unmitigated disaster. It would never have happened to Faith.

After nearly an hour of aimless wandering, Phoebe asked directions back to the train station and managed to find it. Discovering her backpack still in its locker seemed to her nothing short of miraculous. It was seven o'clock; she'd missed the youth hostel check-in by hours. She prayed that Diana and Helen had saved her a place.

The youth hostel was full. "First come first serve," said a kid behind the desk, and place-saving was not allowed. The travelers lounging near the check-in desk looked like advertisements for happiness. "There are many hostels in Amsterdam," said the kid behind the desk.

Phoebe headed back to the street. Her hands shook as she turned the pages of her guidebook, circling names of other hostels, finding their locations on her map. She marked three spots, then rested on the curb, overwhelmed by the prospect of carrying the heavy backpack even one more step. Her mind reeled again and again back to Karl's apartment, as if to lessen the horror through repetition, find some new redeeming aspect of the memory.

Finally Phoebe hoisted herself to her feet. Though the sky was still light, it was evening now, the air heavy with a dreadful sense of too late. She walked ten minutes to a second hostel and found that one full, too; without pause she spun back around and began plodding toward a third, this one back in the direction of the train station along a wide, arid boulevard. Streetcars rattled past, empty and beige. The bottom floor of this hostel was a public bar. Phoebe wove among tables to the owner, whose hands glistened with something from the kitchen. He wiped them, leaving streaks on his apron. Yes, they had a bed; Phoebe nearly folded with relief. His son, a red-haired, insolent boy of about twelve, led Phoebe to a room filled with bunk beds. It smelled of mildew. She longed to open a window.

She was given a top bunk at the very end of the room, beside a window of rippled factory glass. A ring of dirt surrounded each pane like frost. Carefully Phoebe spread her sleeping sheet across the mattress and rested her backpack against the windowsill. The shower was down the hall and cost extra; there were no doors or even curtains on the stalls, but the room was empty. The floor felt slick. Phoebe went back to the bar and paid for the bed and a shower. The owner was smoking a joint as thick as a finger, and offered Phoebe a hit. She refused politely. She would leave Amsterdam tomorrow.

A long, vigorous shower improved her spirits somewhat. It was eight-thirty, and through the frosted glass by her bed she saw darkness finally falling. She took everything of value from her backpack, including the bottle of Chanel No. 5, and stuffed it in her purse. She went back outside.

From a café window Phoebe watched the night descend on Amsterdam. Eating her sandwich and drinking a beer, she found herself longing for company. This was strange, for until now being alone hadn't felt like being alone. She'd been shored up—crowded almost—by her sense of purpose. Now she felt weak, transparent. She longed to call her mother but this seemed impossible, as if by leaving home she'd closed off that avenue forever.

There was a small rack of postcards on the café counter, and Phoebe bought one of the War Monument, where she'd first seen the hippies asleep. "Dear Mom," she wrote, "I just want to tell you I'm fine. I hope you are, too." It sounded ludicrous, stilted. Phoebe wished she could find it in herself to write, "Everything is great, I'm having a ball," but the deception seemed too vast to carry off. "Love, Phoebe," she wrote. The man at the counter sold her a stamp. She had almost no Dutch money left.

Phoebe mailed the card outside the café. It was dark, and the streets in this part of town were eerily quiet. Phoebe had been curious to see the Amsterdam whores in their famous red-light district, but no longer could muster any real enthusiasm. Still, she was desperate to be among people. The thought of running into Nico or Karl haunted her as she followed the general drift to a livelier part of town where whores lounged like department-store mannequins behind plate-glass windows, chewing gum, reading, doing their nails, as if unaware of the audience gaping in from the street. One woman in a black leather bikini was talking on the phone, twisting its black cord around her calf. Now and then a door to one of these parlors would open, releasing a puff of music and usually a man, both of which lingered a moment before dissolving into the night. To Phoebe it all looked meager, the dregs of something better that had passed. What Karl had said about opposites seemed to touch all of Amsterdam; the whole city had turned, gone rotten in the eight years since her sister's visit. Even Karl himself—surely his life had once consisted of more than shooting junkies full of drugs and molesting foreign girls in his apartment. He was his own best example.

Phoebe felt a hand on her shoulder and yelped, whirling around to see Helen, the younger Australian sister whom she'd met on the boat the night before.

"I'm sorry," Phoebe said. "Oh God, I'm sorry." She took the Australian girl in her arms.

Helen stiffened, then relaxed, hugging Phoebe back. "We tried to keep your place," she said, "but the bloody guy wouldn't let us."

"I found another hostel," Phoebe said. "It's sort of gross."

"Well, look, we're all back at that pub you just passed," Helen said. "We knocked on the window, but you were walking too fast. Come have a pint."

The bar was packed with young people smoking cigarettes. Diana, Helen's sister, sat at a table with two American guys who Phoebe guessed were in college. She sat down. The Americans were playing a game of some kind that involved coins and mugs of beer. "You from Australia, too?" one of them asked Phoebe.

She shook her head. "I'm American."

"Where from?"

"San Francisco."

"Fucking A. I love that city, man."

Phoebe smiled. She felt deeply separate from these people, as if her experience today had driven a final wedge between herself and her peers. She longed to bridge the gap.

"What did you do all afternoon?" Helen said.

"Heineken Brewery," said one of the guys. "Plus we did Anne Frank's house."

"I meant Phoebe," Helen said, laughing.

They all looked at her. Phoebe panicked over what to say, and suddenly was angry at Helen for putting her on the spot.

"Nothing," she said dismissively. "Just walked."

She saw confusion in Helen's face. There was a beat of silence, then the boys resumed their drinking game. Diana and Helen opened *Let's Go* and leaned over it, planning their next day in Amsterdam. Phoebe sat in silence, sipping her beer. It was enough just to be near them.

Later, lying on her bunk bed staring at the murky window, Phoebe thought again of Faith's postcards. *At night the stars are so pretty,* her sister had written.

Phoebe had forgotten even to look.

eleven

Dear Mom and Phoebe and Barry, From Namur Wolf and I and some others took off to Reims, France . . .

Phoebe followed her sister's postcards from Amsterdam to Namur, Belgium, where she spent a week. In her own company she felt inhibited, shy almost. After dinner each night at the youth hostel, she would linger at the table, then, dreading to be alone, move to the noisy common room until bedtime.

. . . because someone knew this French guy in Reims who we could stay with. Well but the poor French guy had no idea we were coming and his apartment is so small . . .

When she returned to her room and looked into the mirror, her face looked strange to her, the cheeks hollow, the eyes larger, dark. Objectively, she approved of these changes, but her own reflection startled her.

>   . . . It's a little crowded but I keep asking people please be neat and they are. P.S. The way they say Reims in French, it sounds like someone snorting!

It was time to move on—overdue—but she couldn't bring herself to go. Reims, she thought, Reims, and tried to feel anticipation. She wished she had someone to stay with.

On her second day in Belgium, Phoebe had rented a sturdy black bike and pedaled beside a river to Dinant, a tiny nearby town that Faith had mentioned in her postcards. There she checked her bike at the train station and, still tracing Faith's steps, followed a narrow street uphill until the houses fell away and Phoebe found herself in an oceanic sprawl of land. It rolled and tossed in grassy swells, curves of bright green. Crushed silver rock filled the road. She saw horses, brown, silky gray, hindquarters flecked with white. The distant hills were studded with sheep.

A town appeared in the distance. Reaching it, Phoebe was startled by its silence, nothing but a rush and tumble of wind past empty-looking houses. She went inside a tiny shop and bought a bar of white chocolate from an old woman wearing a silk scarf and bright, heavy makeup. When she left the shop, Phoebe was surprised to find several children waiting for her outside.

"Hel-lo. Hel-lo," they said, accenting the first syllable of the word so it seemed less a greeting than a kind of chorus, like birdsong. There were five of them, all boys, the youngest five or six years old, the oldest maybe fourteen. All were slim, olive-skinned. Like the town itself, their chipped-looking faces seemed shaped by the ceaseless wind.

"Hel-lo, hel-lo, hel-lo," they called, as if it gave them pleasure to say it.

"Hello," Phoebe replied. She offered them her chocolate bar, but the boys shook their heads and turned shyly away. Their bicycles leaned near the door of the shop, and the oldest boy mounted his and rode a few paces ahead. The smaller boys clambered onto their own bikes and followed him. When they looked back at Phoebe, she waved good-bye, relieved to see them go. Children made her nervous. She was used to being the youngest herself, noticed only sporadically, following others' examples rather than setting one herself.

She continued through the village. The road swung out of town and plunged downhill. The cyclists weren't far ahead. Phoebe slowed, waiting for them to ride out of view, but the boys, too, slowed down, until it was clear they were waiting for her. "Hel-lo, hel-lo," they called as Phoebe approached.

She forced herself to smile. *"Avec moi?"* she asked with feigned incredulity, hoping to discourage them.

The boys surrounded Phoebe in a kind of pack. Alarmed, she wondered if her *"Avec moi?"* had been mistaken for an invitation. She left the town with her five companions in tow. They chattered among themselves, weaving their bicycles in S patterns over the crushed silver pavement so as not to outpace her. It was strange, not being able to speak to them. Phoebe felt like a bad hostess.

The road ducked under tall trees, and soon they were inside a forest. Wind hissed and gushed in the leaves.

"Dinant?" Phoebe asked, pointing downhill.

"Oui, oui," the boys chanted.

The oldest rode close to Phoebe. *"Pourquoi est-ce-que vous êtes seule?"* he said.

"Je ne comprends pas," Phoebe said, so haltingly that the boy couldn't possibly have doubted her. She'd abandoned French for Spanish in eighth grade.

"Pourquoi est-ce-que vous êtes seule?" he repeated more slowly.

Phoebe shook her head, embarrassed, and forced a smile. "I don't understand," she said.

"Pourquoi est-ce-que vous êtes seule?" said another boy, loudly

now, obviously sharing in the misconception that repetition combined with volume would get the message across. Phoebe racked
her brains. She'd known the word *"seule,"* but what did it mean?
Then she remembered. Alone. The boys were asking why she was
alone. Phoebe pretended not to understand. She felt as if they had
glimpsed something shameful in her.

The littlest boy rode close to Phoebe and smiled up at her,
revealing a black hole where four front teeth would eventually be.
He said something in French, lisping the words, still grinning his
toothless, open-mouthed smile. When Phoebe didn't answer, he
kept talking, mocking her, she thought, showing off for the older
boys at her expense.

"I don't understand!" she cried. "I don't understand. Please
stop talking to me!" She was shouting, on the verge of tears.

The child's face went entirely blank. He stopped pedaling
abruptly and so did the others, in one motion. They gazed at
Phoebe with dark, serious eyes. Instantly she saw that what she'd
taken for mockery was no more than high spirits, excitement at
the adventure of escorting an American girl into Dinant. Now they
looked stung, as if Phoebe had turned on them without warning.
Her sharp words hung there, trapped under the trees.

"I'm sorry," she said. She wanted to say it in French but could
not find the words. "I'm sorry."

The boys watched her with sad, solemn faces. "I'm sorry!"
Phoebe cried with more urgency, but at the sound of her raised
voice all five boys turned as one and began pedaling quickly away,
back up the hill. The youngest, who was barefoot, lagged behind
the rest. He glanced fearfully back at Phoebe, tiny legs straining
frantically on the pedals. Finally he stood up to get more leverage,
rounded a bend and was out of sight.

Phoebe burst into tears. For several minutes she stood weeping in the middle of the road, the choking, gulping sobs of childhood. Something was wrong; something was wrong but she didn't
know what. She was alone in the middle of nowhere, behaving
strangely, with no one around to help her, and what people were

around she wanted only to escape. Wind rattled and shook over-head. The road felt so empty. Had a single car ever driven down it, or was its purpose merely to flatter the landscape?

Phoebe gazed at the earth beside her, tufts of grass poking up from a rain-beaten hillside. She grabbed a tuft and pulled. The dry, powdery soil released it easily. Phoebe tossed the grass in the road and pushed off against the embankment, walking quickly downhill. Her stomach tightened with the faint beginnings of fear. Trees, road, stone houses with their shutters closed; all of them filled her with dread.

She walked mechanically. The possibility of panic hovered very near, like a cat brushing her shins. Phoebe kept her eyes on the pavement. The rhythm of her steps seemed the articulation of a single question: What am I doing here? What am I doing here? I could be anywhere.

Still, she kept the panic at bay. It would all be revealed, she told herself, when she found a way to push herself hard enough.

> *Dear Mom, Barry and Phoebe, Wolf and I are back to-gether again THANK GOD!! In Belgium they speak French, did you know that? Everyday we eat a new pastry. The people have simple good lives and we watch the women go shopping with their string bags. But it is a flaw in me that sometimes I get bored. Love, Faith*

At last, Phoebe reached Dinant. Too tired to attempt the ride back to Namur, she waited for the train. It was nearly dusk, the air luminous blue. She stood alone on the platform. When the train came, the conductor helped her with the bike, a courtesy that overwhelmed Phoebe with gratitude. She collapsed into a seat, wishing the ride would continue forever. Sheer transit seemed preferable to actually being anywhere. In spite of herself she be-gan nodding off, head bobbing back and forth, knocking against the window as Nico's had, in Amsterdam. Afraid she would miss her stop, Phoebe forced herself to stand for the remainder of the ride.

Finally, after a week in Namur, Phoebe packed her bag and said good-bye to Guy, the youth hostel's director. He kissed her as he did all his guests, left, right, left, but there was a coldness in his eyes, Phoebe thought, as if already he'd forgotten her.

She arrived at the Reims train station at six-thirty. The light was thick with dust. A man rode past on a bicycle, a long, droopy baguette tied to the rear. France, Phoebe thought. I'm in France.

Feeling like Quasimodo under her backpack, she followed her map to a group of beige high-rises outside the center of town. Between them lay large stretches of pavement dotted with benches and skinny trees, suggestive of a park but lacking the density to be one. The youth hostel was inside one of these high-rises, though Phoebe had an eerie sense of being the first and only "youth" ever to utilize it. Everyone in the crowded lobby spoke French and seemed to live here.

On the twelfth floor she followed a strip of aquamarine carpeting between cinderblock walls to room 1203. It looked like a tiny hotel room, cot, Formica desk and night table, flat indoor-outdoor carpeting. Phoebe felt a wave of unease. The place was all wrong. She opened the window to look down at a group of girls jumping rope on the pavement far below. The sound of their rope slapping the concrete ricocheted among the buildings. The children were singing a song Phoebe recognized, though she couldn't remember the words. She closed the window, then opened it again, listening to the song. At the small sink she splashed water on her face and dried it with a rough white towel. She changed clothes quickly and left.

By now the shops had closed. French people were settling down to dinner at outdoor restaurant tables—candles, half-filled glasses of wine, silver crossed haphazardly over plates. They leaned forward, gesturing with their cigarettes. The picturesque scene heart-

ened Phoebe. This is it! she thought fleetingly, and decided to
treat herself to a fancy dinner.

She chose a restaurant set back from the street, with dark
green patterned walls. The tablecloth was white, the cutlery heavy
and silver. A piece of lemon floated in her water glass, but what
cheered Phoebe most was the single red rose in its slender crystal
vase. She leaned back, basking in her own sophistication, wishing
someone were here to see her in Reims, France, dining alone at an
elegant restaurant.

The waiter arrived, a good-looking, careless fellow with longish blond hair. When Phoebe haltingly explained that she would
be eating alone, he removed the table setting opposite hers with a
flourish. Most tables were occupied by several people, and wherever Phoebe looked, her gaze snagged on someone else's. She
thought of asking to move but dreaded the waiter's reaction. She
picked up the saltshaker and turned it in her hand, studying it.

Her waiter brought the wine. He'd begun performing his du-
ties with gross exaggeration, Phoebe thought, uncorking the bottle
like a magician preparing it to flap from his hands as a dove. A
withering gaze failed to quell his merriment. Phoebe drank and
drank, craving that give, that welcome loosening of the world, but
the opposite seemed to happen: her focus sharpened, as if she'd
donned a pair of high-powered glasses that enabled her to see
clearly the pitying looks other diners were casting her way. Her
endive salad might have been weeds yanked from the curb, the
chicken dish a table leg. She imagined smashing her dishes to the
floor, hollering aloud to the room at large, Don't be sorry for me!
Can't you see I'm here for a reason?

Phoebe finished the wine and asked for the bill, which seemed
unreasonably high. She paid it anyway and left, not raising her
head until she'd reached the street. Along the wide boulevard people were strolling, enjoying the warm night. Phoebe walked with
arms crossed. The food sat uneasily in her stomach.

One step, another step; like a machine, she found herself plodding back toward the hostel, the last place on earth she wanted to

be. Her heartbeat spiraled; she began to sweat. She went straight to the twelfth floor and switched on the light in her room. There was no curtain, and yellow streetlights below gave the darkness a sulfurous tinge. It was nine-twenty. The room seemed tiny. It looked so plain—Faith would have done something to brighten it up, bought flowers in town, something. She'd hated dull rooms, had scandalized Grandma O'Connor once by pinning all her brightly colored underpants to the walls of the room she and Phoebe shared in Mirasol. Phoebe dug the little jewelry she'd brought from inside her backpack, hair barrettes, the bottle of Chanel No. 5, and spread them over the night table and window-sill and small desk.

The bathroom was near the elevator. Phoebe paused in the dim hall and listened for movement, intending to knock at some-one's door and ask for an aspirin. But she heard not the faintest whisper of motion, as if she were the twelfth floor's only inhabit-ant.

Phoebe changed into her sleeping shirt, turned off the light and lay on the bed, arms folded. The ceiling was made of white squares that sparkled faintly. Her heart pounded in her ears. Something was wrong. She'd failed, Phoebe thought, but at what? Imagining herself in Europe, she'd always pictured someone else, physically even, a tall blonde with an answer for everything—as if, in the course of this journey, she would not only shed her former life but cease to exist as herself. Yes, she thought, to leave Phoebe O'Connor behind and be reborn as someone beautiful, mysteri-ous. But the opposite had happened; her own narrow boundaries had hemmed her in, keeping everything real at a distance.

She seized the two humps of her ribcage. If I just could calm down, she told herself, but her panic swelled with every second. It flashed through her mind that whatever drug she'd smoked in Amsterdam with Nico and Karl had damaged her brain. She stared at the walls frantic to call her mother, but had no idea where to find an international phone at that hour. She sprang from the bed and pawed through her purse in the dark for the envelope with the hit of acid inside it. Lately she'd wondered if she should just take the acid, swallow it down—maybe that would send her reeling through a last, crucial door like Alice passing through the mouse hole. But Phoebe couldn't bring herself to take it—she was too afraid.

She crawled under the covers and curled in a ball. Just get through this night, she thought, but her body trembled, teeth chattering, heartbeat pounding against her eardrums. Gradually she found herself thinking of home, fog swirling like dreams around the Golden Gate Bridge and white buildings of downtown. Fog lapping over eucalyptus trees, so soft, half-liquid the way it poured against the bedroom window, obscuring every other house from sight and even the trees, like being out on the open sea surrounded by nothing, until finally there was nothing left but to close your eyes.

Dear Mom, Phoebe and Barry, Yesterday we went to Epernay where they make all the kinds of champagne and we took a cool tour of the champagne cellars of Dom Perignon and splurged on two bottles for our poor Reims host but guess what? He doesn't like champagne! So we drank it ourselves! Wolf's gone again. I miss him but we don't get along but I miss him anyways. Life is so crazy. Love, Faith

Phoebe woke the next morning to a square of gray sky. The panic had passed. She lay still a long time before getting dressed and hiding her backpack under the cot. She stuffed her valuables in her purse, locked the room and walked to the train station for the day trip to Épernay.

On the train Phoebe's indefatigable hope rose in her again. Perhaps last night's terror had been a final test, she thought, and now, in Épernay, something marvelous would unveil itself.

At the Moët & Chandon winery she joined an English-speaking tour, listening with passionate interest to how the bottles were stored at angles and rotated to shift their sediments, as if the solution to her troubles lay hidden among these damp tunnels with bursts of silty gray moss springing from their walls. It was a long tour, and the longer it went on, the more Phoebe dreaded its end, the return to her own unreliable care.

She downed her sample glass of Dom Pérignon and then stood self-consciously, holding the empty glass while her English-speaking colleagues discreetly sipped their own.

"Please," said the man beside her, offering Phoebe his champagne. He spoke with an accent. "I have not tasted."

Phoebe thanked him, moved by the kindness. She drank the champagne. He was a young man. His eyes resembled Barry's, the same dark iris nearly indistinguishable from the pupil.

When the tour dispersed, Phoebe walked slowly back toward the station. Épernay was filled with the tart scent of grapes; it seemed to rise from the pavement, the storefronts, even the groggy weeds along the road. The champagne had left Phoebe woozy. It was only two-fifteen, and the empty day hung before her. Across the street she noticed the young man who had given her his champagne, walking in the same direction. Their eyes met. "You are taking the train for Reims?" he called through the dusty silence.

"Yes," Phoebe said. "Are you?"

He crossed the street. He was Pietro, a student at the University of Turin. He had come to Reims today from Paris, and tonight would take the overnight train to Madrid.

Phoebe blithely explained that she was making her way toward Italy to meet her older sister. The lie came so effortlessly, bringing with it such a bolt of delight that she wondered why she ever told the truth.

"She lives in Italia? Your sister?"

"In Rome. Eight years now," Phoebe said. "She writes books."

"Ah, writer," Pietro said, nodding. He seemed impressed. "Maybe I have read something."

"Well, no. Because the first one is just coming out. Actually, three of her books are coming out at one time."

"Three!" He looked amazed.

"She writes fast," Phoebe assured him, flushed.

Pietro stopped walking and pulled from his shoulder bag a small notebook and a green pencil. "Please, tell me her name?" he said.

"Faith. Faith O'Connor."

"Faith O'Connor," he said, copying slowly. "I will find her books."

The train was not due for twenty minutes, so Phoebe and Pietro ordered croque-monsieurs at a bar and ate them outside on the warm concrete steps. They must have looked like traveling companions, Phoebe thought, possibly even a couple. She noticed her voice leaning into laughter, how she tossed her head, each tiny gesture like the sweet ache of a muscle craving exercise.

"Why did you come to Reims?" she asked teasingly. "For the champagne?"

Pietro smiled, apparently not understanding. "I gave to you, eh? The champagne," he said. "No, I come for the cathedral."

"Cathedral?"

Pietro looked shocked. "The Cathedral of Reims? Is extraordinary, most beautiful in Europe."

"I just got here," Phoebe said, abashed.

Somewhere in the town a bell began to ring. Pietro's eyes were filled with a gentleness she found difficult to look at. "So, you are here—because why?" he asked.

"My sister told me to come," she said. "She loved Reims."

Pietro smiled. "Your sister," he said. "I think she has seen the cathedral."

On the train they sat side by side, passing soft fields that leaned and shook as if water were pouring across them. Where the grain had been cut a sharp stubble remained, glinting like broken glass in the sunlight. Pietro's clothes were clean but smudged, as if he owned few outfits and wore them often. Despite his physical slightness, there was a strength about him.

"You seem older than college," Phoebe said.

Pietro cocked his head. She repeated the question more carefully.

"Ah. Yes," he said. "For some years I did not study. Now I have returned, but yes, I am older now."

Phoebe asked why he'd stopped. Pietro hesitated, and she worried she'd been nosy.

"I had some creases," he finally said.

Phoebe frowned. "Creases?"

"Crisi? Crisis? You know this?"

"Oh, crisis," Phoebe said. "Sure."

"Crisis," Pietro said slowly. He tapped his head with one finger. "Crisis."

"A crisis in your head? In your brain?" Phoebe could not keep the eagerness from her voice.

"Sì," Pietro said, then seemed to reflect. "No, I am wrong. Not head. In my so-well. You understand?"

"Your soul," Phoebe said. She could not believe what she was hearing. "But you seem okay now," she said carefully. "I mean, you seem stable."

"Now I am well," Pietro said.

Phoebe longed to ask more, but her own fragility felt so obvious, burdening every word. Yet she no longer feared prying. There was something indefinably public about Pietro, as if the events of his life were there for the taking. "How did you do that?" she asked. "I mean, get well."

Pietro placed a fist against his heart. "Jesu Christ," he said. "I found Him and I am saved."

Phoebe stared at him. "Are you a priest?"

"Missionary," he said. "I am just beginning, in Madrid."

Phoebe wanted to tell Pietro that she was a Catholic, but was ashamed of not having been to church in so long. "How—how did you find Him?" she asked.

"He came," Pietro said. "He came to me."

"You mean you saw Him?" Phoebe's voice was hushed.

"Non 'saw,' " Pietro said, putting one hand on each eye.

"Saw." And placing both hands flat on his chest, he flipped them open like two doors making room for something to enter him.

"Were you afraid?"

He smiled. "When I don't see Him, then I am afraid." After a moment he added, "Still I am afraid, *sì,* but *no* I am alone. I am not alone," he corrected himself.

Phoebe looked out the window. Beneath a layer of thin, frayed clouds the sky was pure blue. "My sister used to be religious," she said.

"Your sister. *A Roma.*"

Phoebe felt as if by lying about Faith she'd soiled Pietro without his knowing it. "Yes," she said, anxious now to be truthful. "Our father was very sick and my sister began to study for her Confirmation." She was aware of speaking slowly, formally for Pietro's benefit, and this gave her descriptions the distilled, monumental quality of events she'd read about. "We went to Mass every day," she said.

"You also—you accompanied her?"

"Yes."

Jesus on the cross, his ribs like a pair of folded wings. Phoebe's mind had wandered far from the priest—a spelling test, a two-square game she'd dominated at recess—no event was too profane to bear contemplation in the house of God. Only at the Last Supper did she finally wend her way back to the sermon in time for the breaking of the Host—the body of Christ in that small, flat disk! Phoebe imagined it tasting buttery, sweet, and for years had watched jealously as adults and older children rose from their pews at the end of each Mass to partake of this wondrous food. As they left the altar, she would scrutinize their faces for signs of transformation. But their expressions gave nothing away.

When finally she'd made her own First Communion—years late, taller than the other girls and wearing the wrong kind of dress—she was disconcerted to find that the Host had no taste at all. It stuck to the roof of her mouth like a cardboard chip from a board game, then melted away. As for the promising wave of intensity she'd felt while coming away from the altar, it proved no more than the dizzying power of her longing for something to happen. By the time she left the church, it had already passed.

"Your father," Pietro said. "He is well today?"

Phoebe hesitated, beguiled by further stories she might invent. But lying to someone so religious seemed deeply wrong. It was almost like lying to God.

"He died," she said. Grade school, high school—"Your dad, what does he do?" As if dying were his sole achievement.

"I am sorry."

Phoebe shrugged. These exchanges always made her uncomfortable; in the end she felt obliged to make light of her father's death, just to get things back on a cheerier note. "It was ages ago," she said.

They sat in silence. Countryside yielded to city, modern apartment buildings, bright laundry flapping on cramped terraces. Soon the ride would end, they would go their separate ways.

The train jerked and swayed pulling into the station at Reims. Phoebe felt lightheaded getting off; from the platform Pietro took her hand and gently guided her down. She heard church bells, big, silvery peals like heavy objects plunging into water.

"I have some hours before my train," Pietro said when they reached the street. "If you are not occupied, I can show to you the cathedral."

"Oh yes!" Phoebe cried, grateful for this reprieve.

He led her to an older, residential part of the city, stone buildings four or five stories high, shallow grille balconies. Dozens of squeaking birds hopped among the fussy trees.

At the far end of a square the cathedral loomed suddenly before them. Phoebe had never seen anything like it, a massive honeycomb of nooks and crannies and statues, points of gray stone rising like stalagmites toward the sky. She and Pietro crossed the square, sluggish pigeons flapping halfheartedly out of their way. The cathedral's massive rounded doors were bordered by carved figurines laid one above the other, up, up and around the top, where the hapless saints looked like passengers stuck on a Ferris wheel.

"We see the West Façade," Pietro said. "There, you can find" —he pointed above the left doorway—"Smiling Angel. She is famous, maybe you have seen from pictures."

With her sly, beatific smile, the Smiling Angel might have been the Mona Lisa's sister. Two pigeons roosted on her head.

They entered the cathedral through a small rectangular door carved in the right portal. A vast space loomed around them, filled with a cavelike smell of wet stone. Phoebe followed Pietro down the nave, feeling cool rock through the soles of her shoes. Pairs of fluted columns rose to the ceiling and curved back down like the ribs of a giant beast. Phoebe sensed them flexing in and out with its breath. The dusky air was streaked with seams of color from the stained-glass windows, purple, crimson, gold, colored puddles on the stone floor. The vast silence was like a sigh, the hum you heard inside seashells.

They traversed the aisles, Pietro pointing out paintings and statues in a manner at once reverent and familiar, as if these saints were his family members. "Here is Saint Sebastian," he whispered. "He was soldier for the army of Diocletian, shot with arrows because he was a Christian. When he recovered, so they beat him to death." His accent, combined with the simple phrases he used, made Pietro's speech sound biblical to Phoebe, the barest, truest way a thing could be said.

They paused at a series of tapestries, scenes from the life of the Virgin Mary. "Visitation," Pietro said of one Phoebe didn't recognize: two women conversing in a doorway. "After Mary learns she will birth the Son of God, she makes a visit to her cousin Elizabeth."

Phoebe found it sweet, Mary rushing to tell her cousin the big news. She gazed at the rich, salmon-colored fabric and tried to listen, but the cathedral's hum seemed louder now, flowing up from beneath the floor as if a giant machine were whirring under the stone.

"In the cathedral," Pietro was saying, "is a three-dimension Bible. All windows, all statues, they tell one part in the story . . ." But Phoebe couldn't listen, the hum was too distracting, a churn of bright, familiar sound like a schoolyard during recess. A wave of pleasure rolled through her, a warmth low in her stomach, a delicious calm in her limbs.

"I apologize," Pietro said. "I speak too much."

"No," Phoebe said, shutting her eyes.

"We can be silent."

She smiled. It felt like her first real smile in days, weeks. She opened her eyes and looked at Pietro.

"You feel something," he said wonderingly.

They stood in silence. The smile just stayed on Phoebe's face, the corners of her mouth rising inadvertently. In Pietro's eyes she saw a fierce, burning strength. "I feel it," she whispered. "All around me."

"He is here, *sì*. With us," Pietro said.

Gently, his arm barely touching her back, Pietro guided Phoebe to a pew. They sat side by side on the ancient, creaking wood. Phoebe smelled its polish. An organ played experimentally; hymns she dimly recognized would collapse mid-passage, change key and resume, each random echoey note floating to the ceiling and lingering there before melting into the larger sound. Phoebe felt the silky pulse of blood through her veins. Pietro knelt to pray, forehead pressed to his folded hands. The position looked so extreme, as if someone had thrust down his head, forced him into supplication. He didn't fight it. He simply bowed, as Faith had bowed day after day in church while their father was sick.

Phoebe found she was breathing in time with the gentle flex of cathedral ribs. Gradually the border between her own body and the cathedral's body began to dissolve, and Phoebe herself was dissolving, melting into its oceanic sigh, and what bliss—to be absorbed, to give herself up! The fulfillment of her journey. The fulfillment of all her life, Phoebe thought, as snippets of childhood prayers began drifting to mind. She whispered them aloud—"Hail Mary, full of grace. Our Father, who art in Heaven. Body of Christ. Lamb of God, who taketh away the sins of the world, have mercy on us"—each prayer like a glimmer from a splendid, holy pageant that had vanished when her sister died: the games of her childhood, the gaudy echo of electric guitars, Faith arranging her rosary in the shape of a heart on the same glass table where barely a year later she would tease through her fingers a soft green heap of marijuana, pressing it to dust, brushing it over the glass before rolling it into slender white joints. Faith deep in prayer while Phoebe dreamed beside her; returning home afterward to the sweet, intoxicating smell of their father's illness.

A priest crossed the altar, long white robes making him seem to float. Pietro finished his prayers and resumed his place on the pew beside Phoebe. Concern made a crease in his face. It was only then that Phoebe realized she'd been crying, her face wet. "You have some pains, Phoebe," Pietro said.

"I did," she said in a dreamy, distant voice. "But it's over now."

"Is good you go to your sister," Pietro said.

Phoebe nodded her agreement. She was floating like the priest, suspended in warm liquid.

"When you can go?" he persisted. "Maybe today. Perhaps we walk together to the station. You have there your bag?"

Phoebe turned, looking him full in the face. "I lied to you," she said. "My sister is dead."

She caught a faint reflexive action somewhere in Pietro's eyes, an infinitesimal quickening. "You are alone?"

"Yes," she said, smiling, for something had opened, the world was flooding inside her.

"We go outside, Phoebe," Pietro said, standing, taking her by the hand. "Soon I take the train, I have already my ticket, but we must speak."

He led her from the cathedral. Outside, Phoebe encountered a blissful metamorphosis, everything sweet to her eyes. Even the skinny boys battering a soccer ball around the square looked gentle as mice. God's children, Phoebe thought, we are all the children of God.

Pietro chose a bench and they sat. Phoebe breathed slowly, deeply, relishing the push of her lungs against her ribs, the satiny passage of air through her windpipe. The distant rant of construction sounded like music. How could this world have so frightened her?

Pietro tried to speak, then halted in frustration. "I wish I have some better English," he said despairingly. "I try to help you, Phoebe."

She looked at him in surprise. "You helped me."

He shook his head. "Is no good you are alone."

"It doesn't matter," Phoebe said. "Everything is fine."

Pietro looked at his hands. "Too fast," he said, and snapped his fingers. The nip of sound startled Phoebe. "Too fast."

He seemed afraid. Phoebe turned to him, filled with sorrow. "I wish you could be happy," she said. "You made everything good."

"I did nothing," Pietro said.

But it was time for him to go. They hurried, breathless, through the twilight. "I wish I can stay here, Phoebe," he said. "But they have bought my ticket and someone will meet my train." Phoebe caught dinner smells drifting from open windows. Each time they crossed a street, Pietro took her arm, looking anxiously in both directions.

His train was already boarding. Hurriedly Pietro retrieved his suitcase and dashed with Phoebe to the platform. At the entrance he took both her hands in his own and held them tightly, looking into her eyes. "I will pray for you, Phoebe," he said. Again he struggled for words. "It needs time," was all he managed to say. *"Non* be afraid."

"I'm not afraid," Phoebe said.

He smiled, vexed. That wasn't what he'd meant. Abruptly he began rummaging in his suitcase, old and frayed, the sort of suitcase a traveling salesman might have.

Pietro copied from one page of a large notebook onto another, using the same green pencil he'd used to write Faith's name. He tore out the second page. "Here is the telephone. Three-four-one, is Madrid, eh? I don't know happens with the phone there, but always you can leave some message, please you will call if you have troubles? Pietro Santangelo. Is me, eh? You will remember? Here I write it." The pencil shook in his hand. The train's whistle blew.

"Go—go! I'll remember," Phoebe said.

Pietro turned and walked quickly down the platform to the train. Phoebe had thought he might hug her, she realized, craved the feeling of being that close to someone for a second. Almost immediately the train began pulling away. Phoebe watched its windows, thinking maybe one would open, that Pietro would wave. But he must not have had time.

She turned and walked slowly back through the station to the street, retracing the steps she'd taken the night before to the high-rise complex where the youth hostel was. Everything seemed transformed, vast and spectacular now.

Phoebe went to the spot where she'd seen the girls jumping rope and lay face-up on a concrete bench. She stared at the sky. It was pale on the side where the sun had set, darker as her eye moved across it. She thought of those children, the song they'd sung as they jumped, and suddenly, effortlessly, the words came back to her:

> *Miss Mary Mack, Mack, Mack,*
> *All dressed in black, black, black,*
> *With silver buttons, buttons, buttons,*
> *All down her back, back, back.*
> *She jumped so high, high, high.*
> *She touched the sky, sky, sky.*

And she never came back, back, back,
Till the fourth of July, lie, lie.
Miss Mary Mack . . .

Phoebe gazed at the sky, singing softly to herself. She thought of how young she still was, all the things that hadn't happened yet. She felt her connection to the stars and the planets, the old men smoking cigars on a bench next to hers, the people in yachts and slums and forests; above all, to Pietro Santangelo, who had saved her. Hope, Phoebe thought. There is always hope. A part of her was with him even now, Pietro Santangelo, riding past the stubbled, glittering fields that were God's work, watching the sky fade to black.

twelve

Paris, Wow!!
Love, Faith

Phoebe sat on a front pew inside Notre-Dame, the white envelope in her hand. The acid itself was on a tiny white square of construction paper, smaller than her smallest fingernail. A red Mickey Mouse in suspender shorts was printed on it, one fat finger pressed to his lips as if to stifle a smirk. Phoebe found him menacing, but maybe Mickey Mouse had always looked like that.

She'd come to Paris after it became clear that nothing she did would revive the spell cast by Pietro Santangelo and the Reims Cathedral. She'd known the feeling was gone the moment she woke the next day in that cinderblock room, had hurried immediately through heavy rain to the Reims Cathedral, only to find it chilly and dark. She'd tried kneeling, standing, praying, slowly descending the nave with her eyes closed, then turning around at the altar and popping them open to gaze with all her strength at the rose window. But the hum was silent. Her wet hair dripped on the stone floor.

Phoebe had taken the train to Paris and arrived late the previous afternoon. She paid for a small blue room off the Place Saint-Michel, with a sagging bed and a window overlooking the street. She bought a falafel sandwich, wrote her mother another postcard and went right to sleep.

Another failure. Even Pietro Santangelo had seen this one coming—even he had recognized whatever it was in Phoebe that kept her from making the final, crucial leap. All morning she'd sensed her sister's mounting impatience, imagined the antsy look Faith got when things went on after her mind had already strayed from them. And it seemed to Phoebe now that her time had nearly run out.

Gingerly she clasped the tiny square of acid and set it on her tongue. It had no real taste, just a faint sweetness at the back of her throat. She chewed until it turned gummy, then swallowed.

Two minutes, five minutes. Anxiety clutched at Phoebe's stomach. The cathedral's blue stained glass and echoey clamber of tourists reminded her of the vast indoor swimming pool where she'd taken lessons as a child: its warm, chemical smell, the dozens of strange children and slender, bushy legs of their instructor, who wore buried in his chest hair a gold whistle, which he blew to make them jump. Gazing in fright at the glossy, viscous-looking water, dreading that whistle—certain, once she'd plunged into the water's sticky depths, that she would not resurface.

After fifteen minutes Phoebe left Notre-Dame for the open air. The acid might not work, she thought. After all, she'd been given it months ago. Did acid even last that long? And the thing was so small.

Following her map, Phoebe took Rue de la Cité across the Seine, then walked toward the Louvre along Rue de Rivoli. Life-sized female statues were draped languorously alongside windows and above them, their arms dangling, loose garments falling open.

Dear Mom, Phoebe and Barry, My French is the worst but luckily we have a friend who translates. Everyone in Paris keeps talking about the demonstrations of two years ago when they tore up cobblestones from the roads and threw them at the cops and they built barricades like the French Revolution. The whole country *went on strike for a couple of weeks literally no one worked or studied they just wandered through the streets talking to each other. Nobody locked their doors people slept in strangers' houses and fell in love and pulled the hands off the clocks outside because time was stopped. (Remember Mom?) Everyone says how it was the most incredible time of their life and how depressing it was when the whole thing finally ended and they were just students again, supposed to take exams and get jobs and all that. Some people say they almost wish it never happened so they wouldn't know how things could be and they'd still be happy. Love, Faith*

Daffodils in white paper.

Waiters shaking white cloths over restaurant tables.

Deep in Phoebe's stomach, something was slowly uncoiling. When she rubbed her eyes, an electric mist hung in the air. My God, she thought, it's actually going to work, and felt a thrill of fear.

From Rue de Rivoli she turned onto the massive Avenue de l'Opéra, but before reaching the Opera House itself, Phoebe veered right onto a smaller street, Rue des Augustins, then left, and soon was lost among a web of tiny streets that lifted gradually uphill into some kind of wholesale shopping district. One store contained nothing but racks of turquoise T-shirts with roaring lions on the front. White sailor hats crowded another. The cheap, garish clothing mesmerized Phoebe, as if her eyes had craved precisely these gold-tasseled combs and fake clotted pearls, necklaces of candy-plastic gems. "Blue T-shirts," Phoebe said aloud, stag-

gered by the power of word and object combined. "White sandals," the phrase whispering across her lips, "white sandals . . ."
whiter and more delicate than any pair of sandals she had seen.

Phoebe began to feel someone else's gaze upon her, taking in
her movements, approving. I've done the right thing, she thought
excitedly and then stopped, distracted by the fluid, translucent
skin of her arms, her opalescent fingernails.

By slow degrees, the landscape was flattening into two dimensions like children's-book lands or religious paintings. Copper
horses leapt from rooftops. Phoebe looked at the azure sky and
laughed, knowing her sister was near, sensing Faith's passion and
humor and wondering why she hadn't swallowed the white paper
instantly upon arriving in Europe, saved herself so much sorrow.

*Dear Mom and Phoebe and Barry, Yesterday at a
chateaux outside Paris Wolf and I jumped over those velvet
ropes that block off where you aren't supposed to go. And
we walked through the rooms nobody ever sees they were so
beautiful and quiet with silk furniture and little glass things
you could pick up. We pretended like we really lived there
and lay down on a canopy bed with carved posts but maybe
some kind of silent alarm bell went off because a guard
came running in and totally freaked and we got thrown out
but still it was worth it (Wolf doesn't think so). But sometimes I think those velvet ropes are all over the world you
just can't see them. In Paris I keep thinking where is the
best most intense part of Paris, where is the absolute center
of Paris and I can't exactly tell, I'm stuck outside the velvet
ropes and I just hate them, it makes me so furious when all
I ever see is the same normal stuff everybody sees. I wish I
could climb over like in the chateaux but the problem is, in
Paris unlike a museum the ropes are invisible, you can't tell
which way is in which way is out. So you just keep trying.
Love, Faith.*

———

The world shuffled, arranged and rearranged itself around Phoebe like a bird puffing out its feathers. The speckled pavement poured downhill, gallons of loose sand. She jumped to avoid it touching her shoes, but the air felt so thick, thick as water, slowing her movements.

At the heart of each sensation lay the kernel of something familiar, a germ of ordinary perception or thought distorted beyond recognition. Sounds became indistinct; traffic, voices, airplanes, everything ran together into one larger sound like a crowd, hundreds and thousands of people assembling nearby. Something is going to happen, Phoebe thought, some tremendous thing is on the verge of taking place and she stopped where she was, stilled by a dragging, irresistible force like the sea's undertow, stood quivering, waiting for the crowd to rumble into sight and sweep her along, but the crowd never quite appeared, it simmered just beyond sight, on the perpetual verge of materializing the way movie theater lights seem always about to dim when you know they're going to. Phoebe looked at her watch but found it inscrutable, tiny bars under glass, deeply beautiful, a work of art no less, except where were the hands? Someone's pulled them off, she thought, time has stopped.

In a window Phoebe caught her reflection and moved nearer the glass, exchanging with herself a look of such mutual knowledge it embarrassed her. What we've been through, she thought. As a child she'd played a game of staring in her bedroom mirror and tempting herself not to recognize the girl who looked back, a delicious fear seeping through her stomach as her own image became another girl's, a stranger whose presence made her shy. Phoebe stared at the slur of her own dark hair, wide-set crooked eyes gazing back through the murky glass, another girl, another person's hand reaching gingerly, gingerly out from behind the glass to touch Phoebe's own, and it was Faith.

It was Faith.

From across the window Faith stood looking out at Phoebe,

their two hands meeting on the glass. Behind its chill Phoebe felt her sister's heat. "My God," she whispered.

Faith was smiling broadly, mirthfully, and Phoebe, too, felt a plume of laughter rising in her chest, for here was Faith, after all this time, at last—I knew it, she cried, but silently, not moving her lips. I knew it, I always knew you'd come back.

I've been here all this time, Faith seemed to say. Couldn't you feel it?

Sometimes, Phoebe said. But other times you disappeared.

I've been in one place, Faith said. You've come all this way.

Phoebe studied her sister, aware of some change in how she felt, being near her, but unsure what it was. Then she realized.

We're the same age, she said, incredulous.

Faith laughed, that big hungry laugh Phoebe had missed and longed for and tried in vain to imitate. We're two halves of an apple, Faith said. You did it, Pheeb. It's almost over.

Phoebe gazed at her sister's narrow eyes and long mouth, a face in constant motion, or else it was just her own eyes moving over it, trying to gather it all in at once. A face so unlike her own.

Two halves of an apple.

How do I get across? Phoebe said.

Faith smiled. You push.

That's it? Just push? And as she spoke, Phoebe pressed her hand harder against the glass in hopes of parting it, stepping through into Faith's warm arms, but the window held fast.

When I say push, I mean really push, Faith said. So Phoebe pushed with both hands, palms tingling against the glass.

Come on, baby, Faith said gently, you've got to give it more than that.

I'm trying!

Faith shook her head. Crossing hurts, Phoebe, she said. It hurts. Otherwise it would be too easy. You've got to be willing to suffer a little.

I'm dying to, Phoebe said.

She set one shoulder to the window and pushed with all her

might, feeling the pressure in her spine. Her sister braced herself from the other side to weaken the glass, and Phoebe pushed and pushed, but still nothing happened. Dammit, she said.

That's not pain, Faith said, not like I mean it, and Phoebe realized with despair that even now she was holding back, even now with only a single pane of glass between herself and her sister, she couldn't get the job done. But I can, Phoebe thought, I will! And she stood back from the glass and threw herself against it with a massive blow, but no, still no, her shoulder and arm felt bruised, but still she was outside.

Harder, Faith urged, much harder Phoebe come on, we'll go together at the count of three, and Phoebe moved back almost to the curb; Faith did the same from her side. This is it, Phoebe thought, she would break through this time or perish in the attempt. At a run she threw herself head-first into the glass and Faith did the same; Phoebe's spine felt severed as she slid to the pavement, her vision stunned to white, yet unbelievably there was the glass, still unbroken, that same thick glass of airport windows —My God, Phoebe thought, how can I get across without killing myself? Head throbbing, blood in her mouth from her bitten tongue and meanwhile someone was shouting—was it Faith?—no, not Faith, another person screaming at the top of her lungs from Faith's side of the window; sensing trouble, Phoebe staggered to her feet and dove at the glass in a last, wild effort to escape the woman running outside in shrieking hysterics, her hair nubbled in tight red curls. The woman grasped Phoebe's arm in a parrot claw, hollering, motioning at the window in an apoplectic frenzy of distress. Faith had vanished, the woman had scared her away and a small crowd was forming around Phoebe, but she didn't care, couldn't care less. She stumbled free of the screaming woman and wandered away.

Her head and neck throbbed; her gums, even her teeth seemed to ring from the impact. Nothing she saw made any sense: a blond, bare-chested woman slouched in the passenger seat of a blue convertible—How? Phoebe thought. Why?—her white breasts hanging down to her stomach—I'm imagining this. She blinked to clear her vision, but it wouldn't stop: everywhere Phoebe looked were bleached blondes in various states of undress, enough to fill several chorus lines. She wandered through the glare of their perfume—prostitutes? In broad daylight, on a busy street? And Phoebe realized then that she must have broken through the glass after all, and this was the other side—this was it!—and hadn't she always sensed the prostitutes would be here, too? Red corsets and garish makeup, flaunting the gash of their cleavages— Yes! Phoebe thought, she'd reached the other side and Faith must be here, too, waiting, hidden among these prostitutes—was one of them Faith? But no, her hair was dark.

Phoebe turned down a long, narrow side street. It was suddenly very quiet. There were no cars, just men on foot and women leaning in doorways, one in a short yellow dress with bruises on her legs; another, a pixie-faced girl with flecks of red polish on her fingernails. Phoebe gazed at them in plain awe while the hidden surging crowd edged nearer, closing her in, cheering her on, air rushing in and out through her windpipe, and now she heard some other sounds, clicking, hissing sounds she didn't recognize.

A man muttered something as he passed, taking in Phoebe with flinching eyes, the hissing, clicking sounds gathering force as her path crossed that of another man, with a walrus mustache and damp-looking skin; Phoebe felt his eyes on her hips and breasts and looked down at them, startled by the presence of her own body here on this street, as if she'd discovered she had a beard or mustache. Hold on, she wanted to say, wait, no—her eyes locking with those of a woman naked under her blue fishnet dress, small breasts, dark pubic hair, the woman making a nasty face and spitting on the street in the expert manner of people who often spit, and Phoebe realized this spitting could only be meant for herself and felt a surge of wonderment that she, like these women, was bones and flesh, breasts and hips—Phoebe felt them moving inside her clothes, prickling slightly the way limbs do when they've fallen asleep and the sensation was thrilling; for a moment it was thrilling, and then the moment passed and she was terrified.

Phoebe glanced behind her, but the way back looked just as long. Hundreds of women seemed to lie in wait for her now, their hostile noises gathering force as she walked, drowning out the cheering crowd. Phoebe noticed garbage, dusty window shades, smells of stale milk and pee. A skinny girl in a torn green dress seemed about to faint, her eyes rolling back in her head as a man pushed her through a door; Phoebe heard coughing, gagging sounds—here it was at close range, exactly what she'd wanted, but entering this world was not the same as eyeing it with longing. Now she had to get out, something terrible was about to happen — No, Phoebe thought. No! Breaking into a run, breasts flapping against her chest, a cramping sensation low in her abdomen as if she were going to bleed and meanwhile the drug was growing stronger by the second like some maniac twisting a dial in her brain. She could hardly run, like dreams where your limbs won't move, but Phoebe hauled them along, her clumsy bag of tools, past the jeering women, past men who bore an eerie resemblance to fathers of her childhood friends, finally bursting from the side street onto a wide boulevard where cars and buses drove merrily past and heat shook the air into streamers.

Something in Phoebe had turned, she'd lost control, was engulfed now in pure unmitigated terror. It was the fear of before, in Reims, the fear of all her life. Every thought struck her with unbearable force, pushing her to the edge of sickness. This is too extreme, she thought. But you wanted extremes. But not this—I didn't want this, or maybe I did but I've changed my mind. Well, too late. Each time she relaxed, the world promptly collapsed into shaking particles; a herculean effort was required just to assemble it sufficiently to walk through, foot after foot. When she reached the curb, Phoebe had no idea what to do, which signal she was waiting for, everything a gnash of colors and lights and roaring sound. She stood a long time until she sensed a pause around her

like held breath and then she was crossing a river, picking her way
among bleached stones with the sound of birds and running water, a waterfall—I'm in the country! Phoebe thought—then she
stumbled against something hard, a metal garbage can, and she
had crossed the street. It was a busy street. She had no idea where
she was going.

She was lost in a sea of molecules, atoms, shifting colored
patterns. Every instant had the dazzling power of retrospect, those
dreams that shiver across your skin the next morning like the
stroke of a feather. This will kill me, Phoebe thought, I can't stand
it. I don't want it. Much of this she was saying aloud, "I can't
stand it. It will kill me. I want to go back," until a man shook her
by the arm and spoke sharply in French and Phoebe jerked open
her eyes which she hadn't realized were shut, and a woman in a
yellow floral dress advised her to hail a taxi and return to her
hotel. But a split second later that same woman was speaking
rapid French to a newspaper vendor and Phoebe realized she
hadn't said a word: it was one of those half-dreams where you
think you've gone to the bathroom but find when you wake that
you're still desperate to go. Phoebe raised her hand for a taxi—a
historic moment—she was standing outside a castle signaling
trumpets to hail the approach of a monarch in a jewel-encrusted
crown, gleaming white horses, shadowy forests hovering just beyond sight, then a taxi stopped and Phoebe got in and the driver
took off, and she opened her eyes to find herself standing in the
midst of a crowded sidewalk, one hand thrust in the air as people
pushed past her.

I need help, she thought, I need help! Seized by unendurable
panic, she burst through the doors to a restaurant filled with
lunchtime eaters, but the room was indecipherable to her eyes like
photographs where some trick of the lens crystallizes the world
into squares. "Help, I need help!" Phoebe bellowed, and the
room fell painfully still. She noticed smoke in the air, a smell of
clams, and thought, My God, I'm really here, I'm not making this
up.

A heavyset man approached, a slim brown cigarette in one hand, mustache resting like a centipede on his upper lip. "I need help," Phoebe whispered.

"Please, mademoiselle, you are ill?" he asked, guiding her gently by the arm to one side of the restaurant, but no, no, Phoebe thought, what can he possibly do? Just holding still for this long was such agony; a terrible force had gathered behind her like tons of water ready to explode through a narrow pipe— No, she couldn't stand it; she pulled away from the fat man and bolted from the restaurant back to the street, heart beating wildly, pushing up from her chest so she wanted to spit it out on the pavement and stop its freakish pounding. Behind her the pressure was mounting, pushing against her like a crowd trying to fit through a narrow door and Phoebe walked, walked faster but still it was behind her, inside her, coursing through her veins, a sick panic like nothing she'd felt in her life. Frantically she reasoned with herself: There's nothing to be afraid of, everything will be fine, but it wasn't true and she didn't have any more time for this; she was running now, a half-pace ahead of her terror, her mind scrambling for the right combination of thoughts to unlock her from this nightmare—numbers, she thought, weren't combinations numerical?—1, 2, 3, 86, 87, or maybe some pattern of words: blade, blithe, butternut, bittersweet, she was going to die, something terrible was going to happen and why is that so bad? Phoebe thought, Faith died young and I've done nothing but admire her for it, but I don't want to die—I don't want to! Her thoughts pounding away like machine-gun fire: I don't want to die I don't want to die I want everything back the way it was before I hate this please God if I can just come down please God if I can just have back what I had before. But that's exactly what you didn't want, said a different voice, you've spent your life longing to throw it away. And Phoebe knew this was so.

She leaned against a building and tried to swallow down her heart. Whisk, wide, water, wattle, the wings of angels, the whiteness of feathers. She closed her eyes but no, it wasn't helping, she would certainly die—it was a horror, the mistake of a lifetime, because even if by some miracle she did survive, she would be brain-damaged for life. She tried to think of Faith, but what filled her mind instead were those poor prostitutes, legs like bruised fruit, garbage and foul smells at the heart of what had always seemed so thrilling, so mysterious—nothing but violence and sorrow and rot.

Phoebe sank to her knees on the pavement. She shut her eyes and tried to pray, teeth chattering although it was hot, hot pavement under her knees, but God must have gone away, she'd lost Him in the swirl of moth-colored stockings and cones of bleached hair. Or maybe there was no God on this side of the glass, maybe that was why Faith buried the rosaries and Bible after their father died, but Phoebe tried praying anyway, hands clasped above her head, eyes shut, lips moving frantically. Occasionally someone leaned down and tried to help her; a man in a charcoal suit even spoke to her briefly in English, but Phoebe couldn't answer, just stared at his face, watching it expand and contract while the man moved on to other languages. "Español, Deutsch, Italiano?" he asked with rising alarm, and it crossed Phoebe's mind that maybe he was God, maybe on this side of the glass God looked like anyone else, a man in a suit, and she found herself clutching his leg, feeling the warm bone inside flesh inside cloth, and thought, Am I holding the leg of God? Then the man wrenched away, disappeared into the crowd but some time later Phoebe saw him again, crossing the street with a man in uniform, a round boxlike hat on his head and he looked like a cop—Phoebe forced herself to stand and walk because every drop of blood in her veins was illegal, polluted and full of poison and thank God, there was a taxi stand, *Dear Mom, Phoebe and* . . . "Place Saint-Michel," Phoebe told the driver with a clarity that startled her, and they drove awhile, classical music on the radio, the milky feathers of doves, the long, silky wings of insects, *Dear Mom and Phoebe and Barry, Here we are in,* 4, 5, 6, Our Father who 7, 8, *Yesterday we went to,*

9, 19, Forgive me, Father, it has been four months since my . . .
Wolf was a drag as usual, next we go to . . .

The driver was talking. They had stopped; the numbers on the
meter made no sense to Phoebe but she handed him bills until he
stopped her with some impatience, pushing the money back, and
Phoebe got out, dropping coins in the taxi, on the pavement. Statues sparkled around her like salt licks. So many people. Phoebe
turned around slowly, staring in each direction until she saw the
river, and yes, she knew what to do, yes she had a plan, the key to
ending this nightmare; a wind seemed to blow her body toward
the river and she climbed on the bridge, traffic roaring past, her
ears filled with sounds of the forest, the jungle, running water; she
knew what to do, the postcards were leading her astray, they were
bad clues leading her to destruction; now a thudding determination rose in Phoebe, 12, 13, 14, 15, *I just hate those crazy,* Faith's
cards in her hand, her sister's photograph, too; Phoebe leaned
over the railing, *Dear Mom and Phoebe and* light, lapiz, lamenta-
tion, lullaby, water swirling below, so many boats but the water
wasn't blue the corruption was everywhere, Faith's cards in her
hand—they're killing me and I don't want to die—the water
sickly, sticky-looking like the swimming pool water she'd dreaded
as a child, hairy chest, a gold whistle meant jump—Phoebe let the
postcards go, they swirled, scattered, grew small so quickly like
confetti, that day once a year when everyone throws white paper
from the windows of downtown, she'd thrown the picture too,
Faith whirling down to the water; I've done it again, Phoebe
thought, sent her to the water a second time—God forgive me
please it was her or me, one of us had to go, Forgive me, Father,
nothing was ever how you thought, a life lesson ha ha, 19, 18, 17,
postcards resting on the water, floating there, she was free of them
now, Thank God, Phoebe thought, she knew where to walk, she
was walking, pretending to walk; if she concentrated hard enough
she could organize the world an instant at a time before it burst its
seams yet again, forgive me, Father, there was her hotel, a miracle

from heaven. "Forgive me, Father, for I have sinned," she murmured aloud while ascending the endless flights of stairs to her room, her blue room, her own backpack crumpled on the floor. Forgive me, Father.

Collapsed on her sunken bed, eyes shut, Phoebe found no darkness or quiet; it was like being inside a radio where the station keeps switching, *Dear Phoebe, You wouldn't believe what . . .* Strands of light, guitar music in bright, quivering strands, cars moving outside her window in yawns of blue, her hands on her breasts, their softness oddly comforting, 91, 92, 93, it would go on forever; summer camp, bottles of beer on the wall the rocking yellow bus, Faith in the front seat the driver's pet, her long hair hot with sunlight, melted like oil, the children's voices, Miss Mary Mack, Mack, Mack, 102, 103, I love you, Phoebe thought, I love you, I'll do anything for you but I don't want to die, I'm sorry I threw them away, please God forgive me but it was all wrong, 29, 30, nothing was working. Phoebe stood, crossing the tiny room to the mirror above the sink. Her reflection a sea of shifting colors, purple, green, pink, eyes entirely black at the cores. A freakish face, a ritual mask carved in her image but her own face, not Faith's, and Phoebe shook her head, closed her eyes and popped them wide again, then shook the mirror, turned away and looked back suddenly to catch the reflection by surprise . . . cloth, cath, mise, wise, 68, 67, 66, but there was her own obstinate face, her own no matter what she did, I've killed her, Phoebe thought, her own empty face, the pounding heart she could practically taste, goddamn this . . . *Dear Mom and Phoebe and . . .* Seized by a spasm of anger, Phoebe slammed her fist into the mirror, shattering her own startled look into several bright pieces that clattered into the sink.

There was pain in her hand. Holding it to her face, Phoebe spied a tiny sliver of mirror wedged in the soft place between her first and second fingers. Warm red blood flowed toward her elbow. Phoebe watched the blood, fascinated by its warm abundance, this wealth of extravagant color hidden away beneath her own plain flesh. Something calmed in her now, cool in her chest, her head, warm blood pushing away the fever, drawing it out of her. No, she thought, I will not die this time; bleeding, cutting the soles of the feet made you well in the old days, it will end like everything else, I believe it will end. Thank God, thank you dear God, *Dear Phoebe* . . . Hail Mary, three wishes, I wish for my life back again, please God the cracks in the ceiling, the tiny insects, please God the moments of silence, of nothingness cool in her chest, the heart gradually calming. Slowly Phoebe slid the shard of mirror from her skin, relishing the exquisite flash of pain that reached to her heart and held it a moment, held it like a fist, then fled her body in one last warm push.

part three

thirteen

Trees were in feverish white flower outside the lavish, dilapidated building where Kyle's cousin, Steven Lake, and his wife, Ingrid, lived. Phoebe lingered on the street, hesitant to ring the bell so early. She'd taken the overnight train to Munich from Paris, giving the Lakes, who had never heard of her, no warning of her arrival. She'd been afraid they might say there wasn't room for her.

Phoebe sat on the front steps to wait. Days had passed since the acid trip. The pounding of her head had been unbearable at first, gray-blue bruises on her forehead and temples and scalp. For two days she'd lain quite still on the sagging bed, listening to scattershot sounds from the street. She'd been afraid to move; the membrane between herself and the acid trip seemed very thin, like the soft patch on an infant's skull. Sudden, drastic movement might puncture it, causing her to fall back through. Carefully Phoebe would creep down the many flights of stairs to pay for her room and buy food. On the third day she'd begun reading her book of Charles Dickens stories: blacksmiths, scullery maids, Christmas roasts, somehow they were what she needed.

She'd thought at first that she might go home. But with time this seemed less and less possible, like turning around on that narrow street lined with hissing women, finding the way back just as long.

When the ache in her head subsided, Phoebe had turned to the task of repairing her room. She moved carefully, as if each bone in her body had been broken and reset. She wrapped the pieces of shattered mirror in a T-shirt and smuggled them out to the street, where she emptied them into a wastebin. Her bloody hand had stained the bedspread, but after several bouts of scrubbing and hanging it in the sun to dry, the stain (the whole spread, in fact) had faded.

Faith's postcards were gone. She'd thrown them into the Seine. Phoebe remembered doing it, the driving, frantic sense that this move held the key to her survival, but she no longer knew why. Now there was nothing to guide her—if you chose a place at random, how could it matter whether you went there? The address of Kyle's cousin, Steven Lake, was still wrapped around the pink joint at the bottom of her wallet. All this time she'd carried it.

Phoebe leaned against her backpack and drifted into shallow sleep. At exactly nine o'clock she woke, climbed the steps and pressed buzzer three. An intercom clicked on, a man's voice spoke in German.

"I'm looking for Ste-ven Lake," Phoebe said, pronouncing the name slowly.

"Steve's in Brussels this summer," said the same voice, but American now.

"Brussels," she said.

"Yeah, I'm renting while they're gone. You want their address? Hello?"

Phoebe felt as if she were sliding down a hill.

"Hello?"

"I was supposed to—give him—" She was stammering.

The intercom clicked off. Phoebe turned back to the empty street. The flowering trees had a sweet, powdery smell. She was in Munich, Germany. When a buzzer sounded, Phoebe whirled back around, throwing her weight against the door.

"Third floor," he called. The hall was shadowy. Phoebe began toiling up the stairs under her backpack. She heard descending footsteps, and through the hair that had fallen across her face, glimpsed a tall man wearing wire-rimmed glasses. She questioned the point of hauling the backpack upstairs when Steven Lake didn't even live here.

"Here, let me take that," the man said, lifting it from her shoulders. Phoebe noticed a slight double-take at her appearance. The bruises were still visible, ashy smudges above her eyes and on her temples. She lowered her head. The man sprang ahead toward the first landing. Phoebe sensed the hurry in his step, an eagerness to get on with his day.

"You a friend of Steve's?" he said over his shoulder.

"No. But I know his cousin, Kyle Marion."

He paused mid-step. "Not San Francisco Kyle Marion."

"Yes!" Phoebe said. "You know him?"

There was a pause. "I went to high school with him," the man said. He waited at the next landing. Phoebe's curiosity had the better of her now, and in spite of her bruises she looked full at him. The recognition broke across her in a single white flash, raising goosebumps on her legs and scalp.

"Wolf," she said.

The color had left his face.

They both stared, speechless. It was Wolf. He looked as if he might faint. "I'm Phoebe," she said.

"I know who you are," Wolf said, and he pulled Phoebe to him, rocking her in arms whose feel was instantly familiar to her. "I know who you are, Phoebe, Jesus." He drew away to look at her, smiling that sheepish smile of older relatives who haven't seen you in years. He gripped the tops of Phoebe's arms, her heavy backpack still dangling from his shoulder. "Phoebe O'Connor," he said. "I'll be damned."

He looked smaller than she remembered. In Phoebe's mind Wolf had grown vast with the years, ballooning in size and strength at twice the rate she herself had, since childhood. Now his chipped features looked almost frail. But his face was the same: white teeth, narrow green-gray eyes like the animal he'd been nicknamed for, the brown hair that once had fallen halfway down his back cut short now, so it stood up a little from his head. He'd lost his indelible tan. But for all that he was Wolf, familiar in every detail down to the hands on Phoebe's arms, hands she'd watched rolling joints, steering his pickup truck with invisible ticks of movement, sifting through her sister's hair.

"What are you doing here?" Wolf said.

"Traveling." It was all the explanation she could muster. "How do you know Steven Lake?"

Wolf shook his head. "Americans in Munich," he said. "I've known him for years."

"But you never knew he and Kyle were cousins?"

"No idea. I mean . . . isn't Steve from New York?"

They were climbing the last flight of stairs. Through an open door Phoebe stepped into a large, spare living room overlooking a backyard. In contrast to the sumptuous decay of the building, the apartment itself was sleekly renovated, crisp walls, knotty blond floor.

"Have a seat, walk around, make yourself at home," Wolf said, setting Phoebe's backpack inside the door. "Some coffee?"

Phoebe followed Wolf into a kitchen. His shape was the same, she decided, broad torso, long legs, but the smallness, the slightness of him disconcerted her. He was no bigger than any other tall man.

Wolf set the kettle to boil and turned to Phoebe, smiling. "You grew up," he said.

Phoebe crossed her arms.

"You were, like, a child the last time I saw you."

"Ten," she said. "I was ten."

"Now you're what, sixteen, seventeen?"

"Eighteen."

"Eighteen," Wolf said. "God, I forget how long it's been."

The kettle sang. He lifted it from the stove with a potholder, pouring an arc of scalding water into the filter.

"Your hair's so short," Phoebe said shyly. "And you have glasses now."

"I always had glasses, I just never wore them," Wolf said, laughing. "My blurred youth."

"You look different," Phoebe said. She couldn't get over it. "You look, I don't know, respectable."

Wolf gave a wry half-smile. "It's a different world."

They brought their mugs to the living room and sat on a striped blue couch. Sunlight poured through the windows. In the bright light Wolf suddenly leaned toward Phoebe, peering at her forehead. "What's happened to you?" he said softly.

"I fell."

Gently Wolf pressed a palm to Phoebe's head. The cool of his hand felt good. "Looks like someone beat you up," he said. "How did you do this?"

"Oh, it's not worth telling," Phoebe said. "Stairs."

Wolf let it go, but she sensed his reluctance, his concern, and they felt like balm. The bright light hurt her eyes; she closed them awhile and leaned back. It seemed an unfathomable luxury, being in somebody's home.

"How's your mom?" Wolf said.

"She's good, I guess. She has a boyfriend. Actually, her boss, Jack Lamont? It's him."

"Get out of here!"

"Swear to God," Phoebe said, pleased that Wolf could appreciate the bizarreness of her mother's choice.

"Well, hey, that's fantastic," Wolf said. "If she's happy, that's fantastic. And the Bear? What's old Barry been up to?"

"He's a millionaire," Phoebe said, and gave Wolf the short version of her brother's success.

"Well, there's some justice for you," he said, grinning. "I always liked your brother."

Phoebe was keenly aware that neither one of them had spoken Faith's name. She wondered whether in Wolf's eyes she looked as much like her sister as everyone said. She hoped so.

Wolf relaxed, spreading his long arms across the back of the couch. "Phoebe O'Connor," he said. "I have in my head the most vivid picture of you—outside your house, waving to us as we drove to the airport."

She laughed, embarrassed. "You remember that?"

"You were barefoot," Wolf said, a catch in his voice.

Phoebe recalled the absolute stillness that had fallen on the street the moment his truck disappeared, as if everything loud and bright in the world were gone, too, packed away among their seashells and bandanas. She'd knelt on the pavement, touching the warm spot where the truck had been, keeping her hand there until the pavement cooled and even after, for many minutes more, until the fog made her teeth chatter.

"Anyway," Wolf said, "I want to know everything that's happened to you since."

Phoebe laughed. "That's a lot," she said, though of course it was really so little.

The telephone rang in another room. Wolf went to answer it, and through the open door Phoebe admired his virtuosic German. The language made her picture someone clipping bushes with a pair of oversized shears.

"You sound totally German," she commended him when he returned to the living room.

Wolf laughed. "I practically am, at this point," he said. "I'm a legal resident, so I'm allowed to work here and everything. And my fiancée's German, Carla—that was just her on the phone. So I'll become a citizen after we're married."

"You're getting married?"

"I am," Wolf said, hesitant. "We were engaged in March."

"Wow." Phoebe felt as if she'd been struck. Her bruised head began to throb.

"It must be tough, hearing that," Wolf said. "I'm sorry."

Phoebe nodded and looked at the windows. A hummingbird hovered outside the glass like a giant mosquito.

So Wolf's life had moved on. The strange thing was not so much that this had happened, Phoebe thought, but that suddenly she knew it. In her mind he'd remained shirtless, sun-soaked, restlessly prowling her thoughts. Now she felt the shame of facing an acquaintance she'd dreamed about, hoping he wouldn't read it in her face.

"How did you end up in Germany?" she asked.

Wolf resumed his seat beside her on the couch. He'd never really gone back to the U.S., he explained, had stayed here illegally for years, working in restaurants, factories. He'd studied German at Berkeley for his biochemistry major, so he spoke the language.

"You dropped out of Berkeley, right?" Phoebe asked. "To go to Europe with Faith?"

There. Her sister's name filled the room. Phoebe wanted to say it again, yell it out.

"Yeah," Wolf said. "I loathed America then. I was dying to escape."

But the name had done its work. A respectful silence descended over them.

"Anyway, I'm a translator now," Wolf concluded. "Mostly technical stuff, brochures, annual reports for companies doing business in the States. Lot of drug companies, so the biochem wasn't a total waste. Actually comes in pretty handy."

"So everything's worked out great," Phoebe said ruefully.

Wolf knocked twice on the coffee table, as if hearing this made him nervous. Or maybe he just felt guilty, parading his happiness.

"Oh, I forgot," Phoebe said, fumbling in her purse for her wallet. "I was supposed to give this to Steven Lake. From Kyle."

She pried the pink joint from the crease in her wallet. It was bent and smudged from the long trip. Wolf took it, smiling at its condition. "We'll save it for Steve," he said.

The bathroom was full of spotless white tile. In the medicine cabinet Phoebe found a bottle of Estée Lauder perfume and several light-brown hairpins laid neatly in a pile. A pair of jade earrings shaped like tears, a bottle of coconut-smelling lotion; Phoebe stared at these items, trying to conjure up the woman who had bought them and worn them, placed them so carefully here. Their neat economy could not have been less like the bright jumble of Faith's possessions, yet when she tried to picture Carla, all Phoebe saw was her sister's face.

In the hot shower her hand began to throb. The cut from the mirror had become infected at first, but was healing now. Phoebe moved cautiously, as if the shower tiles were made of eggshell. I'm in Wolf's apartment, she told herself, awaiting a jolt of elation at this spectacular good luck, but her feelings were dulled. Too much had happened; finding Wolf seemed the fulfillment of a hope she'd abandoned when her journey veered inexplicably from adventure into survival. Why had she come to Europe? Phoebe no longer felt sure; all she knew was that she'd barely survived a nightmare. The prospect of portraying a happy girl on vacation for Wolf exhausted her in advance, made her want to stay in the bathroom forever.

"What's your fiancée like?" Phoebe asked as she and Wolf traversed the wide, regal streets of Munich. The churches looked like big armoires, the sky was flawless blue. Outdoor clocks were striking noon.

"She's a doctor," Wolf said.

"A doctor. Wow." It made the fiancée seem old. "So you must be incredibly healthy," she joked.

Wolf laughed, tipping back his head as if the laughter were a substance, like smoke, which might offend Phoebe. "Slowly but surely," he said with affection. "I'm not an easy patient."

He pointed out sights: the old and new painting museums, the technical university where he would teach a course in translation this fall. Phoebe gave them only passing attention. Mostly she looked at Wolf, filled with wonderment at the thought that he was the same boy whose shoulders she'd ridden down Haight Street, kicking his ribs to make him go faster. Perhaps Wolf, too, was remembering that time, for he asked suddenly how much San Francisco had changed.

"A ton," Phoebe said. "You wouldn't believe it."

"How? I mean, what are the changes?"

"You never go back?"

"Oh, I do," he said. "Occasionally. But my parents live in Tiburon now. I never go to the old places."

"There's no point," Phoebe said.

"What about our high school? What I hear, it sounds almost like the fifties again, cheerleading, football . . ."

"Disco music," Phoebe said. "Everyone goes dancing in discos."

"It sounds healthy," Wolf said, half laughing. "It sounds . . . innocent."

Phoebe turned to him, amazed. "I can't believe you're saying this."

"Age," Wolf said, and smiled.

They had entered the Hofgarten, a large formal park filled with red and white flowers in soft rectangular beds, thigh-high bushes clipped to look like walls. At the far end a square-columned building rose from inside a ring of trees. It was capped with a dark metal dome like a bronze helmet.

"But something must still be there," Wolf said. "From before, just—even if it's nothing." And Phoebe was struck by the change in his voice, a wistfulness. She told him about Hippie Hill, the empty Panhandle, Haight Street full of junkies; and strangely, as

Phoebe described these disappointments, her bitterness over what she'd missed was eclipsed by a sudden, painful yearning for all she'd left behind—for home.

They had slowed to a stop. Sunlight poured over the bronze dome, turning it gold. It looked like a mystical, curative sphere. Wolf took a step or two back and held up a hand, his eyes fixed on Phoebe. "Wait," he said softly. "Stay there."

She glanced at the dome behind her, a shimmering hump of black-gold. When she looked back at Wolf, he'd dropped to one knee. Phoebe nearly laughed, but the noise caught in her throat. Wolf looked as vulnerable, as empty-eyed as someone asleep. "What is it?" she asked softly.

He rose to his feet, slowly brushing dust from his jeans.

"Wolf, what?"

"Nothing," he said absently. He seemed disoriented, as if he himself were unsure what had just happened. "Let's get out of here."

They left the park in silence. Phoebe didn't ask again. As Wolf had gazed up at her from the path, she'd seen a kind of parting in his face, like a door swinging open and shut on a dark room. Phoebe had no idea what this meant. But she was glad, relieved in some way to have seen it.

They ate lunch at one of the oldest restaurants in Munich, businessmen inside glowing cocoons of smoke, smells of beer, salt, oiled wood. Diamond-shaped panes of glass filled the windows. Wolf and Phoebe climbed a narrow flight of steps and were seated at a scarred plank table. Wolf ordered beers, which arrived in bell-shaped glasses tall as wine bottles.

He raised his glass. "To the pleasure of drinking with you, Phoebe," he said. "Legally, no less. Who would have thought?"

Phoebe sipped the sweet, malty beer, cloudy in her glass. The taste was whole, like a meal in itself. She hadn't drunk alcohol since the champagne in Épernay with Pietro. It felt like a previous life.

Wolf watched her drink. "By the way," he said, "my name is Sebastian."

"Sebastian." Phoebe burst out laughing. The beer seemed to flood her brain. "No way. Sebastian?"

Wolf laughed, too, reluctantly. It occurred to Phoebe that Carla was probably quite serious, being a doctor. She swallowed back her laughter.

"Right now I feel like Wolf," he said. "I won't deny it's a pleasure."

"So, should I call you Sebastian?"

They both smiled. The name hung there, ludicrous.

"Call me Wolf," he said, "what the hell." After a moment he said, "I'll be thirty next year, can you believe it?" He seemed sobered by the thought, as if there were untold things he needed to accomplish before that day.

"Thirty isn't so old. Sebastian," Phoebe teased.

"Danke schön," Wolf said.

He ordered sausages, sauerkraut, stuffed cabbage. The food arrived on dented pewter plates, and Phoebe ate until she felt faint. She drank a second beer. Wolf drank two more. Drunk, Phoebe felt her hold on the present beginning to slip; it was less clear to her now what sort of person she was trying to be. The confusion made her quiet.

The restaurant emptied suddenly, as if an inaudible whistle had summoned the businessmen back to their offices. Pale light fell through the windows, cutting the smoky air into diamond-shaped bands. Wolf lit a cigarette.

"I've thought about you a lot, Phoebe," he said, "all this time."

Phoebe was touched, amazed that Wolf had thought of her at all. "Really?"

"I mean it," he said. "Just, hoping you were okay."

There was a pause. "I guess I am," Phoebe said nervously.

"I know this sounds crazy but I have to say it," Wolf said. "I hope you haven't suffered too much."

Phoebe felt herself go red. "I don't know," she said. "I mean—"

Wolf shook his head. "That was for me, not you, that question," he said. "I'm sorry."

"It's fine," she said, unnerved. The truth was, the effect of Faith's death on her own life was something Phoebe rarely thought about. The very event was blurred in her mind; her mother's white face in a doorway was all she remembered, and for some reason a blue plastic horse, just a plain blue horse, square-bodied, round white eyes, a toy she'd pulled from the Wishing Well at the shoe store. Holding that horse and trying to believe that her sister was dead.

"When was the last time you saw her?" Phoebe asked. "Faith."

Again something flared in Wolf's eyes, that pain or alarm she'd seen earlier, by the bronze dome. "August," he said. "Nineteen seventy. We went to Berlin from Paris. I left in August, she died in November. As you know."

He leaned across the table, adjusting himself as if to offset some pain in his stomach. "After Berlin I came here, to Munich. I thought she might come down, but she never did. I was still here when it happened; my parents called. I talked to your mom, told her everything I knew, but it wasn't much."

"I remember that," Phoebe said. "You talking to her."

"We stayed in touch for years," Wolf said. "Four, five years. I'd check in occasionally. She was so great. Whenever I called, she'd say, 'Wolf, it's always wonderful to hear from you. And if a time comes when you don't feel like calling anymore, I'll understand that, too.' " He lifted his empty glass, then set it down. His olive skin looked gray without its tan.

"Faith didn't want me around anymore, is the bottom line," he said.

"I know."

He looked startled.

"Her postcards," Phoebe said. "I saved them."

Wolf shifted in his chair. "What did she say?"

"Just, how she was glad when you left. How you'd been holding her back and now she was free."

Something moved around Wolf's mouth. Phoebe wished she hadn't told him. He took a last pull on his cigarette and mashed it into the ashtray. "I've thought a lot about why it happened, needless to say," he said. "But I don't know. I honestly don't know why."

"Well, I want to know," Phoebe said.

"Understandable."

"That's what I'm really doing over here," she went on, unable to stem the surge of confession rising in her chest. "I'm going to every place she went, all the way to Italy, you know, to Corniglia. Where it happened."

Wolf's narrow eyes widened visibly. "Jesus," he said. But Phoebe barely noticed; for the first time in days—weeks, it seemed —some confusion had lifted and she knew again why she'd come here. To find out what happened.

"What do you think you'll learn, going down there?" Wolf said.

"I don't know," Phoebe said. She felt exhilarated.

Wolf shook his head. "Me either."

Phoebe sensed from Wolf's expression that she'd given something away, that he saw her differently now. But her impression of Wolf had shifted, too; he was a man who had nearly recovered from something. His diminished size seemed part of this evolution, as if growing older had been, for Wolf, a matter of scaling back.

"How come you never went home?" Phoebe said.

He took a long breath, drawing a cigarette from his pack but not lighting it. "I couldn't," he said. "Start up again, like nothing happened? How could I do that?" His face looked bare, stripped of something. "So I waited," he said. "Years kept passing. This ended up being my life."

He opened his hands and smiled his new, hesitant smile.

Phoebe smiled back. An understanding passed between them, as if, for the second time that day, they'd turned in a stairwell and recognized each other.

It was late afternoon when they walked back to Wolf's apartment. Carla's shift at the hospital would end soon, and he wanted to meet her. Phoebe felt nearly comatose, done in by the beer and her lingering frailty. She would go to sleep at Wolf's, they decided; he would stay at Carla's that night and come back for Phoebe the next morning. He would take her to the countryside; they'd tour some castles.

Phoebe noticed Wolf looking at her often now, as if his wonderment at her presence had sharpened with the hours. "Goddamn, this life is strange," he said when they reached the street where his building stood.

"But good," Phoebe said. "Right?"

Overhead, the white trees spilled their blossoms heedlessly, like artificial snow.

fourteen

It wasn't Wolf's old pickup truck, but it felt something like it to Phoebe: an orange Bug, top down, Janis Joplin rasping over the tape deck. Wolf drove as she remembered, sprawled languidly in his seat, one hand nudging the wheel as if it were a fan whose breeze on his face he was adjusting.

They were headed south, toward King Ludwig's castles. Wolf had come back from Carla's that morning with eggs and pears and dark bread, and fixed Phoebe breakfast. He'd made a careful sightseeing plan, a change from the old days, when Phoebe recalled him herding people indiscriminately into the back of his truck, then thundering into the hills without direction, scaring up clouds of silty dust.

Phoebe felt exceptionally clean. She'd showered for thirty minutes in that scalding white bathroom, scrubbed her feet and legs and elbows where it seemed an invisible layer of dead skin had collected. Finally she'd opened the bottle of Chanel No. 5 she had lugged all this way and dabbed some on, a rather too liberal dose it turned out (Wolf teased that his sinuses hadn't been this clear in weeks). It was eerie how far she already felt from the bad time, the many bad times. Only yesterday there had seemed an active need to conceal her troubles from Wolf, but today Phoebe felt she might forget them altogether. The nervous, solitary girl of these past weeks was someone she wondered at, even pitied. But not herself.

The outskirts of Munich fell away, leaving countryside, sheep pressed like burrs into folds of green hill, towns like sunny children's bedrooms filled with cheerful furniture of churches, barns, houses painted in bright pastels and white trim.

"Summertime time time time . . ." Janis sang, her voice like a piece of burlap slowly tearing in half.

Phoebe looked at Wolf. His eyes were narrowed against the sun. He seemed thoughtful today, brooding almost.

"Do you think about Faith very much anymore?" she asked.

There was a pause. "I resist it."

"How come?"

He glanced at her as if the question were surprising.

"It makes you sad?"

"It does, yeah. And I don't trust the sadness," Wolf said slowly.

Phoebe sensed his reluctance to speak of the past and tried to quell her desire to make him. She couldn't. "Remember the Invisible Circus?" she asked.

"Of course."

"Could you—can you tell me what it actually was? I've tried looking it up in books but it's never there."

Wolf smiled. "That's funny, that it's not there."

It had happened in a church, Glide Methodist Church in the Tenderloin. A Digger event, no publicity, no media, just the night itself with the right people there. The Diggers fixed the place up like a funhouse, all these trippy rooms and colored lights, shredded plastic on the floor, punch bowls full of Kool-Aid acid. The usual thing, in a way, except it wasn't usual yet, and besides, this

was a church, pews, altar, the whole bit. The idea was for everyone to live out their craziest fantasies at once. Meanwhile these
"reporters" were taking notes on everything that happened, then
Richard Brautigan—no joke, Brautigan himself—would type up
the notes into "news bulletins" and mimeograph hundreds of cop-
ies that got passed around instantly, so not only were people doing
all this crazy shit, but a lot of times they were reading about themselves doing it before they'd even finished.

"It sounds like a dream," Phoebe said.

"It was," Wolf said. "That's exactly how it felt." He smoked,
gazing at the road. "It was all about watching ourselves happen,"
he said. "This incredible feeling, standing outside, seeing the thing
unfold. Like tripping. I remember thinking, Shit, this is going to
be huge. Whatever it is."

Phoebe wanted to ask what sort of things people did in the
church, what Wolf and Faith had done, but felt timid. "What do
you think it meant?" she said.

Wolf laughed. "The Invisible Circus?"

"No, all of it. The Be-In . . . that whole time."

He laughed again, uneasy. "I don't know. God, who knows?"
He glanced at her. "I have no answers about that time, Phoebe,
honestly. Only questions."

"What questions?"

"The obvious ones, I guess: What happened? Why didn't it
work? Or did it work, but for some reason I can't see it?"

"What do you mean, it didn't work?"

Wolf sighed. Phoebe saw she was wearing him out.

"All I know," he said, "is at one point it seemed clear that if
we just kept pounding away like we were, some gigantic force
would, like, lift us away. And today, the ones who pounded the
hardest are pretty much all dead. So you've got to ask yourself:
How well was that working?"

"Maybe they're the ones who got lifted away."

Wolf's brows rose. "Possibly," he said. "My guess is, they'd
rather be alive."

"Why?"

He turned to look at her, tension in his face. "Because my view of death is not romantic."

There was a long silence. "Anyhow," Wolf said, "I'm the last person on earth to ask about any of this. I was a bystander, beginning to end."

"That's what everyone says."

"Well, that should tell you something."

"Maybe I haven't met the right people," Phoebe mused.

Wolf burst out laughing. "Phoebe, you're wonderful," he said, easy again. "You're so completely without irony—it's like discovering one of those tribes untouched by civilization."

Phoebe was taken aback. She thought of irony as a purely literary concept, an elusive one at that. "I'm even not sure what it is," she said.

Wolf wiped his eyes on the back of his hand. "I think irony may be one of those things you either can't see at all or can't see anything but," he said.

They began to climb, land cresting and falling beneath them. Silvery flashes of lake appeared, as if the car were upsetting pitchers of bright, mercuric liquid, spilling it on the roadside. Far off, Phoebe caught her first glimpse of mountains, magnificent beyond the foothills like a giant white stage above the burly shoulders of an audience. She remembered clattering into the dusty hills in Wolf's truck, how once, on a hot deserted road, he'd walked tightrope across an electrical wire, holding a fallen branch to balance himself. "Don't!" they'd all shrieked when he started climbing the pole toward the wire, dragging the limb behind him. Someone knew someone whose cousin got electrocuted. But Wolf continued up the pole, and when he reached the top, he grinned down at Faith—it was Faith he was showing off for—grinned down at all their worried faces and said, "Hey, come on. Nothing's gonna happen to me." And then he'd done it, cool and white-toothed, taking step after step across the wire with a lazy elegance that had seemed the very essence of Wolf.

"Do you think you used to be arrogant?" Phoebe asked.

Wolf laughed. "Probably," he said. "Did I seem it?"

"I'm not sure."

Wolf grew thoughtful. "When I think of that time," he said, "what I remember most was feeling like nothing could ever go wrong for me." He turned to Phoebe with a hard smile. "That's arrogance."

"So how does irony fit in with that?" she said.

Wolf smiled again. "Blows it to pieces."

Panting tour buses filled the parking lot. Perhaps a mile off, above a staccato of pines, rose a castle whose dimensions were eerily familiar to Phoebe, like a vision from one of her dreams. Crenellated towers, white stone, spires slender and pointed as paintbrushes—it seemed the precise castle she'd spent hours of her childhood trying to crayon. "What is that?" she asked. "I know I've seen it."

"You have," Wolf said, raising the Volkswagen's convertible top and clamping it. "Disney used it as Sleeping Beauty's castle. In the movie."

"Oh." This was not what she'd expected. Phoebe turned away dismissively, then looked back in spite of herself, drawn to the castle by a pull she remembered from encounters with famous people at Jack's cocktail parties. It was never their achievements so much as sheer recognizability that made Jane Fonda and Michael York so luminous across a room, as if, in a random and chaotic world, they alone were meant to be. "Can we actually go in it?" Phoebe asked.

"That's the idea."

They went first to a smaller castle nearer by—Hohenschwangau, where "Mad" King Ludwig II spent his childhood. Trailing their robotic guide, the group sifted past soup tureens, porcelain dishes, faded tapestries of hunt scenes. The walls of King Ludwig's bedroom were painted with tiny yellow stars, and at the foot of his bed a door opened onto a miniature flight of steps leading down to the room below, where his future queen would sleep. But Ludwig never married. There was a brief engagement, broken without explanation, followed by his removal from power and mysterious death.

Phoebe lost herself in the tale of the ill-fated king. Dreamily she followed the group up a curved flight of marble steps that resembled bars of soap, hollowed from a century of footsteps. Upstairs, narrow windows overlooked rollicking hills. Wolf remained at Phoebe's side, steadying her once when she stumbled, so that she couldn't resist stumbling again on purpose, inviting his protection. She was aware of someone watching them, a young girl with pale hair and a frail, birdcage face. Only days ago Phoebe had scrutinized couples herself, ravenous with envy at the tiny gestures they exchanged, the world they made between themselves. She moved nearer Wolf, tapping his shoulder, whispering into his ear, arranging herself for the eyes of this girl and, in moments, believing the picture herself. Her destiny seemed profoundly, irreversibly changed. The girl was alone. Phoebe felt guilty, playing on her solitude, but the small deceit was too sweet to relinquish.

Outside, they began the uphill walk to Neuschwanstein. Phoebe looked around for the blond girl, half hoping she would follow them up and watch them in this second castle, too, but the girl had vanished.

"Was he really crazy?" she asked Wolf. "King Ludwig?"

"Well, it was the middle of the Industrial Revolution and the guy was building King Arthur castles and galloping around in a medieval sleigh," Wolf said. "Not to mention inviting his horse to the dinner table."

King Ludwig had poured money into building Neuschwanstein, Wolf said, his fairy-tale castle, adding wing upon tower upon phony grotto room until his kingdom went bankrupt and the panicked subjects revolted. They put him into custody by a lake, where a few days later both Ludwig and his doctor mysteriously drowned. "In two feet of water," Wolf said. "Nobody's ever figured that one out."

Tourists wobbled past in horse-drawn buggies. A smell of pine filled the hot, clear air. "I think he wasn't," Phoebe said. "Crazy."

"You nostalgics," Wolf said.

Ludwig's Neuschwanstein was the closest thing Phoebe had seen to Oz or Wonderland, lozenges of smooth bright marble in the walls, grotto rooms choked with fake stalactites. Over Ludwig's throne hovered a fat mosaic Jesus made from what looked like broken candy. As Phoebe wandered the gleaming rooms, a swell of emotion rose in her, a sweet sorrow. She understood him, that was all. She understood this king.

At the tour's end they filed down the massive staircase. "Poor Ludwig," Phoebe said. "He was a tragedy."

"Poor Bavaria," Wolf said.

"But look what he made!"

Wolf glanced at the painted ceiling. "This?"

"Don't you like it?"

"Sure, I like it fine. But was it worth the price?"

His knowing tone annoyed her. "I think it was worth any price," Phoebe said.

Wolf stopped, turning to her. "You can't be serious," he said, and seemed to wait for her to admit she was not. "You honestly think this Disneyland was worth bankrupting a kingdom for?"

"Maybe," Phoebe said sullenly.

Wolf made a dismissive noise. "Tell that to the folks who were killing themselves to put food on the table while old Ludwig was picking out curtains!"

They stared at each other. "There were no curtains," Phoebe murmured.

Wolf left the castle ahead of her, boots *tock*ing the marble floor. Outside, he ran his hands through his hair and looked at the sky. Timidly Phoebe approached him. "Why does it matter?" she said.

"It doesn't."

Chastened, they walked in silence through steep, wooded hills behind the castle. Phoebe moved off the path for a better view of Neuschwanstein, like a ghost ship lifted on swells of green sea. She imagined King Ludwig looking down from one of its baked-Alaska windows, promising her that she was right—it had all been worthwhile. Behind her hung the ravine. Phoebe felt its openness at her back, cool air rising from far below.

Wolf passed her on the path, boots crunching the gravel. "Phoebe?" he called. Impulsively she dropped to her knees, crouching among the leafy bushes. Let him search, she thought, let him worry she'd vanished. She waited for some time among the ants and flies and little branches, but Wolf did not call again. The sound of his boots faded away.

After several more minutes Phoebe crawled sheepishly from her hiding place. "Wolf?" she said, but heard nothing except the bustle of birds. "Wolf?" Fear seized her—suppose he'd left, just gone off and left her. Phoebe pictured herself alone again, alone like the girl in the castle, alone as she'd been for weeks, until yesterday. She crashed through the brush, scraping her shins, finally bursting onto the wide main path where Wolf leaned against a tree, smoking a cigarette. "There you are!" she cried, breathless.

Wolf gave her a quizzical look. "I've been waiting for you," he said.

They headed back down to the car. The sun was at an angle now; each tree made a cool bar of shadow on the path. Phoebe felt caught, punished for the whole charade of this day, for turning her back on the awful time she'd had, pretending to be someone else. The fantasy sickened her now, glutted her like long days at the carnival or amusement park—corn dogs, candy, bright spinning rides—excesses that had always left Phoebe longing for the more spartan ways of home. Faith was the opposite. Any sense of an ending had awakened in her a driving need to prolong whatever it was; Phoebe remembered her sister getting off one punishing dizzy ride and starting to vomit, their father lifting her over a trash can and holding her midair, muscles jumping in both his arms as he braced the spasms of her slender body heaving up a day's worth of peanuts and sno-cones and cotton candy. Faith spent her last breath, then frantically sucked in air only to be sick again, more violently than the first time. It was terrible to watch. Faith was crying, tears running haplessly down both cheeks as their father gathered the long hair away from her face, holding it in his fist until at last she'd finished.

He carried her to a fountain and held her over it. They all stood quietly while Faith drank. When he set her on the ground, Faith stood weakly, rubbing her eyes while the color returned to her cheeks, then she smiled and suggested they get back on the ride. Their father laughed, relieved to see her spirits back. But Faith persisted, begged and coaxed and wheedled until it was clear that she actually meant to do it, get back on. But he wouldn't relent, not that time. Simmer down, he said, you're acting like a maniac. Riding home, Faith slumped by the window, stomach rumbling. She jammed her hands against it to stifle the sound, looking so miserable Phoebe thought she might be sick again, but it wasn't that, she just hated going home.

They reached the Volkswagen. The car's interior smelled like Wolf, a peculiar mix of tart and sweet like the backyard after a hard rain. Phoebe remembered that smell from his T-shirts, which she used to find on the floor of Faith's bedroom. If no one else was around, she would lift one to her face, inhaling Wolf's smell, a smell of comfort mixed with something else she couldn't name, yet was drawn to.

She would tell him, Phoebe decided, what had happened in Europe. It was pointless to hide it.

"Wolf," she said when they were moving.

She told everything, starting with London, moving on through each city, marooned in Karl's apartment in Amsterdam, frightening those children outside Dinant, finding God, losing Him again. She'd expected to grope for descriptions, but found instead that they tumbled from her, stunning Phoebe with a wash of unexpected relief, even power. For out of the nightmarish surge of events a story had hardened into shape and it was hers, that story. She could tell it. She'd escaped.

Wolf drove in silence, expressionless. When Phoebe reached the part about trying to throw herself through the glass in Paris, he swung off the road. "I'm sorry," he said, killing the engine. "I can't drive and listen to this."

The car was only an inch or two from a split-rail fence. Wolf leaned on the wheel, staring through the windshield while Phoebe finished. Afterward they sat in silence. Phoebe noticed a cow to her right with a smooth yellowy coat, enormous bones protruding from her backside. She felt calm, light.

"It's wrong," Wolf said. "You going through that."

His grim tone unsettled Phoebe. She searched for some answer.

"It's just wrong," he said.

"Well, God," she said. "I mean, it's not like you caused it."

They drove on, stopping soon after in a village for lunch. A shallow river pushed through the heart of the town, fat geese, soft black ducks paddling near the shore. Bright paintings adorned nearly every building: Christ on Saint Christopher's shoulders, a knight on horseback waving a long medieval banner, the Madonna holding baby Jesus.

They ordered lunch and sat outside, at a black picnic table shaded by a striped umbrella. "What I can't fathom," Wolf said as the waiter brought their sandwiches, "is why you forced yourself to come to Europe at all. I mean, Christ, why put yourself through that?"

"I didn't force myself," Phoebe said. "I wanted to."

"But why?"

"To find out what happened."

"You know what happened!"

"I don't."

Wolf looked bewildered.

"And besides," Phoebe went on, "in the postcards it sounded so intense, everything she did."

Wolf stared at her. "Phoebe, she killed herself."

Phoebe lifted her sandwich and ate, avoiding his gaze.

"She killed herself," he repeated. "I get this feeling you don't really understand that, like you think—I don't know what you think."

"You don't know what happened," Phoebe said.

Wolf pushed away his untouched food and lit a cigarette, swallowing down the smoke like nourishment. Phoebe tore into her sandwich, gulping whole mouthfuls unchewed, nearly choking herself.

"Yeah, but you're forgetting, Phoebe, I was on that trip with her," Wolf said. "When she was writing those postcards, I was *there,* okay? Me." He knocked a fist against his chest.

A wisp of anger rose in Phoebe's throat. She ate more quickly. "So tell me," she said, not looking up.

Wolf rubbed his eyes. The energy seemed to leave him.

"Was it drugs? Was it heroin or something?"

"Sure it was drugs. It was everything that came along, that was Faith. No, it wasn't drugs."

"Then what?" Phoebe pressed.

Wolf threw back his head as if consulting the air. "The problem is, you do something crazy for long enough, it starts seeming normal," he said. "To hold that edge you've got to go further and further out, and Faith had no trouble with that. But it changed her. Made her something else."

Phoebe held his gaze, listening.

"Only one thing I ever saw her scared of: stopping. Like in that quiet, I don't know, like something terrible would happen. All it took was one person egging her on—everyone wants a show, and Faith was usually willing to provide one. But she's the one who suffered. Like the guy wearing the lampshade, the life of the party till everyone goes home, then he spends half an hour puking blood in the toilet."

Phoebe looked away. Her sister in the amusement park, heaving over a trash can. Wolf had kicked the image to life. Faith thrashing in their father's arms, the violence of it.

"All that energy, that incredible hope—it just turned. In the end she was one more person looking for kicks, anything that would take her someplace she'd never gone before. And me," he laughed bitterly, "talk about arrogance, I was arrogant enough, fucking idiotic enough to think I could control this."

Phoebe stood up. She couldn't listen, was physically unable to hear her sister described in these terms. She left the table without a word, a funny ringing in her ears. "Hey, wait," Wolf said. "Phoebe, don't just—hey, come on!"

She kept walking. She heard Wolf leap to his feet, then the anxious protests of the proprietor, whose bill they hadn't paid. By the time Wolf caught up with her, she'd reached the grassy slope of the riverbank. High on the opposite side stood a church, its twin onion domes oxidized blue-green and crowned with crosses, spindly as weather vanes. "Phoebe," Wolf said from behind her, breathless.

He moved in front of her, catching Phoebe's arms and forcing her to stop. She waited, eyes toward the grass, knowing he would apologize.

"What kind of shit is this?" Wolf said.

His grip hurt her arms. Phoebe looked into the angles of his face and found the narrow eyes full of rage. She tried to squirm away but Wolf held her fast. Phoebe thought he might hit her, half hoped he would.

"If you don't want to know, don't ask," he said softly. "Hell, I'd rather you didn't ask. But don't ask and then run away and expect me to chase you."

He let her go. Phoebe stayed where she was, swallowing dryly. A piece of cheese was stuck near the top of her throat.

"You remember Faith however you want," he said, "that's your business. Leave me out of it."

Phoebe turned away in despair. The water looked like dark beer against the rocks. Two old men stood nearby, surrounded by white geese snapping at hunks of dry bread they pulled from their pockets.

"Don't get me wrong, I was in love with her," Wolf said. "Crazy about her, absolutely crazy. I don't expect I'll ever, ever feel that way about someone again. Jesus God, I hope not."

He squatted at the water's edge. Phoebe sat hunched on the grass, chin on her knees. "What about Carla?" she said.

"It's night and day," Wolf said with feeling. "You can be in love and still have a life, you know? You can build something. Faith and I were like thieves. Nothing belonged to us, it was one long spree." After a moment he said, "On the other hand, we were kids."

Phoebe lay flat on the grass, watching the clouds break apart and recombine like railway cars. Wolf came and sat beside her, and she saw that the anger had left him. "I'm not saying Faith was bad," he said. "You know I'm not, Phoebe, you know all this— you must! She was full of conflict. Before we ever spoke I knew that, just seeing her at school, the sadness in her face. Skirts every day, blouses buttoned to the neck. These weird, sad eyes. It's the clearest picture I've got of her, in a way."

"You had a class with her, right?" Phoebe said, sniffling. "Physics or something?"

"No," Wolf said. "We were three years apart—we wouldn't have had any class together. She probably made that up."

Phoebe sensed him debating whether or not to go on, weighing the use of it. "What happened really?" she said.

He'd noticed Faith, Wolf finally said, watched her with mild curiosity for weeks until once he was driving home from school in his truck and he'd spotted her hitchhiking—in her proper blouse and skirt, the most weird, incongruous sight. After that he'd look for her sometimes driving down Eucalyptus, and now and then she'd be there, thumb out. Alone, always. Once he'd driven past just as Faith was getting into someone's car and he'd had a silly urge to follow it, make sure nothing happened to her. But he had a girlfriend at the time, Susan, and she was with him.

Phoebe raised herself onto her elbows. She could hear Wolf sinking into the story, wanting to tell it. There was yielding in his voice, the pleasure of giving way where normally he would resist. "So what happened?" she said.

Once, when Susan wasn't there, he'd driven down Eucalyptus and, sure enough, there was Faith hitchhiking, so he'd pulled over and picked her up. "I think we go to high school together," he'd said, which apparently was news to Faith. This surprised him, he had to admit; he'd kept a pretty high profile. Faith was achingly shy, just looked out the window saying nothing, and Wolf had no idea what to say, either, that's how edgy she made him. Finally he asked why she hitched, didn't she know that was dangerous for a girl to do alone? Still watching the window, Faith said, "The bus is slow."

Well, look, how would she feel about a detour to the beach? Faith said okay, not seeming to care one way or the other, so Wolf drove her to Ocean Beach, wondering what the hell he thought he was doing, it wasn't even nice out for chrissakes, but he parked on the Great Highway and the two of them sat looking over the dashboard at the dunes and ice plant, fog condensing on the windshield. Gray sky, waves lumbering up, nose-diving onto the sand. Faith just stared out there saying nothing. Wolf getting more and more nervous at the silence, when suddenly she turned to him and said, "Hey, want to go swimming?"

He assumed this must be a joke. No one swam in San Francisco—who swam? It was late fall, the water gray and impermeable-looking as rock. But Wolf said, "Sure, why not?" thinking if it was a joke then hell, he'd call her bluff, and he followed her out of the truck onto sand that felt heavy and cold as freshly poured concrete. Faith took off her shoes but kept on the rest of her clothes, a blouse and skirt that whipped her legs in the wind, a

Sunday school outfit. She headed toward the water, Wolf trailing reluctantly, thinking how his clothes would make him sink, how heavy blue jeans got when they were wet, about riptides and undertows and crosscurrents and whatever the hell else people drown in. When his toes touched water, he said, "Hey, you really want to do this?"

Faith just stood there, wind tearing her hair. She said, "Are you scared?"

"Fuck no, I'm just . . . No, I'm not scared."

And seeing no way out of it, he leapt in ahead, like diving through a sheet of glass, such a terrible, crushing cold, but he beat her in at least, though Faith was right behind him. Wolf thought he would die for sure but he kept on swimming, he'd be damned if he was going to look like a coward in front of this freshman, this prissy little girl, Jesus Christ. So with the teeth knocking in his head, he kept going, straight out. Sharks, he hadn't even thought about sharks—after all, this was the fucking ocean. But some distance out a funny thing started to happen: the cold water began to feel almost hot, literally kind of tropical, warming his limbs; it felt pretty good, he had to admit, and on top of that there was this weird power, being out there in that gray heartless sea—as if you'd crossed over to a place most people didn't know existed. Faith swam near him. Wolf had the impression some of that heat he felt was coming from behind her skin, and he reached out, touching her—just did it—they kissed right there in the water, so easy, as if they knew each other when all they'd done was say five words and jump in the freezing sea. When Faith looked back at the empty beach, she was smiling. Wolf had never seen her really smile before; it shook on her face she was so cold, and he wanted to get her back onshore. Around school he was pretty used to calling the shots, being a senior, having the truck and all, but as he breathed the cold salt air and the wind beat his head, Wolf had a feeling those days were probably over and he didn't mind, really. He was actually kind of glad.

Back onshore the cold made them stammer. "You want me to

take you home like that?" Wolf asked as water ran from Faith's
skirt and blouse and long hair all over his front seat. His parents
were in Mexico on vacation. "Or you want to shower and change
at my place?"

And not hesitating, Faith said, "Your place," though she was
only fourteen and had never been with a guy in her life, but nothing scared her, nothing. Or maybe she liked being scared.

Wolf looked away, his sharp, handsome face full of pain.

Watching him, Phoebe felt a weird, elated glow. Her sister
had risen again, untouched, majestic, invincible. The feeling
seemed to lift Phoebe up and crush her, stopping her breath.

Wolf glanced down at Phoebe, who lay on the grass. Their
eyes locked and she saw that parting in his face, a stirring deep in
his eyes, and it seemed to her then that she was pulling him down,
that she could do that. The sensation was eerie, like finding each
other in a dream. Wolf looked away. He covered his eyes with a
hand, as if they hurt. "Let's get out of here," he said.

fifteen

It was fully night by the time they parked the car. Street light swarmed in the flowering trees outside Wolf's building, as if drawn by their sweetness. Rounding the top flight of stairs, Phoebe caught a flutter of harpsichord music and saw a band of light under Wolf's door. Wolf saw, too, and from the brief unreadiness in his face she guessed he hadn't expected this. "Carla's here," he said.

The bright indoor light shocked Phoebe's eyes. Carla sat cross-legged at the table, reading a newspaper. Her cigarette leaned in an ashtray. Phoebe's first thought was how tall she seemed, even sitting down. Wolf greeted her in German somewhat stiffly, but Phoebe noticed the familiar, easy way their lips met.

Carla's short pale hair looked smooth as an animal's pelt. In spite of her height she was finely boned, her delicate face frank, unguarded, its delicacy there for the taking. Her shoulders curved inward a little, as if in apology for the full, soft-looking breasts under her white cotton sweater. "I am happy to meet you," she

said carefully, in a strong accent. She took Phoebe's hand in both
her own, a decisive grip offset somewhat by the slenderness of her
fingers. Phoebe felt the engagement ring. Afterward she peeked at
it, a modest diamond, pure white, as if a drop of light were
trapped inside it.

Phoebe murmured something, overtaken by shyness. It struck
her only now, meeting Carla, how prepared she had been to dis-
like her.

Cloistered in the bathroom, Phoebe listened to Wolf and
Carla speaking German, their gentle voices muting the harsh language as if muffling its edges with felt. A second door connected
the bathroom to Wolf's bedroom, where Phoebe's backpack still
was. While changing into jeans and a T-shirt, she peered around
the room; last night when she'd slept here, she'd been too drained
and dazzled by the turn in her fortunes to notice very much. Now
she was drawn to Wolf's dresser, a scatter of loose change and
restaurant matchbooks. Phoebe hovered at the door, listening to
Wolf and Carla. Was there a difference in the way he spoke to his
fiancée? It seemed to Phoebe there was—a readiness to laugh,
something. She knew only one phrase in German, *Ich liebe dich:* I
love you. At least they weren't saying that.

On the desk lay Wolf's translation work, the unbound pages
of a typeset German text on the left, and on the right, face-down,
an enormous stack of handwritten pages. Phoebe flipped over the
top sheet and found it crammed with minute, painstaking writing
that she thought at first could not be Wolf's. "In order to be
effective," she read, "the brace, which acts as a kind of corset on
the growing spine, must be worn twenty-three hours of each day,
with the remaining hour spent in therapeutic exercise (see Appen-
dix 1)." The pen was one of those black artist's pens whose ink
comes out through a needle. Phoebe lifted a few more pages and
read, "These sores, caused by heat and chafing from the plastic in
the first weeks of use, should be treated with astringents, such as
rubbing alcohol, in order to toughen the skin. Avoid all mois-

turizers, lubricants and balms; these will only prolong the condition.''

There was a knock. The door opened and Wolf regarded her
quizzically. Phoebe realized she was crouched like a thief over his
manuscript. "I was—curious," she stammered.

Wolf grinned, moving closer. Phoebe sensed that he rather
liked the idea of her spying on him. "Find anything interesting?"

"Yes" sounded shameless; "No," potentially insulting. "I
don't know," Phoebe said truthfully. "I'd just started looking
when you came in."

Wolf laughed. "Don't let me stop you."

They stood together, the manuscript before them. Phoebe
smiled nervously.

"It's a bore," Wolf said in a different voice. "Treatments for
adolescent scoliosis." He shrugged, moving to the door. "Will you
join us?"

Phoebe stood by the living room window. Outside, the tall trees
shook dryly in the wind, their dense leaves distilling the white
lights beyond to pinpricks. Wolf sat on the couch next to Carla,
his right knee touching her left. Part of Phoebe refused to believe
in the authenticity of their affection. She'd felt this skepticism with
other couples, too, a suspicion that their closeness was contrived
merely to persuade her, that without her there to watch, they
would move apart indifferently.

Carla asked whether Phoebe had enjoyed Ludwig's castles, her
uncertain English giving the questions a stilted, textbook aspect.
"I am sorry," she said, lighting a cigarette and blowing a stream
of smoke toward the ceiling. "My English is very . . ." She
paused, as if groping for the proper pejorative, but managed only,
". . . bad."

"You never speak it," Wolf said.

Carla turned to him. "I know, but some years ago I am . . ."
She looked away as if embarrassed, laughing suddenly. In that

laugh Phoebe heard an eerie likeness to Faith—the same abandon, as if the laughter were a pair of arms she was letting herself fall into.

"I feel strange, in English," Carla told Phoebe, real surprise in her voice. She motioned at Wolf. "Like he is stranger."

Phoebe smiled, still unnerved by the laugh.

"In English I am not me," Carla said, serious again. The strain of wanting to explain showed in her face. "I have only simple words, like baby."

Wolf made some objection in German, but Carla waved him off. "In English I am . . ." Her eyelids fluttered as she groped for a word. She consulted Wolf in German.

He blustered in protest. "Colorless," he finally said.

"*Ja,*" Carla said, nodding matter-of-factly. "Yes. In English I am colorless."

Carla went to unpack the groceries she'd brought. "German food is very heavy, so we are making for you some Italians," she told Phoebe from the doorway. The room felt deeply silent in her absence. Phoebe sensed Wolf wanting to say something, but when their eyes met, he looked away. An odd shyness overcame them.

"Look, Pheeb," he finally said, "I'd rather you didn't—I'd prefer we not talk about Faith in front of Carla."

"Was I doing that?"

"No, no. Not at all. I'm just saying let's not."

The request seemed reasonable enough, yet Phoebe was stung by it. "Okay," she said.

"It's just," Wolf said, "I hate inundating her with all that."

"I won't mention her," Phoebe said, edgy.

Wolf idled at the door as if he'd meant to say something more, then left without a word.

Phoebe went to the window. Yellow light from the kitchen smeared the dark glass. She heard their laughter, the tinny sound of a radio, and it seemed to Phoebe that her sister's life was entirely effaced, a shadow beside the vivid presence of Carla. Wolf's fiancée reminded her of girls in high school who'd worn their

boyfriends' athletic jackets to smoke cigarettes outside on foggy
days, sleeves reaching halfway down their slim, manicured fingers.
They had seemed to Phoebe so dazzlingly complete, lockets tangled in their turtlenecks, a dozen rings, jade, turquoise; girls who
didn't hesitate, whose very thoughtlessness she longed to copy.

Phoebe began to explore the living room, listlessly at first,
drawn to a stack of American board games she'd loved as a child,
Candy Land, Life, Clue, but as she opened the latter box and
fingered the tiny murder weapons, Phoebe began, as she had in
Wolf's bedroom, to feel an element of subterfuge. She imagined
herself as an undercover agent posing as a dinner guest, with or-
ders to search the premises by evening's end. Like a cat burglar,
she leapt to the stereo and flipped swiftly through an exhaustive
record collection, ELO, Chicago, Journey, all bands she despised,
though seeing their albums in German was amusing. Men at
Work, the Bee Gees; having determined these records couldn't
possibly be Wolf's, Phoebe left them, darting to a set of low, deep
shelves filled with rows of books. She reached behind the books
and found the space crammed with objects. Hands scuttling like
crabs, Phoebe prised free a squeaky rubber mouse, a pincushion
shaped like a tomato, a pair of seamed black panty hose still in
their plastic. But all this clutter was the Lakes', she knew; they'd
thrown it back here to clear out the place for Wolf. At the sound
of footsteps Phoebe jumped to her feet. "Dinner is coming," Carla
said.

Wolf and Carla served tortellini in a cream-and-peppercorn sauce,
spinach and green-apple salad. They both ate quickly and efficiently, forks in their left hands. Still full from the sandwich she'd
devoured at lunch, Phoebe struggled to finish her portion. Carla
asked Phoebe about her travels: Where exactly had she gone?
How did she get from place to place? Was her luggage heavy?
Often she employed the present progressive—you are seeing, you
are going—creating the eerie impression that she was narrating a
voyage in progress. Behind Carla's politeness Phoebe sensed real

scrutiny, as if there were something specific she was trying to nail down. It made her nervous.

"You are living in San Francisco?" Carla said.

Phoebe looked up, surprised. She'd assumed this went without saying.

"Phoebe and I went to the same high school," Wolf jumped in, "about a decade apart." It sounded forced.

"Not a decade," Phoebe said.

"No?" He seemed to welcome the challenge. "I graduated '67. You?"

"This year, '78. Oh yeah," she admitted. "I guess it is a decade."

"You are how many years?" Carla asked.

"Eighteen."

Carla exclaimed, speaking in German to Wolf.

"She says you're young to be traveling alone," he translated, adding with the same tense joviality, "which is true enough."

Phoebe considered alluding to his own youthful travels but thought better of it. That would be almost like bringing up Faith. She shrugged.

"In America we grow up fast," Wolf said with mock bravado.

Carla grinned. "But you are staying children for always."

After dinner Wolf and Carla pushed their plates away and lit cigarettes. They divided up the newspaper, spread it over the glass and began combing the apartment listings. The Lakes would return at summer's end; they had to find one before that. Phoebe left them in their cloud of smoke and brought the plates to the kitchen. "You guys cooked," she said, dismissing their languid offers of help.

She piled everything in the sink and turned on the water. While it ran, she began quietly opening drawers, surprised at how fragrant some were despite their emptiness, cloves, coffee, peppermint, as if the contents had just been removed. She found a sack of prunes, a bag of straws. Phoebe hoisted herself onto the counter and stood upright to inspect the highest cupboards. Here were products still in boxes—the Lakes' wedding gifts?—a cheese board shaped like a crescent, a small hibachi grill and shish kebab set. A dense silence clung to these objects. Phoebe had loved to babysit for precisely this sensation: other people's lives spread open around her, like having the power to go inside rooms you'd glimpsed through street windows. Inevitably Phoebe would open the father's closet door to look at his ties, suspended there as if forever, so still and elegant.

Phoebe stepped along the counter as far as she could go without entering Wolf and Carla's range of vision, working her way through a set of lobster bibs, a fondue pot, some cryptic machine whose apparent purpose was the compression of bread and leftovers into tidy loaves. No wonder the Lakes hadn't used it. When the sink was at the point of overflowing, she climbed back down and washed the dishes, a delicious lightness in her chest. Afterward she left the water running in the empty sink and hid impulsively in the V of the open door, peering through its crack at Wolf and Carla leaning over their newspaper. Carla exclaimed at something she'd found, set down her cigarette and circled the item with a stubby pencil, her other hand groping for Wolf as if for a pair of glasses or a cigarette pack, finding his wrist without lifting her eyes from the paper. The gesture transfixed Phoebe—the inadvertence of it, the thoughtlessness. Wolf rose from his chair and leaned over her, his chest to Carla's back. He kissed her temple, breathing in her smell while his eyes perused whatever it was she'd found in the paper. The sheer ordinariness of it all confounded Phoebe, as if any one of these things might happen several times in a day, with no one watching. They belong to each other, she thought, and found herself awed by the notion—knowing someone was there, just there, reaching for that person without a thought.

Later the three of them moved to the living room. Wolf discovered he'd left his tapes in the car and ran downstairs to get them. "Wolf," Phoebe called after him, wanting him to check for a hairbrush she couldn't find. But she'd missed him.

Carla lay haphazardly on the couch, one leg over the armrest.

Phoebe noticed the curve of her hipbones through her jeans. "This name you are giving to Sebastian," Carla said. "Olf?"

"Oh, Wolf," Phoebe said. "It's a nickname."

"Like animal? Wolf? Yes, yes," Carla said, approving. "The eyes, yes."

Wolf returned, puffing from his sprint. He squatted by the stereo.

"Wolf," Carla called to him playfully. "Why I am never learning this name?"

Phoebe saw Wolf stiffen. Lightly he said, "It's old."

"Where is coming from, this name?"

Her question was aimed at Phoebe. Wolf, too, turned to look at her, and Phoebe knew she'd misstepped. Had Wolf asked her not to use the name? Should she simply have known? Now she was at a loss. Not mentioning someone was one thing, lying to avoid it was another. She couldn't believe Wolf wanted that. "It was Faith," she said timidly, watching his face. "Wasn't it Faith?"

"I don't know," Wolf said tiredly, turning back to the stereo. He slipped in a tape and turned it on. They sat, waiting in the crackling silence before the recording began.

"Faith," Carla said, sounding confused. "Faith." She pronounced it "Fate."

"You remember Faith," Wolf said, as if reading from a script.

"Yes. Of course I can remember Faith," Carla said, frowning. "But why is Phoebe . . . ? I don't . . ." The words seemed to elude her, yet she didn't switch to German.

"I'm her sister," Phoebe said, blood rushing to her face. "Faith's sister." It felt like a proclamation.

Carla's eyes were on Wolf now, her mouth slightly open. She spoke in soft, rapid German. He answered humbly, his throat dry. Phoebe thought he seemed afraid.

Carla ran a hand through her short hair, turned to Phoebe and said, "I did not know that you are the sister of Faith," in the clearest English she'd used all evening.

Phoebe stared at her. There was a change in Carla's expression, as if she were seeing Phoebe clearly for the first time. There was pity in her face.

"I am sorry," she said, moving closer, some delicate smell rising from her skin, and Phoebe was filled with a wave of sorrow such as she almost never felt about her sister, a longing to rest her head on Carla's soft breast and be soothed. She very nearly did it.

Carla cupped her palm around Phoebe's shoulder, her touch gentle but authoritative, a doctor's touch. They sat in silence. Iggy Pop was singing "The Passenger." Phoebe forgot Wolf was there.

The next day was Carla's day off, and she'd bought tickets weeks before to a jazz concert later that night. Phoebe willingly bowed out. They would all be sleeping at Wolf's, so while Carla changed clothes in the bedroom, Phoebe helped Wolf arrange a bed for herself on the living room couch. In ponderous silence they tucked in the sheets.

"Hey. I'm sorry," Wolf said, grazing Phoebe's eyes.

"She didn't know who I was," Phoebe said, her indignation awakened just by saying it.

"I know. I know." His manner was harassed, but Phoebe saw shame in his eyes. "I wanted it not to be a big deal," he said. "It was idiotic."

Carla emerged from the bedroom wearing makeup, her black pants tucked into red cowboy boots. To Phoebe she looked reduced in some way, her delicacy and frank expression no match against the vague, tricky pull of Faith's absence.

A new uncertainty had formed in Carla's expression, as if she herself sensed a change in her standing. "We go?" she said tentatively, asking Wolf and Phoebe both.

Wolf moved to her quickly and drew Carla against him with a kind of urgency, as if the sight of her standing alone were more than he could bear. Phoebe looked away as they moved to the door. *"Ich liebe dich,"* she heard him whisper.

After they'd gone, Phoebe went to Wolf's bedroom and threw herself on the bed. The overhead light was off, curtains were drawn; the green glass shade of an antique desk lamp made the room feel aquatic. The soft mattress dipped like a hammock. She listened as an airplane bored its way through the sky, trying to picture the people inside it, each with a destination, a life, luggage full of belongings they'd bought and packed and cared about. In Mirasol she and Faith used to lie in bed trying to guess the destinations of approaching trains; "Milwaukee . . . Decatur . . . Dallas," they'd propose in increasing volumes, "Europe . . . Timbuktu . . . Florida," and as the train passed, Faith often would leap from bed and run to the dark window, stand like an apparition in her white nightie until the engine had faded to silence and even after, when the whistle arced back from the distance like an echo. "Tomorrow they'll be so far," she said. "And we'll just be here, isn't that weird?"—always with a wistfulness that betrayed her envy of passengers traveling through the night at high speed. It was a mystery to Phoebe, her sister's envy; why, when she and Faith were so clearly the winners, curled in warm beds, with Grandma's rough starched sheets pulled tight across their chests? Given a choice, who wouldn't choose home?

Phoebe roused herself from half-sleep and returned to Wolf's desk. To its right stood a narrow set of shelves, the top ones stacked with technical-looking books in German, crisp catalogs: "New Sulfa Drugs from HAAGER" read one, its logo suggestive of test tubes. Another, by a company called Kat, was entitled "Agricultural Fertilizers: What to Expect from the Eighties." Phoebe made her way down shelf by shelf until finally, on the bottom two, were the first personal belongings of Wolf's she'd seen in the apartment. A tattered German-English dictionary, a pair of binoculars, a single Havana cigar in its silvery tube. A photograph of his parents in a small Lucite frame, smiling in fancy dress. Phoebe recognized them, though she couldn't think from where. An antique pocket watch, pale heavy gold, elaborately engraved with someone's three initials. The paucity and restraint of these objects were painful to Phoebe, as if Wolf had chosen to pare himself down to the minimum, inhabit a life as lean as his body.

On the last shelf sat a broad antique box, its top curved with age, inlaid with bits of mother-of-pearl. The box was too large to be opened without removing it from the shelf; Phoebe slid it out with a grunt and set it on the rug. It was a heavy box. She hesitated before opening it.

Two pink seashells greeted her eye, the kind Faith used to collect on the beach at Mirasol. Phoebe's heart nearly stopped. She held the shells in her palm, so light, smooth and cool as porcelain. Of course they might not be Faith's, shells were shells after all, every beach had them. Carefully she set them by her knee. Next came a diploma of some sort, pronged German calligraphy on yellowy parchment. It curled in a loose cylinder when Phoebe lifted it from the box. She began probing in earnest now, hands shaking with guilty fear, a beat of excitement in her chest. She was looking for something. A particular thing, Phoebe thought, a secret.

Awards, certificates, all in German. A miniature basset hound made from brown and white pipecleaners. Newspaper articles toasted with age, one giant front-page headline with several photographs of young people beneath it, two men, two women; Phoebe wondered if these were criminals, wished she could read what they'd done. Then a manila envelope, at the top of which Wolf had neatly printed, "Pictures."

With trembling hands Phoebe opened it, removing a pile of snapshots that seemed in no particular order. The first was of Wolf—the old Wolf, Wolf as Phoebe still imagined him when his present incarnation was not directly before her. He was deeply tanned, hair hanging past his shoulders, a string of Indian beads encircling one bicep. He flung at the camera a knowing, arrogant grin Phoebe perfectly remembered, a white curve of teeth. He was leaning against his truck, shirtless, the muscles of his brown abdomen stacked like ice in a tray. Phoebe had grown used to the change in Wolf from those days, but only now did she feel it, an ache in her chest at the loss of that confidence, that cocksure swaggering joy she saw clearly in every detail of this picture. It was more than gone, it was impossible even to imagine, as if Wolf today were a pure rejection of that boy, recoiling from him with all his being.

The first picture of her sister produced in Phoebe an eerie, marvelous sensation, a prickling chill from the base of her spine to her neck. She'd grown up surrounded by pictures of Faith, but always inside their house. Now, thousands of miles from home, here was Faith, standing with Wolf knee-deep in a field of blue cornflowers, her face blurred with motion, Wolf approaching her with what looked like a pipe in his hand, or possibly a piece of bread. On the back he'd written in his pinched hand, "Loire Valley, July 1970."

Phoebe sank into a state of trancelike absorption. Faith in Paris, choosing oranges at a market; in an old-fashioned bathtub, her dark hair tumbling from a clip, breasts floating a little, like fish. Phoebe forgot where she was, drifting with Wolf and her sister among a shifting panoply of stoned-looking strangers who gazed deadpan from kitchens and parks and train compartments, blinking through clouds of opalescent smoke. The bleached colors lent a pale, celestial aspect to these pictures, as if starry white light were flooding from some hidden source, dazzling them all into blissful oblivion.

A single picture jerked Phoebe from her reverie.

She rose from the floor and held it under the light. It looked completely unlike the others, its colors stark and crisp as if a different camera had been used, though the effect was that of a strong, merciless light. In the picture Faith's hands were knotted uncertainly at her waist, the smile wavering on her face as if it were a strain to hold. At first glimpse Phoebe thought her sister's hair had been pulled back into a ponytail or a bun, the kind she'd used to make with a white porcupine quill. But Faith's hair was not pulled back, it was short. Someone had cut it off, Phoebe thought, for the cutting seemed a thing inflicted upon her sister, blunt, uneven, as if she'd fought it, as if someone had held her down and done it by force. It made her look older, broken somehow. Or maybe it wasn't the hair, for her eyes, too, seemed off, not stoned so much as bruised, narrowed against the light. Faith stood uneasily, a hand half raised to her face, surrounded by a formal garden not unlike the Hofgarten, where Wolf had taken Phoebe the day before. There was even some kind of domed building behind her. Phoebe flipped the picture over. "Munich," it read. "Oct., 1970."

Wait a minute, she thought. How can that be?

She examined the picture again, but closer inspection confirmed that the park where Faith stood was indeed the Hofgarten, its flowerbeds empty, trees bare of leaves, but the same dome, a fat black pearl in the sunlight. Yet hadn't Wolf said clearly that Faith never came to Munich? Perhaps someone else had taken the picture, given it to Wolf later? But then he'd still know Faith had been here; why make such a point of saying she hadn't? And something else, too—the longer Phoebe stared at the picture, the closer Faith's location seemed to the place where she herself had been standing the day before, when Wolf dropped to one knee and seemed to leave himself.

It was obvious: he'd lied. Phoebe reached this conclusion, then waited in the bath of greenish light to discover her reaction. She felt a wave of fear, then tentative outrage—How could he lie? Why would he lie?—but these emotions were borne away almost instantly by a stronger feeling of promise, a swell of possibility that seemed almost to lift her from the bed. Wolf knew more than he'd told her! What yesterday had seemed a blank, impermeable wall now had sprung wide to reveal—what? Anything. Anything at all, Phoebe thought; what did it matter as long as there was more? This reprieve, this hope, it was all she needed. Like finding out that Faith was still alive.

Feeling manic, almost high, Phoebe slid back to the floor and sifted quickly through the remainder of the snapshots, more bleached-out scenes from Amsterdam and Belgium and France, but these no longer interested her. She'd found what she was looking for. Then another picture caught her eye, and again she set down the pile and lay on the bed, holding the picture in the bath of light from the desk. Faith and Wolf sitting on the brick steps of the O'Connor house, a tiny Phoebe wedged between them, barefoot in her white nightie. They each had an arm around her, leaning in so protectively they might have been her young parents. Phoebe looked at her own small face, the smile modest but certain, as if a giant happiness were pushing out from behind it. She felt a surge of longing disbelief—where had that moment gone? Gazing into the camera, smiling at whoever was behind it—the memory was as lost to her as if she'd never been there. And now it was gone: the moment, the house, her sister. Only this image remained, mocking their absence. Pictures are sad, Phoebe thought. Pictures are always sad.

Eventually Phoebe replaced the snapshots in their envelope, keeping aside the one of Faith in the Hofgarten. She returned the carved box to its shelf and went to the living room, where she paced, photograph in hand. Still holding it, she finally turned out the lights and lay rigid in her makeshift bed, eyes tightly closed, pulse hammering at her throat. It was impossible to sleep, yet she must have slept, for the sound of keys in the lock made her start awake and lie motionless, searching for her bearings. At the front door Wolf and Carla were quietly removing their jackets, a cigarette smell from their clothes seeping to where Phoebe lay. Soon their murky shapes crept toward the bedroom, Carla first, then Wolf, who shut the door behind him. Phoebe heard the bathroom sink, the flushing toilet. Then the stripe of light vanished from under the door and she thought she heard the sigh of bedsprings as Wolf and Carla lay down together on that soft mattress. Phoebe was filled with sudden dread of what else she might hear. Her mind reeled with the memory of Wolf and Carla kissing hello, lips meeting so easily, bodies that had met perhaps hundreds of times in a way Phoebe couldn't fathom. She threw off her blanket, sweating now, fixed her eyes on the door. I'll die if I hear anything, she thought, I will die. But she didn't. She heard nothing at all.

sixteen

She was back in the Hofgarten by noon the next day. Everywhere Phoebe looked were things her sister might have seen: trees sharp as etchings, pebbles like tiny jewels under her feet, the black dome swollen and tender as a fresh moon.

Wolf and Carla had gone off early that morning to look at apartments. When Phoebe returned at three-fifteen, Wolf was already back. On the table lay a map he'd drawn, directing her to the bar where he and Carla had eaten lunch. "Long walk," he said.

"I went back to the Hofgarten," Phoebe said, and peered at Wolf's face. She saw nothing.

"I brought you a sandwich," he said.

He sat with Phoebe while she ate, then went back to his room to work, bare feet snapping on the polished floor. Phoebe removed Faith's picture from her purse and paced the apartment, anxiety and excitement constricting her chest. Finally she knocked at Wolf's door. He sat at his desk. "What's up?" he said.

She handed him the picture. Wolf took its edge, studying the image of Faith as though he'd never seen it before. He turned the picture over. "Where did this come from?"

"Your box."

Wolf shook his head, smiling as if a joke had been made at his own expense. Yet he didn't seem surprised. His eyes wandered again to the picture.

"So she did come back," Phoebe said.

"She did," Wolf said. "She came back."

Tiredly he rose from his chair, took off his glasses and rubbed his eyes hard with the heels of both hands. Then he stepped to the window and looked outside. Someone was cutting trees, an electric saw chewing at the silence.

"Faith made me swear I wouldn't talk about it," he said. "To anyone, especially her family. But I guess you've got a right to know, and anyway, at this rate you'll find out with or without me."

"I'm sorry," Phoebe said, shamed by the memory of pawing through Wolf's sparse possessions.

"You do what you do."

"It was wrong, though," she said, wanting him to forgive her.

"It was."

"You did it."

There was a pause. "Why did she make you swear?" Phoebe said.

"She got into a thing in Berlin she wanted off the record."

Here was a turn Phoebe hadn't expected. "What kind of thing?" she asked fearfully.

Wolf glanced at his desk, noticed he'd left the cap off his needle pen and carefully swiveled it on. "Let's get out of this room," he said. Phoebe sensed his wish to quarantine Faith, away from his work and desk and bed. The thought saddened her.

Phoebe sat on the living room couch. To her surprise, Wolf brought two beers from the kitchen and offered her one—how could he think of drinking? Brusquely she refused it. Wolf started, surprise in his face. He set the beer on the floor. Out of guilt, Phoebe picked it up and drank some.

Wolf lowered himself to the rug and leaned against the base of the couch so he was in front of Phoebe, to the left of her shins. She couldn't see his face. He lit a cigarette, using one bare foot to drag the ashtray over.

"Well?" Phoebe finally said.

"I'm kind of at a loss," Wolf said. He sounded nervous.

"Just tell what happened."

"I'm afraid it'll sound weird, out of context."

"About Berlin," Phoebe said. "What you weren't supposed to tell me."

"Okay," he said, "okay." He dragged on the cigarette as if it were a joint. "Well, we left the States, Faith and me. You know that, obviously." He gave a nervous, smoky laugh. "We left because of this bad feeling."

"What feeling?"

"Just, things going sour. Things having already peaked. There was a mood in the air like something had turned, bad omens or something, I don't know." The cigarette shook in his fingers. "I guess Cambodia was the beginning. April. Or maybe not Cambodia . . . no, but it was, I mean, bad things happened before that, Christ knows, but invading Cambodia after everything we'd done to stop the war . . . you thought, Jesus, has anybody heard us? Then the National Guard just mows down those kids at Kent State. Kids, you know?—just blew them away. It was a level of evil you couldn't cope with."

Phoebe heard the bitterness in his voice, tinged even now by a flutter of amazement, a stung disbelief.

In the Movement, too, Wolf said, something had slipped. Hell's Angels messing people up at Altamont, the Weathermen self-destructing, literally, in a New York City townhouse. All in a couple of months. The Haight was on a slide, full of junkies and runaways, gang bangs. They'd made a wrong turn somewhere back, that was how it felt. Now they were lost.

"Faith and I had been broken up almost two years, barely spoken," Wolf said. "Then in June I spotted her across a court-yard at Berkeley during some rally, another windbag speech. I watched her getting more and more bored, and when she started to leave, I came around and intercepted her. We kissed hello. I said, 'So, what do you think of all this?' 'I think it's bullshit,' she said. 'I don't mean the rally,' I said. 'I mean everything, the whole scene.' She said, 'That's what I'm talking about.'

"It was this warm day, kind of sweet-smelling. Faith looked so beautiful, that long hair catching all the sunlight. 'Let's split,' she said, 'just take off.' I said, 'Cool with me,' so we started walking toward my apartment and suddenly I was dying to be with her again, dying for all that craziness she brought. 'You know, I didn't mean split the rally,' Faith said as we were walking. 'I mean split.' 'I know that,' I said, although I didn't, I had no idea what she meant, but at that point I didn't give a damn what it was, I just wanted it.

"We were gone in a week," Wolf said. "Faith had a shitload of money, from your dad, I guess. Five thousand bucks. I had some savings, too, plus I sold my truck for seven hundred."

"I got that money, too, that five thousand dollars," Phoebe said in a rush, then wondered why.

"We were after something," Wolf said. "We truly were. In a way that's hard to admit, it sounds foolish now but it didn't then, that's the difference. Hundreds and thousands of us, all reaching. It's a powerful thing, that many people believing in something at once."

I know, Phoebe almost said. How would I? she thought.

"I'd see my dad go off to Chubb Insurance every day," Wolf continued. "Year after year in his suit and tie . . . was he happy? I don't know. It was like happiness didn't come into it."

"Or my dad," Phoebe said.

"Exactly! Guy wants to be an artist—is an artist—works at IBM to support his family and the job drains him dry, he can hardly paint. Finally gets sick . . . it's tragic."

Phoebe stopped short of agreeing. If he was a bad painter, was it still tragic?

"He was constantly on Faith's mind, your dad. I knew it when we first were together, right after he died, but by the time we went to Europe, it seemed a lot more intense. I remember on the plane ride over she kept staring out the window. I said, 'What's on your mind,' and she said, 'Gene.' She'd started calling him that."

" 'I think he's out there,' " Faith said. " 'I think he sees us.' "

Wolf lit a cigarette, inhaling deeply from it, then held it in his hand and looked at it thoughtfully.

"In Europe she talked a lot about Gene," he said, breathing smoke with each word, "saying to people out of the blue, 'You know, my father died,' which didn't generate much interest. Then in London a bunch of us were sitting in Green Park and this girl had a copy of *Howl,* and Faith said how her dad knew Ginsberg and Michael McClure, Ferlinghetti, and man, you should've seen the faces—complete fascination. Really, your dad knew them? Knew as in *knew?* But how? Like, who was your dad?"

Wolf had listened as their questions shaped Faith's answers, in that conversation and later ones, until the understanding became that Gene had been one of the original Beats, doing whiskey shots with Neal Cassady, showing his paintings in the galleries where Ginsberg and Kerouac read. It was a strange thing to watch, this myth about Gene taking shape, what he could have been, should have been. Wolf knew perfectly well it was bullshit. But he went along. Why not? he figured. It was only a goof, and it made Faith so happy. And when he overheard people repeating the story— that chick from San Francisco, you hear about her dad?—it took on a strange kind of truth.

"We'd show off for him," Wolf said. "I found myself doing it, too. At wild times I'd look at Faith and say, 'Gene approves,' or, 'I think we got his attention.' Whether or not he was her original dad, this guy had come into existence, this Beat painter, and he was like our partner in crime."

Phoebe sat up, trying to imagine their father watching her,

too, poised to scoop her up as when she'd fallen down as a child, lifting her into the air so swiftly she'd forgotten to cry. But she couldn't feel him. If she fell, she fell.

"All through the travel we kept feeling this restlessness," Wolf said. "London, Amsterdam and Belgium, then Paris. I mean, Paris, Christ! But everyone there was still fixated on '68, the general strike. You couldn't make anything build, it was all aftermath.

"It affected us different ways, the restlessness," he remembered. "I'd kind of hang back, looking for a next move, and Faith would start spending money hand over fist trying to make something happen, you know, find the one thing that would bring everything else to a halt.

"Once, she bought fifteen feather pillows. 'White feathers,' she kept insisting at the shop, 'blanches, blanches.' I'm rolling my eyes—the saleswoman thought she was nuts. A bunch of us carried them up the Eiffel Tower, and at the top we cut them open. It was dusk, this electric blue in the air, the feathers gushed out of the sacks, then floated almost level with us, glowing like bees or something, fireflies. Jesus, what a moment. Someone must have reported back down to the guys below because the elevator door popped open and this guard in uniform came charging out. Faith just pointed over the railing at the feathers, saying 'Look!' like we'd only just noticed them ourselves, and the guard looks out, kind of taken aback, these feathers hanging there like big snowflakes on this summer night, and he stands there blinking like he's forgotten what he came for. After a minute he smiles, this tight little smile under his mustache, shy, like it's not used to coming out when he's on duty. 'Peace,' we kept telling him. 'Peace, brother,' flashing the V, waving as he got back on the elevator. Faith and I just looked at each other, we didn't even have to speak. We knew Gene was loving this."

"Feathers," Phoebe said. "That sounds incredible."

"It was," Wolf said. "It absolutely was. I'll never forget it."

They sat in silence. Feathers, Phoebe thought, searching in

vain for some moment of her own that could rival the beauty and mystery of Faith's act. She felt a disappointment so familiar it was almost a comfort.

Still, Wolf said, plenty of things had gone wrong in Paris. Faith leapt into the Seine on a dare and was sucked downstream, so a tourist barge had to rescue her. Another time she got hold of a bottle of absinthe and spent the night in a hospital with a stomach pump down her throat. "We exhausted each other," Wolf said, "Faith always lunging at things, me always trying to resist."

The final blow had come when someone fell off a roof and shattered his leg at a party Faith helped pay for, a bunch of bands playing outside, people dancing, the guy just slipped. Faith blamed herself—thought she should have seen it coming, should have insisted they put up a railing. In her mind everything flipped, their luck was gone, they had to get out of there fast. She visited the broken-legged guy in the hospital, gave him five hundred dollars in francs. He had no idea who she was.

"The whole time, we'd been hearing stuff about Germany," Wolf said. "How there were all these anarchist groups in Berlin doing crazy stuff. Whenever we met a German, they'd talk about this student leader of theirs, Rudi Dutschke, who got shot in the head by a neofascist in '68, paralyzed for life. It broke their hearts. People literally wept, talking about this guy; they were always toasting Rudi. For the student radicals it was like Kennedy getting shot—this anguish, this incredible rage. I guess by 1970 it was really starting to boil.

"Anyway, in Paris we met a German woman, Inge, who wrote for a lefty German paper called *Konkret.* She was in Paris with her French husband, and couldn't wait to get back to Berlin—Paris was dead, she said, but Berlin was just starting to peak. They were driving back there right after the roof incident, so Faith and I thought, What the hell? We got in the car with them."

Wolf paused, as if gathering his thoughts. Phoebe waited in

silence, craving some grand gesture from her sister, a triumph. She longed for this and dreaded it, too, the way you dread the loss of something.

"On the ride to Berlin," Wolf continued, "Inge told us about this friend of hers named Ulrike Meinhof, a pretty well-known journalist who'd suddenly chucked everything a couple of months before and gone underground with a terrorist group. She'd been the ultimate chic lefty—in her thirties, married for years to the editor of *Konkret* (same paper Inge worked for), had a big house in Frankfurt, twin daughters. Inge had been reading her stuff since university, so when Ulrike left her husband and moved to Berlin, she tried to befriend her. But Ulrike kept to herself, seemed kind of depressed. Her articles were getting more and more radical—she was sympathetic to these student anarchist groups that were starting to use violence."

"What kind of violence?" Phoebe asked. She was thinking of Patty Hearst.

"Guerrilla-type stuff," Wolf said. "Disrupting things, throwing a hitch in the works. They'd all gotten hold of this handbook for urban guerrillas, I think it came out of Brazil. They threw Molotov cocktails, rocks, slashed some tires. Little things. I guess the notion was if you made enough cracks, the whole fascist thing would come crashing down under its own weight."

"Students?" Phoebe said. "Like my age?"

"About, yeah," Wolf said. "Anyhow, Ulrike Meinhof decides to do a TV play and asks Inge to be on the filming staff. A story about girls who run away from a welfare home. So they start working on that, and meanwhile one of these anarchist kids, Andreas Baader, gets thrown in jail for having set a department store on fire two years earlier. He wants to write a book. Ulrike Meinhof hears about this and volunteers to help him. The kid's lawyer, this well-known lefty lawyer, Horst Mahler, strikes a deal with the government so Ulrike Meinhof can meet with Baader a few times at the Dahlem library to help him do research. The first visit comes right after the TV show is finished. It's midday, guards close off a wing of the library and bring in Baader, and all hell breaks loose—masked gunmen come bursting in, Ulrike whips a gun out of her purse, shots are fired, and she and the gunmen go tearing off with this kid Baader in tow. The whole country is in total shock, not only because of this well-known journalist turning criminal, but because Baader's lawyer, Horst Mahler, he's disappeared, too. The TV play gets canned, naturally; they're not going to air a show by an outlaw. A couple of weeks later, early June, right about the time when I ran into Faith at Berkeley, this group issues a statement calling themselves the Rote Armee Fraktion."

"What's that?"

"Literally, Red Army Faction. But 'faction' is more like 'gang' in German."

"I've heard of them, the Red Army Faction," Phoebe said, mildly electrified. "So did you—meet them or something?"

Wolf shook his head. "They were underground," he said, "you wouldn't meet them. In fact, you couldn't get near them. They'd spent most of that summer in Jordan, learning guerrilla tactics from the PLO. I remember hearing that and thinking, Shit, here we just pissed away our summer getting stoned and throwing feathers around."

Phoebe remembered the charge of excitement she'd felt in Harrods during the bomb scare. People her own age changing the world by force. What guts it took.

"So we got to Berlin," Wolf said. "And there was this incredible charge to the place, almost this simmering. We crashed with a carpenter friend of the guy we drove with, he had a big place in Kreuzberg, this tenement district near the Wall full of immigrant Turks, where the freaks had sort of collected."

"And were the anarchists all around, like you thought?"

"Totally," Wolf said. "The Hash Rebels, Black Help, this one group called the Socialist Patients' Collective, literally a bunch of mental patients—and their doctor—who'd decided society made them sick and the way to get well was to fight it. Tupamaros West Berlin, named after some Uruguayan group . . . they were a whole world, these people. Tons of underground papers, *883, Extrablatt, D.P.A.;* they'd print letters from this jailed Hash Rebel named Michael Baumann to his girlfriend, Hella, and I'd translate them for Faith . . ."

Phoebe heard the lift in Wolf's voice, as if the very memory excited him. "We got swept along by the scene," he said. "Clubs, taverns like the Zodiak, the Inexplicable Shelter for Travelers, the Fat Host and the Top Ten. We kept crazy hours, crashing at dawn, sleeping whole days. And whenever we woke up, the good feeling was still there—that was the thing—like finally we were moving, like if somehow we could just keep to this pace, we'd do more than survive, we'd catch hold of whatever it was the Weathermen, the students in Paris, the Hell's Angels—what all these cats had missed. Faith was in heaven. Parties in old blasted-out warehouses —I'd look out through a pane of broken glass and see the moon, smokestacks, ashy glittering stars and think, Christ, here I am, like I was about to be lifted away."

Phoebe listened intently, overcome by a familiar sense that she herself was slipping from the scene as if literally fading, becoming physically less solid. She felt an urge to grab hold of something, anchor herself, but there was only Wolf, and he'd vanished into the story. "What about the Red Army?" she said.

"Oh, you felt them," Wolf said. "They'd come back from Jordan that August, literally just a week or so before Faith and I got to Berlin, and everyone was just—aware of them, you know? Especially in Kreuzberg. Walking around, I kept thinking I saw them. Later it came out that their trip to Jordan was a disaster . . . Baader, I guess, was scared of guns; also there'd been some flap about the German girls sunbathing nude on the compound roof. But no one pictured it like that, I can promise you."

"Did you ever really see them?" Phoebe asked.

"No," Wolf said. "We never did, that was the thing. After a while it got to us."

———

It was August, each day shorter than the last. "You could taste fall on the air at night," Wolf remembered, "this tang under the heat. I'd catch myself thinking of school, the draft, what would happen when I didn't show up for classes—would I be an outlaw? Could I ever go home without getting thrown in jail? And this panic would open in me, like what the fuck had I done with my life? I'd wake up some days and find Faith staring up at the ceiling, brooding, have no idea what she was thinking about. Sometimes not even ask."

They'd drifted among the sights, Nefertiti's bust, the spangled halls of Charlottenburg Palace, Hitler's Olympic Stadium, where, crossing the moth-eaten grass, Faith had turned suddenly to Wolf and said, "We're doing something wrong."

Wolf didn't want to talk, he felt too many things of his own. "Something can't be happening every minute," he said.

"Something is," Faith said. "You're either with it or you're not."

"Hey. Look where we are."

Faith glanced around them at the vast field encircled by walls, long white flagpoles vanishing into the mist.

"I meant Berlin," Wolf said, uneasy.

"Everything is the same," Faith said. "Same people running the world, stomping on the same other people. Nothing is different, Wolf, after all this, nothing!" She sounded panicky. "I've still got fifteen hundred dollars."

"You'll run out."

"I know," Faith said, pensive. "I need to think of something big. It has to be big."

"Let's start a fire," Wolf said, tossing her his lighter. Faith flicked it, the tiny flame pulsing in the fizzy air. She pulled a joint from her antique cigarette case and fired it up, Wolf peering around nervously, half expecting SS guards to come goose-stepping out and arrest them. But no one came. The place was a museum.

Faith took a long hit and passed the joint to Wolf. "If IBM built a stadium, it would look like this," she croaked, holding in smoke. "They're fascists, you know. All of them."

"I'm the converted," Wolf said.

As they finished the joint, the place softened before his eyes, rippling like there was music pulsing through it. Wolf flicked away the roach. "Adolf Hitler built this place," he said, "and we just got stoned in it."

Faith took his hand. Wolf kissed her hair. "When you feel like nothing changes, think of that," he said.

They had gone to a party that night on the outskirts of Berlin, in a massive building where someone said bombs used to be stored during the war. It was a wild scene, acid bands, freaks from all over the world. Faith and Wolf met a guy there, Eric, who wore a pink leather coat and looked a little like Manson: dark, lunatic eyes, handsome with a kind of fanatical edge. Wolf had seen him before at the Gedächtniskirche, this bombed-out church on the Ku'damm where all the hippies hung out. Eric's mother was English, so Faith could talk to him without Wolf having to translate. Somehow the RAF came up, and Eric mentioned the fact that he'd gone to university with Baader's girlfriend, Gudrun Ensslin, another Red Army member.

"Do people ever join the group?" Faith asked. "Or is it just the original members?"

"They're accepting CVs as we speak," Eric said.

Faith looked doubtful. "What's a CV?"

"He's goofing," Wolf said. "It's a résumé."

Faith's eyes narrowed. She hated being mocked. "I shot a rabbit one time," she said, deadpan.

Eric stared at her, and Faith burst out laughing. Wolf laughed, too.

Eric smiled sardonically. "And when did you perform this . . . action?" he said.

"I was ten," Faith said, still grinning.

"A prodigy. But haven't you any more recent experience?" He poised phantom pen to paper, a mock interviewer.

"Coke bottles," Faith said.

Eric looked blank.

"Targets," she explained. "Clay pigeons, too."

"The gun?" Somehow the discussion had turned serious.

"A .38. Revolver."

Eric's brows rose. But he said only, "Americans. Always the revolver."

Wolf tried to lure Faith away from Eric, but there was no budging her. So he ate a tab of acid and hung around, kind of drifting in and out of the conversation. It wasn't long before Faith brought up Gene, how IBM had ground her father down, drained his spirit away until he was empty, until his very blood revolted. She said things Wolf had never heard before: how it felt to watch her father die, how there was nothing she could do, she'd tried everything she could think of, but he died anyway. All her life she'd been trying to fight back, she said, all her life, but she was getting so tired—you couldn't do it alone, what you did alone was always too small. Wolf listened, half disbelieving as she opened her soul to this stranger, handed it over like someone else's wallet she'd found. Sure enough, Eric was staring at Faith as if mesmerized, Wolf flashing on how she must look to him: a passionate American kid, light-years from home, who'd risk anything, everything, who'd give it all away. And suddenly he was terrified.

He lifted Faith's hair, whispered into her ear, "Let's split."

"Not me," Faith said.

Frustrated, wasted, Wolf wandered off to flirt with an Italian girl in yellow hip-huggers, yellow fabric under his fingers, watching the pants move between his hands as he danced with her. Faith's glare trailed him around the room, but she was too proud to come near him—that was his mistake. Although he hardly had the heart for it, Wolf followed Yellow up a flight of creaking metal stairs to this giant roof you could've launched a plane from. They lay down under stars that in Wolf's present state were indistinguishable from the shards of glass around the mattress they lay on. All he could think of was Faith, how he wanted to teach her a lesson but was too stoned and wiped out to recall what exactly it was she needed to learn.

When finally Wolf rejoined the party, Faith and Eric had gone. He wasn't surprised; hell, he'd brought it on himself. But his druggy panic had eased. She'd be back, he thought. They'd been through worse and come out of it.

Wolf turned, meeting Phoebe's eyes for the first time in a while. She jumped at the contact. "You okay?" he said.

Phoebe nodded. She felt empty, as if her mind had no more proper contents than a road awaiting traffic. The feeling brought its own strange peace.

"Phoebe?"

"I'm fine," she said, but her voice was disembodied, as if she'd ceased to be anyone at all. Wolf watched her with a remoteness befitting her own faint presence, Phoebe thought. Her understanding no longer mattered, the story had reclaimed him. They sat in darkness.

Faith didn't come back that night, or what was left of it. No surprise. The next day, either. Wolf hung out, killing time at the Gedächtniskirche, the Park Tavern, trolling the Zoo station looking for her. He drifted into a thing with a Russian art student, a redhead, that was all he remembered about her. Paintings full of DNA patterns.

By the time he saw Faith again, two weeks later, Wolf was half living in the art student's studio. He'd drop by the carpenter's pad a couple of times each day, checking to see if Faith had been around. Her backpack was still hidden in a closet, under a Mexican blanket. One day she met him at the door.

"Welcome back," Wolf said. "What happened to Prince Charming?" Faith looked blank. "You know, what's-his-name," Wolf said, "with the flippy eyes. Eric."

"Oh. I don't know," she said.

"So where the fuck have you been?"

"Don't ask like that! Where have you been?"

She wore different clothes, straight clothes, a blouse with little red diamonds on it. Her hair was trimmed and neat, flat, as if someone had sat her down with a wet comb and worked all the tangles out. Wolf was struck by how unmarked she was; he felt the miracle of this, how the years of wildness had left no visible print. It was all just practice; in the end she would still be a teenager. Wolf felt a thousand years old beside her. "Fuck it," he said. "I'm glad you're back."

"I'm kind of back."

They were alone in the apartment. As Faith came toward him, Wolf noticed she was walking oddly. He couldn't explain it—as if her center of gravity had shifted. He took her hands. "You look like you're here to me," he said.

They lay on the carpenter's bed. Wolf wanted her so much; it never went away, that part. He wanted other girls, too, but never with this urgency, and the truth was, he'd gladly have given them up if he thought he could do it without conceding something. Faith's thin warm arms looped around him, pulling him back to a deep, still place within himself. He'd never loved anyone this much.

Reaching under Faith's blouse, he felt something hard against her skin, wedged in the back of her pants, pulled it out and found himself holding a little automatic pistol. "Holy shit," he said. The gun was warm from her skin. A .22, it looked like.

Faith seemed ready to burst, watching him hold the gun. Wolf grinned, shaking his head. He looked at the gun, then at Faith, and they made love with it right there in the bed, cold and smooth on their bare legs.

Later, Faith rummaged for the gun and held it up, turning it in the light so it made a dark shape on her face. "I'm a good shot," she said. "My dad taught me."

Wolf leaned on one elbow, watching her. "You won't let me smash a bug," he remarked. "It's kind of hard to see you shooting people."

Faith laughed. "It's for self-defense."

"People get shot in self-defense."

"I'd never shoot it," she said, serious now. "I'd only ever use it to scare them."

Wolf flopped back down, his arms crossed. "I don't know, Faith."

She moved close to his ear. He felt her breath, the warmth of her limbs, and pulled her against him. "Wolf, I *found* them," she whispered.

After dark Faith got up, pulled on her jeans and the diamond-patterned blouse so gingerly, as if the clothing were on loan. She slid the gun back down her pants, the front this time. Wolf sat up, resting his feet on the cold floor, trying to clear his head. "Wait," he said. "You're just—like, taking off?"

Faith crouched at his feet, her hands on Wolf's bare knees, and looked up at him. "Listen to me," she said.

"I'm listening."

"You have to find a way in, Wolf. You have to. This is it."

"We've said that a few times."

"No," Faith said, vehement. "The other times were nothing, I promise. Wolf, it's a *scene.*"

"So take me there."

"I can't," she said, moving away. "They're huge, I'm one little piece. I can't even talk to them, except for the lawyer—the other ones don't speak English."

Wolf shook his head. "What the hell do you do for these people?"

Errands, Faith told him. Little things. You couldn't just go to the store when you were underground, someone might recognize you. So Faith went for them. "They need all kinds of stuff," she explained, pulling her backpack from the closet. Then she lowered her voice. "They're it, Wolf. And they're planning something huge."

He left the bed and went to her, still naked. "Baby," Wolf said, taking hold of Faith's elbows. "Don't do this."

She frowned. Wolf tried to clear his head because Faith seemed so clear; her posture, eyes, everything about her said she knew what she was doing, that it made sense. And no wonder, Wolf thought—where else had they been headed all this time? She was right, she must be right, if he just could clear his head . . . the gun in her pants—but when he pictured Faith holed away in some apartment running errands for people she couldn't even talk to, Wolf found the vision so drab, desperate. As bad as everything they'd been trying to escape. "Hold on," he told her. "Just—let's slow this down a second."

But Faith ignored him, counting out her traveler's checks. "Wait," Wolf said as she shouldered the backpack. "Faith, wait." He moved in front of the door, not fully aware he was blocking it until the move registered in her face. When Faith tried to move past him, he held his ground.

"Look, if it's not your thing, fine," Faith said. "I need to split." And she gazed at him so coldly, with such cold disappointment, Wolf felt like the enemy. It enraged him.

"I'm surprised you don't pull your gun," he said.

Faith just looked at him.

"Do it," Wolf said. "You want out? Pull the gun."

"Wolf, quit it." She made a halfhearted effort to push his arm, his chest, but Wolf's limbs were stone, they felt immobile even to himself. Faith seemed to droop under the heavy backpack.

"Pull the gun, come on," Wolf said. "You know what you're doing. So do it."

Faith's face tightened in anger. She put her hand on the gun. "Fuck you, Wolf," she said. She pulled it out and held it, barrel down. "Why?" she pleaded. "Please, let me go! I hate this."

"You hate it!" Wolf said, and laughed. "You'll make a hell of a terrorist, Faith."

An angry vein pulsed at her temple. She lifted the gun, watching her hands as if they were someone else's.

"Safety off," he said.

Faith released the safety. Eyes fixed to the gun, she pointed it at Wolf's chest.

"Touching," he said very gently, his eyes, too, on the gun until the cold round nub of it met his skin, Faith's cold anger behind it. Her face was twisted in pained concentration, as if keeping the gun aloft required every ounce of her strength. Wolf searched her eyes but they looked strange, opaque, and he found himself thinking, amazed, She could actually do it.

"Is he watching you now?" he whispered.

Faith's head jerked up. In Wolf's eyes she must have caught her own reflection, for an awful recognition parted her face and she dropped the gun, which hit the floor and fired, jumping backward several feet, spinning. In the sparkling silence they stared at it. Faith began to cry. Wolf lifted the backpack from her shoulders and they clung to each other, shivering, the gun halfway across the room and deeply still, as if mortified by its outburst.

"Don't go," Wolf said.

Faith shook her head, crying—she didn't want to go. Timidly she crossed the room, leaned down to the gun and put the safety back on. She stood up quickly but stayed there, gun at her feet. Wolf trembled in the night air, wishing he had clothes on. There were splinters on the floor near a moulding where the bullet had entered. After a while Faith squatted over the gun, and Wolf felt the battle in her, two things pulling opposite ways. Which ran deeper? That was the question. By then, somehow, he knew what it would be.

There was a long silence in Wolf's living room. "Why didn't you call my mom?" Phoebe said.

Wolf shook his head. "You didn't do that—go running to

somebody's parents," he said. "Plus, what could she do, your poor mom? Just get terrified." He paused, lighting a cigarette. "I don't know, though. Maybe I should've." He turned to Phoebe. "You think I should've called her?"

But Phoebe was empty, a vacuum. "I have no idea."

"Anyway, I left Berlin the next day," Wolf resumed after a long pause. "I had a friend in Munich, Timothy, who'd lived with my family freshman year of high school. I nailed Tim's address to the wall of the carpenter's pad, went to Munich and waited.

"On the last day of September, I saw this giant headline: the RAF pulled off three bank robberies the morning before. Twelve people involved, three cars, they got something like 230,000 marks. I looked at that and I thought, Oh Christ."

To Phoebe's confusion, laughter rose in her chest.

"I know," Wolf said, glancing at her, smiling uneasily.

Loose, tooth-chattering laughter overwhelmed Phoebe. "Why am I laughing?" she said.

"What else can you do?" Wolf said. "Bank robberies. Shit."

"How many?"

"Three. Four, originally—one didn't work out. Damn," he said, finally yielding to his own mirthless laughter. "The thing is, it really wasn't funny."

The laughter drained from Phoebe suddenly, leaving her tired.

Wolf was working illegally by then, loading boxes at a shoe factory on the outskirts of Munich. He'd sublet a room in someone's apartment, leaving word with his friend's family on the off-chance that Faith would track him that far. Days passed, then weeks, Wolf scouring the paper on the streetcar to work, following news of a police raid on the Red Army, a few big arrests, but no mention of a young American female. It was early October by then, soon to be 1971; Janis OD'd on the fourth, Hendrix had died mid-September, in London. A lot of people were starting to head back home, but Wolf felt paralyzed. "My head was messed up," he explained. "Reading about the Red Army every day, knowing

Faith was part of that, I'd just panic sometimes, thinking I should be there, too, like I'd made the mistake of my life. She was in the world, you know? Out there doing something real, and here I was, following the story in the fucking newspaper."

Phoebe shifted uncomfortably.

"I couldn't disconnect myself from the thing," Wolf said. "So I stayed, I waited. Then, out of the blue, she found me."

It was late October, already getting cold, and Faith had none of the right clothes. Something was the matter with her. She was just—broken somehow. Wolf wrapped her up in sweaters, turned on the oven and burners full-blast so the windows steamed white. Faith shivered convulsively; it took all day before he could get her to talk, but finally she did.

"She was involved in the robberies," he said. "Her job was to cut a hole through the fence behind a building next to one of the banks, so the gunmen could crawl through after they made the hit. Some of them thought she wasn't strong enough to cut the wire, but Faith insisted she'd done it before. So they put her in a dress, gave her a little white purse with a book on Berlin inside it, a subway map—the ingenue tourist. Faith wanted to dye her hair like some of the other girls, but instead they decided she should cut it. Ulrike Meinhof thought long hair drew too much attention; she'd cut off her own weeks before. So Faith had no choice but to go along and have her hair cut short, the last thing on earth she wanted to do. Petra Shelm, a former hairdresser in the group, did the honors, spread Faith's own shirt under the chair to catch what fell from her head. Faith stuffed some hair in her pocket when they weren't looking, but later she threw it out.

"Anyway," Wolf said, "it turned out she really wasn't strong enough to cut the fence. She struggled wildly out there for about an hour, got so desperate she damn near asked some guy she saw down the alley to help her. Tried using her wrists, feet, ended up ripping the hem of the dress. When they came back to get her, she was all disheveled, the fence uncut; they totally freaked. Horst Mahler jumped out of the car and did it right there, everyone watching. Faith held the clippers for him while he wrestled with the wire."

Phoebe tried to imagine her sister struggling, failing so publicly, but couldn't. In her mind's eye, Faith always found a way. "Was it, like, a disaster?" she said, feeling anxious.

"Not at the time, no," Wolf said. "Faith said the whole experience of the robberies was incredibly intense. The adrenaline gets you high as a kite; for days everything had this LSD clarity. The gun, too, carrying it on your body, like having a second heart. Even being 'wanted' she liked; feeling marked, incognito when she walked around, thinking, if that grocer, that streetsweeper knew who I really was, they'd freak. Everything they did went straight into the news—instantly, this druggy out-of-body thing, seeing yourself from miles away, knowing zillions of people were following each little thing you did . . . I mean, imagine it."

"It sounds incredible," Phoebe said.

"It was. I mean, she said it was." He was silent a moment. Phoebe felt a pull of regret in the room, like an undertow.

"She couldn't read German, obviously," Wolf said, "but Horst Mahler would translate for her. After the banks they'd never even had to count their take—it was all over the evening papers, down to the last pfennig. They sent Faith out to buy them. Her hands were shaking so hard she dropped the papers on her way back, got one wet in a puddle. No one even cared, they were too excited."

Wolf fell silent. In the absence of his voice a dullness bore down upon them, Phoebe thought, as if some faint glow had been snuffed. They could laugh all they wanted.

"Anyway, the triumph was pretty short-lived," he said. "About a week after the robberies, the cops busted two apartments and got four Red Army people, including Horst Mahler. After that, the RAF decided it was too dangerous to stay in Berlin, so they pared down their operations, started moving people into West Germany. At that point Faith was out, more or less."

"Out?"

"You know, they cut her out. Sent her on some long errand to a suburb of Berlin, and by the time she made it back, after dark, the apartment was empty. Everyone had just split. Faith had no idea where to find them."

"God," Phoebe said.

"Yeah, it was awful," Wolf said. "Faith just bottomed out, like coming down from a two-month high. Hung around that empty 'safe house' awhile, crashing on a bare mattress. Incredibly dangerous—the cops might've raided it any minute. I think she was almost hoping they would."

Phoebe tried to imagine her sister left behind, abandoned to those empty rooms, but nothing came to mind. Or no picture of Faith anyway; the apartment she saw, littered with the dregs of their haste, half-open doors, a bottle of milk, cigarette butts heaped on windowsills. The only sound her own footsteps. "Poor Faith," Phoebe said, an ache in her chest.

"She kept trying to find her mistake," Wolf said. "Should she have been more bold with them, or the opposite? Was everything fine until the fence, or had they already written her off? It went on and on, she couldn't let go. Meanwhile, she was down to three hundred dollars."

Phoebe felt the air in the room against her skin. It was painful, as if her skin were raw. "I wonder why," she said.

"Why what?"

"They left her."

"Who gives a damn why? They were assholes!"

They exchanged a hot look. Phoebe felt a swell of angry disappointment—in herself and Wolf for sitting uselessly in this dark room; in Faith, too, for failing to meet some expectation.

Faith had gone with Wolf to the shoe factory once, sat in the coffee room while he packed and loaded boxes. Afterward they'd stopped at the pub, a woodsy place with antlers on the wall, where the factory people went. Wolf thought it might revive her, flirting a little with the guys from work, and it did. But without her long hair Faith didn't draw men's attention the way she used to. She was thin, pale, both of which she'd been before, but with that gush of dark hair she'd always looked dramatic, wasted but spectacular. Now she looked more like any strung-out kid. Wolf liked it. It made her beauty his secret, not something every other guy could grope with his eyes as she walked by. But Faith despised the haircut, said she looked like an acorn. It sharpened her sense that the intensity of everything in the world—herself included—had been muted through some failure of her own. That night at the pub she had fun, though, was laughing on the streetcar home, and mid-laugh she turned to Wolf and said in this odd voice, "Maybe everything will be okay," as if this were some crazy wish she hardly dared hope for.

"Two days later we went to the Hofgarten," Wolf said. "I had the ring in my pocket, turquoise and jade, her favorites. Maybe I picked the wrong day. The minute I dropped to my knee she knew. 'Don't,' she said, before I could speak. 'Don't, Wolf, please, I'm going crazy. There's nothing left in me.' I told her fuck all that, fuck it, here we are now, in this moment—zam—the head of a pin, we can do anything! But she couldn't hear me, like some other noise was louder in her head. She just wiped her eyes, saying, 'Please, baby. Please stand up.' When I got back from work the next night, she'd left."

Phoebe and Wolf sat in silence. "And that was it?" she finally said.

Wolf struggled to his feet and switched on a light. The room pounced. He moved to the kitchen stiffly, legs obviously asleep. Phoebe heard the glassy thunk of bottles hitting the garbage.

"You don't know anything else?" she said when he sat back down. "Nothing?"

Wolf looked away. Phoebe gazed at the square of black window, trying to absorb the fact that the story was over. But of course it wasn't over. Faith had simply eluded her, vanished just when it seemed the story might finally be at an end. And here it was, the triumph Phoebe had longed for and dreaded and known would come: Faith had disappeared.

Phoebe looked around the bright room, colorless now to her eye, looked at Wolf and found him colorless, too, one more person her sister had left behind.

He suggested a walk. In silence they roamed among the painted antique buildings of Munich's Old City. The air smelled of sugar-roasting peanuts. Above the central square, life-sized mechanical dolls assembled in cheerful jerks around a clockface, preparing to strike the hour. Phoebe saw all this through a kind of gauze.

"I wish you'd say something," Wolf said as they left the square for darker, quiet streets.

But Phoebe had nothing to say. Her thoughts amounted to nothing, as did Wolf and Carla and all the festive beauty of Munich, nothing beside the spectacle of her sister's life. Terrorism, suicide; like a fast, beautiful car plunging straight down a mountainside. No wonder their father had watched.

"This is a pretty church," Wolf said. "You want to go in?"

He led the way. The church was small and oval-shaped, its interior more ornate than any Phoebe had seen in Europe, all whorls and curlicues and gold leaf. It looked like a bribe to God.

They sat in back. The light was dense with gold. "What I told you back there," Wolf said carefully. "Obviously it upset you."

"I'm not upset."

"Phoebe, you've disappeared. It's like you've gone underwater."

"I'm thinking."

"Thinking of what?"

"I have to leave Munich."

He stared at her. "Why? Did I—is something—"

"I have to keep going," Phoebe said, the words a monotone.

"Where?"

"I told you before." But Wolf seemed not to remember. "Italy," Phoebe said. "Corniglia. Where she did it."

The name impacted on Wolf physically. "Will you listen to me, Phoebe?" he said. "Will you be with me here a second?"

The intensity of his gaze brought Wolf into sudden focus, upsetting the drift of Phoebe's thoughts. She looked away. Wolf exhaled slowly, then stretched, arching his back over the pew, his spine cracking like knuckles.

"Fine," he said. "I'll go with you."

Phoebe frowned.

"I'll go. To Corniglia."

"Oh no," Phoebe said. "No."

"Pretend I'm not there," Wolf said. "I don't care if we speak. But you're not going down there alone, there's no way."

"I'm sorry," Phoebe said. "I'm sorry, Wolf." She shook her head, smiling, and it felt like so many other times, disengaging herself from a boy's car, a party, leaving a football game when suddenly the shouts and bright pom-poms had fallen silent in her mind and she saw the empty truth of them. And then she left them behind. Again and again, she left them. It was only hard for a minute.

"I'm not asking you, Phoebe," Wolf said.

He watched her eyes, his own flicking back and forth between them as if to find some route inside Phoebe's head. She felt the warmth of him, Wolf's physical presence beside her, breathing, watching.

"I don't want you," she said, and stood, leaving the pew and then the church, not running, hardly walking even, just releasing herself to the peaceful drift of her solitude. But Wolf was right beside her. On the street he suddenly took Phoebe in his arms, like that first day on the staircase. She held still, hands at her sides.

"Come back," he said. "Please, Phoebe. Come back." And she felt the pain in his voice, distantly at first, then right in her chest. She looped her arms around Wolf and rested them there.

They stood in silence. From somewhere came the sweet, oily smell of fried bread. Wolf's heart beat loud in her ear. Phoebe thought of him hugging Faith, the gun between them, and was stricken by a grinding, painful sense that her sister had gone away, left the two of them here to fend for themselves. And maybe it was right, Wolf coming with her, maybe it would help. His chin rested on top of her head, he was that tall.

seventeen

High in the Italian Alps, midway through their drive, Phoebe and Wolf stopped for lunch. The town was like an afterthought of the road: a single restaurant, a store with shutters tightly closed, a tiny bruised-looking church. The cold dry air pinched Phoebe's nostrils and throat. She and Wolf stepped from the car into whispery silence, as if the clouds, which seemed only inches away, were gently buffing the tinny sky.

The restaurant smelled of woodsmoke. The proprietress was an elderly woman whose lively face and hands made her age seem accidental, something that had befallen her in a moment of carelessness. To Phoebe's surprise, she spoke German. Wolf explained that this region had been joined to Italy only since World War I. The squat clay jug on their table was filled with red wine.

The restaurant's sole customer was an elderly man wearing oversized black trousers hitched to his chest by a pair of startling red suspenders. A great playfulness seemed enfolded like a prize

among the wrinkles in his face. To Wolf and Phoebe he raised a
tiny glass filled with clear liquid, grappa, Wolf said, pretty powerful stuff. They toasted him and drank.

Their trip had begun that morning, after a week's delay while
Wolf completed the scoliosis manual. At first he'd seemed present
in body only, uttering scarcely a word as they drove south from
Munich over fat green hills into Austria. The air turned bracing,
tangy; blunt speckled rocks nosed their way up from beneath the
soil. The tallest mountains veered straight into clouds, like columns of stone reaching up to the portals of palaces miles overhead. Phoebe had never seen Carla again; Carla was working,
Wolf kept saying, but his strained tone made Phoebe wonder if all
was well between them. He'd spent every remaining night at
Carla's apartment, leaving Phoebe his bed, made up for her with
fresh striped sheets.

They skirted Innsbruck and then crossed the Brenner Pass,
where a handsome, mustachioed Italian checked their passports
and waved them into his country. Soon after, they shifted onto a
smaller road. The slower pace seemed to relax Wolf.

"I hope it's okay," Phoebe said. "You coming with me."

"Sure it's okay."

"I mean, with Carla."

"It worked out all right," Wolf said, hesitant. "It's a tough
situation."

"Because of Faith?"

Again Wolf paused, his wariness giving Phoebe the sense that
his fiancée was nearby, within earshot. "Unfinished business is
tough," he said, and glanced at her. Phoebe felt his life tip open
just slightly, in a way it hadn't before. She crept gingerly toward
the opening.

"How much did Carla know about her?"

"Everything, pretty much," Wolf said. "Early on I kind of laid
the whole thing out for her. But after that I never talked about it
—we never talked about it. Even though I wanted to, sometimes."

Phoebe waited, afraid of stopping him. "Why didn't you?" she said.

"I felt awkward, I guess, bringing it up. I thought, Hey, you're in love, you're not supposed to be thinking about all that. Even when Carla asked me about Faith, I'd resist, tell myself it was self-discipline, putting the whole thing behind me. But I'm seeing now it's the opposite, I wasn't letting go."

He shook his head, as if the discovery confounded him still. Phoebe felt a peculiar warmth. Wolf hadn't let go.

They began a slight descent. It felt like exhaling. Something had finally loosened between them, a change even the landscape seemed to reflect: gentler mountains, exposed rock, yellowish and crumbly-looking like something baked. Punishing turns exposed views of staggering beauty; often Phoebe would stare in confusion before she could even react. "Look," she cried. "Oh my God, look!" By lunchtime she was exhausted.

A strong wind battered the restaurant. Wolf swirled the wine in his glass, then drank. "Do you ever think how things might be different for you if Faith were still alive?" he asked.

"For me?"

"It's a weird question, I know," he said. "But I mean, she's on your mind a lot."

"She would be anyway," Phoebe said warily. "I mean, she'd still be my sister."

"It's funny, though," Wolf said, "how things—people—have a lot more power sometimes when they're not actually there."

"Faith always had power."

"True. True," he said. "But it's one thing to be a precocious kid. Twenty-six years old is different. She'd have made choices by now."

"Maybe you guys would be married," Phoebe said, but Wolf winced, and she was sorry she'd made the comment. The truth was, she found it hard to imagine Faith just living a life the way other people did. It seemed unlike her.

"It's strange," Wolf said.

"What?"

"How when somebody's gone they can start to dwarf you."

"Speak for yourself," Phoebe said.

Wolf started. "I meant you in general," he said. "Not you you."

For dessert they ate tiny mountain apples poached in red wine, thick sweet cream poured on top. A languor overcame them. Phoebe folded her arms on the rough wood table and rested her head in them. Absently Wolf touched her hair. She lay very still, wishing he would do it again, but Wolf had turned to bantering with the proprietress. A delicious prickling climbed Phoebe's spine to her scalp, the sensuality of childhood, long hypnotic hair-brushings she'd traded with friends. Amazing, how easy it had been to touch people then. It felt so long since she'd touched another person.

The old man in suspenders rose carefully to his feet and donned his coat and a hat, which he tipped at the door as he took his leave. "I wonder where he'll go?" Phoebe said. "This seems like the middle of nowhere."

"Maybe he owns that little place next door," said Wolf. "Maybe he's eaten lunch at this woman's restaurant every day for the past thirty years."

"Maybe they're secretly in love," said Phoebe.

Wolf looked at her, surprised, then nodded approvingly. "I'll bet he was waiting for us to get the hell out of here," he said, laughing.

"I don't think so," Phoebe said. "I bet they're just glad to be in the same room."

Wolf glanced at the proprietress as if imagining it. "That's nice," he said.

As the woman added their bill, she spoke laughingly to Wolf, eyes teasing back and forth between him and Phoebe. Wolf made some reply and her expression changed. "Ah," she said briskly.

"What did you tell her?" Phoebe asked as they moved to the door.

"I said we're practically family."

In the restaurant bathroom, more precisely the outhouse, Phoebe examined herself, poking at her flesh, and decided she was well again. Over the past several days a curious malady had afflicted her, sensitizing every cell in her body to the point of agony. She felt sprawling, obtrusive, conscious of her hands and feet and legs, her skin inside her clothing, her face and hair in shop windows she passed. At times her whole body hurt, a chronic, delicate pain like the ache of her scalp when she'd parted her hair a different way, then combed it back. Phoebe could not decide if her body itself was causing this ache, or her keen awareness of it. She tried to ignore her physical self, but for the first time in her life Phoebe found this impossible—every part of her seemed to clamor for attention. Her breasts felt so obvious, and she began plucking out her shirts when Wolf was around, to conceal their shape. Not that he'd paid her breasts the slightest attention; ironically it was her constant plucking he'd finally noticed. "What's wrong, are you hot?" he asked Phoebe once, and though she swiftly denied it, he'd thrown open two windows.

Crazy as it seemed, Phoebe was certain her physical disorders could be traced to that brush with the prostitutes back in Paris— the moment when she'd realized that the women had mistaken her for one of themselves. Alone in Wolf's bed she was assailed by memories of that encounter, broken windows, bruised thighs; she would place one hand on her breasts, one low on her abdomen, and feel an unnatural heat from inside them, a fever, an infection of the tissues or the blood. After three tormented nights she'd resorted to self-medication, first the penicillin tablets and cough syrup she'd brought from home, then a prescription drug from Wolf's medicine cabinet that proved to be a sleeping pill and left her sprawled on the couch in a stupor all afternoon. Finally she'd

tried the birth control pills, sensing as she broke the plastic seal
that there was a certain logic to this choice that the previous reme-
dies had lacked. She'd gulped one down, filled with hope that it
would reign her body in, though afterward she feared the opposite
might be true, that starting these pills might be another step
toward relinquishing control for good.

But the pills had worked. The ache in her limbs had subsided,
replaced by a pleasant calm. As of today, she'd taken four. They
were pink, their colored outsides sweet as candy.

Back on the road Phoebe battled a froth of nervous laughter that
seemed continually on the verge of overflowing her. She'd felt this
way for a while, waiting to leave Munich with Wolf. Their immi-
nent departure had infused the city with fresh exquisiteness—
tumbling church bells, piles of white sausages, the burned smell of
sugar-roasted peanuts—these broke across Phoebe in moody,
shuddering waves, like memory. She assumed her happiness must
come from knowing she was headed toward the danger, the bright
simmer of Faith's activity. At times Phoebe practically saw it: a
flicker of motion, like the shadows of flames, just beyond the
edges of her sight. She wasn't afraid. After all that had happened,
it seemed there was no fear left in her.

As a child, before holidays or her birthday Phoebe might be
doing the simplest thing—say, cutting up a peach—and find herself smote by this same delicious awaiting. The world shivered
around her, winking, complicit, the wet peach opening like a grin
in her hands.

Wolf was laughing, too, but always after a pause, as if
Phoebe's high spirits were bright coins fluttering down to him
through deep water.

The air turned humid, heavy with the scent of eucalyptus. Fingers of cypress rose among the pines. Deep, ragged clefts gouged
at the hills like the marks of recent violence, as if the hills themselves had been torn from the earth only hours before.

For the first time since her arrival in Munich, Phoebe no

longer felt like Wolf's guest. They were sharing an adventure now; it was Wolf who first pointed out the rows of grapevines stitched neatly into the hillside. He pulled over and put down the Volkswagen's top, and they stood quietly outside the car for several minutes, inhaling the tart smells of soil and ripening grapes.

When they were driving again, Phoebe sensed in Wolf the beginnings of a new curiosity, an eagerness to separate her from the tide of history and coincidence that had swept her into his midst. He mentioned her father. "I was sorry I never got to meet him," he said.

"You would've loved him, my dad," said Phoebe.

"How well did you know him?"

She turned to him, offended. "He was my father!"

"You were little when he died, that's all I mean," Wolf said. "Although hell, plenty of fathers live to be eighty and never know their kids. The majority, some would say."

"Well, not mine. You would have loved him." Phoebe realized she'd already said this.

"Sometimes I felt like I almost knew him," Wolf said. "Everything he left behind—that house, all those paintings, you guys . . . when I looked at the shape of all that, sometimes I thought I could see his outline."

Phoebe wanted to ask what he'd seen, but was afraid Wolf might interpret the question as her not knowing her father. "What did you think of his paintings?" she asked.

Wolf considered. Phoebe tried not to look as if she actually cared. "I always wondered why he never painted you," he said. "There were a few pictures of Barry around, not many, about a zillion of Faith. I think I asked her once, why he never drew you, but she didn't know."

"I was a bad subject," Phoebe said. "Barry too."

"What, you squirmed?"

"I was too stiff. I sat still okay but I was just stiff, I came out like a wood doll." She laughed, empty, skittish laughter. She was remembering the deep apprehension she'd felt under the scrutiny of her father's dark eyes, the powerful beam of his attention. "Hold still," he would say, and Phoebe would freeze on the spot, hesitant even to breathe for fear of breaking that attention, scattering it like birds startled from a tree. But it was no good, she couldn't relax.

"It was my fault," she told Wolf. "I didn't look natural."

He nodded, noncommittal. But it was true: at the hospital, during the few times when Faith's energy had abandoned her and she'd stayed at home or collapsed sleeping in the chair by her father's bed, Phoebe had tried to replace her, poised on the hard stool, determined, like Faith, to hold utterly still while giving the impression she was just about to move. But it wasn't enough. Phoebe's stomach would clench as she watched the familiar listlessness steal across her father's face, a glazed inattention his illness left him powerless to hide. Then the merciless exhaustion would enfold him and he would begin nodding off, pencil in hand. "Daddy," Phoebe would say gently from her stool, and his eyes would jerk open, murky apologies at his lips, but he couldn't shake the drowsiness, or rather, Phoebe couldn't keep it off him. If he slipped away a second time, a sick panic would seep through her. "Daddy," she would say sharply, "Daddy!"—hoping Faith would wake up, afraid something would happen to their father and the fault would be Phoebe's. Because she wasn't enough. In Faith's presence alone was he safe.

"I was a bad subject," she said. "Faith was the natural. She had motion in her face." Why was she going on like this? She felt ready to cry. Wolf just listened, eyes on the road. "You think I didn't know my father," Phoebe said bitterly.

He looked at her, his face tense. "I think he should've had more patience."

A painful silence filled the car. "Anyway," Phoebe said, struggling to recover herself, "that's not what I even was asking. I meant what did you think of the quality?"

"Of the paintings?" He seemed surprised.

She nodded. "As art."

Wind yanked the smoke from Wolf's cigarette. "I think he should've varied his subject matter."

The road dove sharply. Before long they had left behind mountains and even foothills, moving past them onto flat, dull farmland. Phoebe melted into sleep thinking of Corniglia, where Faith died. Phoebe had circled it years before with a black felt-tipped pen in the atlas at home, a move she later regretted; it seemed blatant, undignified. But on the Michelin map of Italy she'd bought in Munich, the town was disturbingly absent. Corniglia, she thought. A tricky coil of a name—ideal, somehow, for a place no one could find. Her mother had been there, of course, right after it happened, but that journey seemed unreal to Phoebe. She had pounded on Wolf's door, herding the giant crackling map to where he sat among his X-rays of curved teen-aged spines, which looked like cats' tails when Phoebe held them up to the light. With his needle pen he made painstaking drawings of these crooked spines, taking hours sometimes to finish one. "Don't worry," he'd told her absently. "We'll find it."

"But how? It's not even in my guidebook."

"We'll ask around, go to a tourist office if we have to. I was thinking we'd stay a night in Milan anyhow, otherwise we'll hit that coast in the dark."

"What if nobody knows?"

Wolf had stared at her. "Phoebe, it's a place. It exists. We can find it."

He'd laughed then, shaking his head, and Phoebe's spirits had lifted. Laughter induced in Wolf a momentary helplessness, a flash of yielding she liked having been the cause of.

Phoebe woke after sunset, sore-necked, a warm wind on her face. The sky was frantic with color. She looked at Wolf, so gratified to see him there, driving, and found herself filled with a sharp, peculiar longing; it rolled through her body, leaving a pounding sensation deep in her belly. Phoebe lay still. She swallowed uneasily and tried to think of Faith, but her sister seemed far away, as if, rather

than heading toward her as Phoebe had imagined, they had been
driving the opposite way.

Wolf glanced over, smiled when he saw Phoebe awake. "Welcome back," he said.

Milan gathered around them slowly, then abruptly, like Christmas. The streetlights were puce. Combined with the heat, their
bath of steamy light gave the city a stagy, lurid aspect. Wolf
parked on a quiet street and took their things from the car, refusing to let Phoebe carry even his own small bag. The smallness of it
depressed her. This was all so temporary, their being here, so
purely circumstantial.

"You've found a chauffeur who not only hauls your luggage
but knows the cheap hotels," Wolf said as they made their way
under the gaudy trees.

"You're hired forever," Phoebe said, then blushed in the
darkness. It had come out clumsy, childish.

But Wolf's laugh was full of affection. "I can think of worse
fates," he said.

The hotel was on the top floor of what clearly had once been a
single family mansion. A black cage elevator descended through a
cylinder of cords to greet them. As they rose inside it, Phoebe
watched the grand stairway loop around them in wide ribbony
arcs. At the top they were met by an elderly woman with bulging
eyes and a tight painted face, breathing asthmatically inside her
red suit. Yes, there were rooms, she said. Panting, she led them
down a hallway.

Phoebe's room delighted her: an old-fashioned sink, a floor
made of smooth green stone, a bed with brass posts. Wolf pushed
open a set of French windows, admitting the warm night and
papery leaves colored orange by the streetlights. "How much does
it cost?" Phoebe asked.

He waved this away, wrestling with the second window. "Relax," he said over her protests. "It's one night."

He took her passport and went to arrange things. Phoebe
stood on her tiny balcony looking down at the street. Soon she

heard Wolf's boots on the floor of the adjacent room. The bed squeaked under his weight.

Phoebe was aware of feeling inordinately happy, a rare, startling happiness that had nothing to do with dangerous or important things hovering at close range. They were far away, the dangerous things; her attention had lapsed and they'd sailed out of sight. She was glad to be rid of them.

Phoebe showered down the hall and washed her hair. Returning to her room, she studied her face in the cloudy mirror above the sink. Normally mirrors invited a harsh focus upon her flaws, the unevenness of her eyes, the overall blandness of her features. Phoebe wondered sometimes if Faith's face had been marginally smaller than her own, giving the same components greater resonance. But this mirror allowed only an impression of herself, as if from a distance.

She dressed carefully and sat on her bed, waiting for Wolf to knock. She was nervous, and planned on drinking a lot.

"Look at you," he said, touching the small of her back as they left the room. Getting on the elevator, Phoebe thought Wolf paused to catch her smell, and again she felt that shock of longing, like a heavy object plunging into deep water. It was not quite painful, but had something in common with pain. She and Wolf rode down in silence, patterned light sliding over their faces.

Outside, they agreed to walk. The warm darkness felt good on Phoebe's shoulders, as did the weight of her long hair, still damp, the soft dress brushing her skin. This awareness of her body no longer troubled her; she actually enjoyed it. Perhaps she'd come late to a pleasure most girls her age already knew. Wolf wore a shirt made of soft rust-colored fabric, silk it must have been, big swashbuckling sleeves. A dress shirt, Phoebe thought, that he'd brought to wear with her.

"Good news," Wolf said. "I found a map at the desk with Corniglia on it. So we're all set."

Phoebe murmured her delight. It unnerved her how little Corniglia seemed to matter suddenly.

Wolf shared her sudden thirst for wine, and a bottle was nearly gone by the time their pastas arrived. Phoebe's cheeks burned; she was tipsy, reckless, filled with loud clanging laughter she didn't recognize. Though her mood was clearly perplexing to Wolf, he didn't seem offended; bemused, rather, as if unsure what exactly Phoebe was up to. Above all, she sensed his resolve not to hurt her in the smallest way. It felt like an advantage.

Phoebe asked about his family. He was closest to his sister, Wolf said, a reporter for the *Baltimore Sun* now stationed in Prague. This impressed Phoebe deeply, a woman reporter living alone in a Communist country. "I'm supposed to visit her this fall," Wolf said. "I've scheduled the time." His parents came to Germany each year; Wolf went to the States perhaps a third that often. He took a keen interest in what had become of the people he'd grown up with. "It's incredible," he said. "You look back and feel like you saw it all coming, but you didn't, that's the thing —you never could've imagined it." Phoebe smiled. Her only such experience was of seeing Wolf himself after so long. But she would never have said his present life had seemed inevitable then.

"What about you?" he asked. "What lives do you imagine for yourself?"

"None," Phoebe said truthfully. "It's always been a blank."

"That's funny. I think of eighteen as the age of grand illusions," Wolf said.

"Maybe when you were eighteen."

"What's the difference?"

"Oh, it's different," Phoebe said. "Things are totally different now."

"Well, sure," Wolf said. "But the basics are the same. I mean, you went to high school, you had friends and boyfriends, all that, you went to parties, concerts, am I right?"

Phoebe nodded, pleased that Wolf assumed she'd had boyfriends.

"Well, that's all we were doing," he said. "I mean, we were teenagers."

Phoebe shook her head. "It wasn't the same. By the time I got to high school, nothing was real anymore."

Wolf looked at her quizzically.

"It's true," Phoebe said. "Everything was kind of fake."

"Fake," Wolf said, clearly perplexed. "Why would it be fake?"

"How should I know?" Phoebe said. "It was just fake. I couldn't take it seriously."

Wolf shook his head. Phoebe played with the hot candle wax, letting it harden on her fingertips. "Some things are real, some things are fake," she concluded.

"How about this, right now? Fake?" Wolf asked lightly, but there was an odd tug in his voice, and Phoebe sensed that her answer mattered. She had a perverse urge to tell him yes.

"No," she said. "Right now is real."

Wolf gave a half-smile. "I'm relieved."

Phoebe waited to feel angry with him for prying, but each hoarded truth Wolf teased from her seemed to leave behind it a lightness, like fragile heavy packages being lifted from her arms. Now they were Wolf's, too. He was helping her carry them.

"I think one of these days the world's going to look a lot different to you," he said.

Phoebe was intrigued. "How?"

"Just—yours," he said. "Yours." And he looked at Phoebe with such palpable sympathy that she wondered what in herself could possibly have inspired it.

"I hope you're right," she said.

Wolf grinned. "I'm right."

Veal, chicken, ribbons of salad; like casualties, the empty plates and second empty bottle were spirited away from their table. So much wine had eroded Wolf's usual guard; gone was that studied good nature reminiscent of young male teachers at Phoebe's high school. She found her gaze stumbling against his and leaning there, unable to break away, and again that desire would stun her. She stalled mid-sentence, too amazed to continue.

For all her crushes on boys, Phoebe had never felt so powerfully drawn to anyone. In fact, often when she and the boy finally sank back on the sand or a bench or the seat of his car, something in Phoebe shrank from his soft lips and clamoring heartbeat. Her mind wrestled free, veering back to Faith and Wolf in her mother's bedroom, the white door shut, watching from the end of that long hall, trying to fathom it. "Come on," Faith said, taking Wolf's hand, and Phoebe would try with her mind's eye to follow, always realizing that whatever happened between herself and this boy would not bring her any nearer that door, not make the slightest difference in her life. Finally she would have no choice but to break free as she had that day from Kyle, for already she was gone. Like hearing her name called again and again, louder each time, finally having to turn.

But this was Wolf.

And her very certainty overwhelmed Phoebe now with a riveting sense of power; light seemed to pour from behind her eyes, her smile was a nimble pair of arms reaching out to gather Wolf in. Other people did these things—why not her? Why not this? When Phoebe leaned down to adjust her sandal, the top of her dress fell open just slightly, her thick liquid hair spilled down her shoulders, pooling like oil in her lap, and Wolf watched. Phoebe felt him watching. Her very longing was a thing she could harness; it sharpened her, distilled her every impulse to a single burning knot between her stomach and her breasts, like a star, Phoebe thought, a magnetic field whose pull would either draw Wolf irresistibly to her or cause her to implode. But what had she to lose? Nothing! Nothing, Phoebe thought, and wanted to laugh, for unlike Wolf she had nothing to lose. She was eighteen years old.

Phoebe ate his dessert. Something with pears, a sweet glaze. Wolf laughed and ordered a second. His lips and teeth were stained from the wine. The restaurant was nearly empty.

"All right," he said, mashing out a last cigarette. "Let's make our exit while we still can walk."

The darkness smelled of flowering trees and motor oil. Phoebe tugged in lungfuls of warm air to stop the violent spinning of her head. She nearly toppled off the curb, but Wolf was behind her. "This way," he said. "Here, okay," laughing, slinging an arm around Phoebe's shoulders. She leaned against him gratefully. Right away she felt better; closing the gap between them seemed to ease some tension within her, as if hundreds of taut, quivering strings had relaxed for the first time in hours. A silence overcame them. Wolf navigated briskly toward the hotel. Phoebe drank in the warmth of his skin. This is crazy, she thought, I've gone absolutely crazy. Her blood felt thick, clogging her veins.

When they reached the hotel, Wolf let her go. In the elevator he stood opposite Phoebe, craning his neck to study the overhead cables. Phoebe watched the bones in his chest. She felt predatory, thirsty, already slightly sick.

Wolf took their keys from the desk and led the way to the rooms. The hall was poorly lit. He opened Phoebe's door and handed her the key, kissing the top of her head. *"Schlaf gut,"* he said, but as he tried to move away, Phoebe lifted her arms to him blindly, craving again that relief of closing the gap. And here were his legs against hers, his stomach, so many points of contact that their meeting felt miraculous, irrevocable. The keys slipped from her hand and clattered to the floor. Wolf held quite still, arms at his sides, while Phoebe hung there, foolish and drunk, fastened to the heat between them, chest and ribs, the roll of his throat as he swallowed.

"Whoa. Whoa, Phoebe, hey," Wolf said, half laughing, trying to shake free, but Phoebe heard the falter in his voice and she cleaved to him, turning her head so her lips met the hot skin of his neck. Abruptly Wolf pulled her against him, a swift, fierce tug at the small of her back. He lifted her onto her toes, one hand fisted, holding his keys, his heart beating into her like something come open.

It lasted an instant. Wolf seized Phoebe's arms and forced her away, hands trembling. "Stop," he whispered. "Jesus, we're out of our minds." In the half-dark he watched her, a stunned look on his face as if she'd punched him with a strength he couldn't fathom. Then his grip on her arms softened, as if suddenly he felt her there. One kiss, Phoebe thought. It was that close. The enormity stopped her.

Wolf let go. "It can't happen, Phoebe, listen to me," he said. "Are you listening?" His voice filled the hallway, half-angry, half-disbelieving. "This is not a possibility."

They parted without another word. In her dark room Phoebe clawed the sundress over her head, yellowy street light spilling across her damp skin. Deep in her belly a small ravenous animal lay coiled; Phoebe felt it breathing, felt its heartbeat.

She yanked the bedspread away and lay under one sheet. Across the wall she heard the jerk of bedsprings and realized that Wolf's bed and her own met against this same thin wall; they were practically touching. Across the wall she heard tiny movements and imagined him in his bed, what he must be doing now or be about to do. Phoebe braced her head against the pillows until her neck felt ready to crack, every nerve in her body trained on that wall—this was sickness, sweet awful sickness, her flesh an open wound she could barely touch yet had to, mercilessly, again and again, nothing else would heal it.

Hours later Phoebe crawled from murky sleep and fumbled her way to the sink. Yellow street light soaked the room. Outside the window the city seethed faintly. She drank several glasses of water and ate another candy-coated pill before returning to sleep.

eighteen

Phoebe woke to the sensation of having spent hours turning on a spit. She lurched to the sink and vomited, shutting her eyes afterward while she cleaned out the sink. She flapped the French windows to air the room, then scoured her teeth. When she lay back down, she was folded into softer sleep.

Later she heard Wolf's footsteps next door and tried to remember the last sequence of events between them. Grabbing him and not letting go, that seemed the gist of it, Wolf forcing her away. Remembering made her weak with shame. The room kept turning; Phoebe closed her eyes to still it. They'd played this game as children, you whirled in a circle, then stopped, savoring the explosion of dizziness in your brain.

She would have to get away from him.

Phoebe rolled onto her stomach. Incredibly, that pulse of longing still beat through everything else, Poe's tell-tale heart pounding from under the floorboards. Seamlessly it mingled with her sickness, like two halves of one thing. She had to get away from him.

Eventually Wolf knocked. From the bed Phoebe eyed him in the doorway. Somehow she'd managed to dress herself. Wolf looked unwell, his skin like clay, mouth ringed with white. He was holding her key. Dimly, Phoebe recalled dropping it in the hallway the night before.

In the covered Galleria near the cathedral they stood side by side at a bar drinking cappuccinos, eating brioches to calm their stomachs. Italian men in beautifully cut suits surrounded them, conversing with the fabulous speed of auctioneers. It was Sunday. The sound of church bells rocked through the parks and streets like laughter. The city felt empty. The bells and flood of bright sun made Phoebe think of her father's funeral, a clear winter day in Mirasol, navy-blue sea stirring against the beach. The bells rang and rang—the same small church where her father had gone as a boy, only two blocks from the sea, so you felt grains of sand between your shoes and the tile floor. Something festive, celebratory in the heedless flinging of those bells, the blue sky. Bent cans outside the church were luminous; you could hardly open your eyes. As Grandma led Phoebe toward the doors, a dog had flailed up to her barking, flipping its tail. Phoebe crouched on the sidewalk to pet it. "Oh now, leave him be," Grandma said, her pale, watery eyes full of sadness. Her son was dead. Their mother had not permitted a wake—"It's bad enough they had to see him dying," she'd said. "They're not going to see him dead." Grandma touched Phoebe's head to make her rise, but the church looked so dark, sludgy organ music seeping from its doors. Faith went straight inside, but Barry knelt beside Phoebe and touched the dog, a shabby mongrel of a thing, its wiry tale beating ecstatically at this sudden bounty of attention. Barry leaned down and buried his face in the scrubby fur of its back.

August, Wolf was saying, the Italians were all at the seashore. They'd see them in Corniglia, he said, and smiled, though behind it Phoebe felt him watching her closely, trying to assess the damage.

There was no damage. Only the constant, uneasy desire to move nearer him. Now that it was there, it would never go away.

Their luggage was in the Volkswagen, parked off the cathedral square. Wolf wanted to get back there—Milan was full of thieves, he said. Stone dangled like moss from the cathedral façade. Phoebe's eyes felt dry, raw; the bright light chafed them even through her sunglasses. Wolf unlocked her door and opened it. She looked up at him, squinting through her glasses. "I can't go with you," she said.

Wolf narrowed his eyes. "You're not going with me," he said. "I'm going with you."

"No."

Wolf stretched, the car keys flashing between his fingers, shirt lifting slightly from his jeans. "Shit," he said to the sky.

"I can't." The simplicity of it satisfied her. The matter was out of her hands.

Wolf leaned on the open door. "Look," he said in a dry voice, "we're human beings, okay? We got loaded, the lines got fuzzy for a second. It's the oldest story in the world, Phoebe, come on. Let's not flip out about it." He sounded cool to the point of indifference, but his eyes were begging her. "All right?" he said. "Now can we please get on with this?"

Phoebe rested her gaze on Wolf's soft T-shirt, the collarbones splayed beneath it. Sunlight soaked her hair, heating her scalp. What he'd said last night was true, she thought; nothing could happen between them.

"Good-bye," Phoebe said.

She leaned into the car and seized her backpack. When she slung it over one shoulder, its weight nearly toppled her. The whole thing seemed only half-real. Wolf must have felt this, too, for he did nothing, just watched her go, a surge of pigeons pecking at his boots.

Phoebe crossed the cathedral square, alert to sounds of pur-
suit. None came. When she reached the opposite side, she adjusted her backpack to rest squarely on both shoulders. Still she
heard nothing. So that was it, she thought. Wolf was relieved, or
perhaps he simply refused to chase her. It made no difference.
Phoebe crossed the street, determined not to look back. The bells
were ringing again. The dazzle of light was surreal. A new phase,
Phoebe thought, so long as there was money in her pocket.
Though it was Sunday, of course, and not a penny of that money
was Italian.

She reached a side street and hesitated, debating whether to
cross or turn. Before she'd made up her mind, the Volkswagen
peeled around a corner, cutting her off. Gears crunched, there
was a yelp of rubber on the curb. Wolf leapt from the car, clearly
beside himself. Phoebe stepped away. She felt like a tortoise,
pinned beneath the giant backpack.

"Goddammit!" Wolf shouted. "Goddammit!" He kicked a
tire, *clong*ing the hubcap. Then he wheeled back around and let
fly at the door, where his boot left a soft-looking dent. Phoebe
watched him with unnatural calm. Finally Wolf faced the car, his
arms crossed; from his agitated breathing Phoebe assumed he
must be planning further assaults upon it. Instead, he turned to
her, speaking with a gentleness that seemed to cost him great effort.

"Phoebe, please," he said. "Please, get in the car. It was my
fault, that stuff last night—please, just get in the car. We won't go
to Corniglia, we'll just drive a little. Just get in the car. We'll take
it from there. Please."

He moved close to Phoebe, took hold of her shoulders and
looked into her face. It worked. The fight left her instantly. She
was tired and dizzy, anxious to shed the massive backpack. The
sun invaded her head, filling it with the thought of leaning forward and kissing Wolf, and an awful sensation flashed through
her, a hot blade slicing her neatly in half. Wolf's pupils were di-

lated, shrunken to furious points, but it wasn't anger now, or not just that. He wanted her. "Okay," Phoebe said, and got in the car.

They hurtled from Milan. Phoebe relaxed into the speed. The sun was high. Wolf glanced at her now and then as if to make sure she hadn't disappeared. "Lock your door," he said.

Phoebe burst out laughing, a brassy, unfamiliar sound. "You think I'm going to jump out on the freeway?"

Wolf smiled grimly. "I don't know," he said. "Are you?"

Phoebe leaned against the window and shut her eyes. There was too much saliva in her mouth; she opened the window and spat a few times.

"Are you sick?" Wolf asked in alarm.

Phoebe laughed again, that strange metallic sound. "Yes," she said.

An hour swept past. Wolf drove his car like an ambulance, accelerating until the Volkswagen began to shudder. Phoebe pictured herself as his stricken patient. They hardly spoke. Something had been decided, conversation supplanted by queasy knowledge.

Eventually Wolf turned off the highway onto a smaller road. It was clear they were nowhere near the sea. In the blood-heavy light of late afternoon they wove among tawny, feline hills. Olive trees ornamented the land, flashing silver. Occasionally a town would appear, blunt towers nestled on a hilltop. A drift of church bells, such a beautiful sound, Phoebe thought, like wind chimes, like singing angels. Gradually she, too, began to drift, back to the moment when finally she'd gone inside the church where her father's casket lay and sat in a front pew, next to Faith. Try as she might, Phoebe couldn't feel the weight of the disaster. The sound of birds kept distracting her, lighthearted, fatuous, flapping outside the church's stained-glass windows and luring Phoebe out of its darkness, away from the dour intonations of the priest. Did no one notice? Faith's eyes never strayed from the priest, as if her gaze were one strand in a fragile, delicate web whose slightest disruption would bring the world crashing down upon her. Phoebe leaned forward to look at Barry, on Faith's other side. He, too, watched the priest, but after a moment Phoebe saw her brother steal a glance at the windows, then glance again, reluctantly, as if helpless against their gleam of liquid color, the beating of wings behind them.

Wolf followed a wisp of road up a hill and parked the car outside the thick walls of a town. The bulk of the day had gone. Phoebe wondered if this town had been their destination all along, or if Wolf had simply tired of driving. She didn't ask. All but the most practical conversation had ceased between them, jettisoned like heavy cargo from an unstable ship. Phoebe stepped from the car and looked down at the surrounding sprawl of hills, whose white, shimmering grass made them look like heaps of sand. Here and there stood a yellowy farmhouse with green shutters, a vineyard beside it. The only sound was the wind.

They left their luggage in the car and passed through an old gate to a steep cobblestoned road. Phoebe heard sounds of children playing, but couldn't see them. She and Wolf walked like people in a trance, not even near each other. Wineshops lined the road, colored bottles tilted in their windows. An old woman sold bunches of red flowers wrapped in white paper. Apart from the noisy, absent children, the town was silent.

They reached a sloped rectangular square paved with a herringbone pattern of narrow yellow bricks. Here were the children, eight or nine little boys attacking a soccer ball with such naked aggression that its leaps and jumps looked like desperate attempts to escape them. Houses ringed the square, interspersed with a few old towers and three restaurants, whose empty tables and chairs appeared to have wandered from their doors. It was a quiet hour, between meals.

Wolf guided Phoebe into a restaurant and negotiated with a man behind the bar, handing him their passports in exchange for a key on a leather thong with a block of wood attached. The bartender offered directions, tilting his hand to indicate a turn. When his eyes met Phoebe's, she looked away in shame.

Only as they crossed back through the square did Phoebe notice the birds, hundreds of small black birds circling the square, their wings curved backward like arrowheads. Crazily they swooped and dipped, uttering shrill, squeaking cries not unlike those of mice, only more restless, more plaintive. Like something from the Bible, Phoebe thought, a portent of earthquakes or walls of fire, droughts to last generations.

They turned onto a side street. Though the boys were no longer in sight, Phoebe clung to the sounds of their play, the tinny *thung* of ball against brick. Flowers tumbled from overhead boxes. Wolf stopped at a curved wooden door marked 4 and fiddled with the key. He seemed lost in these practicalities, as if he'd forced from his mind all thoughts of where they would lead. Phoebe felt a kind of vertigo. Wolf held open the door and reluctantly she went in. The dark house smelled of dust and something sweet, ashy, like old flowers. Wolf found a light switch, and an archaic, medieval-looking entry hall sprang into view, cast-iron fixtures, throne-sized chairs. Heavy curtains extinguished any suggestion of sunlight. At one end of the hall was a room filled with covered furniture heaped into teetering piles. Phoebe glanced fearfully at Wolf. He seemed to her now a man of the world who had lured her here by some trick, like Karl in Amsterdam. Yet the situation was her own doing, entirely her own. She could easily have stopped it.

"Is this a hotel?" Phoebe asked, anxious for voices.

"More or less." Wolf sounded odd, strained. "A lot of times there aren't hotels per se in these little towns—you just go to the bartenders and they have access to rooms."

Thick burgundy carpeting covered the stairway. Phoebe swallowed and looked at Wolf, startled and relieved to find her panic mirrored starkly in his face. Man of the world he might be, but

Wolf hadn't counted on this. He was out of his league. Hesitantly he approached her, placing a hand on each of Phoebe's hips. They kissed at the foot of the stairs, deep pulling kisses that shuddered through Phoebe, emptying her mind of every thought. Wolf's mouth tasted fresh, sweet almost, like a child's. He pulled Phoebe against him and buried his face in her neck until she jerked back and cried out. Wolf's hands shook; she felt the pulse of his erection near her hip.

"Come on," he said. Hand in hand, they took the carpeted stairs in twos. The door was right at the top. Wolf opened it quickly with the key. The room smelled of cedar. There was a large bed with a window beside it overlooking the courtyard. The tangled colors of sunset flooded in, indecently bright after the quiet gloom of downstairs. Phoebe heard the slap of the boys' soccer ball against the stones. She shut the door behind her and locked it while Wolf lowered the blind.

They undressed in the dim light with an urgency suggestive of disaster. Phoebe was afraid to look at Wolf. Naked, they held each other, breathing. His skin was hot. Suddenly he lifted Phoebe into his arms and carried her to the bed, where he laid her gently down, then set upon her like someone starving. Missing was any sense of choice. Phoebe closed her eyes. When she opened them, Wolf was staring at her face, as if forcing himself to see what he was doing, as if that might stop it.

She hadn't expected the pain, such a jagged tearing pain at the pit of her stomach. Phoebe winced and cried out, and Wolf knew then, though she couldn't tell if it surprised him. He yelled himself a moment later, his face frozen in a look of anguish, then he fell upon Phoebe, as if barely conscious. For a long time after, the pain was all she could think of.

As darkness fell, Phoebe listened to the tables in the square below being set for dinner. Distinct sounds arrived through the window: dishes, silver, chairs scraping brick. Torrents of Italian, each conversation like an exchange of passionate ultimatums. Noises echoed slightly, ricocheting off the surrounding miles of emptiness.

The bedsheets were stiff against Phoebe's skin, as if they'd been dried in the sun. She lay on her side facing the window, only her feet touching Wolf's. She thought he might be sleeping. An image of herself as a little girl riding his shoulders kept invading her mind, and the memory filled her with horror.

"Hey," he said softly. "How you doing?"

Phoebe turned to look at him. Wolf lay on his back, facing the ceiling. The sheet was pulled to his neck.

"I don't know," she said. "I feel weird."

"That seems reasonable."

There was a long silence. Phoebe grew panicky. "So, what are you thinking?" she asked, wanting Wolf to talk.

He exhaled the ghost of a laugh. "I'm thinking I've lost my mind."

"Is it bad?" she whispered.

Wolf turned on his side, facing her now. The tenderness in his eyes was unexpectedly calming. "I'm not sure good and bad quite figure here," he said.

Below, people were sitting down to eat. Phoebe heard laughter, caught a whiff of someone's cigarette.

"It felt unavoidable," Wolf said, as though thinking aloud. "There just seemed to be no way around it. I tried to find a way but I couldn't."

"That's true," Phoebe said. "I tried, too."

"You did not." He was grinning.

"I did," Phoebe said, indignant. "I tried to leave."

"That's true," Wolf reflected, serious again. After a moment he said, "I was so afraid something would happen to you."

The remark seemed to echo. Something had happened, all right.

"Look," Wolf said, lifting himself on his elbows, "we can get up and leave right now, all our stuff's in the car. It'll be one of those things we just had to get through, since we couldn't seem to get around it."

Phoebe nodded intently, as if taking directions. "Okay," she said. "That sounds good."

They lay still, watching each other. Get up and leave? Wolf's eyes moved anxiously over Phoebe's face, and abruptly she felt it again, a stirring right through the pain, through it, around it, until the pain seemed only to sharpen her longing. She moved to Wolf and he kissed her, tentatively at first, then deeply, her head in his hands. He was hard again—perhaps had been the whole time they were talking. The thought of Wolf wanting her again but holding back, letting Phoebe make the choice, overpowered her. Fearful, curious, she reached down and touched him. She knew nothing at all of men's bodies. The effect of her touch was awesome: it seemed to stop Wolf's very breath. He lay back, eyes closed in a wince. Reluctantly his hand encircled Phoebe's, guiding it in a kind of agony, as if he were caught in a lunatic dream he could not burst out of. Sounds issued from deep within him, as if Phoebe were touching his very soul. Soon he began stilling her hand, keeping it there but not letting her move; for whole minutes they wavered in thick silence, Wolf's hand on hers, his heart beating so loudly she could hear it. Phoebe sensed him teetering at the brink of an excruciating pleasure, his fear of tumbling into it. She moved her hand. Again Wolf stopped her. But after a moment she resumed, gently, resisting his pressure. "Stop," he whispered, eyes still closed, then again, hoarsely, "Stop!"

nineteen

Phoebe tried in vain to keep track of the days. Her time was measured now in journeys between longing and fulfillment, the pace of which might vary from merciless speed to agonizing stillness. The resulting calm was always short-lived. Eventually the trip would be repeated, often so many times in a day that the day itself became meaningless. After four, Phoebe lost count.

Time compressed. She felt herself aging telescopically, older now than she'd been last week, or yesterday, even this morning, before the sun made its lazy arc across the bed.

She and Wolf left the room only rarely. When hunger drove them out, they ate ravenously at one of the town's three restaurants, eyes fastened together across a white cloth, feet buried in each other's laps. They ate mushrooms big as steaks, melting gnocchis in pesto sauce; they washed down lamb and veal and osso buco with bottles of Chianti. Phoebe grew fond of Tuscan bread, rough and saltless, perfect with the dry, tart cheese they were often served. When they'd eaten their fill, they walked straight back to their room and undressed.

Often it was too much trouble to eat. Phoebe lost weight, hips and ribs prodding from under her skin. Every part of her ached, legs and back and abdomen, her raw flesh. Yet far from quelling her desire for Wolf, the tinge of pain seemed to heighten its fevered pitch. At no time in her life had Phoebe felt so entirely her body's citizen, yet at the same time her detachment had never been greater. She felt like a spectator, observing her physical self in baffled amazement as if it were a violent, stricken creature she were nursing through a fit.

Phrases she had heard or read would float to mind: "I melted at his touch," "couldn't keep our hands off each other," "consumed by passion," clichés that still provoked Phoebe's scorn, but not her skepticism. From the depths of sleep she reached for Wolf; mornings they woke to each other's caresses, afterward collapsing back into sleep without having spoken. Their appetite sharpened with the days, until sometimes it seemed only minutes since they'd crumpled helplessly on the four-poster bed that was their home before Phoebe found herself turning again to Wolf, half-ashamed until he pulled her to him with equal readiness.

At first she'd been timid. She knew nothing, absolutely nothing of sex, had always assumed it required certain requisite skills, like golf or tennis. But Wolf seemed aroused by Phoebe's very inexperience, knowing she was feeling these things for the very first time—with him. The hardest thing proved to be letting herself not think, not feel ashamed, and here the sudden compression of time was a help. Soon Phoebe no longer minded lying uncovered in front of Wolf, would not cringe anymore if she made an embarrassing noise or cried out. In moments she felt a kind of madness fall on her, obliterating all traces of self-restraint. She wanted more, anything; she wanted to die. Afterward these spells appalled her. That wasn't me, she would think.

So consuming was their erotic life that everything else seemed circumscribed within it. Thought, conversation—these began in the physical realm and led inevitably back to it. Phoebe assumed Wolf's engagement to Carla was over, but he never said so and she never asked. Their physical urgency drowned out everything else—even Faith seemed faint beside it. Phoebe found herself not thinking of her sister for whole hours, sometimes even a day. At night she would lie awake listening to the echoey silence of empty countryside, thinking how nothing beyond this room seemed even half-real compared with what was inside it.

The purest moments between herself and Wolf were those of repose, recuperation. Lying perfectly still, they would gaze at each other in thick exhaustion and nothing would seem to divide them: they could float inside each other freely as fish drifting through windows of underwater castles. But desire reawakened the distance between them, teasing, irksome, piquing them both to begin again the excruciating journey toward communion.

They kept their window open, filling the room with sunlight, fresh air, sounds from the courtyard below. Still, there were times when they needed to get out, "be vertical awhile," as Wolf put it. A ruined tower stood on the edge of the town, and from its moss-padded heights they gazed down at the sprawl of boisterous landscape. Seeing Wolf clothed, out in the world, Phoebe often was shocked at how unmarked he was physically by all that had happened between them. Their flesh seemed ready at times to fall apart limb from limb, yet here they both were, intact. Somewhat creaky, lips faintly bruised, but unmarked in any permanent sense. If they went their separate ways, there would be no proof. This troubled Phoebe.

During interludes in the outside world they were careful not to touch; in their present state the smallest thing was enough to arouse them both. A kiss was certain doom. It happened more than once that having left their lair only minutes before, they would lose heart and turn back, quickly retracing their steps. These false starts always left Phoebe feeling moody, exiled from the buoyant, carefree world that wafted in from the windows.

"How abnormal is this?" she asked on the third day, lying among bedclothes they'd made up carefully not fifteen minutes before. Outside, it had started to rain. They were still clothed, for the most part. Phoebe's stomach chewed away at nothing.

"It's one extreme," Wolf said, sounding sleepy. Soft hair covered his legs; Phoebe loved how the woodlike bones were encased in such softness. When she touched his knee, Wolf flinched.

"Let's eat," Phoebe said, sitting up.

"You couldn't live this way, that's for sure," Wolf said, turning on one side to face her.

"I guess you'd have a lot of kids."

He laughed. "That would put an end to it."

They'd made love twice that first day before Wolf had even thought to ask about birth control. "What if I'd said 'no'?" Phoebe teased him later, and he'd been embarrassed, perplexed himself by the lapse.

"I would've just dealt with it, I guess," he'd said.

Phoebe lay back down. The restaurant felt so many steps away; an eternity would pass before the food was actually before them. Rain spattered the bricks below, sending a fresh wet smell through the open window.

"It's not abnormal," Wolf said. "It just never happens."

He touched her hollow stomach. Phoebe moved near him. She could wait until morning to eat, she guessed. Each morning Wolf went down to one of the restaurants and returned with cappuccinos and brioches still warm from the oven, which they ate in bed. They were comfortable here, Phoebe thought; she would wait. The smell of that rain was a meal in itself.

The next morning, their fourth day, they awoke determined to visit the tower, and arrived there well before noon. Usually there were tourists up here, but today, cloudy, still wet from the rain, there was no one. Phoebe and Wolf sat side by side on a ledge upholstered with damp moss, and looked down. Without sunlight the hills appeared brown, toasted almost. Phoebe was pleased by the abundance of cypress trees, which Vincent van Gogh had painted so well. She found herself describing to Wolf the first sexual feeling she could remember in her life; it was part of the blown-openness of their situation that any topic, barring Carla or Faith, felt perfectly natural between them. She'd been eight or nine, she said, climbing a pole in a playground during the afternoon phase of someone's sleepover party. The sensation seemed unconnected to her arms. She'd dangled from the pole in a kind of rapture, minutes at a time. She'd urged the other girls to try and they'd all taken turns, enjoyed it so much they'd demanded of the birthday girl's bewildered mother that she bring them to the playground first thing next morning, before their parents picked them up. But that day was foggy, the pole cold to the touch, and nothing happened that time. The spell had worn off.

Wolf listened with great curiosity. "Was it like coming, the feeling?"

"I can't remember. It went on as long as you could hang there."

"You had strong arms."

Phoebe laughed. "They got tired," she said. "But when I started climbing more, I think they got stronger."

"When was the last time?"

"Oh, a long time ago. It would've looked weird after a certain point," she explained. "I mean, by sixteen your feet would touch the ground."

"At sixteen you graduate to the real thing. The real pole," Wolf said, laughing.

Phoebe swung her legs. Wolf took her hand, touching it to his lips. "We're being very good," he said.

Because the place was deserted, they allowed themselves to kiss. They were shy, kissing in public, as if someone watching would know everything. "Let's go back," Wolf said.

They stood up. Before them the brown hills swayed and dipped. "Why not here?" Phoebe said.

Wolf laughed, not thinking she meant it. But Phoebe liked the idea. She was wearing her long skirt, which should make it easier.

"Forget it. Someone could show up any second," Wolf said.

"Maybe there's someplace hidden."

"We'd be thrown in jail. They're all Catholics."

"I'm Catholic, too."

He laughed. "Well, that's a relief."

Phoebe ignored him. A flight of narrow, half-decaying steps led down to the other side of the wall. At the bottom, beyond a wedge of scrubby grass, the hill dropped suddenly away. Where the wall turned, Phoebe saw what she'd been looking for, a nook invisible except from the top of the wall or looking up through binoculars from the hills below.

Wolf followed her down. "We'd be back in the room by now," he said.

Phoebe took his hand and led him into the nook. Tangled in the ivy at their feet were wine bottles, a pair of blue socks. As they kissed, Phoebe felt the responsibility drain off Wolf like an actual substance and it thrilled her, having that power. Wolf leaned against the wall while Phoebe unzipped his jeans—he'd joked about his permanent erection—now he gasped at the touch of her cool hand. The act itself was more awkward than Phoebe had imagined; being taller, Wolf had to bend his knees, but this didn't seem to bother him now that they'd begun. Phoebe's skirt virtually covered them—only the front was lifted. Wolf threw back his head, bracing it against the wall. Afterward he stayed like that, eyes shut, baring his throat while his breathing calmed. After a while he put his arms weakly around Phoebe's shoulders and leaned there. "I'm gone," he said.

And he was. Gone. Lost—in her. In bed he gathered Phoebe's long hair in his hands and moved close to her face, watching the movement of her eyes. "You do what you do" was the nearest Wolf came to explaining all he'd jeopardized to be with Phoebe now. But it was less an explanation than an assertion of the pointlessness, the self-indulgence of attempting one. At times a certain wry fatalism would overtake him, a brooding ill humor whose basis, it seemed, was the belief that everything was lost. These moods terrified Phoebe at first, but their only effect was to drive Wolf back to her with even greater abandon, as if, by surrendering to Phoebe anew, he were proving that this—she—was worth the loss of everything else.

Asleep, he thrashed beside her, often yelling out in terror, but Phoebe had only to gather him into her arms to deliver Wolf from these agonies into far more exquisite ones. Afterward, still clinging to her, he would slide into a deeper, drenching sleep, one hand clutching her finger like a tiny child, and Phoebe would stay awake as long as possible, guarding his sleep, secure in the knowledge that she alone had the power to save him.

Eventually they would have to rejoin the world, Phoebe supposed, but when she tried to imagine it, herself and Wolf sharing a life like normal adults, no picture came to mind. But that was because of the newness, she reasoned; though it felt like ages had passed, it was really only days. They needed time to grow into this thing, would be guided through its later stages as naturally as they'd been led to this first one. Besides, her own future had always seemed unreal to Phoebe when she tried to imagine it.

When several days had passed, they decided to take a short trip, a day trip into the world to remember what it felt like. "Reassimilation," Wolf said. "Rehabilitation." He suggested Lucca, a place he'd not seen himself but heard was lovely.

It felt odd, getting back in the car. A week and a day had passed since their arrival, Wolf said, though Phoebe would never have known. The morning light astounded her eyes. Olive trees shook silver. She felt like an invalid emerging from long convalescence. The world's resilience impressed her, its ability to proceed, unhindered, despite her own lapsed attention.

Maneuvering his car on the curved roads seemed to make Wolf lighthearted. Phoebe wondered if he'd missed it. The last time she'd ridden with him was before, when it seemed, looking back, that they'd hardly known each other. Phoebe sensed she should act differently now, some way that reflected the changes between them, but she wasn't sure how. You couldn't hold hands with someone driving a stick shift.

"Don't you think it was fate?" she said. "How I found you?"

"It was lucky," Wolf agreed.

"But not lucky. You know, predestined."

She explained how she'd come to Europe knowing there was something she needed to find, how she'd flailed, grabbing at possibilities until finally, in the depths of despair, she'd stumbled on Wolf.

"I see your point," he said. "But don't things always look inevitable in retrospect?"

"Which is how you know there's fate."

He said nothing. Phoebe sensed Wolf was letting her think what she wanted. "You don't believe in it," she said, disappointed.

"I'm not sure," he said. "I used to. That's what I liked about getting high, feeling all those connections—a bell rings, the light falls a certain way, a song comes on the radio and you look around and think, Dig it."

Phoebe nodded appreciatively.

"Maybe it just got dull," Wolf said, "having everything sort of converge into one pattern, the Buddhists, the Egyptians, the Apaches, hell, why not the Christians, too—it's all one groovy thing, man. It's all, like, spirituality . . ."

"Stop it."

She'd startled him. "I'm making fun of myself, Phoebe," Wolf said. "Not you."

"Things were a lot more spiritual back then. Period," she said.

Wolf glanced at her. "You mean objectively? As in, God was more present?" He looked incredulous.

"Since when are you the expert?"

"Expert, hell. That's what nostalgia is: you see layers of meaning you never dreamed were there at the time."

"But you did see the meanings at the time," Phoebe said. "The bell and all that—you just said."

"We *thought* we saw meanings."

"Well, if you saw the meanings then, and you see them now, when you look back, how can you tell they weren't really there?"

"Huh," Wolf said, grinning suddenly. There was a long pause. "The weird thing about that time," he said, tentative now, "is in a way we were nostalgic for it even while it happened. I think it had to do with constantly watching ourselves, on drugs, the whole out-of-body thing, but also on TV, in the papers. We were news. Whatever we did felt so big, so unbelievably powerful, almost like it was happening in retrospect. I've never felt anything like that, before or since. It wasn't real life. Which I guess is what made it great."

"I wonder what we'll say about this someday," Phoebe said. "You know, right now."

"Right now is good right now," Wolf said.

The moment felt odd, precarious. "Maybe you'll say it was fate. That I found you."

"That's possible," Wolf said.

From a distance Lucca rose above the land like a gigantic fortress, surrounded by thick formidable walls. Phoebe and Wolf left the Volkswagen outside its ramparts and walked hand in hand into the town.

Inside, rich green lawns ran flush along the tops of the city walls, like an emerald moat on the verge of overflowing. There was a good view of the dry surrounding hills. I'm with my lover, Phoebe thought, and had a longing to be seen, as though the presence of witnesses would seal some final bond between herself and Wolf.

Mansions lined the narrow streets. For centuries, Wolf said, rich Florentines had made their second homes in Lucca. Old villas sprinkled the countryside, some converted into museums. Phoebe noticed Rolex watches in the shop windows.

They stopped at a beautiful church called San Michele in Foro, tiny animals carved in its façade. Inside the church Wolf drifted away from her, exploring the vaulted corridors. Phoebe watched him, making favorable comparisons between Wolf and the other male tourists. She especially loved his gait, athletic yet so elegant, the opposite of that chimplike trot of high school athletes. Naked or clothed, Wolf walked like that. My lover, Phoebe thought, but the word did not seem right. She'd heard it too often in high school, employed by girls who wanted to advertise the fact that they were sleeping with their boyfriends. What was it called— what she and Wolf had? Phoebe watched him arch his back to gaze up at a relief of the Madonna and Child, and for an instant Wolf looked like a stranger, a man she had no claim on. Phoebe waited anxiously at the door for him to finish.

Back on the street Wolf was quiet. Phoebe sensed his thoughts traveling far from her, but was unsure how to reclaim them. In the privacy of their room she would have rolled against him or left the bed to shower, fetch a glass of water, and by the time she returned he would be there, waiting. But without this physical recourse, Phoebe felt powerless. As they wandered the streets, she engaged in a frantic mental dialogue: Weren't fluctuations normal in a relationship? Hadn't the whole point of coming here been to ease their intensity a little, exist in the world like two normal people? But the world proved too distracting, it rushed in like static, invading the space between them. Phoebe no longer knew what to say, how to act with Wolf. Too many subjects seemed off-limits.

They stopped for lunch. The restaurant looked like a cloister; a fountain bubbled in the courtyard. A waiter ceremoniously disengaged the bones from their grilled fish. Their fellow diners were oldish and bejeweled. Phoebe and Wolf exchanged smiles at their expense. Still, a silence tugged at them. What did they normally talk about? Or had there always been these silences, and Phoebe was just too happy to notice? Her awareness of all that Wolf had given up for her sake seemed to turn on Phoebe now; she felt a sudden, paralyzing onus to make each moment of her company worth his while. Wolf crossed his arms. She saw tension in his face, and he leaned back in his seat with a languor Phoebe knew was forced.

"What are you thinking about?" she demanded, unable to bear the silence.

She'd spoken too loudly. Wolf flinched, but Phoebe rushed on before he could answer. "You're thinking about Carla, aren't you? If you are, just say it!"

Wolf began to speak, then stopped. Phoebe saw pain in his face and panicked, words overtaking thoughts. "Do you want to call her?" she cried. "Maybe you should do it, go call her right now! I don't care."

"I'd be doing that for me, not her," Wolf said quietly. Phoebe saw she was making him angry.

An old feeling resurfaced: Carla seemed as fully present at the table as if she were seated between them, smoking her cigarette. Phoebe felt a wild urge to seize control, to comprehend. "Do you feel guilty?" she said. "Is that what it is?"

Wolf ran shaking hands through his hair. "I'm confused," he said. "Okay? I'm just confused. It would help a lot if you'd calm down a second." He looked far from calm himself. "Anyway, guilt is irrelevant," he said. "You do what you do, that's what counts."

"You're always saying that."

Wolf stared at her. "Don't push me, Phoebe. Jesus."

He looked away. Phoebe imagined him wishing her gone, and it crossed her mind that perhaps she should make a scene the way women did in movies, holler some insult, flip the table into Wolf's lap. But instead she thought of Carla, alone in the empty Munich apartment, left behind with nothing but the lovely diamond on her hand. Phoebe's outrage dissolved into pity. "Well, I feel guilty," she said.

"That's ridiculous," Wolf said.

When he looked at Phoebe, really looked at her, something

behind Wolf's eyes seemed to fall away almost by accident. Phoebe saw this now, and relaxed. As long as she saw that opening, there was nothing to fear.

"Please don't," Wolf said. "Please."

"Okay."

"Forget about this, okay?"

"Will you?"

"I will," Wolf said. "I'm trying."

They were themselves again. The relief was terrific. Phoebe finally dared leave the table for the bathroom. On her way back, Wolf caught her waist in his hands and pressed his ear to Phoebe's stomach as if to hear the sea. Phoebe felt that loosening within her, like a knot being cut. Blood filled her cheeks.

Outside, siesta hour had fallen. The shutters were down. Phoebe could think of nothing but lying down with Wolf; the meal, the wine, even the conflict between them had quickened it. As the craving sharpened, it nagged, distracting her from everything but the beat of Wolf's footsteps beside her. How long would it be before they were back in their room? Hours, Phoebe thought, hours and hours, and the knowledge nearly brought her to tears. She began torturing herself with memories of them together, yesterday, this morning, and a demented sort of clarity descended upon her. Nothing mattered but that, having it back. To hell with Carla and everything else.

At a cul-de-sac they stopped. Wolf shut his eyes, kissing Phoebe as if to pull something from within her, deeper than her mouth or throat—from her lungs, heart, stomach. Overhead Phoebe glimpsed tall houses with their green shutters closed. She and Wolf were trembling, even their mouths shook. She wished she were wearing a skirt like that other day. This was torture, like needing desperately to pee and being stranded; once she'd lost a pair of skis that way, left them lying in the snow, and when she came back from the bathroom, they were gone. Afterward she'd lied about it, said someone broke her lock while she was eating lunch. Her own desperation had shamed her. Now her hips were wedged against Wolf's. When Phoebe kissed his neck, he leapt as if she'd shocked him. "Let's get a room," he said.

They'd passed a hotel before lunch. They made for this now, unsmiling, like two thieves who must reach a window before an alarm goes off.

Wolf made the arrangements and they sprang up the marble stairs to the room. It was a fancy hotel. Wolf had trouble with the key but the door finally opened. Phoebe caught a blur of velvet and gold as they made for the bed, but the shades were drawn. The moment they were naked she took Wolf into her mouth, something she hadn't dared try because it scared her—there seemed a danger of choking or damage to the throat but now that very fear egged her on, she wanted something more. Phoebe shut her eyes, taking long slow pulls. Wolf lay very still beneath her. After each breath he would wait a long time before taking another, until suddenly he shuddered, crying out so violently that Phoebe was certain she'd damaged him—she pulled away, her mouth filled with a very strong taste, not bad exactly but strong, too strong; she swallowed quickly to be rid of it. But the taste stayed in her mouth, and for some reason Phoebe began to cry and stretched beside Wolf, sobbing. He lay like a corpse. When finally Phoebe looked at him she saw tears running from the corners of his eyes, a steady flow like something leaking accidentally from inside him. His chest shook when he breathed, but he kept his eyes closed and said nothing. They lay that way for some time. There was a feeling in the air of hopelessness. Yet even now, even amidst that hopelessness, Phoebe still wanted more; she was two people, one despairing, the other greedy and low, overjoyed when Wolf roused himself and moved down to stroke her with his mouth—the sensations were murderous, unbearable, she came almost instantly, like being smacked in the head and losing consciousness. Afterward she lay as if broken, the words "sickness unto death" drifting through her mind from someplace; she was drifting free of everything now, even Wolf. Thank God for these moments of calm, although they never lasted long enough; soon the inevitable pounding started up again like a toothache, faintly at first but mounting steadily until she and Wolf clung to each other and he pushed himself inside her, both of them gasping slightly at the rawness of their flesh.

Afterward they lay flung together. The bedspread smelled of orange peels. Phoebe wondered if there was a potpourri somewhere.

"This is bad," Wolf said without strength. Phoebe nodded. She felt as if someone else had abused them, a reckless, insatiable third party.

"I feel crazy," Wolf said, his voice flat. "I swear to God."

Phoebe looked at the room. It was full of shadows.

"I love you," Wolf said. "I love you, Phoebe." He'd never said this before, although Phoebe had said it to him, many times. He was watching her with a slightly crazy look, yet at the same time he seemed attentive to something else, like a noise in the hallway. Phoebe listened, but heard only the vague beginnings of that pounding deep within herself, like evil footsteps making their approach, and it frightened her now, her whole body hurt and she didn't want any more but she did; some part of her was always empty.

"I love you," Wolf said, between kisses. "Phoebe, I love you." They moved together sorrowfully, with apology almost, like strangers consoling each other in the midst of a crisis.

A drenching sleep overcame them. When they woke, it was well past dark. The day had gone, leaving Phoebe with a panicky sense of having missed something important. They discussed whether to drive back now, in darkness, or wait until morning. The prospect of a long drive at this hour was dismal, but even more dismal was the thought of remaining overnight without toothbrushes or changes of clothes. A mood of failure hung in the room like a smell. Phoebe was anxious to confine it within the present day, keep it from touching tomorrow.

They would go back, they decided. Back to their home, such as it was.

Moroccan tiles glazed the bathroom. Big soft towels were folded over rods. "How much does this place cost?" Phoebe asked.

"The beauty of credit cards," Wolf said. "I have no idea."

"We're paying for the whole night, aren't we?" she said. "Even if we leave."

Wolf smiled haggardly. "I'd say we've gotten our money's worth."

In the shower they gently soaped each other's bodies, but despite their halfhearted efforts to resist, were soon hunched against the tiles, hot water beating against them. Wolf looked paler than Phoebe had ever seen him. She wondered if losing too much semen could be physically dangerous, but decided it was not the time to ask.

A towel at his waist, Wolf examined his beard in the mirror above the sink. He'd been shaving twice each day so his stubble wouldn't hurt her, and so much shaving had made a rash on his neck. Watching him, Phoebe was startled by the look Wolf exchanged with himself: a cold mix of regret and stubbornness, the look of a man who believes he has ruined his life. But when his gaze met Phoebe's, she saw the tenderness again, that helpless opening which seemed to flush away everything else. "Let me dry you," he said, and did so very gently, tamping Phoebe's shoulders and breasts as if wiping sweat from a feverish child.

In the bedroom they switched on a light. The room was beautiful. Their failure to make proper use of it dogged Phoebe. Clothing lay everywhere, though the bed looked surprisingly neat.

"All right," Wolf said, checking to see they'd left nothing behind. "We're doing okay here."

The night was cool and clear, moonless. The only illumination on the empty road came from the sweep of their headlights. To Phoebe the glittery sky had a hapless, random look, as if some precious substance had been wasted there.

"Here's my idea," Wolf said when they'd driven a ways from Lucca. "I think we should get out of Italy."

The suggestion caught Phoebe off-guard. "Why?"

"Because I think we're in some kind of limbo here, and it's having this weird effect on us."

"What about Corniglia?"

Wolf turned to her. The town had not been mentioned for days. "You still want to go to Corniglia?"

Phoebe hesitated. "No."

"So the question becomes, what are we doing here?"

They twisted through the dark hills. The feeling between them was fragile, dangerous. They'd reached the center of something. "So where would we go?" Phoebe asked.

"Anywhere. Greece, Yugoslavia, hell, Mozambique. We can go anywhere we want—"

"Except Munich."

Wolf said nothing.

"What about your work?"

"I've got a few things pending," he said. "I'd just—I don't know, I'd get myself out of it."

Phoebe listened with rising dismay. Not a word of this sounded plausible. Wolf was talking as if they were fugitives, planning a life on the lam. It was ludicrous. He must have felt this, too. "Hell, I don't know," he said. "I don't know what to do."

Phoebe turned to the window. The land flew past. It seemed wasteful, how much of it there was. The world was a rash, chancy place, a hill here, a star there. Even this car, herself and Wolf inside it, hurtling under a pointless sky. None of it mattered; it could be this way or any other way.

But gradually something else began to happen. As they drove, the gritty stars seemed to shift, realign themselves before Phoebe's eyes, and her sister, whom she'd barely thought of in days, suddenly felt quite close again. Faith simply returned. She collected there, gathering in around Phoebe like a mist or a change in temperature until Phoebe felt her presence everywhere, perched between them in the Volkswagen, peering down through the cluster of stars, as if this car, these loping hills—the whole of Italy—were encased within a crystal paperweight balanced on the palm of Faith's hand. She was back. But of course she had always been here. Must have been, hiding as she'd loved to do, giving Phoebe a taste of her absence. She'd been around them and between them, pushing them together—crazy, the thought of leaving her behind, what madness! And what a relief to have her sister back, to feel the world surging back around her in its old familiar shape.

"What are you thinking?" Wolf said.

"That we should go to Corniglia."

There was a long silence. Phoebe wondered if Wolf was aware of her sister's return. It seemed to her now that he was—that he'd known all along Faith was there, and kept it secret. "I guess you're right," Wolf said, sounding defeated.

They rode in silence. As the car plunged into darkness, Phoebe felt herself hurtling forward in time until she was looking back from an imaginary future at these days with Wolf, at this very moment. My time with Wolf, she would think, those first days with Wolf, and pictured even now how the memory would break across her, a longing catch to the throat as she recalled their compulsion and wild tenderness, her worries about fate and whether their affair would last. This vision tumbled over Phoebe with the force of revelation: she would stand somewhere and look back, she would live a life. Until this moment she had never truly believed it.

They reached the town and parked outside its walls. Hand in hand they walked up the same sloped avenue they'd traversed that first day. The town felt abandoned by all but a few skulking cats, raking their backs against houses. As they walked, Phoebe felt herself slipping back inside the present time, enfolded with each step, though it was tinged now by a certain nostalgia. Or had it always been?

Wolf unlocked the front door, then lifted Phoebe into his

arms and carried her up the carpeted stairs to their room. Some pressure between them had eased, and they laughed now, undressing each other and falling onto the freshly made bed. Phoebe looked at Wolf's face, where it seemed she could read every thought. Yet he'd known Faith was there, known all this time and said nothing.

twenty

As it turned out, you couldn't drive to Corniglia. So mountainous
was that stretch of coast that the roads all veered inland; it could
take hours to get from one seaside town to the next. Wolf and
Phoebe learned this in Pisa, where accordingly Wolf parked the
Volkswagen on a back street near the train station and left it.
Phoebe worried about leaving the car when he'd talked so much
about thieves. But he seemed indifferent to its fate.

Wolf's dread of going to Corniglia had grown palpable in the
days since their Lucca trip. Phoebe would wake in the dead of
night to find his eyes wide open, riveted to the ceiling. "What?"
she said. "What?" But Wolf shook his head, seeming not to know.
He made love with a ferocity that half frightened her, as if by
forcing them both more deeply into that moment he might propel
them beyond it, to freedom.

Phoebe, too, was distracted by thoughts of Corniglia, but it
was a thrilling distraction, a promise. The sense of a secret awaiting revelation had grown in her. She and Wolf would embrace it

together, and in doing so, seal a final bond between themselves. Yet for all her anticipation, Phoebe felt no impulse to move. Days kept passing. It was Wolf who finally said early one morning, "Let's just go. Today. Get this thing over with."

In Pisa they boarded a local train for Genoa. The elusive Corniglia was not among its many coastal stops; they would have to get off one town north, in Vernazza, and spend the night. By now it was nearly sunset; packing, driving, planning their next move had taken up the day. The train was jammed with Florentines headed for the seashore. Phoebe and Wolf were forced to stand. There were groups of warbling schoolchildren, also hundreds of adolescents dangling from the windows with cigarettes dangling from their mouths, trading salvos of shrill Italian. Phoebe watched, amazed by their swaggering naïveté, a thoughtless arrogance she could not imagine in herself. She envied them. Yet mingled with that envy was a curious desire to protect these children, shield their innocence.

Eventually she and Wolf landed facing window seats. The surrounding commotion made it difficult to talk. The train moved languorously as the sun dropped to the horizon. Two leathery older women sharing their compartment pulled sweet after sweet from their beach bags, devouring each with furtive pleasure. Before the train had reached the coast, Phoebe sensed the presence of the sea and felt a wild urge to see it, just see the water spread wide into the distance. She was used to seeing the ocean every day of her life. It struck her only now how much she'd missed it.

Phoebe nearly cried out at her first glimpse of the Mediterranean. It looked fragile enough to tear, a sheet of thinnest blue silk, streaked pink from the sky. She couldn't see a beach, but sensed one there, afternoon bathers lingering on the cooling sand, and was overwhelmed by memories of Mirasol, playing on the beach only two blocks from Grandma and Grandpa O'Connor's house while summer days melted into sultry, bluish nights. At dusk the sand glowed like the moon; she and Faith and Barry couldn't leave it. Finally their father would come after them, yelling down from the boardwalk, "Come on, you rascals, it's getting dark." Then he'd wander down and join them, "just for a minute," he'd say, lulled by that curious lag time when, despite the darkness, the world still felt gorged on the heat of daylight. He would lie back in the sand with arms crossed at his chest and they would bury his feet, his legs, shrieking and patting down the cracks when he tried to move. Often they got as far as his neck before their mother came outside, calling into the darkness, "Gene? Kids? Honey, I thought you said you were bringing them back."

Phoebe sat upright in her seat. For days, it seemed, she'd remembered nothing; now she had an almost physical craving to drift, to give herself up to the past. The City of Fun stayed open all summer long in Mirasol, entertaining the Navy kids. After dinner she and Barry and Faith would go there with their father, who bought them garish colored slushes that ached in the chest when you sipped too fast. From the Ferris wheel Phoebe gazed down at the tingling black sea and felt a tremendous worldliness, out past her bedtime, bathed in the amusement park's eerie colored light. One man who worked there year after year had a pockmark deep in the side of his face, large enough to hold a marble. Phoebe would stare at him, transfixed by this hole and what secret disaster might have caused it. She thought of him in the off-season, too, his cigarette pack rolled in the sleeve of his white T-shirt, his mouth cocked in a half-smile. Where did he live? she wondered. What did he do besides pull the lever that made the ride go?

"You look far away," Wolf said over the din of the moving train. He lifted Phoebe's foot and held it in his lap. The sweet-eating women winked their complicity.

Wolf's hands were warm on her ankle, but Phoebe's mind drifted from him. "Wolf?" she said, "What ever happened to the terrorists Faith knew in Germany?"

He looked startled. It had been two weeks since they'd spoken Faith's name. "They're dead," he said. "The main ones anyway."

"What about that one woman?"

"Ulrike Meinhof? She hanged herself in prison a couple of years ago." Wolf spoke slowly, eyes narrowed. "The other ones— Baader, his girlfriend, Gudrun Ensslin, another guy, Raspe—they all committed suicide in jail. Last October I guess—was it? Yeah, last October. A lot of people say they were murdered."

"So it's extinct now, the Red Army?"

"Actually not," Wolf said. "It's going strong. Why, you thinking of joining?"

Phoebe smiled. "Right."

"Last fall they kidnapped a guy, Hanns-Martin Schleyer, this big industrialist. Killed three guards and a driver just getting to the guy, held him two months, then slit his throat."

"God."

"They don't call it 'terrorism' for nothing."

The idea of a link between her sister and such bloodletting sickened Phoebe. It would have sickened Faith. "They must be monsters, the new people," she said.

"Monsters I don't know. A few steps further along."

"If Faith had been there, she would've stopped them."

Wolf laughed. "The entire German police force tried to stop them."

"But, Faith," Phoebe said. "I mean, Faith! When Barry threw snails off the roof, she glued the shells back together with Elmer's glue and they actually lived. You don't believe me?" she asked, searching Wolf's face.

"I do," he said quietly. "She told me that story herself." After a moment he said, "Ulrike Meinhof's still kind of a hero in Germany. A martyr. Kids, especially, worship her, but adults, too, liberals. They see her as an innocent, this pure ideal gone wrong."

"Maybe she was."

"Maybe. Although it's hard to say—she'd been in prison since '72, so there wasn't really time to do much damage."

"I guess if she'd killed fifteen people, they'd be looking for another martyr," Phoebe said.

Wolf grinned, the first real smile she'd seen on him all day. "Irony," he said, "from the lips of Phoebe O'Connor."

"See what you've done?" she said.

They passed beach town after beach town: Viareggio, Lido di Camaiore, Marina di Pietrasanta, Marina di Massa. Rarely could Phoebe see actual beaches; it was enough to glimpse palm trees, a pastel-frosted slice of old hotel. The tang of salt air mingled incongruously with the smell of pine trees. Phoebe craned her neck to seize glimpses of the sea, boats rising and falling on it like buttons on the vest of someone sleeping, and a familiar excitement overtook her, a sense that something tremendous hovered just ahead. In spite of Wolf she felt alone, a solitary traveler. This troubled Phoebe. She left her seat and curled suddenly in his lap, crushing the German newspaper he'd bought in Pisa. Wolf held her, surprised and pleased, the ladies beside them looking away in embarrassment.

As the land grew more mountainous, they began hitting tunnels, inside which the train made loud plunging noises as though boring straight through rock. A dank wind filled the compartment. Phoebe endured these interludes, anxious for the sea to reappear. Her gaze and Wolf's rocked together in the half-dark, but even as they smiled, some tension hung between them. Finally Wolf left the compartment and went out in the aisle to smoke.

They made a long stop in La Spezia. By now it was dusk, the air a phosphorescent blue. Young girls in summer dresses climbed from the train into the arms of much older men in white shoes, men with silk scarves bunched at their tanned, loose necks. Phoebe thought at first these might be fathers greeting daughters, then realized that of course they were not. As the girls smoothed their dresses and looped their thin arms around the men's elbows, Phoebe watched, riveted by a sense that what she saw was forbidden yet, in some mysterious way, attractive.

La Spezia was followed by a wilder stretch of coast. The

hordes of passengers thinned. Wolf returned to the compartment smelling of tobacco. "We're almost there," he said, sitting back down and gathering Phoebe's hands in his own, which felt icy. He looked at her deeply, seeming to verge on speech, yet said nothing.

"I wonder if it's pretty. Corniglia," Phoebe said. Wolf let her hands go.

They sprang from the car in Vernazza, where the train barely paused before burrowing back into the mountain's flank. The town was wedged in a crevice between two bulges of mountain, its pale stone houses groping partway up the cliffs. Phoebe waited outside a bar with the luggage while Wolf inquired about rooms. An eerie festivity permeated Vernazza, a mix of riotous laughter and desultory music. The orange-tinted light appeared carnivalesque. Wolf emerged, key in hand, and they followed a steep, cobbled path twisting sharply up the cliffside, barely wide enough for two people to walk abreast.

Their door was already open. Inside, a man chased a small curly-haired girl through the front hall. Sand fell from her legs on the dark tiles; her feet made a wet slapping noise. From other parts of the house Phoebe heard loud conversation in Italian.

Their own small room smelled of ammonia. Phoebe heard splashing, shrieks of the little girl being given a bath. Wolf opened the shutters to admit a wet, oceanic smell. The window faced a weave of empty clotheslines dotted with damp pins. "What a weird place," Phoebe said.

Wolf smiled wryly and sat on the bed. "Agreed," he said. "Let's split."

Phoebe sat next to Wolf and he wrapped his arms around her, but to her amazement she felt nothing, not the slightest stirring of desire. It was as if someone else were describing the scene and she was listening, with interest and detachment. Wolf quickly withdrew. He lay flat on the bed, arms folded at his chest. Phoebe stretched out beside him. She felt a curious detachment from her body, as if the throes of these past weeks had been its last and now she were rising free of it. Her mind, by contrast, felt bound-less, ready to burst from the small container of her head. She shut her eyes and released it.

"Phoebe?" Wolf said. She opened her eyes. "Stay here with me."

"I'm here."

"You're not."

Phoebe turned to him. In Wolf's face she saw some trouble, like a shadow moving just behind the eyes. "Phoebe?" he said.

She refocused. "What?"

"Talk to me. Tell me what's happening."

"I don't know."

"What you're thinking about."

"Going up there."

Wolf sat up. "Don't do this," he said. "It's freaking me out."

"Do what?"

"Use that zombie voice."

"I'm sorry."

"You're still doing it!"

"I'm sorry," Phoebe said.

"Stop apologizing!"

"I don't know what else to say."

"Fine," Wolf said. "Let's stop talking."

He stood up. With angry movements he gathered a change of clothes and left the room to shower. When he'd gone, Phoebe shut her eyes again, giving herself to that drift, the gentle teasing coax of her thoughts.

Mirasol: the last trip while their father was alive, late summer it must have been, before he'd gone back in the hospital for the last time. By then he was weak, no longer could ride the amusement park rides or even attempt the long ocean swims he'd once fa-vored in the early mornings. Illness forced upon their father pre-cisely the leisure he'd scorned in health; he slept late, lay on the beach fully dressed even under a pounding sun. Still, he rarely alluded to his illness. "I'll sit this one out," he'd say as Faith headed for the roller coaster, or to Phoebe, "Bring your lazy old man an OJ, will you?" They took comfort in the day-to-day illusion that he was just under the weather, and Phoebe recalled that last trip as having upon it a glaze of perfection, her parents walking hand in hand on the beach and napping together in the middle of the day, her father taking Barry to the aquarium, the Naval Museum, outings that overjoyed her brother to a degree Phoebe found oddly sad. She and Faith and Barry were exemplary children, returning from the beach well before sunset each day so that no one would have to come fetch them, going to bed when asked without a word of protest. Yet within this harmony ran a jittery cord of apprehension. There was something studied, artificial in it.

And a strange thing was happening to Faith. She and Phoebe attended Mass each day, and while the priest gave his sermon, Faith would shut her eyes and tense her muscles limb by limb, starting at her feet and moving up, legs, torso, neck, and finally her face, which contorted into a terrible knot. Faith could hold this posture for staggering lengths of time, eyelids aflutter, breath coming and going in gasps while every strand of her slim thirteen-year-old's body stood out in quivering relief. For Phoebe these minutes were agony; she was terrified the priest would notice and halt his sermon, or that Faith would fall off the pew foaming at the mouth or even die—who knew? Mercifully, the congregation was small, and often she and Faith had a pew to themselves. Only when the priest reached the Last Supper did Faith suddenly relax. A tired, peaceful smile would float to her face.

After church Faith usually slept, in the car, on a couch or the sand, devouring slumbers much like the ones their father was prone to. But the exertions in church seemed to drain her of something, leave her weak. On the Scrambler one night she took the outside seat as usual, but when Phoebe and Barry were flung against her, Faith lost control of her limbs; twice her head slammed back against the metal beam with an awful *thung*ing noise. After the ride Barry left the car but Faith sat stunned, gripping her head. "Should I tell Daddy?" Phoebe asked.

"No!" Faith said, sitting up. "No." When they departed the ride, she was smiling again, a manic grin overlaid on her worn-out face, as if by failing for one instant to engage and astonish their father, she would be delivering him to his illness.

"Faith, what's that thing you keep doing in church?" Phoebe asked that night as they lay in bed, Faith cupping one palm around the lump on her head.

"Praying hard," her sister said.

Wolf returned from his shower, wet-haired and somewhat calmer. He and Phoebe were on best behavior now, like strangers sharing a train compartment. Phoebe showered, washing vigorously, possessed of a need to be absolutely clean. She combed the hair straight back from her face, pleased by the plain, childlike result. She wore her white summer dress. The bedroom seemed tiny with both of them in it.

They went back outside. Wolf took Phoebe's hand, less a gesture of affection, she thought, than a desire to anchor her. Huge chunks of limestone were piled in a seawall at the harbor's edge, and they hoisted themselves up to sit on one. The harbor was tiny, like a playground for the painted fishing boats. The sea looked dark and vast, streaked with silver bands of moonlight. Couples dined in the square nearby; sounds of their laughter and dishes lingered a moment, then vanished.

"Which direction is it?" Phoebe said.

Wolf gestured to the left, bulky cliffs a shade or two darker than the sky. "I guess Cornigila's a couple of miles that way," he said.

"Can you really walk there?"

"So they say," he said. "I guess there's a local train, too."

"Let's walk. I like the idea of walking."

"Whatever you want."

"I wish we could go now," Phoebe said.

"We wouldn't be able to see much," Wolf said. "Not that there's probably much to see."

"You're so grim," Phoebe said. "It's depressing."

Wolf turned to her. "It's funny you say that," he said, "because I'm finding your elation pretty hard to fathom."

"I'm not elated."

"You are!" Wolf said. "You act like a goddamn miracle is about to happen." He sounded exasperated, but in his face Phoebe saw the other thing, the trouble, and realized that Wolf was afraid.

"It's like you think this whole thing is some kind of game, like she's up there waiting for you. It's surreal," Wolf said, addressing the stars. "I find it absolutely surreal."

"Maybe you shouldn't have come."

"Are you kidding? The crazier you act, the gladder I am I did come."

Phoebe said nothing. Wolf took off his glasses and rubbed his eyes until they looked smeared. "It's a place," he said. "You'll walk up, you'll walk back down."

"Then what are you afraid of?"

There was a pause. "What I'm afraid of," Wolf said quietly, "is what's going to happen when the ghost you've been chasing all this time disappears into thin air."

"No," Phoebe said. "You're scared to go up there."

But she was only scaring him more. Wolf crossed his arms, looking into the water. "Why?" Phoebe said gently, turning to him. "Wolf, how come?"

"I don't know."

Phoebe put her arms around him, Wolf, her only ally. He rested his head between her shoulder and neck. "Why aren't you scared, is what I want to know," he said.

They decided to eat dinner, more for the ceremony of it than out of real hunger. At a table overlooking the sea they poked at bowls of steaming calamari in a thick red sauce. Couples surrounded them, elderly, teenaged, couples leaning together over glasses of wine, handing kicking babies back and forth. Phoebe watched a man lightly pinch a woman's cheek as they shared a cigarette, the woman laughing, her color high, a white flower wedged behind one ear. We're like them, she thought, taking Wolf's hand across the table, but the gesture felt like bluffing. Phoebe held Wolf's chilly hand and remembered spying through the crack in his kitchen door as Carla fumbled for his arm, Wolf breathing his fiancée's smell while he read the paper over her shoulder. And with sudden, eerie dispassion, Phoebe saw that Wolf would never be hers in the way he'd been Carla's, that the dazzling future she'd imagined with him was out of the question.

In the candlelight Phoebe stared at Wolf amazed, wanting to say this aloud. But his gaze was fixed in the direction they would walk the next morning. Maybe he already knew, Phoebe thought, maybe he'd known from the start. Maybe that was what scared him so much. It didn't matter. What mattered now was why. Why, Phoebe wondered, why was it that all her life the things she wanted most already belonged to someone else?

Back in their room Wolf dove into sleep almost instantly, his shirt still on. But no sooner had Phoebe closed her eyes than she felt again the drift and pull of memory.

The final night of their father's final trip to Mirasol. For the first time all vacation she and Barry and Faith had stayed on the beach into twilight, lying on their backs in the sand watching the first pale stars blink awake.

When their father loomed over them, they scrambled to their feet. "Forget it," he said, waving away their apologies. "I felt like getting outside." He seemed more tired than usual, heavy-headed the way he used to get when he drank. "Maybe I'll go for a swim," he said. "How about a swim, Faith?"

There was a startled pause. "I don't know," Faith said. "Maybe not, Dad."

They stood together in the cooling sand. Their father wore his bathing trunks, an old T-shirt pulled over them. "I can't leave this place without swimming once," he said.

"Let's go tomorrow," Faith suggested, "before we leave."

"Nah. Tomorrow I won't have the energy."

Faith glanced at Barry. Their father threw back his head. "It's gorgeous out here," he said. "Christ, look at that sky. I want to swim under that sky." And to Phoebe's joy he seemed his old self again, full of vigor and impatience. He lifted the T-shirt over his head and tossed it into the sand. Though he'd lost weight, he was still well-built, a different species entirely from the soft, overripe fathers of Phoebe's friends. The patch of dark hair on his chest made the crude shape of a heart. He was more than a father—he was a man, with strong legs and a mustache, a hard flat stomach they'd once taken glee in walloping with all their might, for it never seemed to hurt him. Though their father had once looked imposing, now he was tough and slight, distilled to his very essence.

"Come on." He held out a hand to Faith. "Please, babe," he said in a tight voice. "Come in with me."

It was a strange moment, for although they stood in a cluster, their father spoke only to Faith. Phoebe had a brief, hallucinatory sense that she herself was not actually there, was witnessing a private moment between her father and sister.

A hacking cough shuddered up from deep within him, painful to hear. "Come on," he said, to Faith. "Do this for me."

Faith started to cry.

Their father smiled, a ghost of mischief in his face. "What's the matter, you scared?" he cajoled her gently. Faith wiped her eyes, not answering. "That's okay," their father said. "I'm scared, too."

He took Faith's head in his hands and kissed the top of it. Phoebe wondered if her father had felt the hot bruise under her sister's hair. Then he pulled Faith against him, clasping her head to his bare chest as if it were a precious box someone else were trying to wrest from his grasp. Phoebe felt Barry go still beside her. Faith was sobbing now, her eyes closed. Their father's chest moved quickly, shallowly, as he breathed. Finally he let Faith go and began walking toward the water, feebly, like an old man. There was something terrible in the sight of their slender white father approaching that dark sea.

"Faith, go," Barry whispered fiercely. "Go!"

Faith started as if jerked awake. Without a word she left them and followed their father, who had reached the water's edge and was standing there as if waiting, knowing she would come. They went in together, bit by bit. Little waves were coming in; their father had to brace himself against their faint impact. Faith took his hand. Phoebe strained to see them in the fading light. She felt a pressure inside herself, as if something there were in danger of breaking. When the water reached her father's chest, Phoebe said, "I'm going in, too, Bear."

Barry made no reply. Phoebe ran to the sea. The water was warm, silky over her feet. Faith and her father floated close together; Phoebe saw only their heads. She went in farther, watching the dark water climb her legs, but when she looked up, she found they'd begun to swim away, down the beach. In the dusk they must not have seen her. Phoebe thought of calling out to them but hesitated, listening to the faint plash of their strokes. She thought of jumping in, of trying to catch up, but the water seemed vast and black and she felt tiny, powerless against it. If something should happen, she thought, they would never be able to save her.

Reluctantly she turned from the water and walked back up the beach. Her brother was hunched on the towel. Phoebe sat beside him, and they watched the tiny pair of heads move slowly through the water. Then it was too dark to see them. Barry made a choking sound, and only then did Phoebe realize he was crying. "Bear," she said. She caught the wet gleam of his cheeks and was about to ask what was wrong when she, too, began to cry, deep gasping sobs she neither understood nor could quell. Alone on this beach there seemed no hope for Barry and herself.

"Let's go back," Barry said. Phoebe nodded, turning to the water, thinking she'd call to her father and Faith and say they were leaving, but it was dark and her eyes were too messed up from crying to see anything.

"Phoebe, they don't care," Barry said. "Don't you get it? Let's just go."

They stood. Barry left their towel in the sand and took Phoebe's hand. Walking, she began to shiver, as if her tears were making her cold. They climbed to the boardwalk, then to the street lined with small square houses, each a different color. By the time they reached their grandparents' house, they had stopped crying. What had happened on the beach felt strange, distant. Inside the house their mother was setting the table for dinner, her hair falling from a pin. "Is everything okay?" she asked.

"Everything's fine," Barry said.

From an upstairs window Phoebe watched for her father and sister's return. It wasn't long. They moved slowly through the bleached street light, wet hair gleaming. The sight was ghostly, dreamlike. They seemed to hold a secret knowledge between them. Phoebe assumed this must have to do with the swim they'd taken, that if only she'd followed them in, she would be included. She was six years old. Suddenly Phoebe was mad at Barry for dragging her from the beach, mad at everyone for keeping her here, against her will, in the plain bright house. I should have gone in, she thought.

twenty-one

A carved sign pointed the way to Corniglia.

Phoebe and Wolf walked single-file along a narrow path high above the sea. Phoebe went first. The mood between them was resigned, workmanlike. Every word they'd uttered the night before seemed ludicrous now.

The path rounded a point, then doubled back inland to circle a bay wedged in the mountain's lap. Rocky promontories reached into the sea on both sides of it. The land was staggered for cultivation, lifting from the ocean like a vast flight of undulating steps, each one carpeted with grape vines growing on silvery wires. Phoebe walked gingerly, fearful of swerving off the path and onto the vines.

As the morning mist burned off, the heat became intense. Phoebe and Wolf skirted the bay and headed seaward along the second rocky point. Phoebe's heart began to stammer in her chest. They would turn the corner and there would be Corniglia. But the

turn revealed only another bay, larger this time, followed by another promontory. "Damn," Phoebe said, breathing shakily.

Under a sheen of sweat Wolf was pale. "Are you all right?"
she asked.

"Altitude," Wolf said with a faint laugh. Phoebe didn't get it.
"We're at sea level," he explained.

They began their journey around the second bay. The ribbons
of vineyard gave off a rusty smell. Phoebe wanted to go faster but
the path was narrow; she had to keep watching her feet. As they
neared the hub of the next point, a rush of dizzy blood filled her
head. Here it comes, she thought, expectation nearly stifling her
breath. But again she was disappointed—another bay, another
long arc inland.

"Jesus," Wolf said. He leaned against the cliff, hands on his
bent knees. Phoebe breathed lavishly, startled by the tinge of relief
she felt at not finding it yet.

She pressed her palm to Wolf's forehead. It was cool, wet.
"Maybe you're sick," she said.

He shut his eyes. "That's good," he said. "Your hand."

The sea had clarified with the light, deepening to turquoise.
The sky looked flat as tile. Phoebe kept her hand on Wolf's head,
and for a moment it seemed they could stand there indefinitely,
wind pouring against them.

Finally they resumed walking. The wind quickened, warm,
laced with bracing veins of cool. The clear, salty air stung
Phoebe's eyes. They circled the bay, rounded the far point. And
there it was.

Corniglia lay across another bay, draped over a cliff like a cat on a
banister, legs and tail dangling, looking ready to slide off at any
moment. Its colors were pale and luminous, opalescent pinks,
whites, a flash of orange tile.

Phoebe stared. The light hurt her eyes. She thought of salt, of
San Francisco, its bleached, dry colors. "Do you think that's it?"
she asked Wolf, suddenly fearful it might not be.

"Yes, I do," he said.

Phoebe grinned, she couldn't help it. "It looks exactly how I thought."

They headed inland, cutting around the bay. Wolf led, moving mechanically, his eyes fastened to the town. The thud of wind on Phoebe's eardrums mingled with the rhythm of their steps: I'm almost there I'm almost there I'm almost there I'm almost there. They passed a few dusty chickens in a coop, a small soiled goat on a chain. A white cat, milky fur sliding over its delicate spine as it picked its way downhill. A bell tolled noon as they rounded the bay. Gradually the path eased into a paved street and lifted them into Corniglia.

Tall houses shaded the town's steep streets, giving it a cool, cellar-like feel. Corniglia was crowded, but unlike Vernazza the feeling here was of residents rather than visitors. Women sat outside tiny produce shops, bright tomatoes and striped squash gathered around them like skirts. Bakers adjusted yellowy loaves in their windows. A riot of laundry flapped overhead, sheets and shirts and ladies' slips strung between the windows of opposing houses, flecked with sunlight. The laundry billowed and snapped in the wind like a thousand welcoming banners.

They took whichever streets led them higher, scaling the town like the slope of a pyramid. At last they reached an open, tree-lined square. It faced a church. To the left rose the mountain; to the right was nothing but sky. The perennial cluster of women in black sat huddled outside the church. The echoes of bells still hung in the air.

Phoebe stopped, wondering where to go next. She hadn't seen any cliffs. Wolf's skin was gray. A curious blankness inhabited his face, as if his mind had disengaged and drifted off. Behind him Phoebe noticed a smaller church in a spot higher than where they now stood. The church was hunched-looking, as if from years of battling the wind. Phoebe pointed to it but Wolf seemed not to react. She walked past him toward it.

The church was abandoned, its windows boarded up. It faced

the sea, its small courtyard partly enclosed by a salt-encrusted cyclone fence, candy wrappers tangled in its wire. A damaged-looking water fountain jutted sideways in front of it. Phoebe leaned over and drank, surprised the thing even worked. The water was warm. Wolf caught up to Phoebe and took her hand.

A low concrete wall divided church and courtyard from the sea—a ledge, really, no higher than Phoebe's waist. She peered over it. Directly beyond lay a tuft of dry weeds choked with cigarette butts, then nothing. The land simply fell away. Far below lay the ocean, seething white around chunks of rocks as if the rocks were dissolving in it.

They stared at the drop. Phoebe glanced left and right for comparable spots, fearful of being taken in by someplace meaningless. Wind tossed and flung her hair. She couldn't see another place. "I think this might be it," she said.

Wolf nodded. There were dark circles under his eyes.

Gently Phoebe touched the wall. The plaster was faded, chipped. Like the houses in Corniglia, its bleached surface held a tinge of pink. Faith must have stood on this wall, Phoebe thought; her feet—the weight of her body—must have rested on or near where Phoebe's hand was. Faith's feet. Phoebe turned to face the church, imagining her sister's footprints crossing and recrossing the small space of its courtyard. It seemed possible, even likely, that something was left, some shard of Faith's presence among the dust and pebbles and crushed glass. Some little thing. Phoebe leaned over the wall to peer among the cigarette butts, but Wolf seized her shoulders, pulling her back. "Not so close," he said.

"I'm—let go!" Phoebe said, unnerved by the pressure of his hands. He did, reluctantly, but hovered near her. Phoebe ignored him, trying to concentrate. This is the place, she told herself. It happened here. And she was rewarded, then, by a wave of clarity that seemed to lift her from the ground.

This was it. A ringing filled her ears.

This is it.

And so gigantic an event did not just disappear. Fossils,

Phoebe thought, the earth's shifting plates, everything left a print, no matter how stark or faint or deeply buried. She looked slowly around her, heart pounding. For it seemed now that she'd grasped the true object of her search: finding that trace, placing her hand upon some relic from the scene of Faith's death. As if doing so would correct the accident of time that allowed her to stand in the very place her sister had jumped from, and not be able to stop her.

Phoebe leaned over the wall. Wolf seized her shoulders again, but she let him this time. She was looking down at the sea, thinking what an infinite number of times its tides had flushed and reflushed those rocks, how many kids had sat smoking on this wall, tossing their butts, making out—it was that kind of place, you could tell—and this offended her, the defilement, the efface-ment of what few traces might be left. It was more than wrong, it was inconceivable. The true place would be protected from it. Something wasn't right, Phoebe thought, and the clarity she'd felt only moments before began to slip. She consulted the sky and found it empty, vacant as the silence following loud noise.

"I don't think it was here," she said.

"No?"

Phoebe shook her head. A pressure had risen inside her, a feeling of anger, expectation, so many years of waiting and how could this possibly be right? This. After all that. "No," she said, "I made a mistake."

"A minute ago you were sure."

"It doesn't feel right," she said. The cracked plaster, the dust. She had to get away.

"It's not that big a town."

"What about another town? I mean, how do we know it was exactly this town? We saw lots of towns just on the train."

"Phoebe, she was found here."

"Well I never saw that report or whatever it was, did you?" Phoebe said. "Did you see what it said? Because I never did."

Wolf took a long breath. "You can't suddenly call every fact into question."

"Believe me," Phoebe said, making an effort to speak calmly. "If this were the place, I'd know."

"But how? You were a little girl, thousands of miles away. Phoebe, come on! Listen to yourself." He was pleading with her. He wanted to get away, Phoebe thought, that was all.

"I'd know," she said, "because it would feel a certain way."

Wolf seemed about to speak. Then he crossed his arms. "Okay."

Phoebe looked around. The pressure began to recede. This wasn't the place—this was anyplace, no place. South of Corniglia she spotted another cliff even higher than this one, jutting farther out to sea. "It could be that," she said, pointing. "I bet it is."

Wolf moved between Phoebe and the wall. He braced himself against it, taking both her hands in his own, and looked straight into her eyes. "You could spend the rest of your life running up and down this coast," he said. "Next you'll be saying maybe it wasn't Italy, maybe it was Spain. But this has to end. Somewhere it has to end."

"It'll end," she said.

But Wolf's expression had clarified. There was something he wanted to say, something pushing out from behind his eyes. "Listen," he said. "This is the town, and this is the place. I promise, I swear to you—Phoebe, do you hear me?—I swear to you, it happened here."

He was squeezing her hands, his face so near Phoebe's own that for a moment it eclipsed both ocean and cliff. She began to protest, then stopped. Wolf's expression stopped her. Something had dropped away, laying bare a terrible knowledge she'd glimpsed in him before but never seen directly. His lips were white. Phoebe made a sound and stepped away.

Wolf released her hands. The determination fell from him, leaving a sick, questioning look. Phoebe covered her eyes, breathing into her hot palms.

"You were here," she said softly.

Her words made the certainty fall against her with brutal coherence, unyielding as earth. She felt buried in it. She ran to the church and tried its door, but the door was bolted shut. She looked back at Wolf and found him watching her with that odd remoteness, as if his mind had switched off or simply fled, as if the pressures upon it were too much.

Phoebe approached him. In Wolf's eyes she saw the damage clearly now, like broken glass underwater—obvious, once you knew what to look for. Abruptly Wolf twisted to one side, leaned over the wall and vomited down the cliff. Phoebe fled, sinking to the ground by the church, her eyes fixed to the convulsions of Wolf's back. When he'd finished, he rose slowly, wiping an arm across his mouth. He was looking out to sea. Phoebe's teeth chattered. Wolf went to the water fountain and took a long drink, splashing water on his face and then his hair, rubbing it in, then more on his face.

At last he came and sat on the ground beside her. Water dripped from his hair; he smelled of the sea wind. They didn't speak. Silty dust blew in their faces. Sitting with her back against the church, Phoebe couldn't see the ocean, only sky.

"I started thinking last night you might already know," Wolf said, sounding short of breath. "Or be starting to guess."

Phoebe stared at him. The event gaped before them, so gigantic. There seemed no way of approaching it. "Please talk," she said. "Please."

Wolf sat hunched over his bent knees, forehead resting on his wrists. He seemed unable to lift his head. "I saw her," he said. "I saw her, and I let it happen. Can you believe that?" He looked up at Phoebe, anguish and incredulity mingling in his face as if some part of him were still questioning the truth of these assertions. "I saw her. I *watched* her."

"But—wait," Phoebe said, disoriented. "She was—I mean, that stuff you told me before, was it true or not?"

"What I . . ."

"You know. The Red Army? The bank robberies?"

"Yeah," Wolf said. "All that was true."

Phoebe felt relief. She wanted things to be true. "And she came to Munich, like you said?"

"She did."

Phoebe waited for him to continue. "And then she left?" she asked timidly.

Wolf lifted his head. "Something happened in Berlin that I didn't tell you," he said, the words coming slowly. "Something bad."

Phoebe absorbed it. "Someone got hurt," she said instinctively. Then a dreadful intimation overcame her. "Someone died?"

Wolf just watched her.

"Who?" Phoebe said. "Someone from the bank robberies?"

"No, after," Wolf said. "After the Red Army dumped her. There were these other groups, and she joined in with one of them. June Second Movement, it was called."

"And they . . ."

"They set a bomb," he said. "At the Chamber Court. Faith I guess carried it inside, in a picnic basket. She put it in a trash can in the basement; it went off at night. They thought no one would be around, but a guy was, a janitor."

"And he died?"

"Yeah," Wolf said. "Head injuries."

Phoebe shook her head. She felt horror, not so much at the death itself, which seemed purely abstract, but at the smallest inkling of what horror her sister would feel, having been responsible. "Faith must've freaked . . ." she said.

"You can't imagine," Wolf said. "The papers told everything about the guy's life, how he was thirty-two, four kids, working the night shift and going part-time to the university. They went nuts with the story: working class guy gets cut down, you know, by these kids—anarchists, supposedly on his side."

"But Faith?" Phoebe said. "Setting a—there's no way. Wolf, there's no way."

"I think at that point she honestly couldn't see the danger," Wolf said. "All she knew was that these Red Army people had dumped her, and maybe if she'd been bolder, you know, proved herself more . . . it put her in a frame of mind to do anything. She'd already taken this drastic step, joining them, she'd staked everything on that being right. I think in her mind there was no going back."

Phoebe felt a trickle of relief. She'd found her bearings, could connect even these drastic motives with the person she knew as her sister. Wolf, too, seemed steadier now.

"You'd think she would've left Berlin the minute he died, but she didn't," he said, speaking rapidly now. "She must've stayed another week, went to the guy's funeral, found out everything she could about him, children's names, what kind of car he drove. She actually took a train to the suburb where he'd lived and found his house, stood across the street all afternoon watching people bring food to the widow, saw his older kids come back from school. It's incredible she didn't get busted, or questioned at least, except maybe the cops just figured anyone so overtly curious, plus a for-eigner, couldn't be more than a tourist."

Faith had arrived in Munich in a state wavering between incom-prehension and panic. "I killed a man," she would say, and freeze, staring at her hands or the wall while the fact ricocheted through her another time. She had bouts of uncontrollable shaking, so she couldn't walk or even sit up; she'd have to curl in a ball and shut her eyes until the shaking stopped. "I killed a man," she would say through chattering teeth. "God, please help me."

Wolf held her, trying to get Faith to look at his eyes. "Hey, hey, let's not talk about killing," he'd say. "No one killed anyone. There was just an accident, okay?"

But she seemed not to hear, her eyes closed. "I'm sick," she would say. "I'm so sick."

She was thin as a knife, her skin blue-white. All day long she would sit alone, thinking of what she'd done, as if some answer would come to her by thinking hard enough. But the answer was always the same: "I killed him. Like a gun to his head."

"Stop it," Wolf pleaded. "Look, if you hadn't been there, it would've happened just the same, Faith, I promise you. The guy would still be dead."

"But I *was* there. I had it in my hands. I could've dug a hole and buried it or else thrown it in the river and then he'd still be alive."

"If you'd known there was a guy to be saved," Wolf said gently, "you would've saved him."

"But I thought I was," Faith said, weeping now. "That's what I thought I was doing—saving that guy. That was the whole point of everything."

Wolf begged her to come home with him, back to San Francisco. She needed help, needed long-term counseling and therapy —hell, he didn't know what she needed. But whatever it was, she wasn't getting it sitting alone in his apartment while he worked at the shoe factory. He agonized over calling her mother and just laying everything on the table, but Faith made him swear he wouldn't tell a soul as long as he lived. "No one," she said. "You tell and I'm out the door." She meant it. Wolf's biggest fear was that she'd bolt—as long as Faith was with him she was safe, he thought, he could take care of her. But if she ran away, then who knew? So he didn't call. And as for professional help, Faith greeted the notion with contempt. "Help with what?" she said. Murder was a mortal sin. No one could help her but God Himself.

"Then maybe God will help!" Wolf cried, his own earthly arguments having failed him. "Maybe He'll forgive you."

"He'll punish me first," Faith said. "And I hope He does it soon."

She waited. Day after day she sat, waiting for her punishment to begin. She could not understand what was taking so long, then decided this waiting must be part of the punishment itself. But it pained her not to act; her impulse had always been to act, but now her actions had betrayed her. She was afraid to move.

"She could hardly leave the apartment," Wolf said. "The minute she was outside, she'd start thinking she'd left the oven turned on or a window open and something awful was going to happen. She felt cursed, a danger to everyone around her. We'd get on the bus and suddenly she couldn't find her change purse—she'd turn to me practically in tears, ransacking her pockets while everyone waited, and of course it would be right there, somewhere obvious . . ." He shook his head. "She was constantly bringing up stuff from the past, how she'd pushed some kid in a river and he cut his eye, or hitting your mom on her tricycle—her trike, for God's sake—how she'd ripped your mom's stocking and cut the back of her leg. In Faith's mind her whole life had boiled down to that. Hurting innocent people."

At night she would jerk awake and lie rigid with fear. "I don't know what to do, but I have to do something," she'd say, peering at the ceiling. Wolf would lean over her, putting his hand on her chest, trying to still the violent kicking of her heart. "I have to do something," she'd say.

But no, he told her, that was exactly wrong. There was nothing she had to do except find a way of living with what she'd done. "Look, awful stuff happens," he said. "People live with it, Faith, that's how life works."

"He has four children," Faith said. "One's only three years old."

"That's what I'm talking about!" Wolf cried, seizing on it. "You lived with that—you lost your father, and look, you survived it."

He knew instantly that it was the wrong thing. "Right," Faith said bitterly. "And look at me now."

There were long silences as Wolf spoke, but Phoebe just waited. She felt no more urgency, because now she knew—the missing

piece was in her hands. She was almost afraid to have the story
end, of what she would do when Wolf stopped talking for good.

With time Faith had calmed down, as Wolf had known she
would. Even panic and despair could be gotten used to, and gradually she began meeting people, hanging out a little. At times you
might not have known her from her old self, but Wolf saw a difference: she'd grown careless. That hope, the near-evangelical purpose that had fired even her wildest schemes, was gone. She went
parachuting with some U.S. soldiers kicking around Munich on a
day leave, something she'd never done in her life, but it left her
cold. "Her taste for danger resurfaced, little by little," Wolf remembered. "But not as a road to anything else, she just wanted
the feeling. The distraction of it. That scared the shit out of me."

While he was at work one day Faith met up with a group of
kids drifting south in a van. When Wolf got home that night, she
mentioned the possibility of joining them. Wolf said, sure, he'd
come along, too, but Faith seemed leery of this. "You wouldn't
like them," she said.

"Do you?"

"Not really."

"So, why go?"

Faith looked at her hands. "Maybe you should go home," she
said fearfully. "To San Francisco."

"What the fuck does that have to do with it?"

"We should go our separate ways."

"Why?"

"Because I'm bringing you down. I can see it," she said. "I'm
bringing you down, you need to get away from me."

Wolf wrapped her in his arms. Faith was sobbing. "Baby," he
said. "Baby, this has to stop. You have to let it stop."

Faith spoke into his shirt. "What?" Wolf said, pulling back so
he could hear. She was trembling, her eyes closed. "Baby, what
did you say?"

"I killed a man," Faith whispered.

Wolf ditched his factory job and got in the van with the rest of these kids. "They were dull," he recalled, "but there was an edge of desperation that kept things pretty lively. I've wondered sometimes if I'm the only one in that group that's still alive."

Their ostensible goal was a Jethro Tull concert in Rome, but really it was killing time at sixty miles an hour, everyone tumbling around in the carpeted back of the van, hitchhikers hopping in and out, a jam jar full of liquid LSD sloshing around in someone's lap. They'd lost the eyedropper, were just dipping in their fingers and licking off the drug. There was only one other girl besides Faith, an Italian sixteen-year-old who was shooting speed and running out of money. By the time they got to Rome, she'd been reduced to begging people for the cottons they used to shoot up. Once, in her excitement at receiving one, she'd dropped the cotton on someone's white shag rug and spent twenty minutes crawling around in search of it, running shaking fingers through the dirty white shag, such a miserable sight that finally Wolf gave her the money for a bag. For the next two days she kept staring at him with these beautiful ruined eyes, saying, "Please, baby, I won't ask again. But please."

"Faith kept trying to get me out of there," Wolf explained. "It shamed her, I think, being with these people, the level she'd sunk to. But I was pretty sure if I left, she'd forget what level that was, just lose herself in it."

After Rome, Wolf took over the driving, which eased his worst fears of pitching off the road, not to mention reducing the number of hitchhikers they stopped for. He tried to keep Faith in the front seat, next to him. Otherwise he could barely drive, he'd be so fixated on the rearview mirror, what she was doing back there. Often she would sleep, her head in his lap, fitful terrified sleeps, but at least she was there, at least he could put one hand on her head or rub her shoulders, whisper into her ear that her luck had

turned, everything was getting better now—couldn't she feel it?—
hoping Faith would hear it on some unconscious level and believe
him.

But when they hit the Italian coast, a remarkable change occurred. Faith glimpsed the sea and sat upright, staring at the water
with a mesmerized attention she'd not shown for anything in
weeks, save the ghastliness of her own crime. "It was amazing," he
told Phoebe. "There was just this total alertness, like she'd remembered something that threw a whole new light on her situation. I waited for it to fade but it didn't, she sat there riveted, and
as we drove along the coast, all that anguish, the lassitude, everything—it just drained right off her.

"We got stuck going inland a long time because of the mountains. I practically freaked out, thinking, Forget it, she's going to
slide back into her funk, but Faith stayed cool. After all these
damn tunnels we ended up at this town, Manarola, just one south
of Corniglia. I said, 'That's it, folks, we're stopping here,' and we
spent the night on the beach, this gorgeous beach covered with
white rocks, big pieces of shell—it looked like the moon. Faith
and I sat on a huge rock, and the tide came in around us. She was
calm, calm like I'd never seen her—even at her best she'd never
been calm. It was like she'd reached a new level, or that's what I
wanted to think. I'd been waiting so long for signs of hope."

And sitting there, sea drifting in around them, Wolf had understood for the first time what kind of life he wanted to live with
Faith. Maybe they wouldn't rise up into the sky the way he'd
thought, maybe the real thing was doing what his parents had
done, pay the rent, read the paper, hell, maybe that was the dare.
To live—day in, day out. Just live. It felt like a revelation.

They cleared away the shells and rocks from a patch of beach
and unrolled Wolf's blue down sleeping bag on sand that sparkled
like sand inside an hourglass. Whenever Wolf woke up, he'd find
Faith calmly watching the stars. What a relief it must be, he
thought, for her not to feel that panic anymore.

Next morning he and Faith climbed to Corniglia, packs on their backs. The others straggled far behind, but Wolf and Faith felt wonderfully light, like bubbles rising through water.

They wandered through the town. Faith bought a lavish spread for lunch, figs and mortadella and big cans of tuna. She'd turned in the last of her traveler's checks in Rome, but she didn't care. "Why not?" she said, grinning like the old days, the feather pillow days. They set the bags of food in the shade of the little church, then sat on this wall to wait.

Wolf took her hand. "You're better," he said. "Aren't you?"

"Yes."

"How did it happen?"

"It came to me," she said. "I just knew."

Wolf wanted to ask what exactly she knew but was afraid of breaking the spell, making it all disappear. They looked at the view.

"Beauty is close to God," Faith said. "That's why the beautiful things are so dangerous."

"Is God dangerous?"

There was a pause. "Yes," she said.

"I always had my doubts about the guy." Wolf was dying to hear her laugh.

"God is the end," Faith said, "there's nothing else." She turned to Wolf with a look of wonderment. "All this time, what were we ever searching for?"

"Christ only knows."

There it was—the laugh. "That's right," Faith said. "He does."

At that point their companions straggled onto the scene, and Wolf had a jealous fear of all that nice food getting eaten up. He and Faith left the wall, and they all sat down to eat.

"Where?" Phoebe asked. "Here? Where we are?" It didn't seem possible.

"Right by this church."

"Did it—how did it look?"

"I don't know," he said. "I remember it bigger. Higher or something. The wall."

When he'd stuffed himself, Wolf had leaned back against the church and dozed awhile. A stirring woke him. He opened his eyes and saw Faith standing on top of the wall, her back to him. "Get the fuck off there!" he'd shouted, scrambling to his feet.

Faith flinched, startled, then turned to look at Wolf, the wind pounding so hard he was amazed it didn't shove her right off. "Stop," she said calmly.

Instead of pulling her down the way he'd planned, Wolf reached up and took Faith's hand. It was warm.

"I'm thinking," Faith said. "Just let me think."

"Think down here."

"I can't," she said, this absolute calm in her voice, to the point where Wolf thought, Hell, am I the one who's acting weird?

He held her hand, warmed by the strength of her grip. "Let me go," Faith said.

"I can't."

"Yes, you can," she said. "Trust me this time. Everything will be good."

Wolf clung to her hand, to that strength. He wanted it. Faith towered above him in her torn flapping jeans and lacy blouse like some mythic creature from the prow of a ship. He felt dwarfed. The world was their event, but it had worn him out. Faith gazed at the horizon, then turned back to Wolf. "Now," she said. "For a minute. Let go."

Wolf let go of her hand and backed away. The rest of them were propped against the church, watching Faith sort of goggle-eyed. The whole thing felt unreal. Wolf was terrified but riveted, too, in the grip of something bigger than himself. He leaned against the church. Faith stood on the wall. She had such guts. Someday we'll look back on all this and die laughing, Wolf told himself, die when I admit how goddamn scared I was, and he felt himself reaching for that time, that calm, sweet place out ahead. Faith shielded her eyes from the sun. Wolf kept having the urge to sneak up behind her; the wind was loud enough so that she probably wouldn't know until he was on her, pulling her down—he thought of that and rejected it time after time because it seemed low, so undignified against the vision of Faith alone on that wall facing the sea and open sky, something pure, almost noble in the sight of her, and Wolf found himself thinking, If I let her do this, the whole craziness will finally be behind us.

"She looked back at me," he said. "I saw her face and I knew, I jumped up—" But before he could reach her, Faith had spread wide her arms and dived off the wall into the sea.

Wolf's swallowing made a prickling sound. Phoebe wondered if he might be sick again. She felt sick herself.

"Dove," he said. "Not a sound, not a shout. We sat there totally stunned—this sense of the inconceivable having happened —and suddenly I thought, Jesus Christ, this is all some fucking joke, she's hiding behind the wall, there's some ledge I didn't see, and I ran over there ready to grab her, but when I looked down I saw her shape on the rocks and I started screaming . . ."

He fell silent. "So what did you do?" Phoebe said, the words seeming to come from her chest, not her mouth.

"Well, the rest of them split. Took about ten minutes, they just sort of drifted away. Meanwhile, I . . ."

He paused again. Though his eyes were wet, he didn't cry. Lifting the story out of himself seemed to require all the energy he had. "I tore into town hollering and screaming, got it across pretty quickly that I'd seen a girl jump off the cliff. My hair was cut short for the factory, so I didn't look too much like a maniac. A few guys started climbing down the cliff where it wasn't so steep. They knew what they were doing—I got the feeling it wasn't the first time someone had ended up on those rocks. I followed them down—the whole time thinking, Maybe she's alive, please God, let her be alive—but when the first guys reached her, I could tell by the way they leaned over, I just knew. Still, I thrashed my way over there, half swimming, and then I really knew."

"How?" Phoebe whispered.

"Her neck." He could hardly speak. "Her neck was wrong. I put my hand on her chest . . ." He began to weep. The sound was wrenching, unpracticed. "I can't remember," he said. "I can't talk about this."

All hell had broken loose in the town, meanwhile. People streamed down the cliffs, some weeping, most just excited, as if it were a holiday. Wolf stood half freezing in water up to his chest, and only then did it hit him that what had happened up there was his fault, that he could have stopped it. He imagined Gail and Barry and Phoebe, having to face them, explain what had happened—no, his mind veered away, it was impossible, he could take almost anything but he couldn't face them, couldn't bear having anyone know. Finally, in a last mad effort, he'd sprinted back up to this spot, made sure Faith's stuff was all where they would find it, backpack, passport, all that, right by the wall. Then he'd fled back down the way they'd come, back to Manarola, stood on the train station platform heaving from exhaustion, thinking, What the fuck am I doing? Nothing seemed real, Faith dead, him running—to what? His head was about to explode; he thought he might actually lose his mind right there, just fly away, but then he heard a train coming through the mountain and in that moment Faith seemed to come to him, so clear, nothing to do with that body bent on the rocks. She was smiling, saying, Wolf, go on, are you nuts? Get on the train! Don't you see? she said. We're free, both of us. Get on the train, baby, what's the matter with you, go on! Urging him, her voice rising with the noise of the approaching train until they merged, the pounding train and Faith's voice, and when it pulled into the platform, Wolf got on feeling weirdly uplifted, elated almost, as if he and Faith were escaping the disaster together, one more hair-raising exit.

The feeling didn't last. By the time he got back to Munich, he was a zombie—Faith dead, his own fault, everything shrunk to dust beside the enormity of these facts. He'd been certain someone from the town who remembered would come after him with handcuffs. But no one did. Hell, maybe they'd never given him another thought.

Each time Wolf spoke to Faith's mother he would think, I'll tell her now, I can't go one more second without telling her, but he was always too afraid. He'd promised Faith he would never tell anyone about the bomb or the dead man—her last wish, it now seemed, and he couldn't bring himself to violate it. But without telling that, how could he explain the rest? So he'd find himself saying, "I'm sorry, Gail, I'm sorry, I'm so goddamn sorry," going on like that until finally she would break in. "Stop Wolf," she'd say gently. "Stop. What could you have done?"

Perversely, he'd found this comforting.

Wolf fell silent. "I don't see how you lived," Phoebe said. "After that."

He gave a mirthless laugh. "Tentatively," he said. "I lived—I live—very tentatively."

For years, he said, his life had felt to him like a kind of experiment. The question being, How long could he hold out before the whole thing came crashing down on his head? He'd pictured himself looking back on the present day or week from his jail cell, or while contemplating the grass outside the asylum where surely he was headed. But rather than defeating him, these thoughts had actually fueled Wolf with determination. Fuck it, he'd think, if he had to go down, he sure as hell wasn't going without a fight. And Faith was part of that feeling. Come on, he'd imagine her saying, have some guts, the last thing I want is to bring you down—although later he'd wonder if thoughts like these were merely self-serving. And gradually, as a life of sorts took shape around him, he'd started having them less, not that he'd resolved anything, he just didn't think so much. But meeting Phoebe that morning weeks ago on the stairs, Wolf had heard a voice that said, You knew it was coming; well, here it is. And he'd felt relieved.

"I promised myself a thousand times—until the second I opened my mouth—that I'd never tell you what happened up here." Wolf said. "But maybe I always knew that's where we were headed."

Phoebe looked at the wall, searching her mind for some question to draw Wolf out. But her mind was empty.

She shut her eyes and leaned her head against the church. Something unbearable was happening inside her, a sensation like despair, only deeper, more wrenching. The wind blew dust in her face. She felt as if she were dying, as if this pain were the pain of her soul being torn from her body. In fear she opened her eyes. The wind filled them with dust but it didn't matter, that pain, it was so small. It felt almost good.

Faith was gone. She was gone. Her absence felt as fresh to Phoebe as if she'd watched her sister dive from this cliff.

She tasted metal, the peculiar taste that follows a sudden sharp blow to the skull. A stunning emptiness blinked around her.

Wait, she thought. Wait.

In vain Phoebe tried to push her way clear, but her own thoughts seemed faint beside the vast finality of her sister's act. It whirled like a vortex, dragging every part of Phoebe irresistibly toward itself, swallowing her whole. She couldn't breathe.

Wait, she thought. But I always knew what happened.

Yet in all this time the reality of Faith's act, its brutal finality, had never really touched her. It was cloaked in gauze, in light, a terrific flash of light that left in its wake a soft orb.

Phoebe opened her eyes. The bright empty sky made a buzzing noise. The very air seemed full of panic, a tingling whiteness.

"Come on," Faith had said, reaching for Wolf. Phoebe wanted to follow them, but the door was closed. "Can you feel it?" Candlelight on the kitchen walls. "Can you?" Faith asked. "Can you?" And Phoebe did, at seven years old. She knew what it was.

"Come on," Faith said. Something behind that door. Faith opened every door she found, but Phoebe was afraid to.

A flash of light. Then a long glow.

Faith opened every door.

One gesture. Everything distilled.

Faith spent herself. She gave herself away. And time stopped.

She killed us both, Phoebe thought. Killed all of us.

Phoebe's limbs hurt. She wanted to move. She stood up.

The sea opened before her, wide and still. Cowed to stillness, Phoebe thought, the sea and everything else. She walked toward it.

"Stop!" Wolf cried.

Phoebe gave a violent start. Turning, she saw Wolf on his feet, poised to spring at her. She opened her mouth to speak but found she could not; her own astonishment silenced her. Wolf actually thought she would jump. Phoebe strained to imagine it—standing here, making that choice—but her mind veered away in disgust.

"I'd never do it," she said, staring at Wolf in disbelief. "Never. I would never do it." And as she spoke, Phoebe's perception of the act itself began to shift. It was a choice that appalled her.

Huddling with her mother and Barry on the cliff near the Golden Gate Bridge, releasing Faith's ashes to the wind. Feeling so small, just the three of them together—hardly even a family. And her sister chose this.

"What about us?" Phoebe said. "What did she say about us?"

"I don't remember."

"Something, though? She said something?"

"I don't know." He looked uneasy.

"But I mean, what did she think?"

There was a long pause. "I don't think she thought," Wolf said.

Phoebe shook her head. Her ears were ringing. "Okay," she said, "that guy who died had children. But what about us?"

She looked at Wolf, who knew nothing, and was engulfed by a surge of wild anger. "I can't believe she did it," she cried. "I can't believe she stood here and did that to us!" Each word incensed her further, until she felt crazed with the need to vent her rage. "Was she out of her mind?" she shouted. "Standing here and— goddammit!" She kicked the outside of the church, hurting her foot, knocking flakes of plaster to the ground. She pounded it with her hands, raking them over its rough surface until a hot, delicious pain flashed through her. "Goddammit!" she cried. "Goddamn her!"

From behind, Wolf took Phoebe's hands, scraped and bleeding from the plaster's abrasion. He folded her in his arms, holding her still. "Stop it," he said. "You're hurting yourself."

Phoebe let her weight fall on Wolf. "I hate her," she said. "I hate her more than anything."

"Okay," Wolf said gently, holding her.

After a while Phoebe turned around, facing him. Wolf watched her a moment, as if to gauge her calm. "Phoebe, I have to say this," he said. "The last thing Faith wanted was to hurt you— any of you. In her mind it was a sacrifice. She was trying to right a balance." He paused, breathing hard. "The fact that she caused more misery is just a horrible irony. Her worst fear, all over again."

He let go of Phoebe. She moved away from him and hunched against the church, its stone warm at her back. She shut her eyes.

Can you feel it?

Faith opened every door.

Reaching, reaching. Whatever it took.

Come on, Faith said. Come on, come on. A lump on her head, who cared? A bloody nose? So much the better.

And they'd loved her for it.

Adored her.

Everyone had.

Watching. Silently egging Faith on as she climbed or pushed or mounted the high dive, craving the spell that fell on the world when she risked her life.

Strangers scrambling over rocks, holding her sister's wet head in their strangers' hands. Not what Phoebe had imagined. Policemen picking through her things. A whole life—a warm thing—broken into procedures. Not what Phoebe had imagined. The opposite.

And she was riven, then, by a vision of her sister unlike any she'd had before: a girl like herself, reaching desperately for something she couldn't see but sensed was there, a thing that always seemed to evade her. Reaching violently, giving herself to that violence, only to find, when normal life resumed, that she'd done a thing she couldn't live with.

"I should've known," Wolf said. "That's the thing. I should've guessed."

Phoebe opened her eyes. Wolf was facing the sea. "I walked away," he said, shaking his head. "Just walked away."

In his voice Phoebe heard the unspeakable weight of having seen, having been responsible.

"When I saw you on the stairs that day," he said, "I thought, Thank God, I can finally do something for Phoebe. You needed help and I thought, I can help her, she deserves help and I can help her. Like a brother, almost. But something happened. It was like an undertow, and by the time I felt it, it was already too late, I couldn't stop."

Phoebe went to Wolf and put her arms around him, to silence him. She couldn't bear to have him explain himself. But Wolf went on.

"If I'd just stayed by the wall. Not even held her hand, just stayed. Why walk away? I've asked myself a million times."

Phoebe held him. She wanted to comfort Wolf, to absolve him, but of course she was powerless.

"If I'd just—" he said. "Then running away—"

"Please don't," Phoebe said, holding him. "Please."

"Running away when she—"

"Don't."

"Then, after everything else, I couldn't even stay. I ran."

"But then you came back," Phoebe said. "I found you." And only in speaking these words did their simple truth affect her, the weight of her debt to Wolf, her gratitude. "She disappeared," she said, "but you came back."

"Came back where?" Wolf said. "I sat on my ass in Munich."

Phoebe shook her head. Some door had opened in her mind, a shaft of light she and Wolf could move toward. "You helped me," she said. "There was no one else." She was speaking as much to herself as to Wolf. It was true—he'd helped her when she needed help. "You did," she said.

"No," Wolf said. But he clung to Phoebe as if she were the last thread binding him to the earth.

She thought of him whispering into Faith's ear as Faith slept in his lap in the van, and Phoebe whispered now, to Wolf. "I found you," she said. "You saved my life."

"There were a million things I could've done," Wolf said. "A million things." He sounded tired.

"I found you," Phoebe said.

Wolf said nothing.

After a while they moved apart and stood side by side at the wall, looking down. It seemed to Phoebe that a long time had passed since they'd come up here, more than a day. More than a year.

The light had changed, the sea with it. Now it crinkled like a rind, a deep, luminous silver.

They stood and stood, as if waiting. But what could possibly happen? It had all happened years ago.

Wolf seemed calmer, Phoebe thought. Or perhaps his mind had started to wander. Her own had, she couldn't help it. Her mind just drifted away.

Water moved on the rocks, washing them clean. Yet this was the place, the very place where Faith had jumped. There was nothing left, not a trace.

"Let's go back," Phoebe said.

The sun fell as they walked, burning the sky. Phoebe felt as if she and Wolf were the last two people leaving the scene of an accident.

In the end you had to. What else was there to do? You left and went on with your life.

Phoebe wondered if Faith could have known this when she threw herself away.

Time never stopped, it only seemed to.

part four

twenty-two

Phoebe returned to San Francisco in the first week of September. It was late afternoon when her flight touched down, and pressing her face to the plastic window, she watched the land clarify from a white-washed blur into houses and roads, turquoise fingers of water.

She'd called home from Heathrow Airport, the first time since leaving in June. Her mother had sounded ecstatic. But as Phoebe stepped from the plane into a pool of bright light flooding the thick airport glass, she thought at first there was no one to meet her. She walked on uncertainly until her mother's arms were around her, her mother's hair in a softer, more natural style, small gold hoops in her earlobes. Phoebe hadn't recognized her.

Arm in arm they walked to the baggage claim and then to the Fiat, each carrying half the unwieldy backpack, dusty and strange-looking in its new surroundings. "I can't believe you tromped around under this thing," her mother said. "I'm surprised you're not a hunchback."

"But I did!" Phoebe told her breathlessly. "I got totally used to it."

Riding home, she squinted in awe at the sherbet-colored houses, the familiar brown hill branded SOUTH SAN FRANCISCO— THE INDUSTRIAL CITY like the hide of a cow. The city felt vast, metallic and glassy, so different from cities in Europe.

By the time they reached San Francisco proper, conversation had flagged. Phoebe felt as if she had lost the power to read her mother. The new hairstyle, the short-sleeved black sweater and the thin, graceful arms at the wheel—all of it threw her into confusion. For the first time in weeks the memory of their fight reared up again in Phoebe: the terrible thing she'd said, her abrupt and outrageous departure.

"So. You had fun over there," her mother finally said.

"Not really," Phoebe said. "Not fun."

Her mother's brows rose. She said nothing.

"It was hard," Phoebe said.

"Hard in what way?"

"Scary."

A tender look crossed her mother's face. Only when it had passed did she turn to Phoebe. "I was scared, too," she said.

"I sent you postcards," Phoebe protested. "I told you I was fine!" But only now did it strike her, for the first time, how little comfort her postcards would have provided.

They spent the remainder of the ride in silence.

Phoebe had pictured her first weeks home as a kind of montage: running to classes at Berkeley, coming into the city at night for long garrulous dinners with her mother and Barry and Jack—Jack, whose respect she would finally have earned, going off on her own and surviving.

A letter from Berkeley awaited her. It had come shortly after she'd left, in response to her own request for admission deferral. Since Berkeley didn't offer this option, the letter said, Phoebe's request was being treated as a withdrawal. If she wished to reap-

ply for the subsequent year, 1979, she should note the usual November deadline.

Phoebe reacted to this news with disbelief, then panic. Frantically she called the Admissions Office, but the only concession she
managed to wrest from the officer with whom she spoke was an
agreement to revive her application to be considered for admission in January, versus the next September. She would learn in
late October whether she'd been accepted.

On her second night home, Phoebe met her mother and Jack and
Barry for dinner at Basta Pasta, a new restaurant in North Beach.
Her mother and Jack arrived straight from work, holding hands.
Barry came later, having driven in directly from the airport after a
business trip to Tokyo.

The moment Jack greeted her, offhand, still breathing smoke
from his cigarette, Phoebe saw how deeply she'd miscalculated his
reaction to her disappearance. Jack's pale blue eyes flickered with
skeptical indulgence, a look he plainly reserved for those he
viewed as a royal pain in the ass, yet had to treat well.

Jack had never been to Japan, and when Barry arrived, he was
eager for information. "Barry O'Connor's prediction: next big
electronics fad," Jack said. "Any ideas?"

"I've got it right here," Barry said, and pulled from his briefcase a miniature Sony tape player with tiny earphones attached,
inspired, he said, by the chairman's wish to listen to opera while
skiing.

Jack donned the headset and fiddled with the buttons. "Sound
quality is unbelievable," he bellowed at a volume that made
Phoebe wince.

"What did you eat over there?" their mother asked.

"Raw fish."

"Good God. What did that taste like?"

"Tasted raw," Barry said, grinning.

"You guys act like you haven't seen each other in months,"
Phoebe said, more peevishly than she'd meant to.

Her mother turned to her. "That's because we're usually in close touch."

There was a tense silence. Jack removed the headset and placed it quietly on the table. When he looked at her mother, Phoebe saw in Jack's eyes a tenderness that startled her.

"Walked into that one, Pheeb," Barry said, but no one laughed.

For the rest of the meal Phoebe sat in virtual silence. She'd wondered on the plane how much to reveal about her trip, but everyone's questions had been so perfunctory. And it struck Phoebe then, with sudden, dazzling force, that she knew what had happened to Faith. She knew. She could say it right now, "I found out what happened to Faith," and watch their lively faces go still with surprise. But Phoebe said nothing.

Afterward Barry offered to drive her home. They rode first to Coit Tower, hooded in fog but still swarming with tourists, some gamely feeding coins into the pay telescopes, as if these might have the power to bore through the whiteness. Barry parked and they sat in the Porsche.

"Look, I can see things are tense with you and Mom," he said.

"Tense," Phoebe said, half laughing.

"I think she was too scared while you were gone to really be mad," Barry said. "So you're getting it now."

Phoebe looked out the window. "I think Jack hates me."

"Give it some time."

Phoebe glanced at her brother, amazed that he seemed to take no relish at all in her exclusion. She had an urge to confide in him, tell him what she knew about Faith, but as the moments passed, Phoebe reconsidered. Why? she thought. News of their sister was the last thing Barry wanted.

"Anyway," he said, "I'm glad you're back. For what it's worth."

"I don't see why, Bear."

He looked surprised. "Come on," he said. "You're my sister."

In silence they gazed through the runny windshield. Now and

then a cluster of lights flared up through the fog like live coals under white smoke. "Were you scared, too?" Phoebe said. "While I was over there?"

"Yeah," Barry said. "Especially when you weren't at the Che Guevara screening, I thought, Shit, she's just, like, gone—"

"Oh my God!" Phoebe said. "Mom's film."

Barry glanced at her. "That was months ago," he said. "Anyhow, at the same time I kept having this feeling you'd be okay. That was stronger, I guess. In the end."

"Huh." She was disappointed.

"Not that I wasn't relieved—"

"But you're right," Phoebe said. "You are. I'm the kind of person who stays around." For some reason she laughed.

"You're a survivor," Barry said simply, his earnestness giving the cliché an unlikely ring of truth. "You just are. You and me both."

That night, as Phoebe lay in her sister's bed with the chimes fluttering at the window, she was racked by an intolerable sorrow. For years those chimes had seemed an echo of her sister's voice, reminding Phoebe that Faith was there, somewhere, waiting for her. Now they sounded empty. Phoebe moved back into her old room the next day for the first time in years, sleeping before a bright-eyed audience of faded stuffed animals.

Phoebe remembered a movie she'd seen years before on TV called *Latitude Zero*. When a ship reaches latitude zero, its captain finds himself transported to a marvelous land beneath the sea where the streets are paved with diamonds. He grabs a handful of gems and crams them into his tobacco pouch to bring home with him, prove what he's seen, but back in the real world he opens the pouch and finds it stuffed with tobacco again. No one believes him.

Phoebe's first week home was blessed with a certain novelty despite its disappointments, but as the second week passed, a numbing depression settled over her. Nothing had changed, and against the sameness of this city, her life within it, Phoebe's time away—a lifetime unto itself—seemed reduced to a brief, hallucinatory flash.

She began staying indoors, wandering the house or lying on her bed staring out the window, unaware of the passage of time. She slept and slept, and when she wasn't asleep, she daydreamed about her journey. Phoebe saw herself cloaked in a golden haze, riding trains, waking up beside Wolf with fresh sunlight pouring over the bed—could she really have been there, done those things? Already it seemed far-fetched, an exotic wish. Even her worst times assumed, in retrospect, a powerful, moody allure. But Phoebe gave her present self no credit for them. On the contrary, the subject of her memories seemed another person altogether, to be admired, envied, measured against.

She and Wolf had ridden by train from Vernazza up to Genoa, then into France. "What about the Volkswagen?" Phoebe kept asking as they were making made these arrangements. "Shouldn't we get the car?"

"I'll get it later," Wolf had replied, evasively, and finally, "The thing was on its last legs anyway." Only during their two days of chaste train rides in crowded sleeper cars did it occur to Phoebe that the real reason might be that he didn't want to drive with her. Driving would be like before, with everything between them still about to happen.

Finally they'd crossed the Channel and arrived in London, cool, doused in light rain, looking quite unlike the festive city Phoebe remembered from her June arrival. In a heavy mood they walked to the Laker Airways office and arranged for her return the following day. To escape the rain they went to the National Gallery, trudging dutifully among the portraits and landscapes, then Wolf had phoned some friends, whom they'd gone to meet at a pub on Hampstead Heath.

By then it was dusk, the air filled with a pungent odor of smoking wood. The sky was beginning to clear, a virulent orange behind the last debris of clouds. Phoebe drank a half-pint of cider and grew tipsy—she was going home—watched Wolf laughing across the big table over his pint of Guinness topped with its layer of creamy foam and was struck by the change in him. Wolf's hair had grown, he was tanned, wore two days' growth of beard, but the change went deeper: an absence of some tension in his face that Phoebe had come to assume would always be there. He looked free. And she herself had occasioned that freedom—not Faith or Carla, not anyone else. She had lifted a terrible weight from him. They were sharing it now, though from Wolf's peaceful face, Phoebe wouldn't have guessed he felt anything.

As if hearing her thoughts, Wolf glanced up. Through the smoke and clatter and wet carpet smell Phoebe sensed his acknowledgment, his gratitude.

She left her chair and went outside, knowing Wolf would follow. Loud drinkers had amassed at wet, steamy tables. Amid the humid smell of beer and rain she looked over a hedge at the Heath, reams of lush grass steaming faintly in the sudden, late sun. Wolf came up behind her, wrapped his arms around Phoebe and lifted her hair, putting his face to her neck and breathing her smell. Phoebe turned around and they hugged, but when she tried to find Wolf's lips, he stepped away, releasing her. They looked at each other. And instantly Phoebe knew it was over, that this embrace had been the last of something. The desire had left Wolf's face, and his eyes, when Phoebe looked at them deeply, remained opaque. She felt an ache in her chest.

"I'm going home, too," Wolf said.

Later, as they said a tense good-night outside their separate bed-and-breakfast rooms, Phoebe was despondent. "I feel like it's gone," she told Wolf. "All of it."

He took her in his arms. "It's the opposite," he said. "It'll always be there. We're just moving away from it."

And afterward, lying in her soft, narrow bed, Phoebe had felt the Heath outside the window, dark and still as a lake, and all at once Corniglia had felt so distant, as if two days of train rides had brought them years away, completing their escape.

In her third week home, Phoebe called him.

"Phoebe," Wolf said, sounding taken aback. "You at school?"

"No." Morosely, she explained the Berkeley debacle. Talking on the phone to Wolf felt strange; she'd never done it, except on first arriving home, a brief call to tell him she'd made it.

"How are you?" she asked shyly.

"Hanging in there," he said. "I seem to have a few clients left."

"Did you—"

"At least—" They both laughed, exasperated by the lag time in their overseas connection. "The Lakes are in Brussels another six months," Wolf yelled, as if volume might solve it, "so that's a reprieve."

"How are things with Carla?" She was hoping for the worst.

"Improving."

"Are you still getting married?"

He hesitated, the old guardedness back in his manner. "Unclear."

"But you might?"

"I'm hopeful," he said. "Let's leave it at that."

Phoebe felt a flash of despair. "What about the car?" she asked. "Did you get it back?"

He laughed. "A friend of mine was in Pisa, said it was stripped to nothing. So I'm buying a Fiat."

"We have a Fiat," Phoebe said uselessly.

"You take care," Wolf said. "Keep in touch." Meaning, Phoebe thought, I'd rather we not speak again.

"Okay," she said. "You too."

She'd lost weight in Europe, and despite her unease in Faith's room, Phoebe couldn't quell an urge to measure herself against her sister's old clothing. Finally she succumbed.

The garments released a peppery, cinnamon smell as she pulled them on. And they fit, lo and behold; some were even rather loose. Ecstatic, Phoebe leapt around her sister's room in corduroy hip-huggers and a macramé blouse, the star-buttoned jacket pulled over it. She blasted King Crimson, lit too much incense and posed breathlessly before the mirror in a floppy hat with a long peacock feather attached. Abruptly she collapsed on the bed, drained and lightheaded, resting her eyes on the batik ceiling while outside the window Faith's chimes made their sad, splintering sound. She fell asleep.

It was almost dark when Phoebe woke. She climbed from Faith's bed feeling groggy and soiled, then went to the basement and scrounged up five grocery boxes, which she brought upstairs. She packed her sister's clothing into the boxes, folding it neatly, adding Faith's hats, her Indian beads and poison ring and clay scarab on a leather string. She had to go back for more boxes. When everything was packed, Phoebe sealed the boxes shut with thick plastic tape. She stacked them into a column in the middle of Faith's room and left them there.

Phoebe still paid occasional visits to the Haight, sniffing the bowls of powdered incense at her favorite occult shop, lying on her back in the grass on Hippie Hill. But the pleasure afforded her by these pastimes was fleeting and faint. She felt like the ghost of her former ghostly self, flickering outside even the narrow, shadowy realm where she'd once been at home. And there was nothing to replace it.

Everything should be different, Phoebe kept thinking, now that she knew what had happened to her sister. But that difference had failed to register in the world. Perhaps the problem was that except for Wolf, no one knew what she'd learned about Faith. Tell her! Phoebe would urge herself while she and her mother unloaded broccoli and yogurt from Cal-Mart bags in their quiet kitchen. Go on, say it. But something always stopped her—fear of betraying Wolf, fear of more unpleasantness with her mother that she would be powerless to undo.

During Phoebe's fourth week home, her mother returned

from work one evening and announced, with an odd mix of anxiety and disregard, that for several weeks her realtor had been negotiating with a buyer for the house. As of today, it was sold.

Phoebe took to reading the newspaper voraciously each day. President Carter, Idi Amin, Mayor Moscone—she hung upon their words and deeds as if she might be called upon to respond. John Paul I dead after thirty-four days as Pope, gold at a record high, Isaac Bashevis Singer the winner of the Nobel Prize. Sid Vicious charged with killing Nancy. Sadat and Begin making peace while the Middle East boiled. That was the world. And separate though it felt from the tiny web of hilly streets where Phoebe led her life, she strained to touch it, press her face to the glass. The more she knew of the world, the less painful was its absence.

Early one evening Barry picked Phoebe up and drove her to Los Gatos for the night. He'd fixed up a guest room, daisies by the bed in a blue ceramic vase. They dined at an elegant Indian restaurant tucked incongruously in a vast shopping mall, and both drank too much red wine, nervous, overanxious that the visit go well.

The next morning, still woozy, Phoebe accompanied her brother to work. The friendliness of his colleagues surprised her, to say nothing of their youth; in their Levi's and longish hair, they reminded her of brainy high school students wired from too many all-nighters.

Barry's office building was the diametric opposite their father's at IBM—sprawling and flat, full of glass and light and dozens of the sleek, unapproachable computers, which Barry and his colleagues handled with the same rough ease they might use to operate a sink. There was a grand piano, plus two massive refrigerators stocked with exotic juices. Phoebe had expected her brother to strut and brag in his childish way, steeled herself for it, but Barry's authority seemed effortless. After all, she reasoned later, the company was his own, all the people there his employees. What was left for him to prove?

Phoebe visited her brother often after that, boarding the train at a station near the Greyhound bus depot. In the flat, open spaces of Silicon Valley he taught her to drive, sitting by with apparent unconcern while Phoebe jammed the gears of his Porsche, narrowly avoiding stray shopping carts in Safeway parking lots. When she was comfortable enough, Barry encouraged her to follow the narrow roads twining up the thickly wooded hills. Descending, he taught her to downshift. "If you're going to drive, it might as well be fun," he said.

Phoebe volunteered to help her mother look at apartments, hoping somehow that the project would bring them together. It was dreary business, trudging through abandoned-looking rooms, trying to imagine their lives occurring inside them. Her mother's anger had winnowed down to a tense cordiality that Phoebe found even more oppressive. The onus was on her, she sensed, to break the spell between them, but Phoebe had no idea what her mother expected.

On Russian Hill they saw a two-bedroom apartment with high ceilings and honey-colored floors. The bedrooms were far apart, an advantage (though it went unmentioned) now that Jack often spent the night. In spite of herself, Phoebe felt a certain excitement, wandering the grand, empty rooms as dusk blinked in through the curtainless windows. Her mother, too, seemed inspired by the place. "A dining room!" she exclaimed, though their own was much bigger. "We can start throwing dinner parties."

They discussed rugs and desks and curtains, which of their several couches they would keep. Their voices echoed through the empty rooms. Abruptly they heard themselves, and a momentary shyness overcame them.

"Mom," Phoebe said.

Her mother looked up.

Now, Phoebe told herself—now! There was a long pause

while she wondered what exactly she'd meant to tell her mother. For something else was pushing out from inside her, clamoring to be heard. "I'm sorry I disappeared," she said. "And missed your film." It was almost a whisper.

Her mother crossed the room and took Phoebe in her arms. Her lemony smell seemed to arrive from a great distance. "I missed you," she said.

Back outside, they paused to look at the building. It was of an old California style, salmon-colored, decorations like frosting, lacy black grillwork over massive glass doors. Behind it the sky was a dark, lucid blue, fog rushing across it. Phoebe's pulse was still racing from what had happened in the apartment. What was it about Faith that she'd wanted so badly to impart? It seemed to Phoebe now that she had never named it directly, even to herself. Was it Wolf's having been present when she died? The terrorists? The dead man? But no, it was none of these. The truth was that her sister had killed herself. And everyone knew it.

As they walked to the car, Phoebe's mother took her hand.

They rented the apartment. They would move the fifteenth of October.

Through open windows a wind flushed their house, lifting clouds of silty dust from the floors, bare now of furniture. Moving men with trembling biceps carried everything down the brick steps to a long Bekins truck.

Barry had taken the afternoon off to help with the move. He and Phoebe had the job of sorting through their father's paintings, picking three or so to keep, packing up the rest to give away. In silence they descended the basement steps to the storeroom, a jigsaw of canvases crammed haphazardly from wall to wall. Barry unfolded several huge Bekins boxes and they began, Phoebe handing paintings to Barry, who fitted them carefully inside the box. The older paintings were deeper inside the room, so as they worked, the years seemed to lift from Faith, transforming her from the sad teenager propped by their father's hospital bed to a sweet, grinning child.

Phoebe lifted one painting and paused, holding it up to the stray, weak light from the door. It was a portrait of her sister aged eight or nine, standing on the very cliff where, not ten years later, they had scattered her ashes into the sea. She wore a white sunsuit and was grinning, reaching out, a purple ice plant flower clutched in her fist. "Bear," Phoebe said.

He came over. They looked at the painting. At first glance, Faith appeared in her usual state of chaotic happiness, but the longer Phoebe looked, the more her sister's hectic grin seemed belied by a deeper anxiety, as if with this flower she were warding something off. Phoebe looked away, jarred by the impression, then wondered if what she'd seen was really there. She couldn't tell. When she looked at the painting again, her sister just seemed happy.

Barry seemed about to speak, then didn't. "Let's keep it," he said.

Finally the paintings were packed, arranged meticulously in four giant boxes and part of a fifth. "I guess we should pick two more," Barry said, but he seemed restless, weary of the project. "You do it, Pheeb."

Phoebe looked at the boxes of paintings, drawn by the thought of going back through them slowly, losing herself in the project. But no. It was the memory of a longing.

"Maybe just that one," she said.

They dragged the boxes into the garage, then went outside. The backyard was overgrown, fragrant. Miniature daisies peppered the grass. Barry stretched, reaching toward the sky, then he grinned and dropped to the ground, lying on his back. Phoebe lay down beside him, her head at Barry's feet. The earth was warm, soft. The gloom seemed to lift from her then, like a dark oily bird flapping out of her chest. She breathed the smell of grass and watched the slow-moving clouds.

"You hear those birds?" Barry said, his voice far away, husky-sounding from lying down. "That chattering? You hear it, Pheeb? I don't know why but I love that sound."

As Phoebe sat reading *No Exit* in Washington Square one Saturday, someone blocked her light. "Phoebe?" a man said.

She looked up, recognizing the guy but unable to place him. He was carrying a little girl in his arms. "Remember?" he said. "You trained me."

"Oh yeah. God," she said, shaking her head. "You're . . ."

"Patrick. This is my daughter, Teresa."

"Hi," Phoebe said. She left her seat to look at the child, who had curly red hair and her father's green eyes. "She's so pretty," Phoebe said. "I can't believe you have a daughter."

Patrick laughed. "It amazes me, too." He wore loose jeans with what looked like swipes of plaster on them. After a moment he said, "You disappeared."

"I went to Europe."

"Just . . . up and went."

"Pretty much."

"Art was sure you'd been murdered. He kept saying, 'I know that girl, she's never even late!' I guess he finally reached your mother."

"Poor Art," Phoebe said. "I should go apologize."

"I'm sure he's forgiven you."

Teresa was squirming. Patrick set her in the grass and she tottered toward Phoebe, slapping her fat hands on the bench.

"Do you still work there?" Phoebe said.

"Actually not," Patrick said. "I was down on my luck that month, but things've picked up, so I quit. Spend some more time with this one." He lifted the little girl back into his arms. "I'm a sculptor," he said. "My studio's right over here, on Green Street. Three eighty-five. Come around during the day sometime, I'll make you coffee. Or you can make it—aren't you sort of an expert?"

"All right," Phoebe said, laughing. "Maybe I will."

As Patrick crossed the square, his daughter swiveled her head like an owl, keeping Phoebe in sight. Phoebe waved to her. The bells of the Church of Sts. Peter and Paul filled the air, striking the hour.

Something was gone. But something also was beginning. Phoebe felt this more than understood it—a jittery pulse that seemed to flutter beneath the city. A new decade was upon them. In Barry's office the mood of manic anticipation infected Phoebe at times with a wild certainty that the world was in the grip of transforma tion. Everyone seemed to feel it—the clean, inarguable power of machines, the promise of extraordinary wealth. It filled them with hope. Phoebe was amazed that the world could ever feel this way again, much less so soon. Yet she felt it herself.

Women were cutting their hair. Not the soft, blow-dried Dorothy Hamill cuts of a few years before, but sparser, tighter ones, emphasizing the angles and power of the head. In front of the mirror Phoebe would gather her own reams of hair and hold them behind her, away from her face. The idea of cutting it off appealed to her, the lightness of it, like stepping out from behind a pair of heavy drapes.

Toward the end of November, Phoebe drove to Coit Tower at dusk. By now the tourists had gone, and there were plenty of spaces in the parking lot. Phoebe parked her mother's Fiat and got out.

It was dusk; a charge seemed to hang in the air. There was no fog. Phoebe circled the tower, taking in every angle of the lavish view, the neon-blue sky, and wondering how, when exactly, her life had righted itself. For it had. She'd been accepted to Berkeley for January, that was part of it. But something in Phoebe had also relaxed, and now the loose, random way in which her life unfolded seemed to offend her imagination less and less. She still ached to transcend it, cross the invisible boundary to that other place, the real place. But you couldn't have that every day. No one could sustain it.

Phoebe still thought about Faith, of course, but remembering her sister had become a calmer experience. She was gone. The gap between them would be impossible to cross, and it seemed to Phoebe now that her sister was the loser for it. She would miss everything—Faith, who loved so much to be at the center of action.

And yet. And yet.

What came to Phoebe now, looking down at the city and bay, was a day when her whole family, even her parents, had played hide-and-seek by a field in Golden Gate Park. A sunlit afternoon, an oceany wind, glimmers of moisture on every leaf. Faith hid first. They all split up to look, Phoebe poking through the pinecones and eucalyptus leaves with a stick, then wobbling among the bushes surrounding the field, not expecting to find Faith—Phoebe was four years old at the most, too little yet to win these games, or even really compete.

Yet to her own surprise, Phoebe parted a clump of bushes and there sat Faith in a tiny clearing. She was grinning from ear to ear. "You found me," she whispered. "You won!" But instead of calling out to everyone else and ending the round, Faith had taken Phoebe's hand and guided her to the soft place where she sat. They waited together, hiding, Phoebe folded in her sister's lap surrounded by her breath and heartbeat and warm long hair. She felt the cross-hatching of sun and shadow on her face, smelled rainsoaked earth and eucalyptus leaves and was overwhelmed by an almost unbearable happiness. She'd won the game.

Phoebe squirmed to look up at Faith, but her sister's eyes were attuned to movement outside the branches, where the rest of the family was looking for them. A trickle of flute music reached her, faint, meandering, and something had risen in Phoebe, a joyous belief that at any time her plain surroundings might part to reveal this radiant, hidden place. And Faith would be there, waiting for Phoebe to climb into her lap.

about the author

Jennifer Egan's short stories have appeared in *The New Yorker, GQ, Mademoiselle, Ploughshares* and *Prize Stories 1993: The O. Henry Awards.* A graduate of the University of Pennsylvania and St. John's College, Cambridge, she was the recipient of the 1991 *Cosmopolitan*/Perrier Short Story Award, as well as fellowships from the National Endowment for the Arts and the New York Foundation for the Arts. She lives in New York City.